The ARBHAL Sequence

The tug of history, often very ancient history, is felt throughout these works. A large amount of information about the past is disclosed in the narrative (and a chronological tabulation is an appendix to ARBHAL*), but for the purposes of these extracts a reader needs to know that long before the land was Arbhal it was Owan, and the Owanil, a gifted, energetic, but often arrogant people conquered and then lost a vast empire on both sides of Arnan, the inland sea.*

After some centuries of obscurity, during which their island-based priesthood, the Atarlum, *was essential to the preservation of the Owani culture and language, the Owanil, through a series of opportune events, were able to regain control of their old realm, imposing themselves as an aristocracy on a numerically superior mixed population of Other Races (their own slighting term for all those without a pure Owani pedigree). Their old speech, however (the Owanilú), has become a scholar's language, surviving mainly for ceremonial and religious purposes, and in titles and proper names.*

Until relatively recently knowledge of the Owanilú was part of the elaborate system, Preference, by which the Owanil maintained control, practically excluding the Other Races from high office, and from many crafts and professions.

For half an age these exclusions were a source of unrest and rebelliousness among the Other Races, while many Owanil came to view the system as incompatible with their people's

historic love of justice. At the time when Dolvid *begins,
Preference has been abolished for the best part of a century; the
exclusive Owani grasp of the realm's rewards has been loosened
if not broken. With the extinction of the former reigning house
even the* rabhsai *(the supreme, though by no means absolute
ruler) has a mixed strand in his ancestry, and a conciliatory
Patriarch has moderated the* Atarlum's *dogmatic insistence on
the natural superiority and special fitness to rule of the Owanil.*

*Nevertheless, the old conflict is muted rather than
permanently silenced. The much-intermarried provincial
aristocracy still preserves the purity of its bloodlines, and the
same is largely true with the landowning class of the Heartland
("the Families"). While, as mentioned elsewhere,* Dolvid *is
essentially a novel about the childhood and early manhood of its
title character, and* Arbhal *an epic adventure, the theme which
runs right through the entire sequence is the desire (often the
schemes) of this stubborn Owani minority, with the support
(often the covert assistance) of reactionary elements within the*
Atarlum, *to reestablish their former unchallenged dominance,
and beyond that to somehow bring back the supposed glories of
a legendary Owani past.*

Among the important people Dolvid meets when he's allowed to go to the Residence with his father is the head of the powerful Teaching Order of the Atarlum, *known only by his title,* Menadhi. *His frightening suggestion, that Dolvid come to the* Mankh' *for an education commensurate with his obvious gifts to the boy's relief is quickly declined by Vidukh, Dolvid's father.*

When, four years later, Vidukh suddenly falls ill and dies, Dolvid is virtually abducted and taken to the Mankh' *by* Menadhi, *where he becomes his personal pupil.* Menadhi, *generally expected to be the next Patriarch, is a leader among those who seek the restoration of exclusive Owani privilege and power. These opinions are at first embraced by Dolvid, who had begun to think his father's notions on the equality of races quaintly out of touch with the real world, but in time the very zeal of* Menadhi's *advocacy, together with the evident fraudulence of* Atarlum *history where it deals with the Other Races, begin to change Dolvid's mind. He gradually becomes, in his own view, the silent adversary of a man who still regards him as a disciple.*

Dolvid finds his own interest in the languages, lore and customs of the Other Races is tolerated so long as there's no open clash with the patronizing attitude proper to a true Owani scholar. At fifteen, to supplement the scant available written material on the Froghul, one of the little-assimilated minor races of Arbhal, he's permitted to spend a few midsummer days with a Froghuli clan now camped near Kadon Dinul...

The interim state of peace attained by the protagonist at the end of DOLVID *as he turns thirty is a personal victory, oddly incongruent with objective circumstances: he is unsuccessfully married, pessimistic about the future, and, after some triumphant years, out of favor with a new* rabhsai *who seems determined to restore all the ancient injustices, or wreck his realm trying.*

ARBHAL opens after the elapse of six years, with Dolvid living alone in enforced exile, and the realm at the brink of civil war.

This is the real beginning of the long, complex, but in the end organic yarn, replete with desperate deeds set in varied landscape and townscape, and encounters with a rich cast of characters, including (besides those already met) the half-mad and entirely sadistic Rheduban, Aëlu, Sebhal's serene wife, the entire ruling house of Kargul; the bearlike Tovakh and his formidable wife, the strategist Petakoi, their dashing but unexpectedly complicated son Kamin-Tolagh, a compulsive womanizer, and his equally-promiscuous younger sister, Kamin-Tarú...

Late in the second volume, Dolvid travels with Kamin-Tarú, in search of her brother, who's still in the field as an enemy...

Edwin Ahearn

Edwin Ahearn

The Arbhal Sequence

II

HOSTAGES

HOSTAGES

i

The Visitors

From his shelves Dolvid took down the ink-block with its scraper, his flask of rainwater. For no reason he could explain he left them on the table and went to a small window, the one facing south and east. Nothing to see; night was opaque, a slab pressed against the window. By day there would not be much more: the embankment, drab and muddy till the year wakened. He let fall the double thickness of sacking nailed up to keep in his yellow lantern-light.

Pen repointed, fresh ink made, he crossed through the paragraph he had spent half the day assembling. It was all wrong, and in ways he could not put right; with access to no sources but his notes and his memory, even as historian he had become an exile.

The girl said, "We don't need him. Let us keep in mind there may be other ways. If we find him, how can we trust him?"

The older of the two men ahead, their leader, gave a snort, amused exasperation. "When are you going to stop talking about trust? It is not part of the plan."

"He has every reason to be with us," the tall young man, in his quiet voice, for the dozenth time. His readiness to put their lives in the hands of this man Dolvid was why she kept up her warnings; it was just the same as his refusal to hear any bad of his brother.

"Our knives make one more," their leader, dark-voiced.

The young man said, "He will not be much use to us if we kill him."

"Then we'll do without him." All this had been said before.

A quiet chuckle. "In that case, we could have landed in the north, and saved a good few steps." It was this unexcitability that annoyed the girl. She was tired from lack of sleep, tired of stumbling along this rough track in the dark. She was also vexed to madness with the wrangles, which had gone on for days.

Weeks, really, but when it all began, with the coming and going of mysterious visitors at the Great House, she was simply Sebhal's bed-friend, not asked for an opinion. The secret expedition was decided on, and only then disagreement over its purpose came into view. That, too, seemed settled, till Sebhal drew her into the scheming, promoting her to his confederate. She was gratified by his confidence, but it was largely (she saw) because certain things could be said only to her — and also, less flatteringly, because where she was, her uncle's house, was an ideal place for confidential talk; his unwilling doubts about the younger man, a painful mixture of respect for his character and unbelieving despair for his blindness towards his brother. So she became part of not one but two plots, one inside the other.

She recalled the last day at Kamsilat, a rainy afternoon, when she and Rodlakh had bickered like bored children. In that house, but her uncle was down at dockside making sure the boat was ready, and what Âna wanted was to be alone with Sebhal, so they could be in bed together: tonight he would have to be at the Great House with his wife. Yet when the younger man had gone at last, Sebhal turned on her: "Why must you keep baiting him?"

"I do not. He hates me." Her mother always said there was no quarrel without two to keep it going. Though Âna and Rodlakh had in common their admiration for Sebhal, that did not mean Rodlakh had to approve of Sebhal's bed-friend.

"Nonsense," he said.

That ought to be true, itself a measure of Rodlakh's mildness: Sebhal could have said Rodlakh's rank, not to say the rank he might come to, put him outside ordinary likes. Impossible to imagine the young man firmly silencing Âna by reminding her who he was, and she did not know whether that increased her respect or diminished it.

She told Sebhal, "He does not want his hero to have any other woman." Painful for her, she was saddened this established joke did not fetch a smile. Worship was the only word for Rodlakh's attitude to Aëlu, Sebhal's wife — a moist-eyed passion doomed to frustration, since he would be disillusioned with anything less than Aëlu's complete devotion to Sebhal.

With the gravity Âna found daunting, Sebhal suggested her behaving as if Rodlakh loathed her was sure to make it true. She abruptly grew up a little, acknowledging her annoyance with Rodlakh was part of conspiring to deceive him, which made her feel guilty, because he was genuinely good. If it could be called goodness, when it made Rodlakh stupid.

"I can't help it," not able to describe the contradictions, embarrassed, here with Sebhal, by her own scruples. She wished she had Sebhal's conviction that misleading Rodlakh was no crime, when in fact they were working to bring him to power. Making it necessary, Sebhal said, to be ruthless on his account, protecting him from his own innocence. But with Rodlakh the thought that resisting his brother might mean power for himself would make him all the more hesitant. "It is not manly, his need to have a good word for everyone. We have to choose sides now, forgive later."

"You must find a way to help it. If you come with us — " unyielding as steel, while that *if* stabbed her like a knife. "There will be none of this skirmishing, no questioning of my orders. If you cannot accept that, you will be left here."

She had turned to the window so as not to show the violence of her feelings; Sebhal was never going to know how comfortless loving him was. Circles in standing water made Âna think rain had begun again, but it was only a gust of wind shaking drops from sodden trees. Down where the river opened to the sea, brightness was coming to the sky, and sun might break through before evening. Not there: after almost a year she was still not used to being the wrong side of Arnan, where the sun rose over water instead of setting.

"Did they say, beeches? I believe these are." That, rather breathless, was the third man, her uncle, Sett. Beside her, he had given most signs of weariness, turning ankles in old ruts, and muttering doubt the house they were looking for existed. He had ridden the length of this track more than once, and never seen any such building.

Sebhal quickly confirmed this was the spot. "Do not forget we are not all here with our right names," he warned.

Dolvid's night-ear, sharpened in disuse, could not be mistaken about the sound of humans jolting down the steep slope into his dell. He made sure his sackcloth curtains were properly in place; from outside light could still be seen, but he did not want any chink large enough for a peering eye. The door-bar was already secure in its brackets. By the sulky peat fire he tugged up the loose stone, and stowed his journals in the bricklined pit beneath. Not a hiding-place to elude a real search; he had found it minutes after first setting foot in this tiny house. The question, then, was getting things out of sight; he did not know what, if anything, was illegal about his writings, but there were new decrees every week, and whisper about lawkeepers who, for love of punishing, went out of their way to discover, even to provoke offenses.

Quietly lowering the flagstone, he went back to the table and turned the cowl of his lamp so its light fell on the doorway. Scuffling noises outside, chafe of whispered words, and Dolvid wondered whether the door would be broken in if he refused to open. Soldiers might, robbers might try, though there was no sense to coming here, where there was nothing to steal. His sword, a plain cavalry blade, was out on the table; safer not to strap on his best weapon, the long hunting-knife in its back-sheath, which was within reach but out of sight on the dark wall-shelf.

A knocking, much gentler than he was set for. He waited, and it was repeated, firmer but determinedly polite.

"Yes?"

"Travellers." A threatless voice, a woman's. That, for a start, was strange.

"What do you want here?"

"Rest — " another youthful voice, a man's, not rural. "To warm ourselves. Directions."

This was all nonsense, nowadays, but the tones reassured him. By pulling the peg which secured his door-bar, and moving the beam back one notch, he could open the door a crack, with the end of the heavy beam coming against stone by the hinges to prevent any sudden rush from widening the breach.

He peered out where lamplight touched a nose, folds of clothing, boot-tops, hafts of knives carried at thigh-front, as with hunters.

"How many of you?"

"Four," the leader said. At the door's opening shudder he had drawn the girl back, as if fearing a weapon thrust blind into darkness. Between his shoulder and that of the young man she could see Dolvid's face quite well, all lean angles. It nudged at her memory, though the man was a stranger to her. Pressing forward again she asked softly,

"May we warm ourselves?" No pretense in her trembling; damp of this country deepened with night.

Dolvid's mouth was open, and he could not invent an objection to fit it. He pulled the peg and lifted the beam out of its brackets, leaning it against the wall. One by one his visitors came out of night's uncertainty, shrugging off packs and piling them on the floor.

First was the hard-faced man with strong hands, and he named the others in a voice of hammered iron; Âna, daughter of Konat, small, bright-faced, scraping a loop of dark hair away from her cheek; Sett, her uncle, a trader, rounded-off Mixed features, a man with the habit of trying to please, smiling, bobbing his head. Tallest and youngest of the three men, his name given as Vol, made Hrafi's sign for a grateful guest, right palm held level at breastbone height, and Dolvid was glad to give the acknowledgement, though these courtesies belonged to other more gracious meetings.

"And I am Pir. From westward." Very broad in shoulders and chest, a big man with no spare flesh, powerful from his thick legs and competent hands to the square chin carried high, stubborn line of mouth. A very Owani face, pale eyes, a strongly hooked nose, though the name Pir was not. That a father of Old Blood might be an admirer of the near-legendary Gabhani war-captain, Pir Perus, or more recent namesake, Pir Kallikuk, hero in the Wars of Cleansing, was unusual, not impossible, rarer half a century ago, when this Pir was born.

"Westward?" aware of evasive games being played.

"Westward, aye," allowing his own echo of Dolvid's ironic expression.

Âna had drifted to the dull fire, and was telling herself not to begin liking this man, whose tact might as easily be fear. He had been a high official till he fell out of favor with Ban-Sila, and everyone knew he had started the oppressions now carried out by his former friend, the loathed Bolan, Captain of the Household.

But the poverty here was appallingly genuine, shabbier than anything she could have imagined. This tiny house had not a single furnishing her father's poorest tenant would want, and the man showed too much bone in the face. His clothes, once well-made, were dingy and inexpertly mended.

"And I," he was saying, "am Dolvid Vidukhat, of here, and of no calling." He did not doubt his visitors already knew his name, and enough of his history. They were not here by chance, but none of the four, as they ranged closer to the fire, seemed anxious to tell him anything. Deferring curiosity, not feeling in any immediate danger, he offered hot drink. He had enough milk to make an infusion with dried nettles, the goatherds' brew. At the rough cupboard he changed his mind, and instead took out his precious jar of *raminat*. Setting it on the table he went to the hearth to break a bundle of brush and tuck it into the sullen fire. While he was filling a pot at the water-barrel, the girl unasked knelt to huff up a flame.

"You had a calling once," Pir said.

Busy placing the pot over heat, Dolvid answered, "Where are you headed? There is no road north. If you want Kanzan Tâl, you will have to backtrack, and take the turning just past the village — the way bears south before you can turn eastward, near the shore of Kôbh."

"It takes some courage, these days," Pir said, "to ask a stranger his business."

This was humor with a hard bone in it. "Just to have any business," he returned, "takes enough courage, nowadays." The battle, to whatever purpose, would be with this man, who had the balanced stance of a good fighter. The others were seated, the men on the rough, square stools to each side of the fire, girl on the flock-stuffed sack that did for a cushion, knees caught in the loop of her arms. She watched Pir's lips when he spoke. No mystery about who this Âna was; years ago Dolvid had met her father, Konat, a prosperous landowner of Mixed origin, with wide acres to this side of Nambalus. Sett was Konat's wife's brother, a highly successful trader, with a reputation for honesty, but also for toughness in bargaining, of which the affable vagueness of manner was obviously part. His income must be sharply reduced, since the main part of his business had been across Arnan, and that trade was now illegal. For the past two years the entire Colony had been considered outside the law. Undoubtedly, illicit trading went on, and Sett might well have turned smuggler. Reasonable to suppose some of his most recent cargo was in this room; of the other two men, the one calling himself Pir was surely a soldier, then certainly an officer, accustomed to giving orders to be unhesitatingly obeyed. And "westward" where he came from was the Colony, the Army of the West. The deep-scored squint-lines around his eyes must have been earned in the parching sunlight on Landegh.

"*Raminat,*" the tall young man murmured happily, catching the astringent fragrance as the dried leaves were sprinkled on the surface of the water. Vol was hardest of all to fix, not deferential enough to be a junior officer under Pir, not much like a soldier, though he was not uncomfortable wearing a weapon, and the hands were capable.

"What news do you hear?" Pir asked.

"In this country?" — irritated by the question, obvious bait to indiscretion: as things were it was scarcely possible to talk about events and not betray an opinion.

"You must hear what Bolan's troops are doing," the girl flashed out, making it an accusation. "You have heard about the so-called uprising at Kred Bakali."

"I heard there were some hangings." Executions had for sixty years been rare, and this was a distressing case, though in a world of rumor it was hard to know exactly what had happened. Forrlas, a Mixed magistrate in those parts, had been accused of leading an uprising against royal authority; Bolan had put it down with bloodshed, followed by a number of summary hangings, as many as eleven in some accounts, including two women and some youths of fifteen or less. Whether Forrlas had been killed in fighting or subsequently executed was unclear. Years ago, Dolvid had supported Forrlas's nomination as tax-gatherer, and did not believe he had led a revolt. A step beyond wisdom, he said, "I hear little today about justice. Only punishment."

"Once, though — "

"My time was that of Lambarr *Rabhsai*." Surer than ever this was not a chance visit, he went to the table to fetch all his blue mugs and bring them to fireside. Âna watched him with mouth slightly open, but said nothing, as Pir gave her a frown. Silence stretched on, and the fire flared, fuel shifting with the sound of a cough.

"This rift with the Colony," Pir said. "Saidhan's outlawry — how do people see the rights and wrongs of that?"

"You ask me? I seldom speak with anyone whose opinion means anything. In these parts, I have heard men say it is a shame families have these fallings-out."

This so annoyed Âna she half-stood, noise in her throat of an angry cat. There was no right to indifference, and for Dolvid, who tried to be aloof, she could find hatred more readily than for those who openly supported oppression.

Not understanding the violence of her emotion, he made a placatory gesture, explaining his feelings were just the opposite; a pity, rather, there were divisions so deep that they made enemies of a grandfather and his grandson, and put a brother on either side. Over a year ago, in a try for reconciliation, the *rabhsai*'s younger brother, Rodlakh, had sailed for Kamsilat. Once in the Colony, he had quickly become a supporter of Saidhan's position, and in his turn had fallen under Ban-Sila's sentence of outlawry.

"But you must have thoughts — " Pir's casualness could hammer iron bars into lace, "as to the merits of this controversy."

He had to wait. It was the moment when the *raminat*-leaves rose to the surface of the nearly-boiling water, and the brew had to be given a quick stir while taking it off the fire. Pouring drinks into the waiting mugs, slowly, so the leaves remained in the pan, he was able to keep exasperation under control.

"The question is unfair. The dispute is with the *rabhsai*, so if I were in accord with the Colony I would be guilty of treason." He passed the first of the half-filled mugs to Pir. "But if Bolan himself was here, he would not go out of his way to proclaim loyalty, surrounded by armed fighters, two of them from the Colony; from the Army of the West, I would say."

Sett cleared his throat, and looked around to be sure no one else meant to speak. "We need help. That you were told."

"Directions for the road," sarcastically. "There is no road." Looking at the faces watching his, he gave up the untenable notion these might be spies trying to trap him. "What do you want from me? I have no influence, no important friends. My guess is you come direct from Saidhan. He has my sympathy, if that is worth anything."

Pir said, "He remembers you well. He has only one complaint, I am told, that he can no longer ride to b-battle — " the stammer was momentary, "shoulder to shoulder with his son."

Dolvid nodded, calculating Saidhan's age; eighty-seven. For those who had grown up with Saidhan for a hero, the son, Sebhal, was the young inheritor, but he must be nearing fifty.

"And you?" Âna demanded. "You see no need to take a side?" She was obliged to suspend hostility to proffer grudging thanks for the steaming mug he handed her. Another was already poured, and it was odd that otherwise she would have passed hers on to the young man, Vol. Women of her blood in remote rural parts might even now make sure the menfolk were served before them, but Âna was not part of that fading tradition.

"Side? No side takes me, if there are sides. I am no one — " As Dolvid gave Âna her answer, Vol, hunched over his *raminat*, laughed softly.

"Is that a joke?" she demanded. "Besides the hangings at Kred Bakali, there is torture and rape; your friend Bolan has turned the Heartland into a nightmare — "

"My friend, Bolan?" A tightened throat gave notice this passionate girl could make him genuinely angry. He occupied himself with the squandering of more hoarded treasure, a good-sized beech log, saved for a raw night. Laid on peat it began to steam, with an occasional darting lick of flame.

"What else is Bolan? Everyone knows you let him — "

Pir said, "But that is not our business." The ending she had intended was obviously to do with Khalú, once Dolvid's wife and now Bolan's.

"There is a right and a wrong side — " Âna began.

"A realm, too, Arbhal," lightly. "Let us hope it can survive."

"Arbhal?" Pir said, "Then you are not with those would bring back an older name: Owan?"

When Dolvid merely made a long-suffering face, Âna said, "You are, as they say, *Lekh'Owani*," and the guttural gave her the chance to repeat the cornered-cat noise.

"Âna." Pir did not raise his voice, and did not need to. As she clamped lips over unuttered venom he went as if casually to the door, picked up the bar, and dropped it into its slots. It might be a signal they had reached the moment for truth, and certainly would prevent any surprise intrusion, but it also shut him in a small space with four armed strangers.

Ostentatiously, before answering Âna, Dolvid turned to her chosen companion, so-called Pir, with the high cheekbones and curved Owani nose. "That term was made unlawful by Banak-rai, and remained so as long as Lambarr reigned." On the brink of saying something committal, he drew back once again. "Perhaps I am aging. They say it is a sign, when you lose the knack of changing your ways." He did not blame Âna for looking away in disgust: this was a condescending answer, and the tone of false ingratiation he had used for sweetening would have revolted him. Amazing tribute to instincts having nothing to do with likings that he felt a defunct habit reawaken, to seek ways of retrieving lost ground with this girl, to make her admire him even if she, on the whole, repelled him.

"What about Preference?" Pir said. The question was both expected and odd. The return of Preference, the system which had excluded all those not of Owani blood from positions of power, had been a rumor seven years ago, in the first week of Ban-Sila's reign: as far as could be told there had been nothing behind it except the new *rabhsai*'s early training at the *Mankh'*, natural home of Preference, his continued friendship with the *Menadhi*, head of the Teaching Order, the *Atarlum* faction which above all others had cherished the idea of Owani supremacy. To Dolvid as to many others, it had seemed unthinkable a *rabhsai* whose own blood was not unmixed Owani would try to restore the glories of ancient Owan, and yet, while there had been no overt measures against Others, there was no question Ban-Sila's *rabhsayum* had constantly promoted the interests of the *Atarlum*, and of their favorites, the magnates and landowners of unmixed Owani blood. The result, increased poverty for the Others, was obvious underlying cause of all unrest, hence of the repressive measures, which in turn only heightened the Other Races' already mounting sense of injustice. But while both making of appointments and enforcement of laws had continued to drift in the direction of preferential treatment for the Old Blood, the formal decree that would reestablish Preference in all its aspects, though often rumored as imminent, had never come.

"At Kamsilat," Pir said, "they have heard the Decree of Preference is to be revived, at the next meeting of the Council of Thirteen."

"How can it ever be enforced?" a well-worn question. While the provisions of Preference (as it formerly was) were, strictly speaking, questions of belief rather than race, in practice very few who were not of Old Blood would ever attain the mastery of language, lore and tradition needed to hold high rank. Or to be certain of continuing to own their lands, since failure to meet certain religious obligations meant liability to an *Atarlum*-tax that for many smallholders would be the difference between bare solvency and failure. That was the difficulty with enforcement: dispossession would need troops, but most ordinary soldiers by far, and even a large proportion of squadron-rank officers, were not of Owani descent, and full return of Preference would make it impossible for many to retain the small farms, the reward for long service. To impose Preference on the Colony, where Saidhan would never accept it, and not one man in fifty was of the Old Blood unmixed, would need a war, but what soldiers could the *rabhsai* find to fight against men who were in effect defending their adversaries' best interests?

Grimly Pir explained; at Kadon Dinul it was proposed that those who took part in subduing the outlawed Colony were to be awarded lands of the men they conquered. This, a royal warrant for robbery, as Pir called it, would not just replace one set of Mixed landowners with another; the new holders would have their farms on long-term leases, the lands legally remaining the *rabhsai*'s property. Beyond that, Bolan probably supposed if Saidhan and his son could be defeated in the Colony, Mainland resistance to Preference, too, would have lost its great champion.

But Bolan, even with an army of men greedy for land, could never dream of winning against the Army of the West, toughest, most war-tested fighters in existence, led by the best living captain, defending their own property, the farms they had earned keeping the Frontier safe.

Hardly surprising the young man vehemently agreed on the invincibility of either Sebhal or the Army of the West, but the man called Pir remained hard-faced. Bolan, he said, would have other aid to call on; Tovakh was in Kadon Dinul, and cavalry of Kargul was with him.

"His escort, you mean." Tovakh, as virtual overlord of his province, needed no special leave from the *rabhsai* to go anywhere with four squadrons of lances; for years he had been seeking a royal captaincy, if only as a sign his once-rebellious province was again a fully-accepted part of the realm.

But Pir insisted that Tovakh (according to their informant) was in Kadon Dinul to offer twenty squadrons for an assault on the Colony: the army Saidhan had defeated to make Ban-Sila's grandfather *rabhsai*.

"And will defeat again, or Saidhan's son will," Vol said hotly. "But Ban-Sila would never make such a plan, or approve it."

This, in the teeth of the older man's certainty, was strange coming from a junior officer (as surely Vol must be), but was not to be explained, not yet. Dolvid was remembering a conversation with the dowager, Laluvoi, only days after Ban-Sila's accession, when rumors of reborn Preference had so soon begun, and they had agreed it was too late, too many not of the Old Blood were by now in positions of power and influence, too many had come to realize there was nothing natural or inevitable about Owani domination. Yes, but then as now the danger was not that it could be accomplished, but it might be tried; the realm could not be turned back into the past, but could be destroyed.

"At Kamsilat," the young man said, "they are certain Ban-Sila *Rabhsai* would never begin such a war."

That was twice; it was Pir who made ponderous sense of apparent contradiction, and gave some sort of reason for this expedition. He admitted they had just come from Kamsilat, with orders direct from Saidhan. Led especially by the *rabhsai*'s brother, who, despite having been added to the list of the outlawed, had continued to hope for reconciliation between *rabhsai* and Colony, some there were convinced Ban-Sila was being deceived and misled by bad advisors, basing policy on partial and distorted reports. In this extraordinary view, not the executions at Kred Bakali, the brutal enforcement of curfew, none of the cruelties could be ascribed to Ban-Sila, who, hedged in by cunning men pursuing their own evil purposes, had in effect become a captive *rabhsai*.

Pir did not state his disbelief; it was betrayed in the flat, careful voice of someone who wants it known he is only repeating what he has been told. Vol, however, offered slender support, noting Ban-Sila (according to report) had not been present at the public proclaiming of any of the recent oppressive measures, and the Council of Thirteen had not met in more than a year. This was less than persuasive; Ban-Sila was easily capable of any excess. He did not see how the worldly Saidhan could swallow such a tale; they had been together at the very first Council presided over by Ban-Sila as *rabhsai*, even then trying to protect the interests of the big landowners, all Owanil.

Besides, if not Ban-Sila, who? The Patriarch dreamt Owani glory, but the only army he commanded was his bodyguard; Bolan had troops but was never a maker of doctrine; he had friends among the Families but would always be seen by them as a Mixed with rank and ambition beyond his heritage. Ban-Sila might be weak, but as *rabhsai* was the only one who could be emblematic focus for the realm's policies.

Yet when Dolvid started to say some of this he was cut off by Pir, who frowned, with a sidelong look for Vol, as if he was saying *you and I know this is nonsense, but we must not be unkind to youthful illusions.* The idea of a captive *rabhsai* would naturally be attractive to a young officer in the Army of the West, who could stay loyal by his own lights, while committing acts of apparent rebellion.

As this expedition, at mildest estimate, certainly was, and had been since men from the Colony set foot on the Mainland. Their object, so Pir said, in risking capture, perhaps death, was to be face to face with the *rabhsai*, and present him with messages from his brother and from Saidhan; to tell Ban-Sila what sort of realm was being made by policies carried out in his name, warn him the West would never give up, Preference never succeed.

"And then?" — starting to see what they wanted with him, sidestepping the obvious question about how they could ever achieve this meeting.

Pir shrugged awkwardly, exchanging glances with the girl, silent but wound like a spring. "We are soldiers. You know about how policies work. A new meeting between the big lords, reconciliation, some promises made. What would you say?"

The false note here irritated Dolvid; that and the invitation itself. They were trying to pull him back into a world he was done with, where there was hope, hence bitterness. He had a rush of affection for his eventless life here, not happy, but with a familiar and tested extent of unhappiness. It must prove something that he had not

gone to the village today: his loneliness had not yet become hunger for
sound of any human voice. In the village there were men he could
exchange words with, about weather, crops (past and to come), recent
local births and deaths, peat, pork, weather again. At worst it was
meaningless.

Instead, he had walked north and east in colorless country at
the fringes of marshland. A raw day, sky stony, now and again the
feathering of drizzle so fine nothing could be seen on the back of a hand
held up to make sure it was not imagined. His walk was truly aimless;
nothing yet to look for in the way of food, except the pinkish
mushrooms occasionally found at the edge of persisting patches of lacy
snow, but by exhausting his body he hoped to keep down other pangs,
the lost past jabbing at his careful resignation.

Here it was again, and he was still fending it off. "None of this
has anything to do with me."

Âna leapt at once. "It has to do with anyone who is not a
coward. Or would he rather serve the other side, with his old friend
Bolan?"

Resisting new anger, he gave the quiet story of how, the
autumn before last, about when the *rabhsai*'s brother went to the
Colony, he had been unexpectedly visited here by a genuine friend,
who remained at Kadon Dinul, by no means a young man, who had
risked the journey and undergone its discomforts to let Dolvid know
there were hopes of reconciliation, that it might be the moment to
petition Ban-Sila for an end to his exile.

"Reconciliation!" Pir, bitterly. "As we heard it, Lord Saidhan
made an offer of p-peace, and Kadon Dinul demanded surrender."

"I imagine they tell it differently at Kadon Dinul," Dolvid said. "I am quite certain," he loudly added, forestalling Âna, "what you say is true; Rodlakh, after all, has decided to stay with Saidhan."

"Your visitor?" It was Sett who asked for continuation of the tale.

"Nothing. I was not interested. My friend argued with me into the night, and rode off in the morning shaking his head; I was sorry to disappoint him, after all his trouble. A good friend, and best reader of the Old Syllabary outside the *Mankh'*."

"Reader of what?" wrinkling his face.

"Ancient lies." Pir, turning back to Dolvid. "You worked several years in the Old Bronze Residence."

If not for surmise about what his visitors were doing here, this remark would be a complete orphan. Taking seat at the bench by the stone table, he said, "You have to hope for a fine season and a good harvest, or else there will be famine in the Colony. On this side of Arnan spring is coming in on crutches."

The man called Pir, unlike the smallest of his companions, decided to enjoy the evasion. "You mean to say, we have not been altogether frank with you. You blame us? We are outlaws, in dangerous country. You say, you were not interested, what does that mean? That you could not serve the *rabhsayum* of Ban-Sila *Deghi*?"

"It means, I was not interested." Here, Dolvid saw afterwards, he should have known who his visitors were; no mere officer of the West carrying messages from Kamsilat would ever have debated this point with a former *bôdh'loiki*.

Sett came to life. "Well, state affairs are not everyone's idea of a meal. I'm a man of business, and let me tell you, unless there's some start on accommodation, I don't give it two years, the realm will be on its knees. Without trade, it all dries up — capital, crops, the crafts. Can't have any prosperity where there is no trade."

"Uncle — " Âna's gentleness here was appealing. "You will be lucky to keep your boats, and not end up keeping books for a hook-nose with the right connections."

"That would be very foolish. Who knows the business as I do? But I was taking the larger view." Sett was dignified, while Dolvid used three fingers to feel the ridge of his Owani nose, till he noticed Pir doing the same.

"Once, you would fight, if what Saidhan and others say — " Pir began.

"Oh, once — what were any of us, once? A few years back I would have said I could not go on living in a realm where justice was dead — we had an alliance, then, against the return of former evils. They are all gone, Great Laluvoi, Arvus, Mirrat, Merovas — " to his own ear, this sounded like self-pity; he came back to his theme. "I have stopped setting conditions for life. I did not make these times; if I am going to see them through to their end, I have to survive." Not mattering made its own truth, begun as a pose, a shield against bitterness, and when he said he was of no consequence he had nevertheless wanted people, an ill-defined *them*, to say abjectly what a mistake his exile had been, beg him to come back and save the realm. That was long past, and now he believed what he said, "To survive."

"At any price," Âna said.

"I cannot stake my manhood on what I cannot alter."

"Then how can you be sure you have a manhood?"

Pir again remonstrated, but as a general question it was apt enough. For this instance, Âna was first to lower her gaze.

"Nevertheless," Pir said. "You will help us. We have messages to be delivered to the *rabhsai* in person. Former letters from his brother and from Saidhan *Asai* have not been acknowledged; who can say whether they ever reached the *rabhsai*?"

"I cannot do anything for you at Kadon Dinul," he said again. Pir had called himself and the others outlaws, but Dolvid faced death as *kaël'rolai*, an exile-breaker, if he was caught nearer than three dayrides from Kadon Dinul.

"Are we that far now?" Pir asked.

"My friend took more than four." Patiently, he explained what Pir must already know, that while the capital was north and a little west of where they were, to avoid the marshlands, Shemugrân, required a vast detour, east and even a little south till you could cross a river called Lovu, and turn back north to reach Kanzan Tâl, at the head of the lake, Entun Shelum. That was past a long day's riding, and Kanzan Tâl to Kadon Dinul was an established two dayrides on the Royal Road, though fast-messengers did it in less, with a change of horses.

Pir's face was becoming slyer. "The southern fringes of Shemugrân would be a strange choice for living out your exile, if there was not a way north, through the marshes, a lost trail you found again."

This led to further fencing, till Dolvid said, "If there was once a path, and if I had found it — if you could be led safely through Shemugrân, what? You could have crossed Arnan and landed somewhere far closer than this to Kadon Dinul. You have not come to me for the sport of slithering about in Shemugrân for a day and more." On foot the journey would still be over three days, two to reach

Burantal. But a good guess could be made about why they were here, growing to certainty when Pir began discoursing on Dolvid's reputation for curiosity about lost secrets, the scholar's knack of finding ways through all sorts of puzzles; "Marshlands," Pir suggested, "manuscripts. Perhaps walls."

"Is Arvat still working in the Great House at Kamsilat?" He was the son of Arvus, murdered Master of the Treasury, and when Arvat had also seemed to be in danger, Dolvid had arranged his escape to the Colony, getting him into Saidhan's service. Earlier in that bad day Arvat had briefly been concealed in the very beginning of a hidden passageway Dolvid had rediscovered, one built (or extended) by the long-reigning Plakhsila *Kímukoi*, creator of the New Residence. While that great palace was being constructed Plakhsila continued to hold court in the Old Bronze Residence, and his passage and long tunnel connected the two royal dwellings, old and new.

The attractions were obvious; for a start the Old Bronze Residence was outside the city proper, and could be reached without having to pass any guarded gates. For many years mainly a library, the Bronze Residence was, or always had been, lightly guarded. Its hidden passage, then, was not merely a better way of getting into the heavily-guarded New Residence, perhaps reaching the *rabhsai*, but the only way imaginable.

"There is a passage." Vol had been keeping a hungry watch on Dolvid's face.

"There was, six years ago — " setting off a general near-celebration, Pir jumping up and rubbing his hands together as he strode as far as cramped space permitted.

"But what is the object?" — loudly enough to bring a silence. On his fingers he told off the hurdles. The path through Shemugrân was far from certain, and they risked an unpleasant death, drowning in mud. Avoiding that, they came to the Heartland, a tamed and settled country where they could hardly go unseen, and without tokens for a journey to show the numerous patrols. If they miraculously evaded arrest and arrived in Kadon Dinul all they had to do was get into the Bronze Residence in full view of Harbor Gate watch, and hope the passageway had not caved in somewhere, been discovered and sealed up, or its outlets (three he knew of) within the New Residence blocked off or heavily guarded. "All these uncertainties, all these risks, to deliver messages that may very well be ignored?"

They had been wondering whether they were safe with him, and now he wished he could trust them; there were so many complicit glances, so much that was barely a tenth of the truth. And they offered too many excuses for their presence here: Pir said it was not their place to question instructions from Kamsilat, and Âna contributed that they did not all share in Dolvid's cowardice.

Vol, again to Dolvid's ear the only one who gave entire belief to what he was saying, ventured that more important than the messages they had was the chance of discovering the real state of affairs at the Residence.

"And then?" unconvinced. He filled the silence he had made by observing the packs of the travellers were not overfull for a long journey. "Not much here, bread and a little cold meat —" putting plates on the table. He wanted to think, but did not enjoy thoughts that came.

Pir said, "You are being asked to guide us, that's all."

"Guiding means approval — " trying to master agitation, but his hands shook as he laid out table-knives. "I have been in battle, killed men, weapon to weapon. But I am not going to be part of an assassination." The only answer he could see, convenient removal of Ban-Sila, the Colony having his successor, Rodlakh. The result, he allowed, would be desirable, but logic that said the death of one man could save the sufferings of many was not enough to overcome repugnance at the idea of murdering a *rabhsai*.

"Who said anything about that?" Pir, roughly. "Has assassination ever been the policy of Saidhan *Asai*?"

Vol, too, hotly denied it, and Dolvid, muddled between conviction and embarrassment, kept busy by hunting a stone flask of thin wine from Lower Nîv, put away last year.

Sett gestured at the fire. "Damp country over here, but you never want for good peat. At Kamsilat, with no buyers, they have started burning hardwood, good long-timbers. At Kadon Dinul the price of seasoned oak is six times what it should be, and over the water it's going for firewood. These are mad days for a trading man — for any man, you could say."

That broke the tension, and as they gathered at the table to share his food, Dolvid achieved an apology made grudging by his observation that when armed men look for secret ways to come near high lords, anyone might have disquieting suspicions.

Vol, enjoying some pickled fruit, was hugely affronted. "Assassination, not to be thought of," the high-flown, bookish style that seemed most apt to seize him exactly when he wanted the sincerity of plain language. "Not for any true man to speak of. We quarrel with what has been done in Ban-Sila's name, but in the Colony we are all true *rabhsayanil* — it is because we are loyal we have to reach the *rabhsai*. We might be able to free him."

Asked what that meant, he said soft-voiced, not looking up from food, it might be possible to take Ban-Sila away from the Residence, from the capital, out of reach of men who were deceiving and using him, to where he could safely repudiate the evils done in his name.

"Abduct the *rabhsai*? Take him to the Colony to be Saidhan's captive instead — "

"Free him," Vol insisted.

"In this," Pir broke in, "we are permitted to use our judgment, if it is in the *rabhsai*'s best interests, and can be safely accomplished... " He turned to his bread and mutton as if nothing was left to be said.

Dolvid choked on simple incredulity; how could so much be left to the judgment of underlings, no matter how well instructed? About to say so, he stopped, and changed to a question; what next if they did whisk the *rabhsai* away from his bodyguard? "You then ride down to Owan Sai, and say, please can we have a ship to take us to Kamsilat?"

He wanted to hear the answer, but was only half-listening as the man they called Pir told him; a fast boat would be waiting at deserted Tan Lughsai, less than a day's ride south of Kadon Dinul. A man he evidently admired, Galt, a mounted bowman and half-squadron leader with the Army of the West, would be there with a half dozen of his men, but their main protection would be the ill-omened reputation of Tan Lughsai, where no one went since the disastrous fire seven years ago.

That was good, but what had come clear was that it was exactly true such decisions as whether or not to abduct the *rabhsai* would never be left to subordinates. In that, and some fleeting facial reminder of the father, he had recognized Pir. He was Sebhal.

It explained several puzzles, including the excessive care with which the man, often belatedly, kept insisting he was a follower, not maker of policies. Understandable he would want to hide his identity when the price of betraying him could easily be the lifting of Dolvid's exile, though a little odd, when he could not have known he would not be recognized at once. They had not met, but it was only an accident that in better times Dolvid had never seen him, riding on the Avenue of Treaties at one of the Pledgings.

He had to protect the young man, too. With a shock Dolvid knew who Vol was, and told himself it could not be, knowing it was. Like Ban-Sila *Rabhsai*, he was Sebhal's nephew. Dolvid had seen him only as a small child, but now could see the family features, and only marvelled it had taken him so long to recognize Rodlakh *bi*-Arbhai-Navu.

He would be *rabhsai* if Ban-Sila were to vanish, but though he would have more motive for lying than a nonentity called Vol, Dolvid did not revise that part of his opinion: Rodlakh (at least) was truly horrified by the idea of assassination, and apparently — but this was harder to credit — sincerely convinced his elder brother was in some way not responsible for the wrongs done in his name.

Pir — Sebhal — was talking on about the bowman, Galt, and the ability he shared with all Froghul of the Frontier to go unseen in the barest terrain; after barren Landegh they should have no trouble hiding in the woods at Tan Lughsai. "In ambush," he said, "in case we are being chased."

"With Ban-Sila as unwilling baggage? What if he endorses, after all, everything done in his name?"

"He will not," the young man who must be Rodlakh said firmly.

The beech-log, its wet baked out, was burning well. That, and perhaps the presence of so many bodies, was making the room warm; first Sebhal and then Sett discarded their outshirts. Only marginally aware he was being both cajoled and mildly threatened, his mind ran on whether he should let them know he had penetrated their slight disguise, and on what it meant, arrival here of two who ranked highest among opponents of Preference. When they were simply two valued officers from the Army of the West, he had guessed they must have volunteered for this job (as, obviously, indeed they had), and could not imagine what was in Saidhan's mind, letting good men be squandered on a vague and chancy business with such a nebulous objective. Now he saw how desperate they must be; how could the Colony or the wished-for realm recover from loss of these two men, by far the likeliest outcome of this expedition?

"You admit," Rodlakh said, returning to an earlier demur, "Bolan's power has increased. He has valued connections with the Families."

"Bolan is not someone to impose policies on an unwilling *rabhsai*. You have to know the man. He drifts with the tide." At Narn, fourteen years ago, he had heard of soft sea-creatures that did the same, but could cripple with their stings.

"If you speak well enough of him," Âna said, "in gratitude he may give you back your wife."

"Do you believe a woman can be taken away and given back, like furniture? I do not." Sebhal exploded in a laugh with some history behind it, and Dolvid had won that round; the girl herself must somewhere have said words much the same. Irritation with the girl was not going deep, and he wondered where she was failing in her intent to wound. A long time, certainly, since he had any but starkest dealings with a pretty girl — if Âna was pretty, other than as any girl her age was, clear-skinned, quick, eyes mobile, the hair live. He was not altogether happy that if he agreed to join their hopeless mission she would be as lavish with gratitude, he was sure, as now with her scorn; that was the nature of her passion — for justice, she would say. Not that it could have come from what she had personally suffered; her father was one of those prosperous Mixed who would pasture some more cattle and pay the added tax that would cripple a poor flax-grower; he had no fear of dispossession, and his daughter would scarcely have seen real poverty. Perhaps she had imagination, and it was precisely the complacency of Konat that fueled her fire.

But that was burning down; Sett gave a loud yawn, and after food all arguments, gone over again, were losing edge in the warmth. Sebhal tried a lame threat about binding Dolvid and making him lead them, and Âna said, "At knife-point," but they both saw the weakness in trying to compel someone whose pathfinding they would have to trust.

Dolvid too was growing sleepy, and he wished they would simply leave him alone. He did not want to rejoin the world.

Sebhal said, "Well, as Âna says, we can do without you. Our ship is tied up near Nambalus; we can make a fresh landing farther north. But it is a great pity, Master; we had hoped for your alliance."

Then, while Dolvid pondered whether they could afford to leave him alive after telling so much of their plans, Sebhal became eloquent in a way impossible for the army officer he was passing for, speaking of the numbers of men there must be in every corner of the realm longing for nothing better than the chance to strike a blow against the onset of evil, men and women too who would be honored to give up their lives if they could advance the cause of justice.

Rodlakh obviously admired his uncle, and it was not by design he failed to sustain the lofty level. Preoccupied, his eyelids drooping, he said, "I was looking forward to Shemugrân. A long plod, I suppose, but they say there are otters, and I wanted to see the hawks." Drowsiness and all, this had more life to it than when he talked about freeing his brother, and was more to Dolvid's taste than Sebhal's rhetoric. Sett, puffy, beginning to nod, was with the expedition because business was bad, and because Âna was his niece; Âna was strong for justice, but was there because she loved Sebhal, and he was probably the only one who knew exactly what this venture was all about.

Not that it mattered. He began to see the joke; worried about what would happen when they came face to face with Ban-Sila, yet certain no matter what route they took they would never get to Kadon Dinul without being stopped by a patrol. And his life; he called it worthless but absurdly wanted to hoard it as miser's gold. This expedition was — the word came to him — *ramshackle*; the two extra members added not much more than numbers; with Sebhal and Rodlakh alone (as might well have been originally planned) they would have moved faster and less visibly. But as was, aside from policy there might be some sport in seeing how far they could get before they were caught. Not in wan hope of saving the realm or championing justice, but because it was too long since his body had been tested by cold and rain, distance and fatigue, all the discomforts that became pleasures when met and vanquished.

This was all private, but Vol who was Rodlakh had enough waking left to read his face, and say, "He is coming. He will guide us."

Âna wanted confirmation, but when Dolvid nodded his head, he was careful to hold her where she was with his eyes. He was afraid she would jump up and embrace him.

A night march would have been better for hiding them, but daylight was needed for crossing Shemugrân: they settled on a dawn start, an hour before sunrise. The travellers had sleeping bags or blankets, and Dolvid found his, spreading them by the hearth and banking up the fire with most of his remaining peat; if by chance he survived this venture he would not be likely to come back here while winter lingered.

Unrolling his sleeping-bag, he suggested to Sebhal the wall-bunk had room for two — pure conjecture; since exile his occasional beddings with women had been at Kanzan Tâl or one of the nearer small towns; he had never wanted to bring a woman here, risk starting something more complicated than blunting of his appetite.

Sebhal nodded, said they would talk again in the morning, and took the bunk, dragging off his shirt and stretching out gratefully. Âna went there, and he rolled to the outer edge so she could be next to the wall. In principle, surely, Sebhal would not call it good command for the leader to have his friend with him, while the others went womanless. As Bolan said, years ago, somewhere on the long, empty road to Narn, easy enough to forget what you didn't see, but when the thing was right in front of you, it got hard. Bolan's humor, always with the nervous little kindling-laugh.

While he was making sure his only unholed boots were ready, the young man touched him on the shoulder to murmur thanks.

"I should thank you." It was an effort not to append an honorific, now he knew who this was, but simpler to let them keep their false names. "I had been seeking an honorable end to my life."

"There is always a chance," after wincing, "with him leading us." He wanted to cite some of the leader's successes, but realized they would be instantly recognized as Sebhal's famous feats. "And you to guide us," he substituted. "A good chance."

Dolvid hardly slept, veins wakened by such talk, after long solitude, his whole body shaping for change. He was somewhat surprised he had said yes, relieved, too, but that was mixed with apprehension. Room for an unforeseen and unreal nostalgia over what he would be leaving behind, emptiness.

A charred end of the beech-log not covered with turves shifted and gave out a sudden spurt of flame. By the whitewashed wall Âna sat up with a small whimper, and struggled out of her heavy woolen shirt. For a minute she remained sitting up, young, blurry-eyed, soft undershirt lying quiet on her breasts, shoulders gleaming golden in the firelight. Dolvid did not breathe; she seemed to be staring at him, though he knew she was not awake. The flame steadied, diminished, and she sank back, laying a bare, half-folded arm across Sebhal's back and powerful neck. Working hips into his sleeping-bag, Dolvid subsided into the same revolving muddle of excitement and resentment.

The Expedition

Before light in chilly morning Âna's waking thought was of her home; she seemed to be there. Yesterday, a transforming year away, she had crossed a corner of her father's lands, less than half an hour from the house where she was born, not cramped like this, but sprawling in planless stone as it had grown over generations. She wished there had been a chance to talk to her mother, see young nieces and nephews, but was not certain her father would want to see her. He could hardly threaten her with beating, certainly not with Sebhal beside her, near his own age and far beyond him in rank; before Sebhal, before the Colony she had outgrown any fear, and now she missed him, but he was stiff-necked about a woman's matings, in the Gabhani way of his father (and his), and she would have to postpone the day when she could join up new life to its origins, woman to child she had grown from.

Longings dismissed, the feeling of home lingered, and at last she found its source, a familiar, comfortable smell. Squatted next to the fire Dolvid was stirring a big earthen pot of what could only be porridge. Beside him, mug in hand, was Sebhal (whom she must call Pir). The two men were talking in low voices.

"Truly. They could be back at Konatstead today. But with Âna..." Pir's dark voice muttered to inaudibility, as his face, bowing

over drink, was lost in shadows; except for the flickering fire all the
light came from a dimmed lantern on the table.

"...the legs for a hard journey," Dolvid's voice. "It will be grim enough
in Shemugrân and beyond, without any encumbrance."

As soon as she could work out the subject she was wide awake,
and furious. Quickly disentangled from blankets, she stumbled over
Sett's sleeping form in getting to the fireplace. "Encumbrance!" she
snapped at Dolvid. "When you have marched a day with a pack on, we
shall see who the encumbrance is. We'll see who our warriors are, too,
if there is trouble."

He had already conceded there would be no leaving Âna
behind; his real reservation was with Sett, but he could hardly say so
with the man sitting up to ask the hour.

Sebhal (as it surely was) had begun chiding Âna, but this time
she was not cowed. "I am certain Dolvid would choose better comrades
— from the *Mankh'*, perhaps, and his good friend Bolan. Khalú,
everyone's wife, could come along, too."

"You go too far," Sebhal rapped out, while Dolvid turned away
to conceal choking anger.

"This man wants to say who is fit — "

"We are discussing war," a ponderous calm more threatening
than fury. "War, not the guest list for a jaunt in the meadows. Dolvid
has advised captains in the past, and has a proper concern over the
fitness of our company."

"I was part of the planning, from almost the first."

"And making plans includes choosing who is best to carry them
out. Âna, I would unchoose myself, if there might be a better chance
with me left out."

"I would just follow you."

"Not for long." Here at last there was a smile, but a dour one. "I have lost better trackers than you."

"Left out?" Sett sat up, blinking. "Who?"

"You and me, if the captains and counsellors say so."

Not wanting to watch how bitterness soured the young face, Dolvid began spooning porridge into earthen bowls.

"That can't be right," Sett protested.

"No one is left out, not yet," Sebhal said. "But listen to me, if our success depended on it, I would tie you up here, and send Sett back to release you after half a day's march."

"You would do better to kill me outright, if I am such a danger."

"This is childish." The leader bit at his lower lip in exasperation, but managed to gentle his voice before speaking again. "But let us be truthful. If, at the cost of one life, we could set aside all Preference yet avert civil war, any of us would be willing to die; I would. Good, but that is the easier sacrifice, and I would accept the worse one: to refuse the giving-up of any life would be selfishness, especially a life more precious to me than my own. Leave people behind? For the sake — this is brave talk." With a flat-handed wave, he was about to dismiss his own rhetoric, but Âna, eyes moist, laid her cheek against his chest, with a barely audible moan. He squeezed her shoulders, then put a knuckle under the small chin, turning the face up and stooping to kiss the smooth forehead.

"That is well said." Their youngest companion's unassertive voice. How long had he been awake and listening? "We might all resolve — " he faltered over the words. "Our task comes before anything else."

Âna's quick dart of a look as she parted from Sebhal was unfavorable comparison, but clearly the young man had deliberately lamed his conclusion so as to remain Vol. If Sebhal wanted to pass for a simple army officer, he would have to give up that sort of speech, fine as it was. Not to Dolvid's taste; in real life you could almost never be sure the sacrifice would achieve its object; there might be less futile death in the world if we all did what we could to preserve lives nearest us, and spent less thought on what could be bought with dyings. But there was no quarrel about Sebhal's quality; he was a leader born, not simply illustrious and supremely effective, as his father was, but with the dangerous gift of inspiring devotion.

Sett cleared his throat. "I want to resolve we'll all do better on a good breakfast."

Dolvid was making up a pack when noises outside hushed the room; a creak and chink that might be harness, and maybe the dull sound of hoof on soft earth. Doubt ended when the horse gave a fluttering blow. A voice cried, "Ho, there, Master."

Holding up a hand to keep everyone in place, Dolvid noted Sebhal, interrupted while strapping on his sheath, had the long hunter's blade in his hand.

"Are you home, Master?"

Slipping through a door minimally opened he went out into dank grey of a foggy dawn. He knew the voice, Neldron, who sometimes brought him news, son of the village thatcher. He had taught the boy the common letters and a little about measurement, occasionally telling him stories of life at the Residence, which Neldron, open-mouthed, accepted as no less true (though certainly no truer) than wonders from the *Song of Tales* he had heard from his mother. He was fifteen now, becoming a straightforward lad with a robust laugh and an eye for farm-girls. Dim in the mist, he was slouched in the saddle of his threadbare mount, and wished a good morning.

"You're out early."

"That I am, Master. Thought you might not have heard the news, about soldiers in the village. Horse-soldiers, sir; place is full of them, a squadron at the least. Rode in, I don't know what hour of the night."

"From which direction?"

"Eastward, Master."

Then they had not been pursuing Dolvid's visitors, though he could not imagine what else could have brought so many soldiers here.

Neldron was determined to tell all he knew. "Most slept up at the old mill, sir, but there's a captain and his best officer staying at my uncle's house; I had to walk the nag the back way not to be seen. On the hunt, they are, for somebody, sir, and don't want nobody going out — anybody, I mean to say, sir, pardon me. Come sunrise they'll be out riding — I'm going to my sister, and thought I'd give you a shout and all, sir. Important folks, they say they're looking for."

"What banner are they under?"

"With the Sword, sir — but they aren't any Heartlanders. Men from across the river, they are, by their voices."

He was disagreeably startled. "Across the Kôbh, you mean? Men of Kargul?"

"Would not be wrong, sir, seeing the captain is the young lord from there — the one with such a fancy for the fillies."

"Kamin-Tolagh baKargul? Here?"

"That's him, Master." Neldron's voice became confidential, inclining to sly. "Wanted a girl last night, they say, though it was so late. Why I'm riding to tell my sister, sir; her husband's away clearing ground by Shelum, and she could pass a few days out to the shieling. This Kam-Tola, whats-his-name, is he as bad as they say, Master?"

"I know no more about him than you have already heard." Dolvid was vague, mind preoccupied with all the puzzles; troops of Kargul, captained by the notorious Kamin-Tolagh, riding under the banner of the Household, the son of Kargul's overlord leading a patrol.

"Coming here to stale our girls," Neldron grumbled, echoing someone.

"If his greatest crime is greed for women, Kamin-Tolagh is worse than others only by having power to indulge his appetite, isn't that so?"

Neldron did not exactly understand, but had enough of it to stammer assent in a mixture of shame and pleasure. Dolvid asked if he had heard about what these troops were supposed to be hunting.

"A marshfire tale it sounded to most of us, sir, about raiders coming from the west to kill the *rabhsai*. What would they be doing down in these parts, then? No *rabhsai* down here, sir."

"As you say, most likely nonsense."

"Ah." The boy was reluctant to go.

"I thank you for riding by to warn me, but I do not believe they will trouble me here."

The boy leaned over in the saddle as far as he could, then slithered from the horse's back to be even more confiding. "They were asking questions about you, Master. This Captain, Kam-To' — ?"

"Kamin-Tolagh, yes."

"Kam-Tolak, he was asking, wasn't there an exile hereabouts, used to be a counsellor. Not even Vulnak knew what he meant, till the Karguli used your name, sir; Dolvid Vidukhat, he said. I don't doubt come daylight they'll have somebody show them the way here. Were you a counsellor then, Master?"

To the boy the word might be the name of a mythic beast, and he could have small idea what it meant. "A lesser counsellor, *bôdh'loiki*," fighting for calm. Behind him the door creaked faintly. Neldron's eyes were downward, and keeping them there, he offered, "Surely I'll be stopped by the soldiers, sir, if not going, then on my way back — I'll be afoot, my sister'll take the nag."

"You can account for yourself, you will not be harmed."

"Oh, no, I've learned how to answer up to these patrols. What I was thinking was, is there anything you'd want me to tell them?"

"Do not say you brought news to me here, certainly."

Neldron shuffled a little. "You mean to be here when they come, sir? See, if not, well, I could say about passing you on the road, saying it was some other direction than what's true, sir."

He had undervalued the boy's willingness to help. "Do not put yourself in any danger."

"My Uncle Asdron says it's dangerous to have a piss nowadays."

"Yes. Well, it is a thick morning. Not being too sure, you might have seen me making south, as it might be for the Kôbh-side road. Do not offer this, say it only if asked."

"As for that, they're bound to ask, always do, just the same when they're not looking for anyone particular. Near dawn, it could be, what with the fog. Alone, sir, or — ?"

Neldron bowed with a slight gesture, and the downward gaze had not been new-found humility over Dolvid's former rank. Where the muddy bank sloped next to the house were fresh scorings in clay made by several different heels; here the visitors had come skidding down in darkness.

He met Neldron's eyes, and was in conspiracy with him. "Very well. If you are stopped and questioned, do not be too sure of anything, but you might have seen a small band of travellers, not far from where the trail divides for the south — there is no reason why I might not have been one of them, but they were hidden in the mist before you had a good view."

A nod. "At dawn, just as I was passing Gable Rock. I can't say how many there were — more than two, less than ten, is that good, sir?" He was ready to remount. One hand on the shabby saddle, he said, "You'd never be a part of killing the *rabhsai*, Master. A lot of people in these parts may have hard words for Ban-Sila *Asai*, but killing the *rabhsai*! You'd never be a part of that, Master."

"You know I would not - " fresh resolve as much as assurance. The lad was brighter at once. Knees and elbows, he scrambled up.

"Will I be seeing you again, Master?"

"I hope so, Neldron. My thanks."

"And mine to you, sir, and good fortune."

The thanks were for years of tutoring, and acknowledged what Dolvid was yet to, his term here might well be over; impossible, even if he survived this expedition, for him to to come quietly back and resume his life. Watching horse and rider quickly blur into the mist, he decided to leave the breakfast things unwashed.

Sebhal was sheathing his knife. "Kamin-Tolagh," grimly. "And you let the boy ride away. Why would he not earn a tobhai, riding back to the village with a report?"

"Why would he turn informer after coming out here to warn me?"

"He has more to tell than he had. Only his word these troops were on their way here before he came." A head-shake. "It is too soon."

With that, Dolvid agreed. "You landed — the day before yesterday?"

"At evening, but not at Nambalus proper, the bay north of the port. But I meant, we shall have to be aware of possible trackers, with a chase so close. Are we ready to start?"

Âna finished fastening her pack. "Kamin-Tolagh baKargul," she said, and the shudder she had for the name was hard to understand. Kamin-Tolagh was son of Tovakh, and Dolvid recalled seeing him once, riding on the Avenue in the tunic of Kargul's provincial cavalry, not long after the accession of Ban-Sila. Kamin-Tolagh was then a tall and slender youth of about sixteen, already considered handsome, but only on the brink of acquiring his reputation — his two reputations: as soldier he had since become a known master of both sword and lance, as lordling a notorious womanizer. About the second, women, according to temperament, disapproved either with a frown or a giggle; their faces did not, as Âna's had, go cold and rigid.

She explained it. "They say he laughs when inflicting unspeakable tortures — there was a man roasted to death, and a woman — " she could not finish.

"Rheduban," Dolvid said, together with the young man called Vol, who went on, "Kamin-Tolagh is of the House baKargul, and that makes him heir to plenty of grudges, but he does not deserve confusing with Rheduban."

"He is of Kargul', too," she said. Here, southern Paowan, had suffered most from Kargul's marauding in the long-ago civil wars, and bitter memories faded slowly.

"Karguli, but not *baKarguli*," Sebhal hurried to correct. "Rheduban would never be a commander of their cavalry, except he wed well." Once again Dolvid questioned sardonically how this man expected to be taken for an ordinary officer in the Army of the West, with the pride and preoccupations of the Great Families so plainly on view. True, Rheduban had married upwards, though not directly into the Karguli house; his wife was Radaghi, connected with all the Great Families, younger of two sisters many considered best legitimate claimants to the Bronze Sword, if Banak's seizure of power were ever reversed.

Practically, Sett demanded, "How can Kamin-Tolagh have heard so soon about our landing?"

With an edge to his voice, Dolvid said, "Yes, and it seems I am not the only one evil-minded enough to think of assassination — curious that tale should be told, when, as Neldron says, no one would land in these parts for that purpose."

"Tales walk on legs of their own." Sebhal turned to Sett. "The man, Shardirr, from your crew? He is a Nambalus man?"

"A good man, too. He would never do any gossiping, not if he knew anything, which he did not."

"Not even knowing it, he might have talked to someone spying for the soldiery. I was against letting the sailors go ashore."

"Couldn't be stopped. Some of them had not set foot this side of Arnan in a year; Shardirr has a son he had never seen. You can't have ships and no shore-leave."

"Nor war without inconvenience." Sebhal hitched up his packstraps, and with a pleasureless grin asked if everyone was ready.

Âna was still demanding why troops of Kargul were riding here in the Paowan, but the young man they called Vol, noticing how Dolvid gave one long gaze all round, asked, "Is it hard to leave?"

"Coming back may be harder." He slipped his knife into its back-sheath, handle angled between shoulder and neck.

"A Froghuli trick," Sebhal, tapping the haft.

"One I learned when a boy."

"I had heard you were fostered by the *Atarlum*," he objected, and Dolvid made no effort to explain. Trying not to be affected by knowledge of who this man was, he was shy of his accomplishments; *Sebhal*! He had already fought *jinzal*, and singlehandedly subdued a hostile tribe, when the young Dolvid was trying to learn knife-throwing from the Froghul.

They went in file, Dolvid leading, Sebhal behind him, the young man called Vol at the end. On his right cheek as they emerged from the house cool air swirled, clear water into a muddy pool; light was growing, and the mist would soon lift. Âna asked softly, "Should we wipe away the marks the boy saw?" and Sebhal rasped, "In that clay the wiping-out would show more than the marks." Inconsequentially, Dolvid was inventing what Âna's father would say if he saw his daughter now. In outlying parts the Gabhanil were very strict about men dressing as men, women, women; Konat was more up-to-date, but could hardly approve of her campaign clothes, rough outshirt and breeches — which in fact did nothing to mute Âna's femaleness; rather the opposite.

The small vegetable-patch had a line of flat rocks for boundary, and stepping from one to another he came to where the little rill ran, dry in summer months. For those following, he indicated the large, flat stone before he jumped down to it. A dozen wet-foot paces upstream was a gravelled bank where they would leave hardly a sign of their landing, and the dull, matted grass of the upslope beyond was thick enough not to show prints. Parallel with the line of the track, the land here rose to a treeless ridge, and mounting they were climbing into light; far away, at the village, perhaps, a cock was crowing, while in the bushes on the farther side of the ridge waking birds were starting to scold. The horizon was pale bands of bled color, dark rips showing in layers of mist.

As they neared the crest Sebhal hissed out, "Horsemen," urgent-voiced.

Dolvid stopped, and then they could all hear the thrum and jingle of cavalry at a brisk trot. Just ahead a hollow like an eye-socket scooped under the brow of the ridge gave the tenuous cover of thin brush. In daylight, no cover at all, but with colors indistinct it would be enough to disguise shapes. Crouched there, they looked down. Southward, across the clear line of the track, the country was a mysterious blue and purple-brown, while rightward horsemen were just coming into sight, glint of breastplates and the bob of helms visible before numbers could be counted.

"A half-squadron," Sebhal estimated as the jogging blur separated into individual lancers. "No, not quite — say, twenty." They were in double file, Household standard carried by the leader. For a moment it seemed they would continue eastward, but they too must have been told the landmark to watch for, and wheeled left about the knot of small beeches, taking the easier, circling way down into the gully. A blue cloak, lined in yellow, streamed from the leader's shoulders; he had no breastplate or helm, and his long hair, its reddish color not seen in this light, was worn loose.

The man they called Vol breathed, "You have an eminent visitor, Dolvid. Will you go and greet him?"

"Not I. They lack the courtesy." Not dismounting, one of the riders had used the haft of his lance to rap at the door, while others deployed in a half-circle, points lowered threateningly. After a pause, another knock, and a shorter wait, soldiers dismounted, stacked lances, and drew swords to go cautiously into the little house. When they emerged, there was a murmured report, and Kamin-Tolagh (as it must be) swung down from his saddle, and went in. Men, meanwhile, were ambling their horses up and down the gully, and one quickly gave a shout, drawing attention to the scorings made by feet on the clay slope. That brought Kamin-Tolagh back out of the house, and with others he gathered by the marks.

"Go away," Âna, murderously between set teeth. "Oh, go away." After much gesticulating, and many signs of indecision from the men, Kamin-Tolagh called for his horse, rose fluently into the saddle, issuing orders with a descriptive, wide-circling gesture.

"Not good," Sebhal said. *Péfrapravádal* were dividing off; Kamin-Tolagh took one quartet back up to the track, while others fanned out in the gully. A foursome came down to the stream, and in the steps of those they hunted, crossed to the gravelly bank. Obliquely, they began mounting the slope.

In the hollow, the five were poorly placed; in plain view soon when the sun came up, they would instantly be seen if they tried to move. The top of the hillside was no abrupt crest behind which they could quickly vanish, rather a gradual rounding-off to a slighter reverse slope. The four riders were off to the left, but if they meant to use the height to survey the countryside, one downward glance would be enough. Sett was muttering, Âna scratched at her cheek, while Sebhal squatted on a heel to stretch the other leg in front of him and ease his knife from its sheath. The climbing cavalry were no more than thirty paces away.

Below, there was a shout. Where the gully continued eastward a dismounted lancer was bending over soft ground near the stream. Kamin-Tolagh appeared on the track above, and shouted a question.

"Hoofprints, fresh — " the bawled answer could be heard, and the soldier waved, eastward. Nearby on the slope the four riders had halted, and as Kamin-Tolagh waved them in, they went loping down. Those on the track, a dozen down in the gully, all the cavalry were soon moving off to the east.

"Farther than it looks," answering Sebhal's silent question about the distance to cover. They both nodded.

"Now, then," Sebhal said, and they went rabbiting up the slope. Dolvid felt blood surge, heavy pack on his shoulders forgotten. Yet the brow of the ridge was endless. Trees, birches and poplars, came into view, and Dolvid took a look back, past the face of the young man with its bared teeth, and saw they were out of sight of both house and track. A few more strides and he slowed, the others coming up, Âna a yearling foal, arched neck and looping gait. They were in among bare, slender trees, and went leaping and crashing in the brown of broken fern, where, from dankness beneath, tight little fists of naked green were beginning to push through. An outraged bittern flapped with squawks into the paling sky.

Without pause, he led the way swiftly through this band of woods, and soon they climbed a sandy step, to where thorn grew in bulged islands on a flat base of salt sand and gravel. Sett was blowing like a beached salmon, and they all halted for breath.

Sebhal was nothing but scorn. "Sending all his men to follow a single set of hoofprints! Kamin-Tolagh is a bigger f-fool than his father made him."

"They must think it is a packhorse," the young man said.

"We could — use — one — " Sett's head was down near his knees.

Dolvid was hoping Neldron would have the wit not to recount the story they had manufactured; he was sure to be overtaken long before he reached his sister's house.

"Kamin-Tolagh, after he has questioned the boy," Sebhal said. "Will have to redivide his forces. Before, if he thinks it through. Can he find anyone to tell him what path we must have taken?"

"You guessed I must know a way through Shemugrân. With this rumor of an attack on the *rabhsai*, we could have plenty of hunters waiting for us on the far side of the marshes. If we can reach there."

Each mention of assassination brought about its flurry of innocence, amazement about how such a tale could get its start. The young man suggested Kamin-Tolagh, aware of the unpopularity of his province in these parts, had invented a threat to the *rabhsai* so as to get assistance that might otherwise be withheld from a Karguli.

"Possible." Sebhal nodded. "But could anyone tell him a way through Shemugrân?"

"There are many paths into Shemugrân," patiently. "As far as I have found, only one way through. Old men may remember their grandfathers' tales about winter pastures here for cattle from the hills — or else stories of the pig-herders."

"Pigs?" Sett was interested.

"Tell us when we are somewhere safer," Sebhal said. "As before, single file. Try to pick your footing to leave the least tracks."

Dolvid straightened from his crouch, and at once bobbed back down. "Horsemen."

Sebhal let out a quiet curse. "How many?"

"Three I saw." They must have breasted the ridge not far eastward, and had just rounded the belt of young trees, cavalrymen, going slow, standing in their stirrups for a better view.

Creeping carefully, he led the way into deeper cover, winding among arched growths that tugged at sleeves and breeches. Coming to a swathe of clearer ground, he stopped.

"What is it?" Sebhal's voice came hissing. Silently Dolvid indicated about ten or a dozen plover, browsing earnestly in the clearing. He had no notion what they were finding for food at this season.

Âna gave a heavy sigh. The bushes were thicker and higher here, and they cowered down, hearing not far off the brush and crackle of a slow-moving horse, coming nearer; the trooper could easily ride in among them. The sound of him slithered by to the right, and then the man emerged into the bare patch, turning to his left. Dolvid had a clear view, a leather-faced soldier with a crook of nose, Owani certainly, no doubt of Kargul, as his tunic certainly was. His horse nickered, and birds went up like a waterspout; the man raised a hand to reassure comrades, who could not be far away.

This man's main attention was to the northward, his own right, but he glanced down to his left often, and in a few more paces could not miss seeing the crouched fugitives. Sebhal's arm went across the young man's shoulders, and he mouthed something, Dolvid catching only the final words, *his reins*. The man called Vol nodded, and Sebhal's knife was out of the sheath.

Had the lance been carried on the near side of the horse, that moment of frozen shock might not have given Sebhal the chance to close with the soldier. As it was, the man could not bring his weapon across, and Sebhal rose, a great cat, taking a leg lefthanded, as the young man seized the bridle short, holding the horse. Sebhal crossed with the right hand to drive his knife in behind the ear; grate of steel on bone, jangled thump of the falling body, were the loudest noises. After a nervous backstep the *pefrai* gazed with its warm eyes on the burden it had lost, with the spurting puddle of arterial blood, fantastically vivid. Though the young man dropped the bridle, the horse did not move when Sebhal gave a heavy smack to its rump.

Refusing any thought about this murderous dexterity, Dolvid cautiously raised his head. Another rider was a good hundred paces away, making for a patch of saplings, having seen nothing of his comrade's end, though with the turn of his head he could observe the empty saddle. From away leftward there was a shout, and the third rider was coming at a canter for the thornbrake. The other wheeled his horse, and as if by instinct Sett and Âna went in opposite directions, both with blades drawn. Dolvid, turning to face the nearest enemy, took muddled notice Rodlakh was quickly mounting the vacated *pefrai*, and Sebhal was trying to dissuade him, at the same time passing up the dropped lance.

Taking a low bank of thorn at the leap, the onrushing trooper went for Sebhal, who just dived aside into cover. The young man was already urging his mount, picking a deft path through clumps of growth to intercept the third cavalryman. Wheeling after Sebhal the nearer offered a flank, and without time to consider Dolvid leaped in, knife out. The horse was moving too fast, and he had to jump away from skidding hoofs, as the massive hindquarters came around. Pulled hard, the dark-grey horse reared, rider wisely throwing down the lance, too awkward for these spaces, reaching across for his sword. Here, Âna darted from hiding to aim a hamstringing cut at the horse instead of the rider, and with blood whining in his ears Dolvid was nonetheless dismayed by that attack, and glad when the horse, as if on purpose, danced sidelong away.

Sett, trying to take a hand, was square in the horseman's new path, and flinging himself down barely avoided an overhasty sweep of the sword, horse overrunning the clearing, smashing down thorn and brush on the far side. As the rider brought his mount back, Dolvid was by the flattened Sett, to turn with his knife a better-aimed cut, then a short-arm thrust which almost toppled him back across Sett's body; he was actually brushed by the big horse. Purposeful rather than frenzied, the soldier hauled the head of the *pefrai* around again, and Dolvid gripped hard at his knife, not much liking his chances if the adversary kept his calm.

He vanished. Saddle empty, the horse shied and skipped sideways, and the soldier was down in mid-clearing, both Sebhal and Âna ramming their knives into him.

Dolvid was able to see the finish of the other fight. The man called Vol had evidently drawn the third lancer in a wide circle, till they faced each other with space for a charge. Now, with left or guiding wrist held stylishly high and wide, his back straight, the young man flicked his cantering mount aside from the oncoming lance, while his own point splintered against the burnished shoulder-piece, sending his opponent spinning. With the crash, Rodlakh (there was no more doubt) dropped the spoiled lance, and dismounted, drawing his knife. From among thorn, he could no longer be seen as he stooped over the fallen cavalryman. Two horses whinnied at each other, and suddenly raced away together. The third, nearby, answered their call, and at first doubtfully then with a bound went to join his fellows. The sun shook free of the mists, sending long shadows across the clearing, and many subtle colors started where there had been only dull brown and grey. Âna, blooded to the elbow, was kneeling at the fringe of the clearing, choking up oats, while Sebhal made a cursory search of the body.

He was cleaning the two knives as Rodlakh walked soberly back. After admiring the skill with which he handled a horse quite new to him, Dolvid half-expected a change in the almost-apologetic manner. None was observable; he nodded to Sebhal, who asked, "Safe?" Another nod, and Rodlakh said, "Âna?" moving for the huddled girl.

"Not hurt," Sebhal said. The girl gave a vigorous shake of her head, but did not refuse the kerchief the young man handed her.

"Bad training," Sebhal, as if it annoyed him, no less in an enemy. "Had they fought together, we would have lost. If one had ridden for help, seeing the first empty saddle."

"Three to be seen now," Rodlakh said.

"We must not linger."

"Good riding," Dolvid told Rodlakh, as together they pulled Sett to his feet, rubbing at a bruised shoulder.

"It is a good *pefrai*, and I had luck. Let us hope the mounts are no homing-birds." A quarter-mile off, two of the horses had found something green to nibble at, privet perhaps.

Sett flexed his arm. "My thanks," he told Dolvid. "I'm not yet tired of owning a head."

That he had done his part in the fight made a difference. Mutedly horrified by how easily killing had begun, he did not seek to be, all at once, a full member of this circle and its plans, but it was good that Sebhal, following in his footsteps, was no longer a threat.

Their course was north and west, and before noon the tangle of Shemugrân should free them from fear of pursuit. The ground fell away gradually, and soon they were passing among man-high clumps of reed and rustling, dun-colored marsh-grass. At a sluggish stream Sebhal and Âna washed away blood, and they all waded across, finding firm ground on the opposite side to show little sign of their landing. But for birds chattering, or whirring away as they approached, it was silent, quiet enough for the surging whisper of the wind to be heard from far off. In general the view was seldom beyond yards, but soon, over to the left, was one of the landmarks, tops of a sickly-looking group of pine crowning a bulge of hill, visible for miles in the featureless country. Bearing more westerly, they climbed a gradual rise, and were back into bracken and slender trees. After a few rough yards they came to the path they were looking for. Sebhal halted, questioning recent wheel-marks of a loaded wagon.

"Peat-cutters."

"Where does this go?" He gestured back to the south.

"Everywhere. It branches off in all directions. One way goes to the village, one cuts across to join the other track. But this is the only way for us to go. Many people use this path, cutting peat or hunting birds, without guessing they are on the southern end of the ancient herders' trail."

"All right," conceding. "But we shall have to listen hard for following horsemen."

"Some of us," Sett put in, "have been listening hard for following horsemen."

They made better speed now. Mist had yielded for an hour to vivid sun, but the day steadily clouded, and a cold drizzling rain closed in the landscape about them. Keeping carefully to where no prints would show, the mossy and pebbled margin of the path, they were mostly in spindly woods, where often the rotten corpses of older trees were lumpy in the undergrowth. Once, seeing a shape approaching, they drew aside into cover, and watched an ass-cart piled high with turves roll by, its wheels in need of trueing. The driver was known by sight to Dolvid, an old man distantly related to Neldron — but most of the villagers were more or less relatives. Otherwise, they saw no one, and heard nothing but their own sounds, with very little talk.

After a crudely-made plank bridge set low near the surface of shallow water, the trees soon gave out, and they were back with thorn-bushes, parchment-colored shocks of swordlike grass. The sparse woods had led them along a narrow spur of higher land, a causeway, and they were already deep into the fringes of Shemugrân; left and right the pools and hummocks of the marshlands spread under dull sky. Dolvid led the way up a low hillock by recent cuttings, sharp, tarry smell of peat hanging in the air. "If the day were clear, you would not see much in any way different from this."

The rain was now only wafts of damp moving on the cool wind. Among the bushes, they sat to share food; Âna especially swallowed dried meat and kiln-bread with greedy appetite.

Sett was musing none of the crew of his ship had been told this trip was anything but a visit to the Nambalus country. "Still, Kamin-Tolagh won't find it hard to divine we have gone north, if we leave a trail of bleeding corpses to mark the way."

"Not only trackers," Sebhal said. "The whole object of this way was secrecy. Once they are convinced we can pass through Shemugrân, fast-messengers could have the news at Kadon Dinul by tomorrow afternoon."

"It could not be helped," Rodlakh said.

"I was wrong to risk — " Sebhal looked from face to face — "so many lives. If we can reach Burantal safely, we'll divide. I had always intended at least two to go direct to Tan Lughsai — the meeting with Galt is essential, more than ever now we may be pursued."

"Five," Dolvid concurred, "is too many for crossing the Heartland. From nearby Burantal, it is a simple journey to Tan Lughsai by the coastal way; no need to go through any town."

Âna's chin was set. "I am going to Kadon Dinul." She challenged Sebhal: "If you are lost, what am I?"

"A life saved."

"I am going to Kadon."

Rodlakh uncharacteristically snapped, "You will go where it is ordered you go."

"And keep the soup warm till the men come back from their manly hunt?"

"This is not because you are a woman. Am I not under Pir's orders?"

"You have my father's disease, great sir. Nothing was ever forbidden because I was a girl, oh no. Only because I was Konat's daughter."

"Go to Konatstead and be peevish with your father. There is no room here for tantrums."

Her eyes flashed dangerously, but Sebhal broke in. "Nothing is final. If we get through Shemugrân, then I shall decide who goes where."

Rodlakh's lips set in a vexed line, and his annoyance was not properly with Âna: their leader had belatedly concluded it was wrong to risk the life of the *rabhsai*'s brother and heir on such a venture. The crisis that had brought about this desperate expedition was clearer now; in their morning talk Sebhal had told him that while the Decree of Preference was no more than a recurring rumor, the lords at Kamsilat had definite word Ban-Sila, saying it required no confirmation in Council, was about to reintroduce one of the chief tools of Preference, the old Loyal Oath, which required all officers and magistrates to swear in the name of Raëdh. Nearly two centuries ago the great Plakhsila

Rabhsai had brought in an oath of allegiance a man or woman of Other Race could also swear, without calling on an alien god, and revival of the older form was not much short of excluding unbelievers from office.

Sett, with a gloomy gaze for Shemugrân, said, "A mouthful of mud would end any argument."

Even at this season and under this sky there were stretches of brilliant green among the pools, the stands of marsh-grass, tangles of reed. At intervals hillocks rose, often crowned with dead and decaying trees of ghostly grey. Eastward, pale hills were doubtful under the overcast, but their northward goal, the long brown Hills of Burantal, were too distant.

"It looks as if you could walk straight enough," Rodlakh said.

"Straight out of history," Dolvid answered. "Firm-seeming ground can be a thin crust on black custard. If you do not drown, you will soon be lost in the maze of pools."

"How did you ever find a way?"

"Following the pigs."

"Wild boar?" Sebhal, decidedly a hunter, was interested. "Here?"

"There may be, but these were domestic pigs, dead and eaten long ago. When this was a cattle-trail, and for generations after, it was also a pig-drove. Whenever the price of pork at Kadon made it worthwhile, pig-farmers of the Lower Paowan would drive their animals north."

"Lean bacon," Âna, laconically. "The prices at Kadon would have to be high, to make up for flesh lost on the drive."

Sett frowned. "How did this help with the trail?"

"Have you heard of the acorn-trade?"

The trader snorted. "I've heard of cloud-pulleys, and left-handed bale hooks, too. My grandfather used to joke about paying debts in acorns."

Dolvid was in his element. "But the trade was real enough. It was after Kamsila *Rabhsai* had reestablished the realm west of Arnan, and founded the port that has his name. As now, long-timbers from the forest at Kamsilat were what they wanted, but the forest also had ton upon ton of acorns for the gathering up. Smaller ships bringing men and supplies to the Colony began using acorns as ballast for the return journey; feed was never plentiful down here, pigs eat acorns. That," he told Âna, "is how your father comes to have a few stands of oak on his lands."

She left off refastening her pack, but only scowled, either at the simple mention of her father, or because she resented being instructed her about her own birthplace.

"So when the pigmen took their bacon north, they carried big loads of acorns for the journey, in carts or on pack-animals. Pigs are not the neatest of eaters, bags must have spilled, farm-lads in those days as in ours had their little wars, and threw what was small and handy at each other. And Shemugrân was creeping back; a vast, impassable marshland in the earliest accounts, and becoming so again. The trail became marked by a line of scattered oaks — no doubt they grew elsewhere, too, but as the marshes refilled the trail became the Causeway, and there was little other dryfoot ground where oaks could flourish and drop their acorns. Even where the trail was, most of the oaks have died off, their roots rotted away."

Rodlakh said, "The Mainland never has luck with trees. Then how do the oaks guide us, if they are mostly gone?"

"Living or dead, it is hard to mistake an oak. But there is also a butter-yellow toadstool that grows nowhere except on the rotting wood of oaks."

"How can you be sure?"

"I have tested it, three times."

"So we follow the pigs?" Sett lifted his pack.

"With care. The ground may change, and no one could learn every step."

Beyond peat-cuttings, some new, the clear track ended. Dolvid took his bearings half-west, and stepped out boldly, wanting to convey a confidence that he rarely felt. Necessary to hold firmly to logic; often there were ways that appeared more promising than a sighting on the next stand of dying oak. Before long, underfoot was squelching; at Dolvid's instance they had all provided themselves with good-sized staffs while in the woods, and a prodding pole might slide through crumbly surface into soft blackness that had no bottom, while drier-looking ways left or right tried to tempt them into dead ends. The sky was clearing in long pale streaks, sliced by a breeze defying any mention of spring, reddening cheeks and noses, numbing hands.

After a groping hour the way led up onto one of the low hillocks where a good-size oak was still standing, though the trunk was hollowed by rot, and the biggest remaining limb had folded down in winter storms. From this small eminence they could scout the country, and also look back the way they had come.

"Horsemen," Sebhal said, squinting in watery sun. Movement was easier to discern than the figures, horsemen indeed, threading where trees gave out and the peat-cuttings were.

"Have they seen us?" Âna said. "Will they try to follow?"

"If they do, Kargul will have another heir to mourn. There is not much I don't dare, but I would not try this crossing on a horse for the B-Bronze Sword itself."

The Household banner could be seen as the distant riders circled at the edge of the marshlands, ants frustrated by some obstacle. That they would see their quarry was improbable, though there must be footprints where soft ground began.

"Shall we be across by nightfall?" Sett wanted to know, as the journey resumed. "I don't fancy bedding down in a swamp."

"At worst," Dolvid told him, "I am making for a place, not all the way across, where we can sleep dry, if the rain holds off."

The sameness of Shemugrân's sad face became confusing. Narrow strips of drier land were all the same, and patches of water to be skirted, the slow streams where fording had to be found. Sett made feeble jokes, while Rodlakh went in silence, head never still, eager to see everything. Âna was tense, Sebhal stern-faced and thoughtful, placing himself at the rear. At times it was plain they were doing it all again, passing the same tufts of reed and marsh-grass, stepping over the same corpse of a long-dead oak with its frills of yellow fungus, the same oozing patches of malodorous bog. Sightings from one marker to the next became mechanical; all his life had consisted of these probings with his beechwood staff, tentative steps onto what posed as firm surfaces, quick tiptoes over mossy levels where the top skinned away to bare the glisten of black and quivering mud. Plunging in to boot-top was common, and everyone fell, including Âna, most surefooted of them. Mud caked on breeches and shirts, their filthy hands, added to weariness.

"Are you going right?" Sett asked, after a longer hesitation than usual. "It's firmer here."

"This is the way."

"Where are your oaks?   I can't see any of your yellow toadstools."

"This is the way."

"What is it?" Sebhal called, as the little column closed up.

With cold patience Dolvid pointed out the birds, bluish-grey, a variety, he understood, of plover, half-a-dozen hopping about a faint swell of ground; in summer there would be dozens or hundreds. The yellow fungus put out a sticky sweat which must be sweet, because it attracted swarms of small, bright-blue flies, and the birds came to feast on the insects. It was too soon for any flies, but the birds had the habit of settling down where the fungus was or might be. "Does this have your approval?" he asked Sett.

Armored in innocence, Sett nodded. "So when we can't see oaks, dead oaks or toadstools, we look for birds."

"In summer," taking it one step farther, "you could just about trace the way by the circling falcons, who wait to see the plovers well-fed." With something to teach, his good humor came back. "You could say Ban-Sila would not be *rabhsai* if Kamsila had not had his famous taste for oysters."

"How is that?" Rodlakh, understandably, was eager to hear.

It was fairly simple; legend said the estuary of the Navu and therefore the forests of the Colony had been rediscovered when Kamsila, enjoying oysters brought to him, had sent the ship back to fetch more. Without the acorns, pigs, oaks, toadstools, flies and plovers, there would be far fewer falcons in the Kafan Burantali —

"I see," Rodlakh broke in. "A falcon-netter of Burantal saved the life of Great Banak, when he was still a youth, after he escaped from captivity in the First Karguli War." The young man gave a broad smile. "I wonder how Ban-Sila would enjoy hearing he is *rabhsai* because of the high price of pork at Kadon, three centuries ago. Not only *rabhsai*, alive at all; if Banak had died then he would not have met Laluvoi, and Lambarr would never have been born." He frowned, obviously lost to the always-perplexing conjecture about accidents of birth.

"Can we not move a little faster?" Sebhal called out.

As they plodded on through afternoon, Sett caught a little of the speculative mood. "It's a fact, best walnut once fetched the same as a mixed load of green oak. I could not begin to guess how much reading it takes to find out all about the pigs and acorns." With a quick glance over his shoulder he verified he and Dolvid were some paces ahead of the others. "Âna, too," lowering his voice. "She had fine education, her mother saw to that, not that my brother-in-law — well, it's a pity."

"What is?"

"Well, he is married, our, um, Pir. Married. She could have any man. I was the one brought them together — took little Âna across Arnan for the boat-ride, and there it was. The world knows he is a splendid man. Konat blames me, but it has been a good thing for Âna, though he'll never change his wife, the world knows that. Me, I'd do the same, if I began again, I suppose. Who can say what is right?"

Dolvid made sympathetic noises, no longer asking why Sett was on this journey.

The sun had gone and dank mists were gathering in darkening hollows. Sett groaned, "It's my knees," and Âna was panting between clenched teeth.

"We are all weary," Dolvid said. Hours had passed since they had rested, and stiff as they were they had not been sorry to resume the march, with a cold wind making them aware how damp had permeated their clothes. They were all mud to the waist, with daubs and patches on jackets and outshirts, yet Dolvid had not made any serious mistake (*except agreeing to come*, he amended).

"How much farther?" That was the one they called Vol, though his concern was not for his own weariness.

"We have arrived," leading to where the cattle trail had once mounted to and along the shoulder of a larger hill. Reaching the slab of solid rock he stamped in triumph, and Sett gave a feeble cheer.

Partway up the slope he turned aside to find the sheltered spot where, years ago, he had spent a night, when he first reached here, coming from northward. He was far from first to camp here; where the rock-face was scooped out in a shallow cave were the marks of many old fires. The ground was flat and dry, a shelf above Shemugrân, and just past the corner of the rock a stream rushed icily from the hillside, to go tumbling and circling down, dawdling at last to annihilation in the still waters of the marshes.

Legs trembling, startled by hard ground, Dolvid swung off his pack. With the wind cut off by the hill, it was noticeably warmer.

Sett, also dumping his pack, pounded his back. "Who else could have done it?"

"It is not done. You have a nasty little stretch yet to cross."

"Lovely. Our morning treat, after cold breakfast and a cold wash."

Âna was arriving. "Aren't we to have a fire?" plaintively. "There is dead wood everywhere." The hill was crowned with firs, chiefly.

"Do people come here?" Sebhal asked with his normal wariness.

"Could they?" hedging. "They might. I found two ways here from northward, long before I solved the pig-riddle. But a fire would be no danger, kept small. We are facing the main width of Shemugrân, and it could not be seen from northward. In effect, we are on an island."

"Safe as Kamanta," Rodlakh quoted. Âna made a face, but was already raking in rock-crevices, finding dry twigs in abundance, old leaves from the few oaks and beeches. The dead wood in the open was less damp than might have been expected; at the end of this day it was amazing there was anything in the world that did not squeak with moisture.

"If we have a fire, we must keep watch." Sebhal brought out his stone, steel striker and tinder-cord, and as he fussed at the fire, outlined watches: "Dolvid, you did not sleep much last night — "

"I do not need much sleep."

"We need a clear-headed guide. After we have food, I shall watch alone, then Âna, who sleeps and wakes as a cat does, can join me for the second hour. Sett can wake to watch out the next two hours with Âna — that brings us to midnight."

"You have time-wicks?" Sett asked, and Sebhal pulled out a bundle of the treated cords, two-hour lengths marked at the center. "At midnight Âna sleeps, and you, Vol, if you will, see out Sett's last hour, and wake Dolvid. With him, you will watch two hours, and get in an hour's sleep while Dolvid and I watch the dawn."

Âna said, "Do we need two on watch?"

"They keep each other awake. They will also keep the fire burning — burning, Âna, not blazing. We can collect enough wood before dark. Let the clothes you have worn dry on your bodies, but rinse socks in the stream; they can be dried by the fire, with any spare clothes that are damp. Boots not too near the fire, or we'll have lame warriors tomorrow. Sett, you have the mattock?"

Sett pulled from his pack the small digging tool with folding blade, and Sebhal advised them to choose soft earth for their needs. Under the fir trees, Dolvid said, recalling the soft padding of needles, the mattock would not really be needed.

The fire was well started, and Âna, taking out her cup of beaten metal, asked about heating water, suggesting, in accord with a growing willingness to allow Dolvid some use, that he might find herbs for a drink. "The year's young for that," he said, although on this sheltered south-facing slope spring was more advanced; maples were ready to break out in rust-colored blossom, and buds on the beeches were fat. "I might find roots for an infusion, but I do have this — " taking from his pack twists of parchment wrapping white, crumbling lumps. Âna rubbed a little between thumb and finger, and sniffed at it. "Goat's milk?"

Sebhal knew. "That is a Froghuli trick, too. They heat milk in a pan, and just before it boils skim off the cream, then let the rest stand in sun and wind. Shaken up in water, it is milk again." He stared hard, as if he could penetrate the unexpected connection with the Froghul.

Yet cups of foaming hot milk made their fireside supper more cheerful than it might have been. Hands and faces had been scrubbed clean (and numbed) at the stream, and all, including Âna, enjoyed when Sett recited an inventory of his aches, from a bruised elbow to a blistered big toe. Face shining from cold water, she was far younger when she smiled — or young in a more appealing way; she might, after all, be called pretty. And there was a sadness here, pondering might-have-been, an Âna blithe and teasing, in a different land that did not turn everyone into a fanatic. In the real world, was there ever a good season? A plant can grow straight and perfect, but had there ever been soil and weather for humans to flourish in? Perhaps not, but he was sure there had been better than this, when the sorrows were one's own, not those of a whole realm gone askew. Innocence (he wrote in his head) is doubly murdered by injustice, which kills the innocent, and makes haters of those who survive. A few more years of these oppressions, and there would be little to choose between those brutalities and the brutalities of resistance.

"We all hate it," Sebhal said, misreading his fierce stare on Shemugrân. "But we shall miss its safety tomorrow."

As he willed sleep under a sky darkening without color, the last picture was Âna, picking her way back from the stream, where she had bravely bathed, teeth wildly chattering, blanket wrapped on her white body. Sebhal drew her near the fire and hugged her, chafing the blanket against the slender back, reaching down for a corner to rub at her lank hair.

"Her heart, I am sure, is mostly right," the young man said. They were talking softly by the dappling fire, while Dolvid kneaded cramp from his calves. "But she will talk as if she is first ever to explore a new-found country of justice and fairness, when all she is saying is what any good man would know."

"That can be annoying — " and might be much more so for one with Rodlakh's rank, lectured in that passionate style. "But it may be the things all good men know still have to be said, over and over again, even among good men."

"Would that stop Bolan from doing as he pleased? Or a creature such as Rheduban? They say he is pleased, watching a girl being flogged to death."

"If half what they say about Rheduban is true, he is mad. We cannot make rules to deal with madness — or with greatness: Banak and Rheduban are outside discussion. But for the Bolans, who can put swords in the hands of madmen, yes. We should never stop saying what all good men agree to. They forget so easily." There was memory in this.

"Are you warm? Will you walk up the hill?"

Soon treading the soft carpet of fir-needles, they climbed to the top. North and south, nothing showed in blackness but the occasional waver of pale marshfires. Stars were overhead, and the warm gleam of fire reflected faintly from the rock-rim of their camping-place.

Dolvid expanded his comments, recollecting a man who believed nothing and everything, who tried on opinions as others did clothes, to see if they became him. "Always, in private, in answer to food riots or disturbances at Pledging, he would advocate monstrous severities, and found a better audience for them, I know, in the Residence Quarter. But I never did better than to turn them aside — if I'd had the courage to keep saying what all good men know — "

"Bolan would be different?"

"No," after thought. "But it would soothe me; I would just have anger for him, instead guilt for myself."

"Âna hates too hard." This was unexpected.

"None of her feelings are exactly half-hearted."

"Yes, but after — " the young man was struggling. "We have to try for an understanding of those we oppose, or else it will go on till one race slaughters off the other. If you were *rabhsai*, how would you have the races live together. In peace, yes, but how would it be kept?"

He grunted, not sure this was fair. `If I *were* rabhsai' might be a fine game for children, but Rodlakh knew how near to that he was. "If I were *rabhsai*, my whole life would be otherwise, and I would not choose as an historian would, or an exile."

"Great Banak was not brought up to rule."

"Well, then, I would look for ways to make sure the races had positions of power proportional to their numbers; bring about some changes in the Treaty — impose them, if need be."

"In the West — well, it is true the *Atarlum* has very few admirers there, but we have not heard the *Mankh'* has had any large part in — in the miseries we see."

"It is everywhere. Behind Ban-Sila, the attempt to introduce the Decree of Preference, surely behind the new oath — where else but from the *Mankh'* does it come from, that the Owani race was made to rule, and all Others are their natural servants?"

"You are Owani yourself. Can you not imagine how one whose blood was mixed might try to be more Owani than *g'Asalladh'* Himself?"

"Bolan, you mean?"

"Ban-Sila," saying what Dolvid had avoided, and there was no mistake about the pain in the young voice.

Rodlakh's intention to let the man he called Pir sleep through to dawn was defeated by the leader's innate time-sense; without waking Âna he uncoiled from next to her bent form, and told the younger man to rest an hour. Protesting he was wide awake, Rodlakh stretched on his sleeping bag, and was asleep in a moment. Dolvid spread his own bag over him.

Not a hint day would ever come. Mists had obscured the marsh-fires, and this was more than ever an island, blurred stars the only sign from a wider world.

When Sebhal came back from relieving himself among the trees, Dolvid, who had a small bag of *raminat*-leaves in his pack, was balancing metal cups on hot stones. "Is it quiet at the Frontier?"

"Far from it," pondering what to say next. "Between us, one reason they are so anxious for this accommodation with Ban-Sila is concern over the Frontier. Lord Saidhan and his son the Captain b-believe some on the Mainland would strike at Kamsilat just when we're hardest pressed at the Frontier."

"Is it tribal raids?"

"There are always the tribes. You would think Banak's offer would have ended that for good, not so? the Frontier open to anyone who comes in peace? The tribes are all cousins to your Froghul, and they could be full subjects with the Fro', just for asking nicely. Or they could have been," he amended, "till this reign; Ban-Sila and his cronies are the only full citizens today. But no one is going to question a tribe that wants to settle quietly in the Lunu Tezh' — land for the clearing there, and they pay no taxes. In any reign, there are some who think it manliest to wander on Landegh till they are near starving, then raid across the border for a chicken, a cow — I can understand that, Dolvid; not everyone can be tamed to a plot of land. But the Army of the West has its manhood, too, and its mission."

"I would guess the tribes know that, or understand it by instinct. There is no disgrace on either side in such wars."

"Or was none, till Ban-Sila *Deghi* called us outlaws. But worse trouble is brewing up in the Farther West. Everything is restless, and the Shâl Mines road is ambushed every week. That's out beyond the Frontier."

A vague assenting noise. The West was muddled visions of dry and bony country, from which *jinzal* could emerge, bringing death and terror.

"Yes, there are *jinzal*," and Sebhal's matter-of-fact tone was a strange thrill. "More than we have seen in years. The rumors are worse, and with spring coming — Landegh is the breeding-ground for tall tales, but this year it is madness. I have heard about *jinzal* marching in ordered companies, a *jinzai* army, *jinzal* who have learned to use weapons — well, one may pick up a weapon from a fallen soldier, but sword or lance, it is just a club to a *jinzai*; now we hear about *jinzal* archers, and rumors have them wearing helms and breastplates. Every tribesman who tells the tale heard it from someone who knows someone who saw it, almost. It is absurd; *jinzal* have no skills but killing with hands and teeth; they could never forge their own armor, and what other would fit those chests? Still, credit a tenth of what you hear, there might be some half-civilized tribe on the march, one new to us, and if the Colony were to be overrun — "

"Overrun?"

"You Mainlanders never realize how precarious it all is, there in the West."

"But if they could overrun the Colony, why would they be stopped by Arnan? They could learn ships, and if they are too much for the Army of the West, there is no force this side of Arnan to defeat them."

Sebhal was grave. "All true."

"Then you are talking about a new Night."

"Now you know why, why they want to be sure the *rabhsai* has these messages in person."

Dolvid was silent. Sebhal's tale was too far-fetched (had he himself not expressed disbelief?): skillful *jinzal* marching in ranks were as unimaginable as if wolves or eagles named captains and worked out strategies for conquest. There might be much unrest at the Frontier, and rumors of worse, but Dolvid suspected he had just heard *the story*, agreed-on in advance, a tale of crisis to justify desperate actions. Through much of history, warnings of imminent doom had often told less about dangers than about the ambitions of soldiers who uttered them.

A blurring of night came, shift of distances to recreate land and sky. "Truthfully, do you see the *rabhsai* as a captive of his advisors?"

"I am a soldier, under orders. You do not?"

"Only as we are all prisoners of our beliefs — " disliking his own sententiousness, but unhappy, too, with Sebhal's bland feints. "But can a little talk with Ban-Sila alter everything his reign has striven for, since the day he was proclaimed?"

"It is thought his mind might be changed. Not necessarily in the way young Vol thinks. Care is needed in how the *rabhsai* is told about danger to the Frontier — it would be invitation to attack to let on how few Army of the West can be spared to defend Kamsilat. But then — no, I must not burden you with these policy questions; guiding us is enough. What is our goal for the day's march?"

"You spoke about dividing." Dolvid would like to get inside Sebhal's mind, but was not unhappy to be spared more of his elaborate evasions.

He made a mouth. "Can we postpone that battle?"

Dolvid, evening off the water he was heating so all would have half a cup of *raminat,* explained he had thought of heading due west along Kafan Burantali, staying on the near slopes. To cross the hills and go straight down into the Heartland would make for an easier journey, but they would also be much likelier to run into patrols. All going well, they could reach the Gap of Burantal in the afternoon. "That is equally the road for Tan Lughsai. If it helps, I once found a safe hide above the headwaters of Shuburu. You can put off till morning the fight over who goes where."

"Excellent."

iii

Burantal

"We agreed before we set out, I give the orders for this expedition."

"This is nonsense," the young man answered in a fierce, low voice.

"In war there must be one commander."

Rodlakh lowered his voice again. "I am the one, of any, who..." he became inaudible.

"...dangers have increased since then," the end of Sebhal's rebuttal.

"Hranakh take the whole lot of you," Dolvid shouted silently. He was stretched taut with the strain of pathfinding, bored and irritated with this circling debate, which had gone on for hours, returning again and again to the same simple propositions. When there was a stop for food, the argument also halted, and he sat among glowering faces, assertions held back to be made in these rasping whispers as they resumed the march.

As if left to his own game he had led them west along wooded skirts of Kafan Burantali, well up on the south-facing slopes. The going was rough, slower than anticipated, mainly among rocks and brush, slowed more when they had to descend into a gully, often to cross a steep-sided stream. As on the gentler, grassed northern flanks, the rim of the Heartland with its rich farms, progress would be easier near the foot of this slope, a well-worn way, but they were safer here, seeing no one in the woods or on the trails they crossed, rutted tracks of wood-cutters or goatherds.

" — not a boy, to be packed off when there is a chance of danger." Denying his youth, Rodlakh's querulous voice seemed to confirm it.

"That is not the reason. There is danger everywhere."

"Pir will have his way," Âna, softly, just behind. "When it is plain he means what he says." Evidently there was no longer any doubt she would go to Kadon Dinul; she could hardly be imagined so even-tempered otherwise.

"If this was the way of command in the Army of the West," sourly, "*jinzal* would be dining in the Great House at Kamsilat." His annoyance was exacerbated by the ridiculous pretending; he would have to be very stupid not to see Vol was important, a life so-called Pir was reluctant to risk, now yesterday's fight had increased everyone's danger. And Rodlakh, logically enough, was insisting the whole purpose of this expedition was for him to confront his brother.

"What would you be fierce about, I wonder? I suppose, whether it was Plakhat Gabh'Owan or the Patriarch Kamanasalladh VI who first tried to use Gabhanil letters for writing the Owanilú."

"As a matter of fact, so far as can be told, it was neither, but a scribe named *Ifbleni*, if 'Seventh' is a name. I never found out whether he was a seventh child, or someone's seventh scribe. Happily for us all, his way with the letters did not become the fashion. Ifbleni spells as the fancy takes him." Dolvid glanced back at her. "Sett told me you had some learning."

"Enough to be annoying to the learned. Tell me, Master, if a proven descendant of Plakhan could be found — Lost Plakhan, I mean, of the Bride Quest — would he have a claim on the Bronze Sword?'"

He did not see any possible way she could have discovered the Bride Quest was one of his pet mysteries, nor why, after all her calculated insults, she would flatter him with feigned interest. He discussed it; even ignoring that Plakhan's abdication had been irrevocable, a claimant would have to prove uninterrupted descent over four centuries. That would be in male line; if cognate descent was allowed, there would be many nearer claims; the Finú whose sister had married Rheduban, the House baKargul itself, among others.

"Kargul?" brought up to believe they were nothing but criminals. Dolvid explained all their alliances with Gabh'Owan, the former ruling house, and it came as a new idea to her that the baKargul' were quite sincere when they called Great Banak the usurper.

"Banak Navuni, except the remote one coming from his marriage to Laluvoi, had no conceivable claim on the Sword. Legitimist claim, that is; a good case can be made for the right that comes from being the only man able to rule. But baKargul can tell you a dozen with more lawful claims, all the way down to Kamin-Tolagh, or his sister."

"Would you want one of that house for *rabhsai*?" she asked (or challenged), but there was no talk now, as they were busy clambering over a fallen tree, then hoisting themselves up through a tight notch between age-smoothed rocks. They turned to watch the others follow; Sett showed most signs of weariness, no longer placing his feet.

"*Rabhsai* is *rabhsai*," he told Âna when the march resumed. "Eventually, the crimes of the House baKargul might be forgotten; it has happened with others. But *Lekh'Owan* is finished; we need a *rabhsai* of all the people."

"As Ban-Sila is?"

"Like young Vol's Ban-Sila, waiting to be set free."

"Vol is obliged to — " she swallowed it. "If the *rabhsai* is the *rabhsai*, he should be the right *rabhsai*. What is this?"

"Seeds from sunflowers." A favorite snack, his own harvest, kept in his pocket yesterday, so as not to lay a trail of empty hulls across Shemugrân.

"Yes," he resumed, much happier with this new Âna, who asked real questions and expected answers. "*Rabhsayum* is said to

descend from Yoëlladhu Founder, who was named by Raëdh Himself
— " He made the pious sign, and she grimaced. "Yes, yes, but we must
begin somewhere. With your father's people, lordship comes down
from Otti, and just as with Raëdh *Toladhi*, Otti is end as well as
beginning; what is good can have ascent as well as ancestry — we can
come to the right *rabhsai*."

"*Mankh'* talk." She bit open another seed.

"And dangerous, unless the Will of Raëdh, or of Otti, returns
through the people. If not, there is nothing to prevent anyone who
thinks he can hang on to it from seizing Sword in the name of
betterment." Though this was pure doctrine, it was also, as he meant it
to be, about Sebhal. Âna was frowning.

They had been winding deeper into the hills, out of sight of
the flatlands where, distantly, they had glimpsed the sheen of Arnan.
The land was craggier now, and they mounted a long hard slope to
reach a broken shoulder and a clear view ahead. Dolvid pointed. "You
see the tower? That's Burantal."

It was the ragged top of a partly ruined watchtower which
overlooked the Gap of Burantal from the farther side, where the name
of the hills changed to Kafan Lughsai. Though Âna strained forward
eagerly, not much of the city was seen from here. Mainly, Burantal
shelved down northward from the Gap, into the green bowl that
opened on the Heartland, a situation celebrated in more than one
admiring song, the best-known comparing the city to a precious jewel
between a woman's soft breasts.

"When we came to Kadon for the Pledging in '34, we did not
come this way. But I remember the Marionettes of Burantal."

He nodded a little sadly; though as far as he knew the
Marionette Guild had continued its travels from town to town until
quite recently, for him the joy of puppet-shows on the Avenue of
Treaties was in a past too remote for memory, read of or rumored. He

had never actually met Nentirr, celebrated Master of the Guild, though had once sent him a note about a glaring historical error in one of his pieces. Not that it mattered; Nentirr's bold imagination could not be judged by the same rules as sober history. Nentirr and his brother must also be going though some hardship, with restrictions on travel taking away their livelihood.

Sebhal came up. "Are the hills garrisoned?"

"Not now. The watchtowers have no occupants but bats." In the years when Shemugrân was passable, guarding the Burantal Gap had been important, but Kanzan Tâl was now portal to the Heartland.

"Tobhsila took and held Burantal for a few weeks, in the War of the Widowed," Sebhal said. "They keep a garrison of General Cavalry here."

"Down below," with a wave, "The city incorporates an elbow of the main road, with gates facing east and north."

"And a decent hostelry," Sett, wistfully. "Shall we spend a night there?"

"Is the debate done with?"

"I doubt it." Sebhal's mouth was grim.

Dolvid led the way up scree, warning against loose stones. Bearing to the right they crossed one of the lesser crests, keeping low on the skyline, and cut back to enter a narrow but widening gorge. Ahead there was the sound of rushing water, and as the setting sun struck their faces the bottom of the gorge dropped sharply away, leaving them on a wide and almost level shelf. At the right was a steep, stony face, and leftward past tenacious bushes on talon roots they could look down on a stream that came from the rock, turning sleepily in a burnished pool before spilling over the rim, where the gorge opened into the Gap. In late light circling clenches of foam were blood-red.

"Shuburu?" Sebhal asked. "The f-failing stream?"

Dolvid brushed aside portents. "It means nothing, except this is where ways part; rightward for Kadon Dinul, leftward to the coast and on to Tan Lughsai. Shuburu is the only stream flowing away from the Heartland; if it rose only a few paces northward, on the other side of this bluff, it would find a way to the Paowan, instead of flowing direct into Arnan."

"But Banak-rai took it as an omen," Rodlakh said. "Strange that one who had to fight for everything he won also had his fey side."

"The omen was a f-false one," Sebhal, brusquely, and to Dolvid, "You said there was a safe place to camp. We have well-travelled roads to cross, and I would rather do that near dawn. We shall stay together for the night." It was the only time he had over-elaborated a decision.

The path they were on, though now little used, wound down into Burantal, but a short way along the present shelf, still with no view of the city, they came to the remembered place, a narrow cleft about man-high on the rock face. It was like the neck of a fat wine-flask, and at the rounded end hidden behind there were dry caves, with the stump of a long-abandoned watch-tower on rocks above.

Dolvid hoisted up into the cleft, warning the others there was seepage here, the rocks slimy. Âna sprang and wriggled up easily. Sett, attempting something between leap and giant step, missed planting his left foot, and flopped on his front, clinging with frantic fingers as if the drop were many feet instead of a few inches. Rodlakh gave a boost from behind, and everyone was smiling till they saw Sett was in pain, standing unsteadily, hands pressing the hollow of his thigh. The face actually went chalk-white, eyes acquiring the sad, bewildered look of a wounded animal.

The night was a bleak one. Supported each side, Sett hobbled to where they camped, gasping at every step, and was put to bed in dim hope a night's rest would bring a cure. A fire would have been risky so near habitation, and there was no wood here; well-sheltered from wind their chief real loss was a warming drink.

Whenever Dolvid roused from uneasy dozing Sebhal was awake, talking in a low voice with Âna or Rodlakh, or standing quiet in feeble starlight. He shook Dolvid's shoulder for final watch in the cheerless hours before dawn, as Rodlakh groped a way to his sleeping-bag.

Wanting to talk, Sebhal waited till the young man had settled, soft sniffs and throat-clearings giving way to steady breathing.

"I cannot blame Âna," at last. "Her kinsman, she will not hear of leaving him. My mistake, permitting a man in middle life to be part of this." He gave one of his mirthless chuckles. "You could say I am in middle life, too, not so? Older than Sett — but I am Owani, and I have not spent my life adding accounts and jogging from meal to meal on the back of a sedate mare."

"He came because Âna came," Dolvid could not help observing.

"It is she I should have had the strength to refuse. But she was in the secret and we wanted — they, the lords wanted, to keep it among as few as might be. It is all changed. Did we not swear, before we began, no one life would stand in our way? Then how can we let our attempt be wrecked, for the sake of a man whose name history is going to forget?"

No response, and the atmosphere grew heavy before Sebhal resumed. "If he were someone of name, it would be just the same. I am not talking about killing a man, like a horse lamed in the wilderness. Sett could be made comfortable enough here, and each of us could spare food to give him rations for a week or ten days. Our embassy to the *rabhsai* will succeed or fail in three or four days at most; if we are killed or captured, he will be no worse off than the rest of us."

"Just as dead, you mean?" He imagined being left here, lame and alone, staying alive with mouthfuls of food, waiting in the stink of his own waste for possible return of friends. He said, "If you end by abducting the *rabhsai*, who will come back here for Sett?"

"His lameness may heal, with a few days' rest."

"Not likely — " in his mind laying hands on the skeleton learned at the *Mankh'* long ago, the smooth ball at the end of that longest bone, the polished matching socket. "I am afraid the thigh-bone may be jolted out of place. You saw how the foot kept turning in. I am no *ramidu*; I hope I am wrong."

"This would cripple him."

"Normally, the sinews knit, after a fashion — you have seen old wrestlers who have had the same injury, how they walk on the toes of one foot. A good *ramidu* might be able to work the bone back in before the sinews start to shrink."

"Could you?"

"No," very swiftly. "I would not risk trying. My guess may be wrong, and I could cause the injury we were trying to treat."

"But there is no chance of getting a *ramidu* here, and you have the learning — "

"Pir — " much of his annoyance with the silly false name was in his voice. "I'll go with you on this crazy venture to my own death; I was not doing much with my life. But I am not going to help cripple a man for any reason."

"What would you do in war, if you had to choose a man to die protecting the retreat of others?"

"That is a different case; anyone might be ruthless if sacrifice had a plain object. Our chances of success are, at best, so slight — "

"Pir's job — " Âna's voice rose softly in the blackness, and she came after, brushing hair away from her face. " — is not counting odds, but to deal with each obstacle as it arrives. But lower your voices, or else go farther off. Sett could wake, too."

They moved for the narrow neck of the fissure, Sebhal saying, "He would not hear anything he does not know."

"But hearing himself talked about as damaged goods... and he has his knife."

"Sett would never do that." The tone was ambiguous, and most likely if their leader were the injured one, he would surely solve the problem in that way. Dolvid would also concede there was sense to leaving Sett here, so long as that was not taken to mean they were going to do so.

Where they were, the noise of Shuburu came to them, the distant roar of an immense crowd. "I wish we had come some other way," Sebhal said, and it was a shock to see he was troubled by omens and the Failing Stream.

"Wish?" Âna, sharply. "We make our own fortune, and can always will it to good — so you taught me." Plainly she was quoting him, word for word.

"Well — " it was as if he shook himself like a wet dog. "What? I did not relish our long debate yesterday any more than Dolvid, and now it is all wasted breath. If we cannot leave Sett, what? Sit here till our food is gone and we all starve?"

Âna touched Dolvid's arm. "You said you had good friends at Burantal. Would they take in an injured man?"

He had no need to ponder. "With no questions — but I am not the one to ask them."

"You had a falling-out."

In the afternoon he had enjoyed the fresh, intelligent questions, but she had not lost this bustling habit of assuming the worst imaginable explanation for what was unclear.

"Untimarr is a true master-carpenter, and a true son of Burantal. He lived near Kadon Dinul for a few years, and managed what small estates I had. His wife, Morú, would have been our midwife."

"Would have been?"

"If children had come."

"Oh."

"They are good people, of some consequence here, not all that fond of Great Family authority, or Owani conceit in general."

"Yet they served you, when you were in favor."

"As friends friends."

"Âna," Sebhal, with beetling patience, "you asked Dolvid for people he trusted; are you going to condemn them for trusting him?"

Dolvid reminded he was *kaël'rolai*, an exile-breaker, to be killed by anyone with impunity, unlawful to assist. Untimarr and Morú, he was certain, would give him any help, which was why it was unfair to approach them.

Not noticeably abashed, she said, "But you know their house?"

He did; it was on the far side of town. Unclear just what Âna had in mind, but plainly Sebhal was against entering Burantal. "He may yet wake up with less pain."

The last time-wick burned away. Sett woke with a low complaint about the cold; he had slept with bags over and under him, unable to get into one.

"It doesn't seem anything like as sore," he announced. In near-dark it was a moment before he saw the hands Dolvid and Sebhal proffered. Supported on each side, he stood carefully, using mainly right leg. He had a fragile smile, and then stiffened as pain came. Breath whistled in between his teeth. "Curse it," bitterly. "Curse it."

Pir at his left side said, "Stand on your right foot only."

"I'm not sure — "

"Stand on the right foot, or I'll let you drop." Sebhal reached across to have Dolvid let go. Leaning into him, Sett obeyed the rough order. Sebhal kicked aside bedding, and stepped forward, and Sett half-hopped, half-hobbled a couple of untidy paces.

"How far could you go like this?"

"You must be mad."

"An hour? Ten paces? All day?"

"I don't know, it's not so bad. But for concealment — "

"Rest, have your breakfast." He worked the injured man to where he could sit on a rounded rock, and Âna brought food. Rodlakh, coming back from morning observances, looked a long list of questions.

"The path down to the city," Sebhal asked, "is it watched? Would it be wide enough? Could we do it, with Sett supported like that?"

There had been unrest at Burantal, and everywhere there was a watch and a curfew, but troops would hardly be spared to guard the back way into the city, with all the other troubles there were. Âna said her idea had been for someone to go to Dolvid's friends and tell them where Sett was, but Sebhal said, "Too much coming and going. We shall all go together, and see Sett safe."

"But one person alone should go ahead to Untimarr's house," Dolvid said. Since it was not to be him, he suggested Âna, for whom Untimarr would be readiest to open his door in answer to a knock at dawn.

"I made sure you would leave me. I am putting you all in danger."

"We have all been in danger," Sebhal, and with mirthless satire: "The general feeling is, it cannot be added to."

The worst came at the start; all three uninjured men were needed getting Sett through the neck of the bottle back to the shelf. Sebhal crouched, hands under Sett's armpits, while down below the other two tried not to cause him too much pain, as they caught at waist and knee. He gave one bitten-off cry, but then he was down, leaning on Dolvid. Once on the path, there was no place half as difficult; where Shuburu spilled over the edge the way went sharply right, and its downward course was in long bends and mainly easy slopes, for most of the way with room for a man on either side of Sett, hopping and hobbling. Sebhal and Rodlakh were crutches, while Dolvid walked ahead spying out the way and telling the girl what to say, meanwhile reflecting what this reign had brought them to; he would very much like to see his friends, knew they would be glad to see him, and instead he was coaching Âna in how to lie to them. She and some kin were on a journey from the Nambalus country —

"To visit a sick grandfather," Rodlakh contributed from behind.

"Good, near Kadon. He is thought to be dying, and you could not get permission or tokens for the journey, so by the heartless standards of the day, it is illegal — that explains why you are creeping around before sunrise. And your uncle is injured, and you don't dare take him to a hostelry, even if you could find one open."

"Let me have money — " she turned and took both gold and copper from Rodlakh, who had produced his washleather purse. A marvel how she, with her lowly standing, kept up pretence the young man was no one in particular, giving not a hint of deference.

"Come to that last," he cautioned. "They may accept payment for Sett's food and other needs after they have said they will take him in, but if you begin by chinking money, Untimarr will say unpleasant things, if Morú has not already slammed the door in your face."

"I shall like this couple — " not being ironic.

"We shall have to see whether they take to you, or anyone waking them at this hour. But Untimarr was always an early riser, out of the house before sunup."

"No more," Sebhal said, "all praise to Ban-Sila." A reference to the curfew.

"We are coming near houses," Dolvid warned. The sky was steadily lightening, with a ghostly yellow creeping in. Having crossed Shuburu once, now a quietly running stream, they recrossed it on a rough bridge of brick and stone. The path looped across a patch of bare land with a few lightless houses, and ahead were the roofs of the city, gleaming faintly. Across the gap was the steep hill with the gloomy old watchtower, while leftward the terraces of the upper city mounted, windows a grey-gold glitter.

Broad, shallow steps led down into the dark gorge of a walled lane, and they had crossed the city walls unnoticed, the path having been built up to the level of the former battlements. In the street the quiet was reassuring, and at a divide Dolvid chose the right-hand way, past low stone houses with darkened windows, a few shuttered shops. He did not know Burantal street by street, but was unhesitating about general directions, with the watchtower ahead, width of the Gap to the left. In a straight stretch of cobbled street a cat went nosing across, and stopped to stare over its shoulder at the approaching group, eyes shooting a quick spear of emerald before it vanished into the side way.

Âna, halting, said, "Hush." The admonition was hardly needed, but standing quite still they heard the irregular clatter of a few horses, ambling on cobbles. As quickly as they could with the injured Sett, they flattened against a black, windowless wall. Into the cross-street where the cat had gone rode three spiritless soldiers of the watch, one with a lantern casting a sickly puddle of yellow light. They were ready for the end of curfew and start of their rest, and their glance down the way where the travellers huddled was cursory. The ironshod hoofs rattled off in the stony silence of the city.

"Oppression," Sebhal derided. "Where in this realm would there be discipline to maintain it?" Dolvid was tickled, then saw the soldier was not aware of any humor; it was a serious professional concern.

When silence came again they moved ahead, rapidly as they could, Sett's breath coming in sharp gasps. Past the crossways they were among larger buildings, several with the thick pillars and decorative corner-carvings typical of this city. Down a side-alley they saw the glare of fire thrown on the wall facing an open door; the clink and huff of bellows told them a smith was getting an early start. The main street had broadened, and they were moving on smooth and solid stone. Nearby, a door banged, making them all jump. Dolvid led them to one side, in under a deeply shadowed colonnade, carved pillars supporting terraces above, continuing up to and then around the Market Square, pride of Burantal. Not far short of that wide, paved expanse, he made a halt.

"What is that sound?" Âna whispered.

"Laluvoi's Fountain. Come, I'll show you." Staying under the colonnade, he led the way to the corner. Six ways in all led into the great square, which sloped down slightly left to right, in the direction of the main road. Loyal citizens of Burantal insisted their central street was fully equal to the Avenue of Treaties at Kadon Dinul. That could be debated, but it was true Kadon had nothing to match the forest of columns which fronted the Market Square on five sides. The fountain was off to the right a little, a graceful upsweep of fretted stone set in a broad, six-sided basin, Laluvoi's gift to Burantal in memory of the man who had saved the life of Great Banak.

"We can make our way around the fringe of the square in shadow. But we should be sure of Untimarr before starting again with

Sett.   The house is quite near — " indicating the narrow opening directly past the fountain.   "That is Arrow Way.   It runs perfectly straight, a hundred paces or so, and meets a wide, curving avenue — "

"The Bow," she guessed.

"Exactly, but it is one name in this city in the Owanilú, Utalai Course.   Untimarr's house stands in some grounds, just to the right of where Arrow Way comes in.   The gate-arch has elaborate carving, and his door is from a single slab of oak — " recalling this, he was poignantly reminded of happier times — "there is a laughing sun at the center."

Rodlakh said, "I'll go with Âna."   Steel glinted in his hand.   "I can stand watch by this unforgettable gate-arch while she is waking the house."

Sebhal, having left Sett with his back against the wall, also had knife drawn.   "Do not throw bait to any trouble.   If you run into any early citizens, grunt good morning and walk on."

After the two agile young figures, short and tall, had gone flickering past the fountain across the breadth of the square, time yawned, while light grew with steady hostility.   Sun up, curfew would be ended, but that was not the worst.   In many parts toughs recruited for curfew-duty, emulating Bolan's Special Forces, went riding through the streets just after the start or just before the end of curfew, in hopes of catching violators.   Again in imitation of Bolan's cut-throat band, summary punishment had become commonplace, cruelty often mixed with brutal humor: a painter of miniatures at Dônshei was said to have had his fingertips blistered over a forge for starting home half an hour late, and there were many similar tales.   In those describing what might happen to female curfew-breakers could be heard a shuddering relish that made it impossible to judge how much was true.

"If troops come," Sebhal was telling Sett, "and we are far outnumbered, we may have no course but to leave you. I am saying this because there might not be a chance for farewells or regrets."

"Regrets," he echoed. "I am the one that should ask forgiveness for the trouble I've caused with my clumsiness."

"Nothing; you have caused nothing — we made a choice. But when we have peace again, I'll show you rock-climbing."

Dolvid was to come back to this memory of the great captain bantering away Sett's remorse. Deep inside the lower building across the side-street a light showed, growing and shrinking behind a barred window as if a lamp or rushlight was being carried from room to room. As Dolvid reached back to be sure the knife was free in his shoulder-sheath, Sett slouched lower in the recessed doorway, lifting his injured leg two-handed to move it. From the direction of Market Square there came sudden sharp sounds, hoofbeats, and there was no explaining why these had so much greater menace than those heard earlier. Rhythms crossed and recrossed, echoes bounding from wall to wall, so it was only gradually certain the sound was coming up from the direction of the main road, over beyond the Fountain from their former vantage-point.

"Two mounts being walked," Sebhal determined. Keeping back where gloom was deepest Dolvid returned to the corner and peered out between columns. Laluvoi's Fountain sent cold lace against the blue-grey of stone under dawn light, pallid sky diluted with faint green where stars were ebbing. Then he saw horses, two, on the far side of the fountain, evidently haltered together, led by one man — one soldier, as his helm reflected a ray.

The light across the way flared close behind the window, and a door opened with such force it banged against the stone. Glimpse of a woman, a white figure, white-clad, white-faced, holding a lamp up, but attention went at once to the man who gestured her a brusque farewell, wheeling from the doorway and coming to mid-street. He was very tall, loose-limbed, slender, but with wide, level shoulders. The neck was long, big head set at a curious angle that thrust the mouth forward. The boots that rang on stone were military, and so were the breeches, or as much of them as were visible. Above, he was wearing an extraordinary outshirt of dark shuzi, probably purple, reaching almost to his knees. The sleeves, coming to mid forearm, were very wide, with flapping fringes in red and gold.

Tangled hair stood out from the man's head and sent straggles across his forehead. The light eyes were large, set very wide above high cheekbones. Beneath a strong hook of nose there was a broad band of moustache, and it was the man's mouth that made him most sinister, long upper teeth curved, so stretched lips stayed permanently parted, as with a rodent or venomous snake. Dolvid shivered. He couldn't guess why the man should be in Burantal, but was quite certain he was the notorious Rheduban.

He might be somewhat drunk. Hand to a hip, swaying a little, he called out, "Dheruli!"

"Master?" The servile voice of the soldier with the two horses. Rheduban moved loosely in that direction. "Late again, slug. Bring my *pefrai* here." The voice had the nasal drone often heard in western Kargul, provoking the thought that if Rheduban had been born to his rank he might have gone to meet his mount, instead of insisting it be brought to him. The rattle of hoofs began again.

Continuing to drift slowly for Market Square he half-saw Dolvid, and peered in under the colonnade, eyes doubting. He reached across for his sword, a slender blade. "Men," he said. "You there, curfew-breakers."

Neither Sebhal nor Dolvid moved. Still trying to penetrate the shadows, Rheduban backed away a nervous step or two.

"Come into the street, let me see you," gaze flickering back and forth, uncertain, perhaps, how many men there were. Sebhal began a stealthy movement away from the Square, after motioning Dolvid to stay put.

"Dheruli," Rheduban called. "You have your bow? Curfew-breakers here." The sound of hoofs halted again. Dolvid sidled one half-step, so he could see the man Dheruli, too far away to be rushed, reaching up on the back of the nearer and smaller horse.

"You there — out in the street, I say," stepping in Dolvid's direction, and Sebhal sprang out between pillars, coming at the right side of the Karguli captain, who turned very quickly, sweeping a low backhand with the sword. Sebhal jumped back, crouching, knife up across his chest.

Dolvid leapt into the square, ignoring Dheruli and his bow, trying to get behind Rheduban. A long sword-thrust, then Rheduban went back in small tiptoe steps so as to keep Sebhal in view, backing farther as Sebhal tried to get on his opposite side. Their hunting knives were no good against a skilled sword unless one of them could come blind-side. Quick breathing and shuffling steps were all the sounds, and then creak and slide of a bow drawn with arrow ready. Not confident against the full length of shining steel, Dolvid feinted a rush, and had to jump back, wristing down another lunge, Sebhal jumping in before Rheduban could follow that retreat. Then the Karguli twinkled back again with his dance-steps, blade swinging side to side, long face filled with anger. Dheruli had left the horses and was at mid-square, perhaps fifteen paces from his master. Dolvid turned slowly to face him, keeping a corner of his eye for the swordsman, and thinking it was bad luck to run into so experienced a sword with the support of a bow. He wished Rodlakh would return; Âna, too, was a useful knife.

"Shoot that man, fool," Rheduban rapped out, and Sebhal was going farther left. There could have been no real pause, but the many times he reviewed the scene Dolvid saw how all forces locked into balance, sword an overmatch for any one knife, but unable to deal with both, bowman aware he would have the chance for only one shot if he was rushed. The moment trembled and snapped, as Dolvid sprang, not straight for the archer but rightward, and an arrow hummed by his left ear, as Rheduban made a charge at Sebhal, who could only give ground.

Rheduban wheeled and strode to the soldier, who cringed as much from his own captain as from the fight. Cursing a lost chance, Dolvid went forward, and so did Sebhal from the left. Running feet from the far side of the square, and Rheduban swivelled to see Rodlakh coming at the charge. Having wrested the bow away from Dheruli, he swung back just in time to shoot the oncoming Sebhal, hitting him high in the chest. He went down at once on elbows and knees; Dolvid by instinct changed course for the wounded man, and Rheduban, flinging down the bow and making no attempt to recover his sword from the unwilling Dheruli, made a bolt for the horses. Uninterested in the fight they were taking a drink at the fountain's basin. Rodlakh, coming hard, swerved to make a slash which ripped Rheduban's blossoming sleeve as the man flung himself on a horse. Flat on the *pefrai*'s neck he raced away, and Dolvid, having changed direction again to round the fountain, had no chance at the man, and was almost run down by the second, riderless horse, who came shrilling, halter twanging taut.

The abandoned groom gave a despairing cry and cowered, too fearful even to drop Rheduban's sword properly, as it leaned against him. As the man cringed to his knees, Rodlakh, knife high, checked his thrust, and with his free hand cuffed the man hard, once, twice. "Curse you, run!" He shoved at the man, and went into the Owanilú to thunder, "*Sobha', ran'ghai — sobadh nidaën'!*"

Dolvid hurried to Sebhal, and was conscious of Sett's pale face looking out from the colonnade, Âna's quick feet, running from the far side of the square. Sebhal had rolled onto his back, arrow sticking up obliquely.

Âna and Dolvid reached him together, just as a loud gong sent trembling waves through all the city, not an alarm, signal for the end of curfew. Sebhal's eyes were opened, clouded with hurt, and there was a pink foam at corners of his mouth.

Âna dropped to her knees next to him. Put against his chest near the arrow, her hand came away with only a small smudge of blood. At the range, even with a small Owani bow, an arrow hitting squarely would have gone through him. Weaving as he charged, he had been hit slantingly, arrow perhaps striking breastbone or a rib. He was snatching breath in a bubbling wheeze.

Rodlakh had at last kicked the groom into a stumbling run. The tall young man stooped to pick up the crafted sword. He examined it, and then with all his strength pitched it away; it went clanging, end over end, after the retreating groom in the empty, lightening Market Square. Rodlakh came slowly to where Âna and Dolvid bent over their leader. The young man's eyes were bright with tears.

"Can we pull out the arrow?" Âna in a flat voice.

"Not yet," Dolvid warned sharply, and Sebhal seemed to groan out what might be a *No*.

"We have to get him out of the street," Rodlakh said. "We shall have more enemies. You know that was Rheduban?"

Âna had not known; she gasped dismay. "We cannot leave — him."

Rodlakh looked the query at Dolvid, who nodded and mouthed *Dying*. Blood was on the lips, and Sebhal's eyes were fluttering.

Hopeless to dream of carrying Sebhal and helping Sett all the way to Untimarr's house. Rodlakh was looking wildly about the square.

With a neat pace, a small, weaponless man was crossing to them; he must have come from the pillared building facing the northwest corner of Market Square. A shadowed doorway was being held open there, a hand and forearm visible.

"If your friend can be lifted, you must bring him this way. Can be? Must be lifted. Come." He was grave, smooth-faced, nose small and flat, dark, kindly eyes set very shallow. His age might be anything above thirty and short of seventy.

Âna said, "If we move him — "

"But he must not lie in the street, you see. There is the ordinary Burantali watch, as well as these foreign rats sent to plague us. Rats, above anything, I'd say." Briefly his mouth shaped into a chilling reminiscence of Rheduban.

"Two for legs, young man at the head?" the small man suggested. "Swiftly, I implore you."

"We have another injured friend," Dolvid said. "If you, sir, with this woman, could take the legs."

"Large man, great warrior, but one small dart — yes. I am stronger than you would suppose."

Sebhal moaned as he was lifted, and it sounded like a wish to be left to die. As Dolvid crossed to him, Sett asked, "Will he live?"

"No. Well, he might. I don't think so. Come."

Sett's curse as he hauled up was only in part from the pain. Told to make haste, most of his weight on Dolvid's shoulder, he started across the square in giant hopping strides. "Where are we going?" he panted out. "Are — these — friends?"

"You have other invitations?"

They came up to the others staggering with Sebhal's cumbersome form, Rodlakh laboring with his burden. Guided by the small man they jostled through a wide entranceway, a door of decorated bronze swinging shut after them. In the dim there was the elusive notion of a corridor enclosing a central block, windowless at ground level. The man who had been holding open the outside door went trotting ahead to open double doors; he was a slightly taller, definitely plumper replica of the first, the same bland plateau of a face. "I do not believe you were seen," he was saying as they passed him at the doors, as breathless as anyone struggling with a load.

"Rheduban," the smaller one said, "brings on epidemics of blindness."

They worked their way down a few shallow steps, and a third set of doors was opened. The room beyond was high-ceilinged and long; shafts of light slanting through dusty gloom made muddling shadows. At his first glimpse Dolvid was sure he must have gone mad. High up at each side of the long room a seeming row of human corpses was hung, men, women, a few children, their little feet dangling. On tables beneath, set against the wall, dimness permitted a horrid impression of dismembered bodies and detached, staring heads, hands severed at the wrist, bundles of hair, white shins, a scattering of pathetic eyes. Then he saw the knives and files, brushes and pots of color, stacks of billets and bolts of cloth, the strung harnesses, and knew where he must be.

The stouter man used his arm to sweep half-finished clothes from a low worktable, and fetched a bundle of cloth to set under Sebhal's head as they laid him down. Sett disentangled from Dolvid, who was overtaken by weariness, and sat or leaned on a high stool, gazing about in stupefaction. The smaller man looked from one to another of the travellers, nodding. "You will be safe; we'll make you safer. I'll bring better light."

"Water — warmed water. Bandages," the other one, surely his brother.

"Yes — Falis is coming. A sip of *raminat* might not be amiss."

"We thank you, Master Nentirr," Dolvid said.

"Ah, you know me."

"By your fame." He had in fact seen him at a distance, years ago, at Kadon Dinul, receiving the applause for one of his shows in the Avenue of Treaties.

"Yes, well, many talents go into it, really. My brother Ondir, master maker of our figures. Fame has many faces, too — the Guild is sad, but honored." Nentirr, whose vaguely archaic manner must come from his puppet-plays, made the flicker of a bow, and went nimbly away.

The brother Ondir stayed, as one of those who gathered about Sebhal. Âna pulled open the outshirt, and used her knife to cut stained inner clothing away from the shaft of the arrow. Ondir, whose plump hands and thick fingers made him an unlikely-looking master-craftsman, brought heavy shears from one of the work-tables. Steadying the shaft he quickly cut it off, a handspan from where it made a ridge in the muscling of Sebhal's chest. With a blunt forefinger he cautiously tested how firmly the point was lodged, and gave an asthmatic sigh. The short, fluttering rise and fall of Sebhal's big rib-cage had no countable rhythm, the shiver of his heart to be seen not far below where the arrow had gone in.

"The point, broad or slender? Who was there?"

"Broad," Sett supplied. "If it was the same as the one that went by Dolvid's ear and landed at my feet."

"Like a leaf, or tanged?"

"Tanged."

"Ah. That's what I was afraid of, from the wound. Well — " he straightened. "With some light we shall see better."

He must mean a lamp was on its way; he was not talking about the new rays of sun, coming through grimed windows as moted blocks of light, striking the row of marionettes hung opposite, highlighting faces known from history — known, rather, in these representations by the Guild, good faces, grotesque faces, a bulbous nose, winglike ears, the horned head, half bull, of Enardak. Aside a little Ondir whispered hoarsely, "The arrow might be dug out, and perhaps we could stop the blood. I am no healer; I may kill this man."

Catching a flavor of his own fears over Sett, Dolvid sympathized with the man's dilemma. "Rheduban killed him. We must take any chance of bringing him back."

"Aye, but this man." The fat fingers were weaving in distress. "I do not want to blame myself for the death of Sebhal."

Rodlakh, overhearing, was ready to deny the recognition, but the Guild's profession was to know famous faces. Âna was obviously relieved pretense was finished, and when the man she had been calling Pir opened his eyes she was able to speak his real name, "Sebhal, oh, Sebhal. Sebhal," as if the word held life and could be rammed into failing heart and lungs. In Sebhal's throat there was a snoring sound, and when Rodlakh gently raised the head Âna cried out at the blood that came welling between clenched teeth. Ondir pressed a folded wad of soft cloth into her hand, and she wiped blood away from mouth and nose and chin, sniffing back her tears.

Nentirr came back carrying an oil-lamp, followed by a plain woman with a bowl of steaming water, strips of white cloth draped over her arms, while Nentirr had a pot of white crystals, alum, perhaps, or some medicine. Ondir was browsing along the worktables, selcting and discarding tools, settling on a slender-bladed knife, slim bronze pliers, clamps, and a bundle of the flat-tipped sticks used in modelling clay.

On the table Sebhal gave out a noise like an agonized hiccup. Staring ferociously into Âna's face he reached to grope for her hand on his chin, gripping hard at the small fingers. "Moon," he fumbled. "Moonsong." Grasping Âna's hand, he died. Ondir put down his collection of implements with a slight rattle, and Rodlakh let the stilled head sink back.

Âna said *Sebhal* blankly, her face set and hardlipped. Rodlakh's cheeks had two shining tear-tracks. Above their heads old and mythic heroes looked down, Maëdhi the Wise and Odi Kukkuk, Yuvakh Martyr, stone-chinned Shâl IV, Pir Perus whose name Sebhal had borrowed. There was azure-haired Fiunuvoi Flood-Tamer, Lost Plakhan, the warrior Larghai. Great Banak, of course, his brave, imperturbable face, Rodlakh's grandfather, best friend to Sebhal's father. Real and legend ran together, and Sebhal's fame would remain bright as any.

Âna had strayed to the worktables and was turning over parts for marionettes in the making, finding out how jaws were hinged, and what was the device that allowed wooden fingers to grasp a sword. She was like a bored child on a rainy day, when nothing can be taken up wholeheartedly. Questions were crowding about the future of this expedition, the Colony, the Army of the West, the realm.

First, though, they had to mark the passing of Sebhal, and make it real. The little Master of Marionettes felt the need, or sensed it in his guests, a ceremony to take away unique disorder and give it pattern. He must have simply adapted from one of his plays, puppet rites for a puppet hero, but his actions were no worse for that. He unfolded a glowing square of stage-tapestry to drape the body, and before covering the face intoned, "Here pass great deeds and the good hopes of many. Be unforgotten, Sebhal Saidhanati."

"*Olagh am*," Dolvid murmured, "*rashud' y'ai n'olaghan*."

The cloth was lowered. After a muffled sob from Sett, nothing, till Âna said, flat-voiced, "Now what?" Something was coming between her and proper grief.

"Pardon, my wife says soldiers are already in Market Square — not foreigners, troops from the gates, and most of them, I venture, would as soon your meeting with Rheduban had come to a different end. The rat-man has few friends in Burantal; it would be hard to find witnesses if he were slowly pummeled to death at noon by the Fountain.   Still, orders are orders, questions are being asked; Rheduban's own sewer-pack may come back. Talk of a search, house to house, for the missing body and the curfew-breakers."

Obviously, he had better concealment in mind, but Rodlakh was curious. "Back?" he said, "Rheduban has led troops of his own, Kargul, here at Burantal?"

"Oh, aye, when he began favoring our city, a few weeks back. There was a to-do about shirts and fruits taken in the market and not paid for, and they caused bruises shoving aside good citizens. We're not sure, day to day, whether we have found new allies or been invaded. Reliable news was the first traveller kept off the roads by the new laws. However that is, lately rat-man has been coming back by night, alone."

Falis returned to the long room carrying a tray with small cups of warm *raminat*. At first she had seemed plain, but her features were not unlike her husband's, except that while his face was an unwritten page where any startling thing could happen, hers had settled into the pleasant ugliness of a defined personality, seen too in the assured way her feet met the floor. The traditional public deference of the wives of Gabhanil was not always reflected in private; Dolvid remembered the tough old warrior of the Northeast, Ott, who listened in deep respect to the opinions of his wife, Mandellis.

"General Cavalry," Falis announced. "Standing all about the Fountain. No officer higher than a file-leader as yet. They've stopped some passers-by for questioning."

Nentirr nodded soberly. He and his brother went to the far end of the room where there was a raised platform, with a rough-built gallery above, obviously for trying out new marionettes, perhaps for rehearsing scenes. Together the two brothers slid the platform aside, revealing a trapdoor. Nentirr pulled it up. "Our cellar, where many things have been stored." Stone steps went down steeply.

"The air is good," Falis assured them. "We'll bring food to you, when it is safe."

At head of the steps, about to enter, Âna turned. "What about — ?"

"The Captain of the West will not be seen by any intruders." Into Dolvid's head flashed a grotesque vision of Sebhal's body hung for concealment among the marionette heroes. As if reading his mind, Nentirr assured, "He is to be accorded every respect."

On the narrow stair there was no room for supporting Sett. Ondir went up a ladder to the gallery, and lowered harness for suspending one of the life-size figures.

"Is this safe?" Sett wanted to hear, as he passed his arms through the loops.

"Safe, sir?" Ondir wheezed from above. "Some of our figures — take the Yuvakh Martyr, armed and armored with the brocade overmantle, outweighs a larger man than you, sir." He worked pulleys while Nentirr guided the lines; Rodlakh stood at the foot of the stair to take part of Sett's weight as he came swinging down, with a self-conscious grin.

Falis handed down the lamp. As the trapdoor closed Nentirr's face appeared in the last space. "Have no fear. We'll open up, as soon as it's safe." The hatch thumped shut, and soon there was the sound of the platform being dragged into place.

Evidently the cellar had been used to conceal the valuable properties of the Guild, though most things were less costly than might be assumed by a hurried or ignorant thief; arms and armor too flimsy for real use, furs mainly dyed rabbit. Some of the breastplates were encrusted with glass gems, and there were glistening bracelets and coronets that blazed in lamplight, a high crown as worn long ago by the lords of Vrobhan. Most precious were bolts of shuzi and other fine fabric, a rich red and blue brocade, a fine teased linen.

Farther into the cellar were pieces of furniture, a heavy table and four big oak chairs. Massive piers, part of the building's foundations, jutted at intervals, and in between were a number of bunks with blankets and bolsters, each bed in its own alcove.

Sett remarked, "Others have been hidden here before."

"Tactful not to ask about that," Dolvid recommended. In the past there had often been rumors implicating the travelling guild in various unlawful sidelines, smuggling of monopoly goods, help for those who, for one reason or another, wanted to travel in secret.

Soon Sett was lying on the bunk nearest the stairway, while the others, setting the lamp on a table, gathered by the next bunk, finishing the *raminat* they had been given, and trying to make plans. Before that, Rodlakh's discomfiture at the supposed deceiving of Dolvid had to be overcome.

"Sebhal did not want you to be burdened with knowledge of his rank."

Dolvid's face was a match for the *raminat*, which had the brackish taste of overlong storage. "Or was reluctant to put the price of a pardon in the hands of an exile."

"That was never in his mind."

"Yes it was," Âna, in the voice of one wearied with games. "Dolvid," she argued, "has risked his life in two of our fights. He has earned honesty."

"Sebhal, anyway," in half-apology, "believed the deception necessary."

"More annoyance than deception. I was not in doubt for long. I knew in the first hour, *Asai*."

"Not *Asai*, let us not begin that." His quick glance was eloquent about her lack of respect when addressing him. "I was never in favor of this pretense. The battle is already half lost if we give in to suspicions and lies."

"What are your plans?" deliberately abrupt.

"Plans? Sebhal is dead. You realize what a disaster that is — for the West, for justice?"

"Yes. What will our plans be?"

"What can they be? South of Shemugrân, we began in bad luck, and it failed completely at Burantal. If Sebhal had been only wounded, we still could not move ten paces without being captured. With Sebhal dead — "

"*Valrabh'*, for what I was told the scheme was, would your capture not serve better than anything I could do to evade it? Once you proclaim who you are, no officer would dare do anything but see you were taken to your brother, the *rabhsai*."

"If I could be sure of that, I would never have let others risk their lives; I would have returned to the Mainland alone. I tried to arrange a meeting with Ban-Sila, sent him letter after letter — I can not accept that he is his own man. You will say you know him, too, and it is true he is intoxicated with the *Atarlum* — for all that, he never refused simply to listen. And, look, he is surrounded, not just by Bolan's Household and the Heartland friends of the *Mankh'*, but Kargul as well, Kamin-Tolagh and Rheduban. If I fell into Rheduban's hands, you think he would take me for a talk with my brother?"

Rodlakh's captive *rabhsai* remained nonsense, but, yes, nonsense sincerely believed. Once again he did not want to explore what this meant about the hero they had just watched die: there was no need to recall their talk, the night before last, to be absolutely certain Sebhal had not come on this expedition in hopes of rescuing Ban-Sila

from over-zealous advisors, but he — and Âna — had let Rodlakh go
on under that assumption.

"I was puzzled from the start, that such important lives were
risked on this doubtful business. If Rheduban had kept a few men
standing by, we would have lost you, too."

"We have lost the only one who cannot be replaced."

Âna, dry-eyed, asserted, "It is no honor to Sebhal to say, after
all these years and all the men he has trained, he has left an army that
cannot fight with him gone."

Rodlakh protested without much force he had not said any
such thing, and all energy had gone from the discussion. With soldiers
hunting them in the streets, they would obviously be here a while, and
could decide soberly whether any purpose could be served by going on.
If Rodlakh insisted on trying for Kadon Dinul, it might be possible; the
hunt was up, but as far as the soldiers knew they were hunting a few
curfew-breakers who happened to be armed, and the search surely
would not go on for long.

"What about Kamin-Tolagh?" Âna said. "The hunt here will
be that much more serious, if they connect Burantal with three we left
dead south of Shemugrân."

"Two," an embarrassed confession. Rodlakh explained the
man he had unhorsed was clearly out of the fight, with a definite
collarbone and probable leg broken. Instead of finishing him off with
his knife, he had made sure the man's water-flask was filled, and left a
little food nearby for when he regained consciousness.

She was scandalized. "If Sebhal had known — "

"Sebhal was more used to the necessities of war than I am."

As with the action with Sett responsible for their catastrophe,
Dolvid approved of Rodlakh's clemency, though it was poor policy.
The soldier spared might be able to give the number and a fair
description of the travellers; perhaps he had only a fleeting glimpse of

any except Rodlakh, but it might be enough to connect them with the attack on Rheduban here.

"Is it true men from the Army of the West are coming to Tan Lughsai?"

"If they make the crossing safely." Rodlakh's initial tendency was to laugh at this skepticism. "Most of what you have been told is true."

"With some important omissions, *Asai*. Well, then, if this Galt — is that his real name? — is coming, it might be better for us all to make straight for the Cape." Back in the Colony, Rodlakh would be both safe and useful.

He stood and paced, and his style still came from Sebhal. "I am of no special use to the Army of the West — one more lance; they have Saidhan if they need a name. I want to hear approval of what is being done from my brother's own lips. To make him his own *rabhsai* again would be better than anything I could do at Kamsilat."

Âna's eyes, perfectly expressionless, came to meet Dolvid's, and he was shocked to recognize she was making a plea, let it drop for now, till they could talk.

"Besides," Rodlakh confessed. "I am not eager to reach Kamsilat with the news we have — for Saidhan, loss of his only son, for the Army, their beloved captain. And Aëlu, Aëlu is there at Kamsilat. Who will give her the news — where will the words be found?"

He was very young, and what he said had real emotions behind its stilted bookishness. But Âna turned away, her lips twisting, whether with fury or sorrow.

"We'll beggar you," Rodlakh in reproach, reaching under his shirt for the wash-leather purse. Only a step from fear for our lives to good manners, without a breath between: when they heard scrape of the platform being slid back they turned down the lamp and waited tense in the shadows, weapons ready, till the hatch opened and the voice of Nentirr called reassurance.

With his wife and brother he came down into the cellar, and having resigned themselves to another meal of dried meat and kiln-bread the travellers were glad to see a roasted fowl, fresh wheat-bread, a mash of cooked beans, a welcome flask of red wine. This, in the midst of shortage and confiscation, was a feast.

Nentirr became sly, face fleetingly usurped by that of Okseti, Odi Kukkuk's deceitful companion in several stories. "The Guild keeps its friends."

"Its old boastful ways, too," his wife said.

"There is nothing that can't be found, if you have the money to pay for it. The old story; if you can't buy rations, buy the rationer."

"But it makes prices double and treble what they ought to be," his wife said.

"We would be honored if we could call you our guests — " Nentirr accepted coins, and Falis took them away. "With the Heartland as it is we cannot travel, and Burantal has little left to spend on diversions. Well, night can't go on all day, as the Fool says in the tale of the Devil-Bride." His own joke; there was no Fool in Dolvid's translation of the story, nor in the old *Mankh'* edition.

Falis huddled forward, hands clasped. "We've had soldiers at the door, asking if we saw what happened in Market Square. Hunting, they said, known outlaws and breakers of curfew."

"Sebhal Saidhanati," Nentirr said. "This is the same breed that once put Great Banak in fetters."

"But men of our own, not foreign filth. Let this Bolan try sending his curfew-keepers and food-thieves into Burantal, and we'll see where the garrison stands. Still, they all wear boots to leave tracks on my clean floors; it's said there may be a house-to-house search."

"Rheduban, when we first saw him, was leaving a woman — not his wife, I would say. She must have seen some of what happened."

"Safer if she did not," Nentirr said.

Falis had a rancid look. "Svondais knows she's lucky, here in Burantal, to keep ears on the sides of her head. She has her calling. It might be, money aside, she has no choice but to take care of his filthy needs, but she had better be careful."

Rodlakh objected, "The woman may have a liking for him." Âna looked as if she might spit.

"She has studied and follows the *Epranda*," the Marionette-Master explained darkly. "That is what brings my Lord Rheduban here by night."

A minor puzzle, and the woman's odd name, neither Owani nor Gabhani, was part of it. The *Epranda* (some people said it should be *Asprandha*), a faith or body of knowledge kept stubbornly alive through centuries, was rarely heard of these days. Apparently it had originally come from one of the minor races or tribes subdued by the Gabhanil in the Wars of Cleansing, before the Owanil had returned from the Island. The *Epranda* had never been the religion of a whole people, but a kind of forbidden, or at least hidden, set of beliefs. Strange healings, a method of foretelling that involved use of smokes and drinks to produce trances, mutilation and sacrifice of animals; some of this might still be alive behind drawn blinds, but what the *Epranda* meant, for most who had ever heard of it, was its study of pleasure through pain. This had long ago been condemned by the *Atarlum*, and all extant versions of a secretly circulated, frequently recopied book were supposed to have been destroyed (though a complete set with all variants was said to be preserved in the restricted collection at the *Mankh'*); the *Epranda* had been surreptitiously fashionable in the reign of Plakhval, who decreed against it, and since then it had faded away.

Rheduban was famed for enjoying other people's agony, but beyond that he had married Radaghi, once courted by Tholat, the then-Heir, who died at Tan Lughsai. Dolvid had very good reason to know about Tholat's repellent tastes in mating, since it was Khalú's desperate wish to escape Tholat that led to his own marriage.

"Aye," Falis was saying. "Let her take to spying and tale-telling, and she'll lose more than her ears. Eat while the food is good. We'll have to seal you up again."

"What is the *Epranda*?" Rodlakh asked. Âna was equally baffled, but too jealous of her knowingness to ask.

"Needs that might shame any man," Nentirr proclaimed.

"It seemed peculiar he would be here at dead of night, with only a single groom for company," Rodlakh said.

"Filthy," Falis said. "Not that half Burantal does not know." Nearly to the steps where Ondir had been standing impassive guard, Falis came back to speak with Âna as if confidentially, though Dolvid and Rodlakh were sitting at the same table, and Sett yawning on his bunk nearby.

"There's a thing with many sharp needles and little cuts with knives," woman-to-woman. "He loves blood. Whips, too. At times he puts on a woman's shift, and she whips him, and then they do goatish things. For money she serves him."

Sett was ready to laugh when it came to the woman's shift, but Âna's expression of disgust turned to what seemed pitying disbelief, and she shook her dark head sadly.

"The same beast," Rodlakh said, "who shot Sebhal and would not stand to fight."

Nentirr came padding back from the steps. "Not so long ago, my people would have sewn such a creature into a well-rotted cowhide, cudgelled him to break his bones, then rolled him over a cliff. That's how they dealt with freaks."

"Your people?" Falis objected. "Aren't they mine, too?"

"Women, whether they spring from Gabhan or Owan, Froghu or the moon, are of the woman-race."

"Well, I could say a man, however bred and no matter how old, is always of the boy-child race."

"Wife!" His face took on the autocracy of the Shâls.

She went past him to the steps. "Your dolls are waiting for you." Above, Ondir wheezed his amusement, and Nentirr could not have enjoyed it more if the final hit had been his.

"Hoy, Sett!" Rodlakh proffered a heaped plate. Sett, who had been dozing off again, sniffed hungrily. He hauled himself up straight with a grimace. "Ah. This is better than being whipped wearing a woman's shift, any day."

No one failed to eat, though with Sebhal's death so near they all felt uneasy: meat-eating in such circumstances had an eerie sensation not to be examined too closely. After good food and the rough, sweetened wine they all felt drowsy. Sett snored with a plate on his chest, till Âna took it away and spread a blanket. Rodlakh, with his own burdens, stretched out on another bunk. Dolvid in a third was beginning a complicated dream when Âna whispered, "Are you awake?"

"Of course, yes." He rubbed at mouth and nose, and scratched his scalp.

She gave him a last half-glass of wine. "Dolvid — you advise we should make straight for Tan Lughsai."

This was not going to be the real subject. "I'll follow the *Valrabh'* to Kadon Dinul, if that is where he wants to go — though I would love to hear a better tale why."

"You do not hold with Rodlakh?"

"Given that Ban-Sila *Rabhsai* is his brother, I cannot judge."

She sat next to him. She had been mistress to a great man not yet interred; it would be inappropriate for his pulse to flicker. "I am certain he believes the *rabhsai* is a captive."

"His sincerity is not a question."

"He and Sebhal differed about this."

"Sebhal was not the man to look for curious and far-fetched explanations where simple ones would serve."

"He knows, he knew Ban-Sila better."

That could hardly be true; he had spent years in the South, and had not seen much of his brother since he, Rodlakh, was twelve, but Sebhal's visits to Kadon Dinul had been brief and far between, and Ban-Sila had never been in the West. "No. Sebhal knew life better."

"He said, it is a mistake to regard the Family as a family; the scent of power changes all feelings."

"But Rodlakh — " lowering his voice further, "is his father's son, as Ban-Sila is not. Their father, above everything, believed in a family." That was exactly true; the mild and amiable Lambarr would have minded losing *rabhsayum* much less than permanent separation from his wife and children.

"Sebhal warned me never to doubt out loud Ban-Sila was to be rescued from evil advisors."

"For my sake, as well as Rodlakh's?" — puzzled by what was happening: Âna's new mood was confessional, as if she wanted him for a friend, and had to begin with truth. But if the death of Sebhal left her in need of an ally, Rodlakh, surely, would be a more promising choice.

Dolvid had not forgotten the sting of her early, aimed insults. "Sebhal, then, only pretended to fall in with Rodlakh's views."

"You can have strange scruples, you of the Families."

"My grandfather was a chandler, my father began as a chandler's apprentice, and ended as a librarian. Only my nose has a pedigree."

She bowed her head. "I am always making rules before I think. Rodlakh's birth is Mixed, whereas Sebhal — don't you shudder, when some Gabhani or Other talks about the good old days when men could be sewn in cowhides and pitched over a cliff? Those are my people. But Sebhal was yours, and he did not mind a few deaths, a small price, he said, for setting the realm straight."

"And then a few more. That road is hard to get off, once started."

"But surely the realm would be better off without — " her voice dwindled — "Ban-Sila *Rabhsai*."

"No doubt, unless we found a worse one to put in his place." This resumed their discussion yesterday, but far more dangerously when it was nearer a real *rabhsai*. Dolvid was now altogether convinced Sebhal's intent from start to finish had been removal of Ban-Sila. She must know she could never carry that out alone, but surely, having heard Dolvid's views on assassination, she could not see him taking Sebhal's part? Disliking pomposity, ruefully greeting another of those times to keep saying what all good men knew, he enumerated the flaws in murder as a policy: it allowed nothing to the chance the murderer's opinions might be mistaken, to kill a *rabhsai* was to kill law itself, and justify all future murder and revenge. She was patient till he talked about a condition "worse than the worst law," and then she challenged; "Worse than the Decree of Preference would be?"

"Worse," he insisted, and she turned her head away in disgust at the smug Owani. Sebhal had charged the Mainland always forgot how fragile the Frontier was, how little protected their safe-seeming lives from the ravages of wild men and *jinzal*, and surely the same was true with their precarious safety behind the flimsy barriers of law and custom, the chaos they held back. Not only the monstrous Rheduban, but equally their host, a mostly mild man, who, if there were not laws to prevent it, would take delight in the lingering death-agonies of someone whose tastes, merely, were different from his.

"My father has often spoken about how fine it was when thieves were dragged behind horses, and anyone who lied at law had his tongue burnt out. Men would band together to geld the stealer of a man's wife — as if a woman was, was — a piece of furniture to be stolen with nothing to say about it. There is terrible cruelty in the world, but with laws or without, the bullies rise to power. Sebhal — " She stopped.

"What would he have done, let us say, if Ban-Sila had caught a bad chill and died, and Rodlakh still refused to be *rabhsai*?"

A stare. "How do you know that? As if he was joking, Sebhal did tell Rodlakh there could be a sudden vacancy. He blushed, he does that often, and said he would accede and abdicate both at once; his delicacy would have no part of power seized unlawfully."

"But Sebhal did not change his plans."

She hesitated. "After that he stopped disputing with Rodlakh about how much, or how little, Ban-Sila was maker of his own policies, and that was when he warned me to do the same. I suppose he judged Rodlakh, when it came to it, would have to accept the Sword."

Yes, but with a realm's future in the balance, Sebhal would have had a second plan, in case logic was wrong, and Rodlakh, adamant, went off to the South. There was a third brother, Orbanak, only twelve and sent by Ban-Sila to the *Mankh'*, but Sebhal, uncle to all three, was not unreachably distant from power, and a distaste for assassination should not obscure that he would quite probably have made a good *rabhsai*, enormously popular, endlessly competent, a practised compeller of armies, and with a lovely and well-loved wife at his side. Perhaps the Sebhal who spoke so easily of sacrificing any one life to the general good could no longer be sure where singleness of purpose overlapped into personal ambition. He was ultimately acquitted by the bloody irony of having turned aside and found death for the sake of a companion he regarded as negligible, or said he did.

"I am glad my uncle was not left to die, but I am the one who forced Sebhal to come into Burantal. I killed him."

"No one wanted to abandon Sett. Why try to take on whole guilt for a death brought about by all of us, by Rheduban — by bad luck, above everything."

"He would have overruled you, and persuaded Rodlakh. Only my obstinacy — "

"A death," in sheer puzzlement, "you have yet to weep over." She regarded him numbly, and he quickly begged her pardon. "Tears are your own business."

"And there is another one to do the weeping."

"Who, in turn, unless I am blind, is loved by another one."

Âna rolled eyes slightly. "Not loved, revered. As you have seen, he reverenced Sebhal; Sebhal's wife is to be worshipped, and that leaves only Âna to despise — Sebhal's seducer, in his eyes. But Sebhal's heart stayed with Aëlu."

This was bitter. "He died holding Âna's hand."

"Did he? Could you hear him? You are the translator, translate. I was no more there than Odi Kukkuk, who was also looking down."

He did translate; moon, moonsong — *êlu, êlolu*. The name *Aëlu* was indeed the archaic form of the Owanilú *êlu*, moon.

"At Kamsilat," mockingly, "though the Old Tongue is honored, it is never spoken at the Great House — even their endearments are translated." Dolvid recalled Âna, moments after Sebhal's passing, toying idly with marionette-parts, and knew now her seeming-numbness had been a struggle with this bitter anger.

Now she did begin to cry, leaning her face against his chest. He patted at her shoulder, and meanwhile part of his mind where feelings never came was marvelling that Âna, with all her rancor, yet wanted to protect Rodlakh from seeing what Sebhal really intended. Did she perhaps suspect Rodlakh would again make it all her fault? Or was it that if she could keep Sebhal as an unflawed hero in Rodlakh's eyes, she could still catch the reflection she wanted to see? As an historian, yoked to the search for cold truth, Dolvid knew very well the rival appetite for heroic myth, and had warmed himself at the embers of uncritical legend while busy proving it could not be true.

"I am crying for myself," she tilted back her head to inform him.

"That may be all we can ever do." He stroked the thick, dark hair, which seemed damp, but could not be.

"He wanted her there."

"Some men can love more than one woman." These mawkish responses were horribly apt, as if bereavement reduced everything to formulas.

"Or none," between sobs, and with a joyed alarm he observed his flesh heard that as a cryptic challenge. Âna was soft and moist, her salty breath very warm. Tentatively, he kissed her, and far beyond expectation her mouth reached for the kiss. Soon they came to be lying nose-to-nose on the bunk, she on her right side, he on his left.

"I have discovered there are men — " her sniffs were subsiding, "who are kind to a woman because they never learn to love her."

"And women who can love without being kind." It was nothing, play of a wordsmith, yet she was earnest, or sad. "I'm not. Only... ambitious."

"Nothing else?" and when she insisted; "The *Rabhsai* Ban-Sila does not have a wife. If he asked, would you marry him?"

"He is not going to," then, vehemently, "No!"

"Then ambition is not all your story." His hands were restless, and she let him enquire, her head half-sunk in the bolster, nose flushed from weeping, the one eye he could see very brilliant.

"You're not, are you? Ambitious? Yet you have been high."

"I am, in my way," truthfully. "For the power to be left alone." Here, they lunged together in a kiss that grappled and was long subsiding.

Overhead there was the scraping slide of the platform uncovering the trapdoor. "Later, tonight — " a fierce whisper, and she was gone in the wing-flap of unfastened clothes.

Tonight, his mind growled, old gloom descending immediately, *if tonight ever comes*. The trapdoor bumped open: *if this is not Rheduban with his men*. He felt for where his long knife was stowed.

Ondir had come panting down to see if anything could be done for Sett's injury. He claimed (the phrase would not have recommended him to Dolvid) to have "had some luck" with healing, and Sett was eager to have something tried.

A man who knew joining, Ondir watched with understanding as Dolvid, using a stick of charcoal, sketched what he could remember of the bones. He gave no sign of noticing the stain on Dolvid's breeches; Âna seemed to be napping.

When Ondir ran thick, capable hands over Sett's thigh, it was plain where his healing experience had been; he kept making little clicking noises, tongue on teeth, as grooms did to steady a nervous horse. Not saying much, Ondir pressed and twisted at the injured leg, using far more force than Dolvid would have dared, but either because of his skill or his somewhat forbidding silence (broken by wheeze of his breathing) Sett cried out only twice in a quarter-hour's kneading, though eyes became tear-bright in a scarlet face, while a yellow and purple patch of bruise formed outside the thigh, echoed at front by a patch of brownish-blue.

In the end Ondir said, "No bone out there. Fitting's what I know best. I'd wager there's no bone out."

Sett felt at each of his thighs, trying to compare one to the other. Ondir, having done the same, said, "Might be there's some of those, ah, teldons out of place. They grow back."

"Tendons," seeming encouraged. "At Konatstead, there was a hound they all said was lamed for life, good as new in a month. Lived to be fourteen, and never so much as limped."

"Dogs... " Ondir had evidently finished his manipulations. "Cats, even better, healing in their tongues. Only for cats, though. You rest it, that'll grow back good as new, or I'll enlist in Rheduban's personal squadron."

When Ondir had gone, Sett, massaging gently at his leg, grudgingly allowed, "Some good to the *Atarlum*, after all. What should we do if there were no *ramidul*?"

"Learn."

Dismal news came with their evening meal; Rheduban was back in Burantal, with men of Kargul. Nentirr had brought cold food and extra water in case the cellar had to remain sealed for the present. "The Siege of the Guild — we'll do a scene about this, when we can."

Soldiers, it was told, had been billeted on Dolvid's friend, Untimarr. "Mistress Morú," Falis said, "will not be pleased at her guests. A good job their daughters are away by the fords with their uncle."

He remembered the girls, pretty children of about six and nine when he had last seen them. The elder, certainly, by now would be of an age to hide away from soldiers. He said, "Rheduban is not at Untimarr's house?"

"No, with his whore. You know Master Untimarr?" Nentirr had not pressed his guests for names, but had recognized Dolvid's when given.

"I did, well."

"Good man, a fine craftsman, our families are many times akin. He carved some of our faces, the newer ones."

The brother said, "A better carver than I. Oh, I might catch a likeness better, when it comes to a famous face, but he has the greater skill. The Flood-Tamer is his, the new Shâl Four, the Yuvakh Martyr, the Okseti — beautiful work." Ondir's admiration was generous and genuine.

"The best house in Burantal," Falis chimed in. "Not excepting up on the Ridge, though it is full of filth just now."

Âna suggested when it was safe Morú should be told, if she had not guessed, that the curfew-breakers who fought with Rheduban were connected with the injured man she had consented to take in, but never seen.

From regular cavalry at the gates, there was a rumor Rheduban had wanted to seize citizens, hold and perhaps torture them, to make someone tell what had happened to the man he shot, and his companions. For this he would need more men than he had with him, and the garrison commander, while joining the search, had refused to be part of any hostage-taking. "Which," Nentirr said, "has done wonders for Lord Rat-man's temper."

Rodlakh was sitting up very straight. "You see? Good soldiers everywhere, not wanting to terrorize the law-abiding, just waiting for a sign."

"A sign of change," Âna baited him a little.

In one of the dull evening's long silences, she said, "Do you think our hosts have recognized you?"

"Why should they?"

"They knew Sebhal right away."

"Their trade is to know famous faces." He fought with an incipient blush. "How would they recognize me? They were not in Kadon Dinul after I came back from the South. I saw their Rodlakh figure; it is more Orbanak. My height came late."

"With better reason to," Dolvid said, "I did not recognize you, only knew who you must be."

"I remembered you," revisiting happiness. "When my father was alive, when you were teaching my brother the scripts — not Ban-Sila, but Lambakh, who died at Tan Lughsai."

"A good student, as far as his attention held, and he was permitted to go."

"He was my idol. Tholat and Banak-loi, as he was then, were too far away, part of the world of men. Lambakh was nearer me, but with everything I wanted — audacity, cleverness, humor. He never did not have time for me, nuisance as I must often have been."

"He was my favorite, too. I used to wish he could be the Heir."

"Then my hero began bringing back tales from the Bronze Residence of one whose learning surpassed his. I imagined a snowy-bearded giant with brows like the cliffs at Thenimala — Maëdhi in the picture at the Treasury, with his robes and the lightning-bolts. When Lambakh brought me to the Bronze Residence one day, I was in terror."

All at once it came back. "You peeped in at the door. You had a Household tunic with captain's insignia, and were — " he held out a hand at the three-foot level.

"I could not have been as small for you as you for me. I was looking for a mountain, and there you were, shorter than my father and younger than the Heir."

"Two years older."

"Well, you would have had to surpass Plakhsila *Kímukoi* and Odi Kukkuk together to come up to my expectations."

"My brother was always finding someone to make into a giant — Sebhal, for one," Âna said. "Do all boys need heroes?"

Dolvid almost gave the facile answer that what boys strove to emulate, girls made up their minds to marry, but saw in time it would be too cruel in these circumstances. "Maybe the heroes of our boyhood," he offered instead, "help us to choose the men we would be, taking what we admire, or wishing to, from this model and that. Otherwise, we would only try to be copies of our fathers — Nentirr and Ondir would be less distinct than they are."

"Ban-Sila and Rodlakh," the others said together.

"I think I am who I am," she said, "not chosen among this person and that."

Her uncle said, "Yet your every fourth word used to be, *I wish I were a man, like* — whoever your heart was given to that week."

"A wish happily not granted," Rodlakh, unexpectedly and with an ornate bow venturing into gallantry.

They were shamefaced about not mounting any guard, although they had decided their hosts of the Marionette Guild were completely to be trusted. If not, a watch would make no difference, since an enemy could simply sit on the trapdoor till they starved.

All but Dolvid had done plenty of sleeping through the day, but he continued not to sleep, wondering whether Âna was going to keep her word. In his exile he had learnt how bitter it could be to rely overmuch on such lightly-given words — which he also had surely given lightly, and failed, in the days before loneliness closed in. In logic, weighing flickering fact against immovable conjecture, he supposed it was far from certain she would come, and he would never dare go to her bed. Her pain had been real when she confronted who was in Sebhal's mind at the last, and there might have been quick desire for revenge, a mood that would change with a quiet for considering.

Nevertheless, his hearing leapt and fastened to every small sound: Rodlakh turning with a groan, Sett's snore broken off with a shift of position, creaks and twitches of the building itself. Marvellously, dislike for Âna was gone, if ever real, and the youngness, at first so irritating, had become a delight; there had never been a Dolvid who did not admire the white throat, alert eyes, lithe body. Once he believed admiration added to hunger made love, but not now.

All breathing except his had steadied into sleep; he had primed himself for disappointment, but that had nothing to do with his brooding mood, and he no longer saw why she should be allowed to go back on the promise of *tonight*.

He heard a rush and a rustle, muted footfalls from where she had her bunk, but did not turn his head while the passing of too many minutes and elusive sounds began to convince him she had risen only to make use of the earth-closet in a far corner of the cellar. All at once there was breathing, very near, and he twisted impatiently. Âna kissed him.

She had dressed in a brocade robe from one of the storage shelves, mingling faint odors of rose-water and camphor leaves. Quite calm, she lay down beside him, and they stayed flank to flank, conversing with backs of their hands. When one of his turned and began to roam, she captured it, and breathed, "I should hate you."

"For my race?" It was the same as Sebhal's.

"Your calling. The past only poisons minds. Better if we burnt all histories."

"Burn truth and minds will be poisoned worse with lies."

"Except for history, Sebhal would be alive. He was always speaking of getting Tovakh or Kamin-Tolagh or Bolan sword-to-sword, and where did that come from, if not history? He once said it was not a fair fight."

Her tone had changed and she was seeking answers. "Not a fair fight?" The riddle unscrambled. "His father's feat, slaying Tobhsila in the War of the Widowed?"

"He said his father's mount was fresher, and Tobhsila was weary, too, and that was why Saidhan wanted single-combat."

"Every account I have ever seen says they fought on foot. The Karguli chronicler, even, who took every chance of lessening Banak and his allies, concedes Saidhan gave up an advantage, agreeing to dismount. Our own Nilradh Last-Poet chided Saidhan, ever-so-gently; a noble act, but his death would have prolonged the war."

"But he won."

"For Banak."

A long wait, and he was quite content to still his body's greed, if it was a listening friend she wanted.

At last, "He would have killed you for blinking at the wrong moment."

"I know that." But was proud of keeping his voice steady.

"I was truly convinced he was against injustice," in wonder. "But he would have seized the power and was ready to kill anyone in the way. Rodlakh could never — "

"Hush." Her voice, not loud, was made penetrating by passion.

"He would never — he made Sebhal into everything he would want to be himself."

"In life, Sebhal kept the Frontier, performed famous feats, built an army strong against *jinzal*, made sure his followers of every race had land. At the last he was killed for the sake of saving Sett — everything else is words, that die in air. Remember what he was, forget what he said."

"I would be pleased to forget his last words of all."

"Your hand he was holding."

She did not answer, but Dolvid's fingertips found in this talk most of the tight resentment had gone from her slim neck.

"The Rat Lord has left us," Nentirr announced. "Untimarr's guests have gone with him."

It was the third morning after the death of Sebhal. Days had been active only in talk; Âna had twice returned to Dolvid's bed and lain beside him, but with no more to say about Sebhal's contradictions; she had actually achieved calm, and he was astonished they could be lighthearted together, even silly; scholars of fixed habits are not teased without a twinge of anxiety over their dignity. But by day they were sober as could be, and good friends, although it was not easy to put out of mind how much he wanted all of Âna.

The troops who had been in the city had gone farther afield, on a rumor of fugitives seen in the country north-eastward. Feeling less immediate danger, the four took turns leaving the cellar for a soak in the large bronze bath Falis was proud of, standing in its own brick-lined room, with a pump of its own, and a wide, low peat stove where kettles were kept steaming, a room filled with smoke and warmth, the smell of hot metal.

Nentirr had promised to bring writing materials for Dolvid who, not having kept a journal for years, was waking to the fact that he was living in the middle of history. The death of Sebhal, unless he recorded it, was going to be a stubborn crux of future controversy; indeed, muddle was already beginning. Nentirr and his brother, doing their best not to be inquisitive about Sebhal's reasons for being here, had still dropped remarks that must have wild speculation behind them, and the simple events of the fight — to which both had been virtual eye-witness — were being altered by these made-up tales; the phrase 'Rheduban *and his men*' had been heard, and the word 'trap' in connection with Sebhal. Dolvid could see the gestating story, invitation to a parley, courageous, honorable Sebhal, treacherous Rheduban, the brave stand against impossible odds... These might supersede history at the Marionette Guild, but to his taste untidy truth had more drama than neat conventionalisms.

Its recording had to wait on the threshing-out of later news. "Rheduban was on his way before dawn, but not singing for joy, ready to hail his brother the Sun." Since finding out who Dolvid was, Nentirr had missed no opportunity to quote from the *True Song of Tales*.

But there were fresh troops in Burantal, Bolan's. Not hunting fugitives; these were looking to buy food, feed, livestock, wagons, draft animals.

"Nothing to match it since Great Banak," Nentirr said. "Something is afoot in the warfare line, a great campaign. All the threats and bullying this winter about illegal storing of food, as if that doesn't make farmers just find safer hiding-places. And now they can have their price, and something over, in gold, and there are passguard tokens for anyone with wheels and wit to take his goods to Kadon Dinul for the better price."

Falis had an improbable explanation. "I say, the *rabhsai* has decided at last to chase this sewer-filth from Kargul back over the Kôbh where they belong."

"The Nanakh," Rodlakh corrected, preoccupied with other things.

"And these men are Bolan's?" Dolvid asked.

"Unless other Heartlanders ride under that banner. Not that cut-throat rabble; these call their captain Kish'nai."

"Kizhunai. He is Household." A long exchange of glances with Rodlakh.

Nentirr said they must want talk of their own, but before leaving he rather shyly made the suggestion that, while he had no idea where they might intend to go, a farmer carrying a wagonload of grain to Kadon, with tokens to show for the journey, might take them with minimal fuss.

Rodlakh said, "We are not sure, but you might make discreet enquiries."

"A friend," with the sly Okseti face, "can be asked to leave a space in his loading, and never need to know why."

When the pair had gone Âna said, "Supplies for a large campaign. Where? Against whom?"

"Not one foreseen," Dolvid said. Spring was the season for campaigns, but they could be planned all winter. "Is it possible Rheduban recognized who he shot with his bow? Or that Nentirr or his wife have let it slip? They are good people, but that is an immense secret to keep, to have Sebhal Saidhanati die under your roof."

"What are you suggesting?"

"That Kadon Dinul might be tempted to try subduing the Colony, with Sebhal gone."

"There might be other places, other uprisings." Rodlakh laid aside a piece of bread smeared with honey Âna had handed him. "We must go to Kadon Dinul, find out what these preparations are for, and I have to persuade Ban-Sila the Army of the West is no threat to him, only to Preference. He must see."

Sett, almost forgotten, was attentive. "I made sure you would want to head for Tan Lughsai, and so back to Kamsilat, to warn them about the chance of an invasion."

Agreeing a journey along the coast should be safer now, Rodlakh was stubborn about his intentions; Dolvid could go and keep the rendezvous with Galt, while he went to Kadon Dinul alone, with careful instructions about finding the passageway from the Old Bronze Residence.

Dolvid did not need Âna's glance to tell him Rodlakh could not be allowed to go alone. "I was weeks finding all the hidden levers and bolts, and I could not explain them in months. If you are going to Kadon Dinul, it seems I am, too. But Âna — "

"I was thinking Âna could stay in Burantal."

"To sew shawls and practice my lettering?"

"I thought you might want to stay with Sett till he is better." Not expecting his unwelcome guests to come back, Untimarr had agreed to shelter Sett while he recuperated. In less pain, he was unable to put any weight on the injured side.

A few days ago, she might have spat out her fury in a bitter retort, but now, though anger was there, she drew a deep breath and decided to be reasonable. "Sett knows I would gladly be his nurse, but the women of Untimarr's household would do as well — better; Mistress Morú has had training."

"I am not giving birth," Sett commented, "so far as I can tell."

"I can go to Tan Lughsai, to be sure Galt waits for you."

"Alone?" Rodlakh questioned.

When Nentirr came back he had not forgotten the writing things, and had fresh news. Arlimas, a farmer friend, had come into town to borrow tools for mending an axle. His farm was a few miles westward, facing north from the Lughsai Hills, and he was tokened for a journey to Kadon Dinul, having a wagonload of oats and barley to sell. "If he gets his price, perhaps he will buy a mallet to call his own — he has been borrowing mine the past fifteen years."

He was setting out near sunrise, and with his team it would be a full day's pull to Kadon Dinul. "Birds get fat on flies that pester cattle," Nentirr quoted from one of his plays. "If Arlimas had horses to be sure of crossing Arbhu Hills, he would be headed for Dônshei Bridge instead of Kadon — the officer who tokened him said he would get a quicker sale and the best price there, or Dônshei itself, even better. His nags would be a month on that little trip."

"Northward?" Dolvid, perplexed. A campaign against the Colony would assemble at an Arnan-port, Owan Sai most likely.

"As our piece tells it, brave Bolan settled all troubles up north in twenty-eight. Is the Red Bull of Narn on the loose again? I heard some Household troopers thanking Hrafi winter's over."

Dolvid said one word to Rodlakh, whose face remained closed; "Shumat." Almost the only answer. Dolvid had often conjectured about the Army of the Northeast; composed of many races, it had not a shred more reason to welcome the Loyal Oath than Sebhal's Army of the West. But as he told Rodlakh when Nentirr left them again, it remained puzzling.

"I have known Shumat since we were both eight. He is a good soldier and a good man, but he would never interfere in policies on his own initiative, and I cannot imagine him allowing a revolt. Oh, if they tried to enforce Preference, or Mankh' belief east of Yuvakh Din, he would have to resist it, rather than, in effect, meekly dismantle his army, but what happens east of Yuvakh Din does not cause a panic in the Heartland."

"The changes are changing a lot of men," reluctant to speculate. "We should find out all we need in a day or so." They would sleep early; Nentirr would wake them at midnight, and give them directions for his friend's farm. Arlimas would have his wagon loaded before dark, and would carelessly leave the cover undone on the left side. In the morning he would fasten it down without looking to see what might be there.

Sound sleep always came to Rodlakh at once, and Sett was snoring. Settled, Dolvid heard Âna approach like a faint breeze. Allowing washed things to air a few hours, he was naked for the first time in days, not counting his bath, and she soon shuffled away her clothes to be naked next to him.

"We have three hours. No need to hurry." She was calm, her skin touched with cool, and he was glad to be told her intentions.

"Say my name," when he rose to prop on an elbow over her. He did, and could guess her smile; somewhere she had said Sebhal never spoke it, except in annoyance and reprimand.

Her absolute trust of him was impressive, and her smoothness belonged to happy memory that exalted him in its sudden recall: he was glad his maleness was waiting when at last called upon again. She decidedly knew how to be pleased, and hugged him down avidly as she gulped air.

He dozed, perhaps no more than seconds, and found her real and wakeful. "But why, then, did she leave you?"

That amused him, but recollections clotted and had to be cleared away. "Khalú made no bargain that foresaw a tiny stone cabin on the edge of nowhere."

"You reminded me of my great-grandfather. He is dead now, but he was stone deaf, and you had the same look. Aëlu will be lonely. Saidhan too — he has always wanted an heir."

A dubious grunt; Ban-Sila, Rodlakh and Orbanak were as much Saidhan's grandsons as any son of Sebhal's would have been. Âna, perhaps, meant a direct heir to overlordship in the Colony.

"In a fair fight, Sebhal would have bested Rheduban — bow against knife, what man fights so? Will you kill him?"

"Will I?"

"It was your fight, too."

Dolvid wanted to say he was no champion as in the romances; their day was past, if it ever existed. "If we met again, I would do all I could to kill him — in a fight." The vow was not displeasing, and was unlikely ever to need living up to.

"You are going to Kadon Dinul?"

"So it seems." Wry that if he had been in love, he would have implored her to come too, quite probably to be captured or killed (or captured then killed). As was, he could be glad his friend would have the safer journey.

"Why? You are letting Rodlakh risk himself, and you know it cannot come to anything. You could make him go to Tan Lughsai."

"He is the *Valrabh'*. Besides, there is no other cure. He cannot be a leader for the West, until he admits what his brother is." It was becoming clear from Rodlakh's evasions he could not really maintain Ban-Sila's innocence, but used the possibility of the captive *rabhsai* to avoid the choice he had to make, between his family feeling and his convictions. "You could call this his coming of age."

She thought that through, and laughed. "Should I waken him, too? How can he face death, never having had a woman? Would it make you angry?"

"As you wish," though the hurdles were getting higher. "How are you so sure it would be his initiation?"

"Why should I be chaste? when we could all be dead in a day or two. Rodlakh — look how he blushes. And his reverence for Aëlu — that is virginal. But everyone loves Aëlu; you will too, if you meet. Her voice is low, soft music, and she is a span or so taller than I am." Âna was straying into perilous paths.

"No, better not — " she regained the lightness. "If I offered to break the colt with Rodlakh, he would know I was depraved, so soon. Is that what you think?"

She waited, really wanting an answer, and the one he gave, despite deliberation, he regretted instantly. "I think there may be ways aside from weeping to express grief."

"Is that what you think?" incensed. "Loving you — I do not say I ever could, but it would not be all sweet wine; after all, your Khalú may not be altogether crazy."

"As I said." But he was offended by her shot at the facile target.

"My sister married a simple man, and she is happy. I can only meet giants, bowed down by their wisdom. Just because you ponder enough to find misery, it does not mean you have found truth."

He did not answer, though to him he was the easy one, easy to understand, easily pleased, and she was full of complications.

"You, you lie there while I talk about bedding other men, try to teach me to love the memory of a man who would have killed you — understand, forgive, is that manly?"

He was rising again. "What would you say about my manliness?" He felt a sleepy smile had come into her face, and her hands were wakeful.

The night was clear, cool and silent. In the air there was change and the promise of change; the day of Sebhal's death had been the eve of Halving-Day, but it was not only by the calendar a new season had come while they were huddled underground. Next to Dolvid Âna whispered, "Spring increase you," giving his hand a quick touch.

"Spring increase you, Âna." This might have had a farewell note: they had clasped hands in turn with Sett, who was near tears, and Nentirr was also sorrowing; handed gold from Rodlakh's purse he passed it on to Falis as if forced to handle vermin, and mumbled shamefaced about hospitality. Dolvid had entrusted him with a sheaf of notes he had made, using the Old Syllabary, incomprehensible to all but a few, and putting some important words and phrases in Froghulú, which hardly anyone could read. Nentirr was also left with Sebhal's remains, and promised there would be embalming and a temporary interment, till, as he said, "There can be rites befitting his renown." Âna, to Dolvid's relief, did not ask for a last view of the body.

But while it was clear a time was ending between him and Âna, one that could not recur, this was no farewell after all; she was coming to Kadon Dinul. On the road, or at the capital, they expected definite news of what the martial preparations were for, and Âna would then head for Tan Lughsai, the meeting with Galt, so Kamsilat would have the news even if Dolvid and Rodlakh (as it was nicely put) were delayed at Kadon Dinul.

Going swiftly through quiet streets they were briefly on the tree-lined curve of Utalai Course, not far from the house of Untimarr. Dolvid would have given a lot to see the man again, resume their old debate about window lintels. The Course held to the rim of Burantal's bowl; it ended, as recalled, in steps descending to the elbow of road enclosed between two gates, once a good spot to sit and chat with travellers at the end of a dusty summer's day, while horses lapped at long stone troughs fed from springs in the hills behind.

They bore left between unlighted houses, and went up an overgrown slope, where the thrashing panic of a rabbit made them all jump. They were following Nentirr's directions, having needed both tact and firmness to decline his brother's offer to be their guide. Concealment would not be made easier by Ondir's hoarse breathing.

The world was lighter as they climbed. Behind, points of yellow were scattered through the city, sprinkling the terraced rise to the Gap, where a brighter light marked a guard post. From the crest they saw the Heartland, starry sky curving down, a blade of moon past its zenith. From where a fierce watchfire marked the north-facing gate, the feebly luminous road wound over soft black till it vanished in low hills. Âna gasped softly, not from exertion but for the beauty.

For almost an hour they were on common pastureland, the northward skirts of Kafan Lughsai, open grassland with scattered bushes they would never have dared cross by daylight. "The sheep here," Dolvid said, "have longer legs on the side they keep to the Heartland — " a joke old as hills, still good for a polite chuckle. In profound dark the going was often unexpectedly rough, with jolts into unseen cavities, stumbles on sudden hummocks tougher than tufts of grass. After days of inaction, legs stiffened fast.

"How much farther do you make it?" Rodlakh sounded anxious. Night was marching, too, and eastward it was easy to imagine a flawing in darkness, hints of dawn.

"According to Nentirr, we have to strike the cart-track, and then it is a few minutes more. I do not believe we could cross a cart-track without noticing."

"I am sure there were ruts when we crossed that bald part a mile or so back," Âna said for the fourth time.

"Cart-tracks," an icy reminder, "are to and from somewhere, not just bare patches in the middle of pasture."

"But we — " Her rejoinder was interrupted by Dolvid's cry of pain. His shin had been bloodied by a granite marker, standing at the margin of a well-worn path.

iv

Rabhsai and Court

Throat prickled by chaff, Dolvid jerked and choked from a doze, and accepted a skin bottle from Rodlakh. Cold *raminat*, and it helped with piecing thoughts together. In the dim, air was thick with oat-dust from the sacks surrounding them. It was a common kind of wagon, heavy spoked wheels, high sides with two-inch gaps longwise between boards. Stakes all round stuck up above the sides, and over the top was lashed a set of overlapping covers in heavy tarred canvas.

They had found where one securing-rope was left undone, and clambered in near dawn, discovering a clearing among bags of oats piled high all about. Much later they heard and felt the hitching of the team, and briefly saw the gnarled hand of the farmer Arlimas when he tied down the loose rope, slipping the knot inside, content, it seemed, to be unsure whether or not he had passengers. In a high, cracked voice he had advised the horses they were in for a full day, and could expect to meet with bands of cavalry to challenge their journey. "Howso, we've got tokens to show, eh?" — with a jingle of the wrist-chain where the tokens must be hung. "And you don't mind bumping noses with one of they handsome *pefral*, eh, girl?" All the talk was aimed at one of the team, a mare.

Soon there had been the starting jolt, and while wheels rumbled and timbers creaked, Arlimas began a song, tuneless and endless, its tedious refrain filled with *heys* and *hos*. The passengers dozed often, and when a bump shook them from napping, there was the dreary song, winding its way into half-dreams, all one with the stuffy air and jouncing floor, grind of the wheels. The jerk and pitch taking them up to what, by the increased smoothness, must be the main road, was what wakened Dolvid.

Not far away was a small, bright L-shaped tear in the canvas, but when they took turns peering out they saw nothing except the far side of the road with its stony edging. Arlimas interrupted his song as a faster cart came up behind to overtake, and called a greeting as it crunched past, "I'll see you at Kadon, then?"

The answer was unclear for the passengers. Arlimas shouted back, "Aye, so would I, if these beauties would do it." Clearly he was regretting he could not take his team the harder way through the Arbhu Hills. He could have set out eastward, and taken the Royal Way north from Bathrâd, a long journey, but with no forbidding steeps. If he was afraid of missing his market by doing so, the call for supplies must be urgent indeed.

Dolvid said, "Soldiers in the field need feeding, campaigning or not. An uprising of citizenry would not disrupt normal supplies. Preparations on this scale must mean they are dealing with an army, that can block roads, besiege camps and cities. It must be Shumat; there is nothing else in the north to frighten Bolan."

Rodlakh's mouth set in a line becoming familiar, patient, undecided. Âna said, "They would be allies of the West if they have risen, wouldn't they, the Army of the Northeast?"

"Oh, Âna — " he sought inspiration. "It is not that simple. We are not sure of anything. Widespread disaffection, it is true, might be a way of showing my brother these policies cannot be made to work."

"And if he persists? There should be a plan for that."

Rodlakh continued to struggle making his sentences; apparent reluctance to anticipate contingencies was in fact the wish not to have to declare himself in rebellion. "This is the *rabhsai*, to whom I have sworn allegiance as a subject."

"You must owe something to the Army of the West," she insisted, "Sebhal's army, and others in the Colony who have lost their champion."

"You were not at the Great House. Saidhan himself said he could never draw a sword against *rabhsayum*."

"Saidhan *Asai* is past eighty. At his age, he can retire from any battlefield with honor intact."

A wince for the audacity of her goading; the clear implication was Rodlakh at twenty could not.

He was not visibly angry. "Small honor in any course I choose."

"Here they come, then — " Arlimas left off his song to impart news to the mare. "The horse-soldiers, girl, eh?"

In the back they huddled lower as the beat of hoofs and jingle of harness approached. A barked challenge, and the rattle as tokens were displayed. The young-sounding officer told Arlimas to drive on, and the patrol rode back the way it had come, sounds soon fading, while the rumbling of the wheels resumed, and with it the eternal song.

"We lost Sebhal just when he was needed most."

"He is dead — " brusqueness came from her absorption in debate. "If he were alive, you could not lay it all on him. You are Banak's grandson, and Laluvoi's, the one to rally resistance."

"Or turn it into usurpation?"

"Why not, *Valrabh'*, if it brings a better *rabhsayum*?"

The face was rigid; he looked physically chilled. "Behind any treason a worthy purpose is imagined."

"How can it be treason, when the people are crying out for change?"

"Âna," wearily brushing back his hair. "Do you remember that tale about the little grandson in a family of dyers, who thought everyone's hands went purple as they grew up? A great deal of this realm you have never seen; it is not all the Colony and your corner of the Paowan. Down in Ninkufu they would rather have the Old Blood for *rabhsai*, and Kargul would agree — "

"Kargul!"

"Well, but it is all part of this One Realm we talk about. Kargul, the *Mankh'*, the Great Families, the Families of the Heartland — if they want to see my brother deposed, it is not for your reasons, and they would want in his place someone you would dislike still more."

"And all the rest must suffer."

"The *rabhsai* has to strike a balance, bargain among conflicting interests."

"Then Ban-Sila *Rabhsai* will show his even-handedness by letting the Army of the West run loose in Kargul, as Kamin-Tolagh's men do here in the Paowan."

Rodlakh did not answer this taunt, and Âna, with a deep breath, asked the forbidden question. *"Valrabh'*, can you swear your brother is victim of his advisors? How could they keep him captive?"

"Whatever my brother is," again sidestepping the choice, "he must be made to see this Arbhal is on the brink of shattering into many petty realms, not much more than tribes or clans."

"Would that be an evil?" becoming cautious. "A Prince of the Blood must consider the majesty of Arbhal, but would a cluster of petty states be worse than one realm ruled to serve the greed of one single race?"

"Everlasting war." Dolvid had stayed out of the dispute so far, not wanting either to see him as part of a hostile alliance with the other. But this was different, his proper field. "Break the realm into a dozen, or twenty, or thirty little realms, and none of them would be whole. Borders breed wars, as they will tell you at Drin Navuna, whenever those on one side have something the other side has not — water, grazing land, iron, salt, timber, any of thousands of things. Differences of belief, of language — of accent, merely — can be a reason for war where there is no common overlordship. Petty states, like the tribes of the Farther West, use up all their energies in quarreling." He was remembering the ride back from the Narn campaign a dozen years ago, when he and Shumat had dreamed about a land where a man could ride safely, where a woman could go without fear of molestation, from Narn to the cliffs at Thenimala, or Drin Navuna in the West, paying no toll, carrying no weapon, and goods could pass as freely, for everyone to enjoy the bounty and skills of all, still a worthwhile ideal. "I admit, *Valrabh'*, that with Âna I believe Ban-Sila *Deghi* fully responsible for his own *rabhsayum*, but we must do all we can to keep this a whole realm."

"I am alone, then." He meant, about his brother, but Âna had a wry face, as if, on the contrary, the men had combined to exclude her. Dolvid just touched her forearm, and she looked at him with no particular expression.

Going over what had been said, he had perhaps been mistaken in assuming Âna knew his complete opposition to Preference; she might think he was ready to see the Others dispossessed for the sake of his single realm. Too late; any correction would sound smarmy.

Arlimas broached a new song, a sadder one, about homelessness, as plodding progress of the wagon slowed to a creep. The team was straining up a long slope. "Must be Abfekhi Hill," Dolvid suggested. "There is a cavalry post just this side of Tâl Abfekh." The village crowned the hill.

"They will stop us? Make a search, perhaps?" Rodlakh straightened a leg so as to slide his knife from its sheath, and stick it in the floorboards beside him. Âna did the same, while Dolvid reached back to be sure his was free to draw. He hoped there would not be more fighting, here or anywhere. What he would like most was to go with Âna somewhere tranquil where they could spend an untroubled month getting tired of each other. His ache for her had begun again at a touch. As life went, he supposed with free access to each other, one of them would be bored just as the other decided that here, after all, was the companion for a lifetime. Better, perhaps, as was, suspended well short of satiation, with neither epitaph nor promise.

Not yet at the top of the slope the wagon creaked to a halt. Noises, restless hoofs, the groan of boards, confused cries, told them they were halted behind at least one wagon, probably others. They heard the snort of nearby horses, as yet another came rumbling up behind. Again, Arlimas was anxious to keep his animals informed.

"Stand quiet there, hey, girl. We'll be on our way before long. Horse-soldiers got to be sure it's not gold bars we're carrying, eh? Easy." He clicked his tongue, and they jerked to roll forward a couple of wagon-lengths. A challenge came in the bored, dry voice of an officer. "Your name, farmer?"

"Arlimas of Arlimasstead, by Burantal, Captain."

"My rank is *kímukan*. What is your cargo?"

"Oats, for Kadon, where they say there is a need."

"Do you — " the question was broken off, answered in advance by the chink of passguard tokens on their chain. The officer, who must be mounted, had edged nearer to examine the discs; his voice became indistinct, though the farmer's replies were clear enough. "Ah — day after tomorrow, all being well.

"Hostelry by Market Gate, always did before." The tone of the next question was very confidential, and the reply had to be strained for. "No, no, I've not, not a leaf, not since, oh, must be last *Shu'sai*, as you'd call it... they do tell the *margú* up by Bakali is open again — they would have it to serve. I know you do, it's a shame."

Hoofbeats moved slowly down each side of the wagon, ordinary soldiers, no doubt. Their *kímukan* was apparently asking Arlimas to pick up any *raminat* he could find at Kadon Dinul. "Gladly I will, Captain. Not more'n what I have to pay for it. Aye, I'll look for you, Captain."

At the rear, the canvas cover was lifted. Strong light rushed in, and crouched among sacks the travellers held collective breath.

"Oats, all right — " a rougher voice than the officer's. "Hranakh's breath, I wouldn't want to be with the levies. They'll be eating their boiled oats plain, if the north's what they say."

"Oh, they've got sheep up there." A pleasanter tone, with the soft buzz of the downs near Kred Bakali. "Even you have heard of Dakbân fleece."

""You fancy stewed fleece, you can volunteer," the former speaker crowed, then, "Oats, sir. In sacks."

"I did not expect them in jars. Very well, Arlemirr."

"Arlimas, Captain."

"*Kímukan*. Here, put that on your chain, and do not forget to hand it in when you come back. Drive on."

The flap of cover descended, and the wagon creaked into life. "My thanks, Captain."

"*Kí-mu-kan!*"

There was news to be sifted out here; the soldiers had mentioned Dakbân, far to the north and east, the cold river marking the boundary between the provinces of Dramal and Ân. Questionable whether Bolan himself would ride so far, with such unrest in the Heartland. If not, who could be trusted?

"Kamin-Tolagh," Rodlakh offered, "or his father."

"Would they go? Kamin-Tolagh might be hungry for glory, but his father would want a good price to send troops of Kargul that far to fight Ban-Sila's war."

"That might be the reason Kargul is here, to fight this uprising, if that's what it is."

"Or else to take over the task of keeping order in the Heartland, while Bolan goes north with all the cavalry he can collect."

"No one would be fool enough to permit that."

"What would be the difference?" Âna, bitterly. "If the *rabhsai* is willing to make use of the butchers from Kargul, what does it matter where?"

"The *rabhsai* would — " Rodlakh shut his mouth. Forcing calm, he said, "No use losing our tempers over speculations. We are going to the right place for answers."

Dolvid sighed faintly: Rodlakh had been about to say Ban-Sila would be a hostage to the lances of Kargul, and had broken off because he maintained the *rabhsai* was a prisoner already. But there was a distinction, if not one to be understood by Âna, for whom all oppressors came to the same thing.

He struggled from more sleep, assailed by noise.

"Rain," Âna said with a smile for his bewilderment. That was the pummeling overhead, unlike the wagon's normal range of rattles, grumbles, groans.

"And stone," beginning to function; the bumping of the wheels had become a steadier roar. South of Kadon Dinul, the Burantal Road was paved for five miles from Market Gate. They must be on this last lap.

His feelings took him by surprise. He could picture the city by late light, mellowed line of the walls and noble cliff of the New Residence; he had usually returned to Kadon this way in his final years, and what he felt was revulsion mixed with tender regret, a nostalgia that insisted on recalling happiness when he had often been fiercely miserable; it was bad that mourning always came for the past as such, a kind of illness that surrounded everything once possessed and lost with the blurry radiance of pleasant melancholy.

"Will there be a search at Market Gate?" Rodlakh asked.

Dolvid's eye was to the rip in the canvas; evening was thickening under low cloud, and he could see the familiar hedges, the well-kept fields. "Arlimas told the *kímukan* he meant to stay in the hostelry — we are not going to pass through any gate tonight, and I do not think Arlimas expects us still to be aboard in the morning." He was sure the hostelry would be the one outside Market Gate, with its large walled compound where wagons could stay overnight.

In the last two miles the way was marked by the glow of *ôdul* set next to the highway, signal for Arlimas to begin a new song, barely recognizable as the traditional one about Coming Down to Kadon. Soon the wagon was swung hard left, jolting up onto cobbles, a wheel scraping as they passed through the archway, out onto the beaten earth of the wide compound. Rain had stopped, or nearly so.

Jockeying back and forth, a longer backing movement, and rear wheels crunched against curbing. "Ho, beauties, steady work. Earned your hay, you have."

The passengers squatted there while darkness came on, thump of shafts when the horses were unhitched and led away, and also the sound of other carts rolling in, horses nickering, a mule giving out a bellow, happy shouts as friends greeted each other after long absence from the capital.

"We are back to the old days," Dolvid said. "All it took was civil war."

"Not that, not yet," Rodlakh, fervently.

The compound had guards with bows. Their job was to keep thieves out rather than travellers in, but on the whole it would be better to sleep where they were, and make their way out in the confusion of dawn's light, when, if old customs held, there would be a feverish race among farmers to be first through Market Gate.

"Then we sleep on oats," Âna said.

"Unless you would want to slip out and risk getting a bed at the hostelry."

"You and Âna could. I might be recognized here."

"Âna could. If I am recognized, I am *kaël'rolai*, for any hero to kill."

Âna sighed. A young woman coming in alone for a bed here would scarcely pass without comment.

No detailed plans for tomorrow could be made before they could see how the Bronze Residence was guarded; Dolvid was confident it could be entered by night. If so, and they could reach the hidden passageway, there was, of course, no assurance of finding Ban-Sila where they could safely approach him. That might take several attempts, Dolvid said, with the feeling all this was make-believe, and Rodlakh would see the foolishness of it before they went another step.

"I am going to confront my brother, if I have to stay hidden here till leaves turn brown. But Galt will not know what to do."

"I shall take your message," Âna said. "Now we are certain the preparations are not for an attack on the Colony, I can start for Tan Lughsai, as soon as you can make up your mind how long you want Galt to wait there for you."

"If he does not come, for reasons we have not foreseen?"

"I shall make camp and wait for you there. When my food gives out, if you have not come, I shall make my way to Burantal, and stay with Sett."

Dolvid said, "How much food do you have?"

"You can each give me part of yours — here at Kadon you can find food, steal it if you have to. With my own, I should have enough for eight days, ten if I take care."

"I wish we could get you a mount, and roads were safe for a solitary rider."

"I'll walk."

Rodlakh was able to say what Dolvid could not: "It troubles me to see you go so far alone."

"With you I would just be an encumbrance." Her eyes flashed at Dolvid as she again recalled the galling word.

There seemed not much more to say; everywhere was dangerous, and he could not cite a sensible excuse to keep Âna with him, as he wanted. They opened packs and had food, tormenting themselves with rueful talk of the hot drinks and farmer's stew the hostelry would be serving. The night would not be a warm one.

Before day they were fully waking, shivering. They unfastened the rope and slipped over the side to huddle between wagons. Inside the hostelry there were already signs of life, lights showing from windows in the long, plain building. It was two levels high, an older central inn having years ago put out two wings at right angles to half-enclose the compound. The large stables across the court were also incorporated into the walls of the enclosure, which had space for more than twice the dozen or so wagons at present standing there.

The archway gate was to one side of the original central portion, and soldiers were there, stamping their feet as they exchanged remarks, puffs of breath showing in lantern-light. Behind rain winter had slunk back for a final meal, and the cold was enough to make spring into an idiot's dream; all three travellers were chilled to the bone. As well as wanting to imitate the stamping of the soldiers, Dolvid had a huge need to relieve himself. Arlimas had thoughtfully provided an old, lidded pot in the wagon, but it had become inadequate, though they had nothing to drink but a little cold *raminat*. If there had been a horse hitched he would have chanced standing beside it and pissing on the ground; he was sure his bladder had enough to give a convincing imitation.

Sternly banishing those frivolities, he considered how they could change unnoticed by either farmers or guards from hideaways to open, innocent travellers. The key, he had told the others last night, was boldness, but this morning, chilled, agonized by continence, it was a scarce commodity.

Fastening cloaks and outshirts, jangling their token-chains, some chewing or wiping mouths with the back of hands, farm-folk were emerging from the hostelry doors beneath the archway. They shouted to ostlers, on their way to open up the stables, and coins were tossed as farmers tried to bribe boys to bring their animals first. Loudly talking, with boisterous laughs, half a dozen were coming along the flagged pathway between hostelry and the row of beached wagons. With no advance warning to the others Dolvid stood clear and began industriously lashing down the canvas cover. Rural patter came from days as provincial quartermaster. "Good grain, stored dry, mind, not a speck o' rot or rust. Now, I hear of this'n, Kanzan way, got eleven a measure for his rye, nothing choice, run o' the mill."

"Seems a fair price." Rodlakh was unsure with this, but Âna could manage the style.

"Ah," she agreed, as a pair of real farmers passed with a glance. "Best mind they don't bid on your oats, take your wheels, animals and all, before you can shout it's not for sale. These soldier-boys are always short of wheels, that's truth."

"As for the old mare," cheerfully, "They welcome to'r, they can get a day's work out of'r."

The compound was attaining the desired state of uproar. Early risers shouted and whistled at stableboys, and differed with each other about who had called first for his team. Sauntering easily, Dolvid led the others to the far side, away from the flagged path, past grounded shafts of wagons. Their packs were nothing unusual, many farmers habitually wore them; Dolvid's was slung slackly over his shoulder hiding the knife there, Âna's and Rodlakh's carried at hip-front for the same purpose.

Under the archway a few who prized talk above the race for Market Gate were gathered, some chatting with guards in a holiday mood, not watchful, obviously glad of this sudden surge of activity.

Two boys were throwing pellets of bread at each other, till a farmer's wife cuffed the nearer, most likely her son.

Guards paid no particular attention to the three as they approached. Carefully inconsequential, Dolvid led the way, remarking a good job they turnips was in, to get the good of that rain there. Âna, right in the gateway, turned and signalled to someone in the compound they would wait up by Market Gate; it was done so naturally Dolvid almost turned to see who she was waving to. The guard shadowed on the right made breakfast out of a long viewing of Âna as she came out of the dim, brushed Dolvid with a glance, and was held by the face of Rodlakh, a perplexed pucker appearing between eyebrows. The *Valrabh'* gave a noisy hawk and spit, country fashion, wiping mouth with palm, nose with the back of his hand.

They were through the arch, out into the main road. Âna gave a sigh or gasp. She was a child when she last saw the walls of Kadon Dinul, and one who was here every day might yet be moved by this vision, walls tawny in the unyellowed light before sunrise, a warmth of aged stone. Softly lit, with here and there a harder gleam, the New Residence floated on the darker, bluer city beyond those kindly-seeming ramparts. The watchers were at the same level as the hostelry, though with an intervening dip in the road to put doubt into distances. At their backs white *ôdul* traced the southward curve of the road, till it merged into the dispersing mists of the fertile plain. Rodlakh's eyes were up on the Residence, face unreadable.

The line of shops and eating-shops over to the right let them feel sheltered.

"Pardon my manners at the archway. I seem to recall that Household man had duty at Pefrai Gate when I came back from Ninkufu. He recognized me just now without realizing it, so I did a thing no one of Family would. He was still worrying it out."

"Would it matter? While you were there for anyone to see, he could have shouted your name and been believed. What is he going to say, *it was the* Valrabh', *I'm certain it was, in old breeches and a stained outshirt, talking about turnips?*"

"He may try it with his wife, tonight," Âna offered.

"And she will say he was always a fool about remembering faces, it's just like that time when he would have it, and so forth."

"I am not eager to meet Lady Khalú — " Âna puzzled Rodlakh.

"Come." leaving the road just past the bottom of the dip, they rounded a knob of rocky outcrop, and cut uphill across waste ground. They could enter the Gardens of Kamzhinu with no need to pass any city gate. There was an entrance at the corner near the road, in sight of Market Gate, perhaps locked. Instead, they vaulted the low stone wall, and they all went stumbling and skidding down a short, steep bank.

They ran, the Gardens, a narrow ravine, not far from the line of the southern walls to the city. During the long reign of Plakhval, in relative tranquillity, the *rabhsai* had decreed that with its strong new inner ramparts Kadon Dinul could survive very well without the ancient outworks, which took up much valuable land near the walls. The outwalls demolished, a large section of the vast, now meaningless defensive ditch was converted into public gardens, and they were named after Plakhval's eldest daughter, Kamzhinu, whose idea it was said to have been. She was also credited with designing the best features of the Gardens.

Fragments of immense blocks from the dismantled walls were, after so much time, hard to tell from natural boulders. Both slopes were planted with trees and shrubs, many of them dwarf varieties. Down near the bottom a brick pathway ran the whole length of the Gardens, making many crossings of a tiny rill by means of varied stone bridges, some absurdly ornate, some plain high arches. Other paths and tracks wound, making the most of the narrow compass, and there were small half-hidden shade-houses, lichened sculptures, unexpected waterfalls. At Kadon Dinul were many things richer, grander, more imposing, but Dolvid knew nowhere in the realm where craft had been used with more love, or more care to conceal craft. As a child he had played here with Shumat, he walked here with Valnoi, his first love, first consummated love; the Gardens wound through all his life.

Now, after vanishing behind bushes for longer than usual, and emerging sane, he could note a pervasive air not just of neglect, but abuse. Trees had been removed, shrubs torn up. "Perhaps," bitterly, "it is judged too good a hiding-place for fugitives."

Rodlakh shook his head, and all at once began quoting: "*No new dangers brought this about, but return of fears once outgrown, as if men reverted to children, terrified by long shadows in the evening.*"

"I believe it is *at twilight*. But I am astonished you know it so well. I was told publication was *suspended*."

"Not before I had my copy. I have been looking forward to the continuation, ever since."

Dolvid told him where the unfinished manuscript was hidden. What Rodlakh had recited was from the short book *The End of the House Gabh'Owan*, intended as introduction to a longer history, but published alone when it became clear he would not be allowed to finish *The Rise of Great Banak and Laluvoi*, a subject for which Rodlakh's interest was hardly surprising. "And I left sheets for another book at Burantal to be hidden away; I am more squirrel than historian."

"You will finish your books," Âna predicted, a touch of sweetness.

With new sun skimming down into the Gardens, they followed their long, bobbing shadows. The city wall bent north of a true westerly line, so the Avenue of Treaties emerged very near the southwestern corner of Kadon Dinul. This was Harbor Gate, giving on the spacious square with the Spear of Yoëlladhu, where the road came up from the royal port of Owan Sai. Directly across the paved square

on a level mound like a grassy platform, the Old Bronze Residence
stood, and all this could be viewed from the abrupt knoll behind what
was known as the Grottoes. A last humped bridge, up shallow steps to
a six-sided court paved with six-sided stones, a spray of river-birches
at the center in a six-sided bed. Over there, where the rock receded into
a slight cave, Dolvid had kissed impossible Valnoi for the first time, and
nearby, a summer later, for the last.

Clambering the chalky bastion was for goats or energetic boys,
not joints made stiff by a day's cramped ride and a night's cold sleep.
None of them was sorry to reach the top, where they dropped into a
crouch among skeletal bushes.

"Guarded — " he had expected it. Where the portico of the
Bronze Residence jutted above broad steps, pikemen could be seen, and
soldiers also at the entrance on the nearer side.

Dolvid pointed out the small, dark iron doorway, below the
platform on which the building rested, near the middle of that side.
"Once a guardroom, in my day used for storage."

"But kept locked."

"After intruders came in that way one night. But I have a key."
By pure oversight he had taken the key with him into exile, but had
hunted for it purposefully the night south of Shemugrân when he
agreed to be a guide, and it was hooked onto his belt now.

"How do we get to the door?"

"We shall have to wait for night. Here in the Gardens, if we
cannot find anything better."

Âna indicated the road on the south side of the Bronze
Residence. "Is that the way for Tan Lughsai?"

"No," sharply, too sharply. "That is the *Mankh'* road. Down
here, under our chins, that is the road south, Lambarr's Way."

The name had begun as a joke. After they had drawn back
from the summit, making themselves invisible on the backslope,
Rodlakh let himself reminisce about that innocent world. "You

remember, people would gather by the gate and around the Spear to wave at their favorites? My father was loved — beyond his merits, a writer of history might say. I am afraid his disdain of documents, of policy, then, laid up much of our present troubles. I can't help it, it was good to be his son." He was sober-faced as they made their way back down to the Grottoes, Dolvid braced for the farewell that was going to come from a stubborn Âna.

Halfway down, footsteps moving briskly on the main path made them halt, flattening to the slope. They had a clear view to the nearest bridge; squatting, Dolvid watched as the feet came nearer. That anyone on the path would glance up at the hillside was not likely, and less so that any eye could discern the dull-clad figures against dappled rock and patched earth.

When he saw the slender man on the hump of the bridge, stoop of shoulders, sharp jut of nose, he knew he must have recognized the footsteps all along. Jumping up, to the bewilderment of the others, he went recklessly down the slope, bounded across the court, and caught the tall man where ways divided. "Faëdhal!"

A suspicious, frowning start, a face full of happy shock. "Dolvidh. Hrafi smile on us, Dolvidhai. Is it you?" They clasped hands warmly.

"We need talk — " leading him away from the main path, up the low steps.

"Is your exile ended, then, in these perplexing times? I, notwithstanding discouragement, as you are well aware — ah!" He caught sight of Rodlakh, picking his way down to the foot of the rock, Âna behind. With a preliminary flourish, Faëdhal gave an exemplary royal salute. "*Asai...* "

"Faëdhal Fenuvalati," Dolvid announced, "Master of Tongues."

Rodlakh gave a keen look. "And best reader of the Syllabary outside the *Atarlum*," he ventured.

Faëdhal protested mildly. "I had not been informed the *Uzh'freladhai* Dolvidh had rejoined the *Mankh'*," he said. "But we are acquainted, are we not, *Valrabh'*? I gave you a lesson, perhaps not quite your first lesson, in the Old Tongue, it must be twelve years ago, not less."

The embarrassment this might have caused, with Rodlakh plainly having no memory of Faëdhal, was covered by Dolvid's introduction of Âna, "Konatilayu, or Konats-daughter as she would prefer, of Konatstead."

She amazingly returned half-deference to Faëdhal's bow — or not amazingly; this was Faëdhal's talent, to rescue old courtesies from disuse.

Faëdhal's presumption Dolvid's exile was over was not unreasonable considering his company, or would not have been, if they had been less meanly dressed. Dolvid confessed they were in Kadon Dinul secretly, and that as before Faëdhal was breaking the law just talking to him.

"Ah, well. No one has ever accused me of cheating, or taking anything that was not mine, or brawling... a greater risk as things are, if I may say so, is letting ourselves be frightened out of our good manners, which I take to be more than saying `if you please' in the right places. Respect for others is good manners, and so is loyalty."

They were by the shallow central cave of the Grottoes, where a bench was formed by a shelf cut in solid rock. Faëdhal circumspectly waited for Rodlakh to be seated, and slightly raised one eyebrow when the others, made casual by shared adventures, sat without waiting for leave. Once he was sitting Faëdhal could relax his court manners a little, although Rodlakh lacked experience to put him fully at ease, to an extent taking his tone from Faëdhal.

"You were on your way to the Bronze Residence? We do not want to make you late."

"*Asai*, no, not at all, to the contrary. We have been working at a private task — one which concerns you, Dolvidh — but there is no real need for me to be there before the eighth hour. Later, if I wished."

"What is this task that concerns Dolvid?"

Faëdhal explained. Since turn of the year all activities at the Bronze Residence had been returned to the supervision of an *atarlai* of the *Manadilum*. "Shortly, Dolvidh, I, and all those who remain of, ah, your crew, the scribes and copyists we trained together, are to be forced into retirement. For the present, to be sure, the *Atarlum* needs our knowledge and our skills; we are said to be laboring to *undo the errors of the former period* — which is to say, your tenure there as *Uzh'freladhai*. It was for this reason — " redirecting his speech to Rodlakh — "as well, may I say, as more personal ones, that made me hopeful Dolvidh's exile was at an end. The *True Song of Tales* is to be suppressed."

While Âna put a consoling hand on Dolvid's, Rodlakh demanded, "At whose orders?"

"*Asai*, immediately, those of *Menadhi*, though it is generally held the former *Menadhi*, our Patriarch, is the real source."

"*G'Asalladh'* has His powers," Rodlakh said, "but not over servants of the *rabhsai*, working at the Bronze Residence."

Faëdhal cleared his throat. "The power of the *Mankh'*, if I can put it so, *Asai*, has no swords of its own, and lies only in belief, unless some adherent provides the swords to do its bidding."

This was tactfully to say what was obvious; the *Atarlum* could not be running the Bronze Residence except with express consent of the *rabhsai*. Rodlakh was glum, while Faëdhal returned to his theme. "I say, is to be suppressed, but by that I mean only those are the orders. As you in particular are aware, the *Manadilum* retains, in its own way, a love for learning, and so many well-considered words could not be destroyed without an attempt to discover where the *True Song*, notwithstanding its, hem, its impieties, is a clear improvement over the *Mankh'* translation. Therefore we are engaged in a page-by-page collation, to determine which of your alterations can be taken up into a new recension — this would, may I say, be a fascinating task, if one could be indifferent to the motives behind it."

"To restore all the lies, depicting the Gabhanil as servile people waiting for an Owani leadership to show them the way — when, in truth, the Owanil were keeping safe on the Island, letting the despised Gabhanil do their fighting for them." This speech, nothing new to Faëdhal, was largely to make sure Âna did not mistake the *Mankh'* view for his.

"Exactly. But it should be borne in mind, for the two editions of the *True Song*, quite forty copies were made; it will be no simple hunt to find and destroy them all — "

"Saidhan will not give up his copy," Rodlakh, with a broad grin. "Neither shall I."

"Quite aside from that, together with two or three of our own copyists, I have taken it upon myself to make doubly sure the book as written will survive. Fresh copies are being made from the best manuscript — the grey-parchment, you will recall — and written on small squares of soft vellum, easy to carry away piecemeal at the end of each day. Long before the new so-called restoration is complete, there will be fully five or six complete perfect copies of the *True Song* hidden away, and hidden rather well. If everyone who worked on the Bronze Residence edition was dead, the book could not be lost."

"This is very good, Faëdhal, excellent. Isn't it risky as well?" Odd that here, discussing literature, he could be quite clear about his differences with Ban-Sila, with no marsh-fire about an impenetrable ring of evil advisors.

Talk of the dangers of smuggling the manuscript out of the Bronze Residence led easily to a discussion of how in general the building was guarded. Though by day there was more soldiery than formerly, Faëdhal did not think nighttime strength was above the few watchmen and guards it used to be.

As always, he was not the one to go to for detailed news. There had been talk about uprisings in the North, and he had heard Shumat's name mentioned, but could not say any more about it, except troops were being assembled for a large-scale campaign.

He glanced up at brightening sky. "These Gardens — forgive me if I am mistaken, but my impression was, with all respect, that *Asai* does not want to be known at present, while Dolvidh, inexplicably — "

"Is there somewhere we would be safe till it is dark?"

"*Asai*, my own home would be honored beyond its merits by your presence, and can be reached from here without undue difficulty." He began untying a key from the cord at his waist.

Dolvid objected; they could not hope to pass any of the city gates unobserved, or without being stopped.

"Nor do you need to — ah, I forgot; talking with you here makes me forget you have been away so long. I no longer live where I did."

The move had not been a happy one; since Faëdhal had no pupils left at the New Residence, Ban-Sila had reduced his salary, making it impossible for him to maintain the house where he had lived as long as Dolvid had known. "To be just, I was offered quarters at the Residence, or it was suggested I might remove myself to a board-hostelry. Hah! At my time of life, obliged to make table-talk in the morning, my best hour for quiet thought. I was fortunate to find a small house outside the walls. The lane which runs behind the enclosure by Market Gate — you may reach it and never venture on any main road... "

"The Alúsidhai?" marvelling at Faëdhal, who never mentioned these troubles when he made the long journey to see him last year — and at the self-centeredness of exile, that had let Dolvid allow almost all talk then to be about himself.

"Aha, you have not forgotten your Kadon Dinul. Southward, off to the right, there are three small houses. Mine is the middle one — my sign is on the gatepost." Saying it would help reassure his housekeeper, he took off and handed them his copper bracelet with the same device taken from his seal, a fully-opened book.

"An under-captain of cavalry occupies the house I had for forty years. Is it not, to say no more, is it not strange, *Asai*, that we have laws, however unjust one might think them, meant to restore privilege to those of Old Blood, and there is this man, Dolvidh Vidukhat, springing from the best blood of Ninkufu, related, as I read it, to the noble house which brought forth your grandmother Laluvoi of blessed memory, suffering exile? And I myself, claiming no rank, but with blood unmixed through all recorded generations, am turned out to accommodate a soldier of dubious breeding and his still-more-questionable mate? For myself, *Asai*, I have no use for these distinctions, yet it must remain an oddity that those to whom blood means so much — "

"As you say." Rodlakh's face was a carved mask, but confusion had come to Faëdhal, who had remembered in full flight of his eloquence that the *Valrabh*'s descent was not unmixed.

"We shall see better times again, Master. We are in your debt."

"One attains a certain age, *Asai*, and it is, you will pardon me, no longer a question of *better* as such, only restoration of what ought to be when men deal honorably with each other. Not in the three previous reigns of my recollection — ah... " again he had strayed into trouble, but Âna rescued him, unexpectedly reaching up with a kiss for his forehead. "Hope is never dead, Master, where good men remain."

Considering Faëdhal's lifelong aversion to her sex, his pleased response was astonishing; he took Âna's small hands together between his long, lean ones, and pressed them warmly. About to go, he recollected himself, and asked Rodlakh's leave. Odd, to watch him stride briskly away, bound for where they had shared so much work together.

"He is beginning to show his age," not at all clear what that age might be in years.

Rodlakh laughed softly. "To be sure, he has no use for these distinctions of blood."

"We take in the glory of Owan with our mothers' milk, Faëdhal more than I, since he is of the Families. But Preference, or any holding down of men or women because of their race, he sees as intolerable bad manners."

"He has a kind heart," Âna said. "He is lonely."

True, Dolvid allowed, but the defiant loneliness of a man who would not befriend fools just for the sake of company.

"Let us find this house of his," dangling the key.

"I must start for Tan Lughsai."

"By daylight? You could spend the day at Faëdhal's house, and set out when we start for the Bronze Residence."

"Isn't it a full day's travel to the Cape?"

"On foot, avoiding the road, as you must," Dolvid said, "More; nearer a day-and-a-half."

She hoisted her pack. "I shall start at once."

Last night there had been detailed discussion of the journey, and he went over the main dangers again, repeating she must avoid patrols.

"If I do not try to fight, at worst I shall be captured, and all they can charge me with is illicit travel."

"It is not what can be done in law that worries me."

She held his eyes with hers. "My father," with a dangerous calm, "in common with any man he would have though proper for me to marry, would sooner see me dead than *dishonored*. As I already am by his system, anyway. That is not just a way of speaking for him; death would truly be better — mine, not his. I do not agree."

Not growing happier, he warned her again about straying too far westward of the road before turning south. The *Mankh'* estates were in that direction, and the *Adanum Plakh'* was always to be feared. "If you make good progress today, you can find your way across Preghala Ravine as soon as there is light. You must avoid — "

"I shall avoid what has to be avoided," gently. "Stop trying to frighten me from a task I can do."

Rodlakh gave final instructions, saying if he and Dolvid failed to arrive in Tan Lughsai, Galt was absolutely not to attempt coming to Kadon to look for them, but must go back to Kamsilat.

She gave him a smile, and Rodlakh bleakly echoed it. On an impulse, she kissed him, then kissed Dolvid, who muttered, "Do not go. Stay at Faëdhal's house, and in a day or so we can all make for Tan Lughsai."

She shook her dark head. "We'll meet there."

"Then we must all be careful to stay alive."

"Friend, Dolvid."

"Friend, Âna." Some tremendous thing he could say might make her not go, but he could not think of the word. They went in opposite directions, Âna moving briskly for the longer set of steps that mounted to the westward gate. He was standing on exactly the spot where he had said farewell to Valnoi, centuries ago.

"I wish we had not let her go." Rodlakh, boots off, sat on Faëdhal's couch. A small room, made smaller by Faëdhal's understandable reluctance to part with any of his treasured furniture or furnishings. Even in the larger house within the city Dolvid had always felt hemmed in by fragile things careless elbows or feet could destroy, and now to breathe was an adventure.

They had been greeted at the door, at first warily, by Abdanai, Faëdhal's housekeeper, a somewhat vague-eyed young man, slack of jaw, who had not identified Rodlakh, but thawed at once on hearing Dolvid's name, and took them on a tour of the little house, drawing attention to everything of Faëdhal's said to have any association with the fabled Dolvidh. Abdanai had then done his best to make them comfortable among delicate little tables, the cases of books and rolls, glass-sculptures, miniature-seeming chairs. He brought wine, offered food, gave a prod with a tiny poker at a slow-burning fire, and left them to their talk.

"Short of force, I cannot see how we could have stopped her."

"She is willful. She would contradict Sebhal — Sebhal! More than once he said she would be the better for a sound Gabhani beating, but he never dar — he decided against it. In disputes with her father, Konat's side might be worth hearing. But she is changing. What have you done with her?"

"What have I?"

Rodlakh had intended the question to be absurd. "Is it the loss? Last week, I would have had less worry about her going off alone. I have never seen her how she was with your friend. She is forgetting how to hate. Is it true you belong to Lalakh's line, Laluvoi's kin? That is who I lived with in the South."

"Faëdhal's genealogies are probably sound enough, though complicated beyond what most of us would care to trace or trouble to claim — he can end by connecting practically any three people in Arbhal."

"Then we are related."

"If so, distantly, *Valrabh'*, through my mother, and twice over, if it is true your other grandmother was also cousin to Laluvoi, as I have heard said."

"You can ask Doleni, if, or I should say, when we get to Kamsilat." After a minute Rodlakh said, "We could still overtake Âna, if we started at once."

A hint he might consider abandoning the attempt to see his brother, and Dolvid almost missed hearing it; his ears were hot with shame. He had remembered what he wanted to tell Âna at parting. This morning, before, when she followed him without hesitation into improbable farm-talk, when she waved to an imaginary companion, he had felt a flood of unmistakable love for her. That was all, perhaps not so tremendous after all — he ought to be thankful, in fact, that he had not been fatuous enough to think of spouting such sentimental nonsense — and still it lurked with the troubling persistence of unspoken truths. He stood, but pacing was not practicable in these cramped surroundings, and after one half-step which brought him up against a gilded wooden chest set on a wrought stand, he sat again, and gave his attention to Rodlakh. "What makes you change your mind?"

The reply was longer coming. "No, it has to be seen through," at last.

"Have you considered what you would say to your brother, *Asai*?

"Have I thought about anything else? But there are so many different ways it could go."

"Not so many."

"Run them through for me."

"Well." Dolvid began by ticking off points on his fingers, but soon abandoned the gesture. "One, Ban-Sila learns from you about the crimes being committed in his name. Or, two, he already knows, but has no effective power to prevent them. Here, you might persuade him to escape with us from the Residence. From the safety of Kamsilat, as it might be, he could then decree revocation of the new measures, lawful reinstatement of Saidhan, dismissal of Bolan. In those circumstances, there would not be many officers to go against their *rabhsai*, and if Kargul remained intransigent, most of the armies would be aligned against them, just as in 2878, when they were beaten." This fantastic tale must be quite close to what Rodlakh had set out with from Kamsilat. Since then, there had been plenty of chance to see the flaws.

"That would not be your story."

"I have no opinions at the moment, *Valrabh'*." Not his fault if his voice had. "Next: suppose the *rabhsai*, with his known closeness with *g'Asalladh'* and the *Mankh'* in general, approved the Decree and other actions promoting Preference, but is dismayed by the anger that is the outcome of these policies. Or is not yet aware how tragic the consequences are — news is being, not kept from him, but watered down; he knows there is unrest, but not how serious, and Kargul has loyally offered its services to help restore order; his rebellious kin in the Colony is bound to come around — half-truths are easier to tell than outright lies, and harder to refute. In this case, he might not listen to what you have to tell him, and if that is so — " giving this all the weight of a dramatic pause — "Or if, in the last extreme, Ban-Sila is fully informed and in favor of everything being done in his name — "

"That I cannot believe."

"In *zhabhu* you have to consider even the most unexpected turns. I am talking about what might be so — if this was 2642, let us say, under Plakhval. In any event, unless the *rabhsai* is truly a captive, and wants to be set free, you do not need a plea. You need an ultimatum."

"To the *rabhsai*?"

"Not unprecedented — your own grandfather, before he had risen as high as Captain of Armies, told — "

"Very well, very well," with an impatient motion of his hand. "What would the terms be?"

Not a real question: he must have the only answer. "You will promise civil war, no? If the new oath is not withdrawn, neither you nor Saidhan can prevent the Army of the West from acting in its own best interests."

"Saidhan has said as much, in bitterness."

"This trouble in the North must be the same thing, with Shumat's army. Together — "

"You are telling me to make a weapon out of the threatened shattering of the realm, our people killing each other — everything that fills me with fear and dismay."

"Your grandmother would have said, a definition of statecraft. But it would not be a threat, would it? It is simply true; in the end men of the Colony would have to fight against their own dispossession."

"I could explain this to Ban-Sila," Rodlakh slowly assented. "He also must be told about unrest and the rumors at the Frontier."

Dolvid bit back the impulse to shout *No!* Rodlakh's decency was beyond question, but why must he be such a blockhead when it came to his brother? Ban-Sila should imagine the Army of the West poised to descend on Kadon Dinul, not preoccupied with the distant Frontier.

With all the tact used in conveying this notion, it brought them as near to a quarrel as they had come. At last he told Rodlakh he must go carefully, and not begin bargaining by emptying his purse; he owed that to the risks they had taken and the price already paid. Mainly Sebhal's life, Dolvid reflected, and his object had been to stick a knife in Ban-Sila, probably without any debate.

"Very well," as if humoring him. "If we can reach Ban-Sila, I shall not say a word about danger in the West, unless he has given a clear sign he is interested in a peace and not just our submission — is that what you want?"

"In short, a sign he is prepared to abandon and rescind the Loyal Oath, and all measures tending to promote Preference."

"You can be very like Sebhal at times. His gifts could make him too cynical."

Heroes always flaw, Dolvid noted, while acknowledging the complimentary part. Here, probably, was the first criticism of Sebhal Rodlakh had ever uttered. Strange that in coming to see Sebhal as a real and fallible human, he had found the worst possible example.

Stumbling against a sun-dial, hurting the same shin again, Dolvid swore if he survived this bandit period of his life, he would never willingly make another journey by darkness.

Night had been long enough coming. At Faëdhal's they had passed the afternoon playing *zhabhu*, using Faëdhal's board inlaid in contrasting colors of stone, the tiles ivory, war-standards delicately carved from boxwood. After two long, indecisive games Dolvid won the third more resoundingly than he deserved, drawing the tile called Four Bees at a stage where, while he led in captured standards, Rodlakh had a slight advantage in territory. These were the swerves of fortune that helped make *zhabhu* so fascinating, and also contributed to the legendary bad temper of some players. Happily, Rodlakh was a graceful loser, quoting from a much-copied essay, ascribed to Shaël himself, which held no amount of bad luck in drawing tiles could bring defeat to a flawless player. Most *zhabhu* enthusiasts blandly endorsed this rubric, but it could not be proved one way or the other, since the game was too complex to say what was perfect play. In the end the essay had only its undeniable antiquity to recommend it; for reasons to do with how the Syllabary was used Dolvid was fairly certain it was not by Shaël, but somewhat earlier.

This had brought Rodlakh's demand for a decision: who was the better translator, Dolvid or Faëdhal?

"There is no answer. He is better with history of the Syllabary, and also of the Script. For example, the sign we use to write the initial sound in borrowed words such as *jinzai* — a tribal sound in origin —

began its life in Shâl's Script standing for a Vrobani vowel, something near an *i*. It later shifted to consonant-*y*, and at various periods was used by various writers for our own *zh* in *zhabhu*, and ordinary *sh*. In any event, it is important to determine the period for your page of the Script, or else you can produce absurd readings. Now Faëdhal, if he is told this is Late Island, or Blossoming Age before 1500, whatever it may be, can read off a page with hardly a pause. I can seldom do that. But if he has not ascertained the period, he can make mistakes; he never had much interest in anything outside text, and could seldom make guesses from context, as I could — my wild leaps, he called them. So it goes; I know more about the glyphs, but still insist he is better with the Syllabary. The two of us together probably make up as good a translator as you will see in this generation."

"That is very pleasing."

Faëdhal, when he came home before curfew, had spent the day trying for news, but could not add much that was definite. As well as the unknown number of Kargul' troops at Kadon Dinul under Kamin-Tolagh and the loathed Rheduban, Tovakh and his wife Petakoi were here, staying at the New Residence. They were Kamin-Tolagh's parents, and Tovakh overlord of his province in everything but formal title, his father, Tobhan, being in bad health and almost blind. The tough, pugnacious and reputedly quarrelsome Tovakh had wanted a royal captaincy for many years; it might be he would get his chance at command with the northern rebellion.

As for that, Faëdhal could report numberless rumors, a progression in unlikelihood which had rebel forces in Sebira, Drin Dakani, central Dramal, at the gates of Dônshei. The rebels had burnt whole shiploads of shuzi. They had come ashore in Dramal from trading ships. They were using shuzi to purchase support. *Jinzal* were fighting on their side. The lords of Dramal and Ân had been murdered, and a Northern Free State declared. The insurgents were already defeated, and had taken to the hills as bandits. An imminent shortage of everything from mutton to buttons was predicted.

None of the nonsense was more impossible than the one apparent fact, Shumat, or certainly his Army of the Northeast, at the heart of the uprising; what could never be imagined did not become truer by confirmation.

Kadon Dinul near midnight was never as silent as a provincial town; curfew or not, there was a rustling stir composed of many small noises, and in some distant street the tramp of feet or beat of hoofs. Dark was not complete enough for comfort, though the capital was gloomy compared to former times when doors would be thrown open, lamps and tapers burnt through the night, yellow flame contrasting with cool pulsing of *ôthu*-light from wealthier dwellings. That light still frosted the facade of the New Residence, but most illumination came from the ramparts and guard-posts at the gates.

They avoided the Gardens, using a narrow, rutted lane farther from the walls, so they could cross the Tan Lughsai road out of sight of Harbor Gate. Where they chose, a hollow with an apple-orchard close against the road, could not be far from where Âna must have crossed by daylight, about sixteen hours ago. Dolvid wondered about the comfortless spot where she might be huddled for the night, and his mind, groping south, could not in imagination find her.

Soon, they were at the embankment by the *Mankh'* road. On its mound to the far side the Bronze Residence was quietly lighted with *ôdul* at cornices and within. Nothing was moving on the road, and the glow from Harbor Gate off to the right was not enough to reveal the two fleet figures as they went across the stones and vaulted the low serpentine wall. Bent over, they scuttled up the bank, and crouched under the slight overhang of the platform where the building rested. Nothing else moved.

While Rodlakh, knife ready, kept watch, Dolvid worked at the stiff double lock to the old guardroom door, which might not have been opened since it was locked about eight years ago. He was sore-fingered and hot with impatience when the bottom wards at last rasped back. The iron door swung out with a low moan. Inside with Rodlakh, Dolvid pulled the door closed behind, and secured it with one of the turnbolts. They were clamped in absolute black.

Nothing seemed changed; he groped his way past boxes and loose stacks of musty parchment to reach the inner door which, giving on a narrow passageway, he had never known locked. It opened now with a small creak, and the darkness yielded a little. Not far from where they were, up a short set of stairs, was the dimly lighted main hallway.

Standing by the guardroom door they could not be sure whether a noise they heard came from inside or out. Halfway tiptoe up the steps they knew; a footfall came close by, and a man, gaping mouth plainly silhouetted, leant against a wall, yawning, in the opening to the stairwell. Not a young man: in Dolvid's day this night watch was given to half-pay veterans and men not fully fit, but they always had means of summoning aid.

Dolvid and Rodlakh had no need to compare ideas; as the man turned away, scratching his neck, they moved together, with no thought of drawing blades. The man went down with Dolvid's forearm clamped over his mouth; there was a thump, a short scuffle and a dull thud. Rodlakh used a kerchief deftly to bind the man's mouth, while Dolvid kept a disabling twist on arm and shoulder, scared eyes going to and fro. They took the man's belt to lash his feet together. Lips next to their victim's ear, Rodlakh breathed, "Don't struggle, and you'll come out of this with your life." A length of time-wick did for tying his wrists behind his back.

All this took less than half a minute. Between them they carried the man down to the foot of the stairs. Dolvid drew his knife to cut a fat little pipe from the lanyard around the man's neck, an ox-call, then held the blade in front of the frightened man's eye. "Do not make us kill you. Rest quiet and your friends will find you before long."

If there was any notion of questioning this man about other guards it faded when a voice, not distant, called out, "South side? South side — is anything wrong?" The thump of the sentry's fall must have been heard.

"Stay close," Dolvid hissed, and went swiftly back up the steps. On very familiar ground, he took the main hallway, wheeled left up another short stair, and was in the Square Gallery, where tiers of rooms surrounding what was once the Royal Suite soared all the way to skylights. Leftward were broad, polished steps down to the main entrance, right the double doors of forged bronze, smooth-opening, through which they plunged, as the voice, nearer and angrier, called, "South side? South side? Answer me!"

"Old Audience Hall," Dolvid informed as they hurried through the lofty room where a few ôdul gave some light. "Our main work-space." No time to assess changes; he did note that the great maps on wooden panels made for him by the carpenter Untimarr were gone from the side walls: it must be blasphemous in Ban-Sila's realm to know where places were.

He had worried about the doors to the Old Throne Room, and was relieved they were unlocked. Inside, he pointed at the dais. "Where the Chair of State used to be, from Plakhat Gabh'Owan to the earlier half of Plakhsila's reign."

"Is that where you had your writing-table?" elaborately over-innocent.

No noise of pursuit. They picked up two ôdul in the metal carrying-cages that made them into useful lanterns. To one side of the dais Dolvid pushed aside musty brocaded hangings, and was in the space he had often used for sleeping, though there was no bed now. Going to the rear wall with its carved stone, he soon found the blocks that moved on its solid-looking surface. Beyond curtains and doors, other doors slammed, and a voice was barking out instructions.

Now a second block could be turned. It went stiffly, and the oblong slot appeared. As Dolvid reached in, the doors to the Throne-Room were banging open. He pushed right as hard as he could, sending back what was in effect a thick bolt. A man-high slab of stone turned quite easily on its pivot with only a faint scraping sound. With feet clattering just the other side of the curtains, he urged Rodlakh inside, and followed. Once the stone had completed its turn, he pushed the inside handle of the bolt back in. The displaced key blocks on the other side could not be put back, but would never be noticed, unless bright lights were brought. Finding the blocks, years ago, had taken days of hunting among the carvings, and he had known what he was looking for.

The sounds from beyond the wall were indistinct; Dolvid and Rodlakh were inside the thickness of a big wall. Going a dozen paces brought them to the top of a tight-turning stair leading down into forbidding dark. This was within the square bastion at the northeast corner of the Bronze Residence. A steep descent of forty or fifty feet came to where a narrow passage led off, walls of finely-worked stone, the air unstaled.

"This must have been here from the earliest building. In a moment we'll be where Plakhsila's masons began their work." Dolvid peered, but while the light of the ôthu-lanterns was comforting in its steadiness, it did not pierce far ahead. The loudest sounds were thud of his own heart and Rodlakh's breathing, till they reached a sharp-angled descent where, from deep below, the hoarse roar of rushing water came. Continuing down, they soon came to where the newer work began. Easy to see where Plakhsila's workmen, less than two centuries ago, had chopped through the side wall of the original passage to make a new tunnel, its stonework skillful, but not to be compared with the fineness of the original work. The older way went twisting down, while the new led off straight, and for a while perfectly level. Then steps sloped down, and they descended farther by another square-turning stair. Here the air was musty though not foul, and the muffled noise of running water was everywhere. "I estimate we are under the Avenue of Treaties." Dolvid had attempted measurements by means of pacing on one of his earlier explorations.

As the steps ended, their lanterns struck nothing ahead to throw back any light; the going was straight and flat for what seemed a very long way, till they began climbing once more, first on a straight and gradual slope, then steeply up a series of ramps set at irregular angles, so it was soon impossible to judge their direction. Beside a densely carved pilaster, Dolvid stopped. "As near as I can make out, we are directly under the foot of the Residence Steps." The Avenue, which ended there, ran precisely east and west, so that along its axis, the throne room in the New Residence was exactly aligned with the old.

"So soon?"

"From Yoëlladhu's Spear to the Disc of Aëlovoi is ten thousand five hundred and forty-eight *rodukh'*, a span for every season from the Descent to the accession of Plakhsila — two thousand, seven hundred and thirty-seven years. From there — "

"From there I know the distance very well."

"We have come a longer way, of course, but they did build marvellously straight."

He told about two outlets he had discovered in the New Residence, the more promising of which was not far from the Personal Suite. "But before that, we can listen for a while where the passage runs behind the carving in the General Audience Hall. We may hear something valuable; people go there to talk policy."

"The Oak Wall? That could not be. The carving is set back flush with the windows."

So indeed it appeared, but the passage was cleverly accommodated by an extra course in the outside wall, and there were tricks of measurement to make space behind the famous carving.

"Then you have eavesdropped there before."

An expected thought. "Certainly not. All my exploring was done in summer, when Lambarr *Rabhsai* and court were at Tan Lughsai."

The continuation of their climb was a tight, steep-pitched spiral; after consideration of various possibilities Dolvid had concluded the passage here was deep inside the massive buttress on the south side of the New Residence, which divided off the Court of the Ram from the stables. Becoming breathless, they came to a door of solid oak, deeply cracked at the surface, good for perhaps a further thousand years. Holding up his lantern so Rodlakh could see, Dolvid put a finger to his lips. Carefully, he swung the door outward. A tight squeeze between stone and stone, widening abruptly as it angled sharply left, simultaneously reducing overall height to an awkward five-and-a-half feet. There was decidedly more light here, and the left-hand wall had changed to the dry, warm surface of somber wood, with odd-shaped patches of light thrown on the stone opposite. They were actually behind the gigantic carving, *Plakhsila Receiving the News of His Accession*, which depicted that event as it occurred, in the forests near Kamsilat. Chroniclers called this a spontaneous tribute to the great *rabhsai* from craftsmen of the Colony, and Dolvid often wished he had never seen a letter in Plakhsila's neat handwriting, demanding why the gift was so delayed, and repeating unignorable specifications as to size and subject matter, with many details of the composition. Despite this, he ranked the *Kimukoi-Rabhsai* among best and justest of rulers.

As they edged their way along this gallery, a loud voice boomed up from the hall, "*Hranakhai*, this had better be worth my lost sleep, and there had better be hot drink coming." With the Karguli rise and fall, as with Rheduban, but this voice was rougher, older, and had prouder authority — a voice remembered from long ago. "And where is Bolan?"

"He is washing." Another Karguli voice, this one younger. "He only came back half an hour ago."

"'*Ghai*, you drag me out of bed at this hour to tell me Bolan is having a wash? Some of use our beds for sleep. Hoi!" The last was a call for servants, presumably so he could have his hot drink.

By sidling a short way and bending his knees Dolvid could bring an eye in line with one of the apertures, an odd-shaped one, widening outwards. His view was partly framed by a saw-toothed silhouette he was at last able to identify as a drooped elm leaf, carved so as to disguise the peephole. His view was diagonally downward from above head height, in line with the fretted stone canopy where the *rabhsai* would sit when receiving formal petitions or making judgments. Just getting seated in one of the heavy oak chairs ranged next to the canopy was a thick, powerful man whose breadth had no fat to it. The face was lined and weathered, and but for the wiry, grey-streaked beard would have strongly resembled Sebhal's, as did the corded forearms emerging from short sleeves of his dressing gown. This was Tovakh baKargul.

Nearer, standing, a younger man was in light breeches and a loose blue shirt. The hair, almost to his shoulders, was a red-brown color, and as he half-turned, displaying a firm profile, he was indeed the officer of cavalry last seen south of Shemugrân, Tovakh's only son, Kamin-Tolagh. At his elbow, slightly back, a girl was standing, young, to judge by slender form and dark glossy hair, which spilled down to the long, gleaming robe of yellow shuzi. Beneath this dazzling garment the body was lissome, and Dolvid was reminded, as not for years, of being in the streets of the city, and how urgently necessary it always was to overtake, so as to see whether face confirmed the impression conveyed by an attractive back. This one was proudly held, and his greedy curiosity kept willing her to turn. She was not Kamin-Tolagh's younger sister Kamin-Tarú, who was said to have grown tall; this girl did not quite come to Kamin-Tolagh's shoulder. Besides, Kamin-Tarú could never have this girl's raven hair, while Tovakh's remark about sleeping in his bed had been a side-comment about his son's habits, hardly likely if this was his daughter. She did not have to be anyone in particular; there were not enough women of family to sustain Kamin-Tolagh's voracious reputation.

Nearby, Rodlakh, tensely absorbed, had also found a peephole, higher up, and not giving an unobstructed field of vision, to judge by the bobbing of his head.

Servants arrived with cups of what might well be hot *raminat* with spiced wine and honey, and just behind them, unhurried but purposeful, came Bolan. He was thicker in the waist than remembered; the hair, untouched by grey, had crept back a fingerspan or so from the rounded forehead. He had shaved away his moustache, and more than half-a-dozen added years of weariness and worry were stamped into Bolan's face as he turned to greet Kamin-Tolagh. With Tovakh the exchange of salutes was wary, the Karguli asserting superior rank, plainly delaying so as be the one to acknowledge. Kamin-Tolagh remained standing, but shifted a chair up for Bolan. If she moved at all, the girl, as the men drew in closer, drifted slightly back, graceful under the fluid shuzi.

Bolan, clearly, returning from a long ride, had been the one to call this meeting. Yet he did not begin by saying why, asking instead about important news during his absence from Kadon Dinul. Kamin-Tolagh started an account of his patrol south of Shemugrân, but Bolan stood to enquire pointedly about the girl's presence here.

"My son is putting in extra duty," Tovakh, with ponderous playfulness.

"Lovely," Bolan said, and to the younger man, "Would you mind keeping this one for a day or two, so I'll recognize her next time?"

For Bolan to talk so settled the question of the girl's rank; she had none, but might have been picked off the streets or from a Heartland farm. He went on to say in ironic regret this was, after all, and despite the *rabhsai*'s absence, a council of state.

"She does not understand anything," sullenly. "It cheers me to have her here." His father did not lose the crooked smile, but when his son looked to him was not sympathetic. "Cheer yourself with memories, and dreams of later. Bolan is right."

Kamin-Tolagh took both the girl's hands in his own, and bent over to speak into her ear. She must be very simple if her dismissal needed explaining, but it might be he was simply making an opportunity for nuzzling soft hair.

He beckoned a servant, and told him to show the *lady* to the Karguli Wing. Obediently the girl turned to follow. It was Âna.

Rodlakh gave a sharp gasp, but it could not be Âna, who must be beyond halfway to Tan Lughsai, wearing a shabby shirt and breeches. In a familiar movement the girl tilted her head to shake hair away from her eyes and in doing so was full-face to Dolvid. There was no doubt; it was Âna who meekly followed the servant from the hall.

Kamin-Tolagh went on recounting his adventures, his loss of two dead, and the account given by his one disabled man suggesting the outlaw band, one a woman, had fled into Shemugrân; Bolan counter-conjectured the man must have been delirious. Kamin-Tolagh was about to connect the incident with the one in Burantal, with similar descriptions for the four curfew-breakers, again a woman among them, except Bolan, at the mention of Rheduban's name, declined to listen to any more of what he called gnat-piddle. That, as perhaps intended, annoyed Tovakh, who growled about *péfrapravádal* of Kargul keeping order in the Paowan, making up for deficiencies of Household and General Cavalry.

"Oh, aye," Bolan, airily. "Hrafi knows who would be skinning housecats alive, or putting out the eyes of mice, if we did not have Captain Rheduban here to do these things for us." Without rank or ancestry to compare, Bolan was taking a high line so as to avoid complete eclipse.

An automatic assessment, while mind tried to grapple with the problem of Âna. Strange how the many good arguments why she could not be here gave way to the single unreasonable fact she was, under no observable duress, caressed by Kamin-Tolagh.

When his attention returned fully to the Audience Hall there were new arrivals, and all powers of the realm were represented. For *rabhsayum* there was Rhunilat, long-necked, growing to resemble his father, the *Bôdhrai* Rhunsilakh, killed with so many others in the Tan Lughsai disaster. Rhunilat, so far as Dolvid knew, had not been promoted beyond his old rank of *bôdh'loiki*, lesser counsellor, with no precisely defined duties.

Beside him, much shorter, was an *atarlai*, slight of build. Like Rhunilat he was carrying materials for writing. His dull-blue robe, bees-wing loops in gold, showed he was of the Patriarch's personal retinue, though with his smooth face he at first seemed very young for that position. He was expressing *g'Asalladh's* regrets, or rather what he was sure would be *g'Asalladh's* regrets, at being unable to attend in person, and Dolvid decided the little man was, after all, somewhere near his own age.

"You speak for *g'Asalladh'*, then?" Rhunilat wanted be told.

"I am no more than his ears," the *atarlai* said, and made a self-deprecating gesture. *Exactly my age*, Dolvid corrected; he knew the man, or had known the boy. They had been pupils at the *Mankh'* together, and then as now he was small, smooth and ingratiating. An Island boy, Zhâlai, at-Zhâlai as it must be since his oaths.

The situation in the Northeast had brought them all together, and Bolan said the news was bad. At the head of what he called the mutiny, Shumat had used the luck of an early thaw: the rumored fall of Yuvakh Din was confirmed, no surprise, since the garrison there was part of Shumat's command. Much worse, Sebira in Upper Ân was invested to landward, and Tovakh's kinsman, Daënakh, was powerless. His wife and cousin, Leghayu, was safe; she had brought the news westward, having been given safe-conduct by Shumat.

"Safe-conduct!" Tovakh jumped to his feet. "Who does this Shumat think he is, Larghai?"

Bolan said, "He is calling himself First Captain of the Free State of Arbhal. I haven't seen it, but there's said to be a Manifesto, inviting all those who stand against the rebirth of Preference to join Shumat there." He shook his head. "This is not Shumat." At last, a point where he and Dolvid agreed.

"Who in Hranakh's name is it then?" Tovakh demanded.

"I mean, not the Shumat we know. Could it be Dolvid has found a way to go there? He and Shumat are friends from boyhood." Bolan gave a brief, not very accurate history of Dolvid's career as troublemaker, not mentioning he was Bolan's wife's former husband (which they probably knew).

"If he is in the Northeast," Kamin-Tolagh said, "he flew, and quickly. A week ago I visited his house by Shemugrân, and missed him by less than an hour. He may have been with those who waylaid my men."

Bolan was interested, and would have pursued this subject, but Tovakh, angry over that safe-conduct, brought them back to the main issue, the uprising in the North, the strength, composition and command of the forces needed to put it down.

Many themes here to prolong and embitter discussion; Kargul's long exclusion from Royal Captaincy and their possession of far more cavalry than the law permitted; Bolan's desire for help cooled by mistrust of Tovakh and the wish to maintain control of any campaign. Tovakh was determined to get the best price for his assistance, but here his son was not much support: clearly Kamin-Tolagh wanted to ride in battle, and would have paid Bolan for the privilege. And there was deeper conflict perceptible between father and son, Tovakh repeatedly contrasting his own mature good judgment with the rashness of Kamin-Tolagh.

For whom, nonetheless, he wanted honors; apparently renewing an earlier discussion, he spoke of his sharing Captaincy of the Household with the present Captain-designate, Kizhunai, a calm and sensible officer.

That was how Dolvid understood the proposal, but the discussion, on territory the debaters had been over before, was not for the benefit of eavesdroppers, often tantalizingly incomplete.

Also, the two principal adversaries (as Bolan and Tovakh certainly were, though looking for workable alliance) were trying to bait and bluff each other. When it came to strategy Bolan boasted about levies already raised for defense of the strong places in the north, some thousands of foot, armed mainly with bows. "Foot," Tovakh sneered, centuries of cavalry tradition behind his contempt. "Can you put down rebellion sitting in garrison, making Shumat a present of all the food grown north of Dônshei? You need cavalry, to hunt down the rebels, bring them to open fight."

"How many squadrons do you suppose that might take?" Bolan, very bland, and it might be those levies had been a feint to bring Tovakh to this juncture. Bolan, in addition to all cavalry garrisons with their auxiliaries already in the north, wanted the astonishing total of forty new squadrons, of which Kargul (he suggested sweetly) would contribute sixteen, not counting four squadrons already attached to the Household.

Tovakh's teasing disbelief any province could loan so many *péfrapravádal* was purely ritual, but he enjoyed playing on Bolan's contradictory fears, openly telling him it was foolish to distrust Kargul, whose aid he sought. Poignant for the eavesdroppers when he insisted everyone that with Sebhal still to fear, strength had to be maintained here at Kadon, in case the Army of the West seized the opportunity to come storming across the Arnan.

So far, the little recorder from the *Mankh'* had not done much except try to cool tempers when name-calling became too fierce. Now he made an enigmatic contribution, saying that while he was not able to give details, *g'Asalladh'* permitted him to say that for now there was no need to fear invasion by the Army of the West.

All three soldiers stared at at-Zhâlai, and Tovakh put the question into words, "In Hrafi's name, how could *g'Asalladh'* — my humble and sincere devotions, naturally — how in all creation can He say that?"

At-Zhâlai made modest mouths, spoke of the *aën'modha* of *g'Asalladh'*, and when that met with respectful skepticism, noted it was no secret the *Mankh'* had reliable informants at Kamsilat. In reality, as he admitted, he did not know the reason for *g'Asalladh'*s confidence. Nor need to, he dutifully insisted.

"Dissension at Kamsilat?" Bolan wondered. "I could imagine a cause for that, an appetizing one."

Tovakh gloated. "Or trouble at the Frontier. But it could come to the same thing. The young renegade could find excuses to stay at the Great House with his accomplished aunt, while Sebhal rides off to the manly West."

Dolvid heard Rodlakh sniff with annoyance. Below, talk of Aëlu was making Kamin-Tolagh fidget, and Dolvid thought sickly of his taking that restlessness to where Âna was waiting.

"As a true son," Tovakh said, "I shall accept *g'Asalladh'*s assurances; guaranteed absence of Sebhal gives us the chance to smash Shumat. Utterly." He brought a heavy hand down on the arm of his chair. "As a soldier," he added, "I may glance over my shoulder from time to time."

The meeting was winding down in fatigue, with nothing quite settled. The proposal to put before the *rabhsai* came out to be that at the price of the Household joint-captaincy for Kamin-Tolagh, Tovakh would provide the forces wanted. About actual command of the campaign, there was wrangling yet to come.

Bolan stood, yawning cavernously. "I must stay awake to report to the *rabhsai*."

"Kargul can ride in mere days." Tovakh said. "Remind the *rabhsai*, the sooner Shumat is defeated, the quicker we restore revenues from the shuzi trade."

"He is not much interested in trade."

"Oh, yes. A *rabhsai* bored by money... " The two moved down out of Dolvid's view. Kamin-Tolagh wheeled abruptly and left by the same door where Âna had been led away. At-Zhâlai and Rhunilat looked at each other with nothing to say, and servants moved in to carry off empty cups.

After squeezing through a yet narrower spot at the far end of the gallery, Dolvid and Rodlakh went down steps to a smooth-walled space with no apparent outlet.

"What — ?" he began, ready for something to explode over, but Dolvid stooped to pull up a trap-door, swinging by his fingertips down into the dark. Rodlakh passed down the two lanterns before following. Brushing at his breeches, he said, "Is there a place where we can sit and put our ideas together?" Dolvid felt no less shaken by what they had witnessed.

They were in a wider passageway, and after further changes of level and direction Dolvid discovered the low door he was looking for. He held up a hand. "This takes us out of the hidden passage. A room never used during my years, but — ?" Rodlakh nodded, easing the knife in its sheath.

A bronze loop slid stiffly right. Inside, an ornamental plaque was moving, exposing an aperture. From this side, Dolvid reached into the same hollow, and tugged up on the iron bolt. The low wall-section swung out, Rodlakh stooping to go past, blade ready.

As always, the room was dusty and bare. Opposite where they had emerged first streakings of dawn showed in a murky window.

"Is this kept locked?" indicating the outer door.

"On the outside. But they put some ingenuity into this; we cannot be locked in; the inside handle grasps the end of the key."

Rodlakh sat on the floor, back to the wall. From his belt he unhooked the small skin bottle Faëdhal had refilled with cold *raminat*. He took a sip and offered it to Dolvid, asking blankly how *g'Asalladh'* could have learned about Sebhal's death. It seemed the only explanation for at-Zhâlai's hints. "Tovakh does not know, and neither does Kamin-Tolagh — if Rheduban had carried the news, Kargul would surely have it before the *Mankh'*."

Rather than this, Dolvid would be gratified by a Rodlakh angry enough to prove *g'Asalladh'* wrong, by going to Tan Lughsai, crossing to Kamsilat, and putting himself at the head of the Army of the West. There were ways for the *Mankh'* to have found out who it was had died in Burantal: with all their virtues both Nentirr and his wife were fond of gossip, and there were sure to be *ramidul* and *edhradul* in or near Burantal who would report such a story to the *Mankh'*. The larger puzzle was why *g'Asalladh'* was keeping the news to Himself. If He had any question, He surely would not be giving the assured advice at-Zhâlai had conveyed.

Other puzzles were to be discussed. Rodlakh did not understand the ascendancy of Kargul, and how it was Tovakh had apparently won in the wrangle with Bolan. Dolvid was not tactless or brave enough to give the eventual answer, *the threat of Preference, your brother's policies*, but talked about Bolan's difficulties and fears over finding troops.

"Back in twenty-eight, at a bad moment in that campaign, he confided to me he often had a dream where he rides into battle and his squadrons do not follow him. That is coming true." The confession, oddly, had been at Yuvakh Din.

"He tried to pass off how the Yuvakh Din cavalry had gone over to Shumat. Yuvakh counts as part of Shumat's overall command, but the garrison there is General Cavalry, not Army of the Northeast. Bolan is not certain he can call on any troops in the North to pit against Shumat — that is why he was so firm about wanting forty *fresh* squadrons."

"But why Tovakh, why Kargul?"

"Race," simply. For most of the realm, especially the Paowan and northward, the Owanil had come back from the Island in 2477 as aristocracy and the Craft Families; few were laborers, which meant even today many officers but very few ordinary soldiers of General Cavalry, Household, most Provincial forces, were of the Owani race. But in mountainous Kargul (as in remote Ninkufu where Dolvid was born), a stubborn pocket of Owanil had persisted all through the Night, still by far largest part of the general population of that province, so the Cavalry of Kargul did not consist, like others, of men who, enforcing the start of a new Preference, were being asked to fight for their own eventual dispossession.

This had to do with the outstanding question of whether Rodlakh, after all he had heard, still wanted to confront his brother. True, there had been nothing said that absolutely refuted the notion of a *rabhsai* manipulated by his advisors, but that was meaningless; no one had mentioned, either, that Ban-Sila had the normal numbers of eyes, ears, feet and fingers —

"And Âna — " at last.

"Âna," despondently. "Can she have been a spy from the start? Sent to Kamsilat to get near Sebhal — did she arrange for Rheduban to be waiting at Burantal? I knew our luck was too bad to believe."

Dolvid did not think so. She had helped down a soldier of Kargul, and if a trap had been set in Burantal it would have been a better one with more troops; Rheduban as soon as Sebhal could have been the one killed.

Rodlakh could not be told all of Dolvid's reasons for trusting Âna, her sobbing in his bunk, unmistakable torment in her changed view of Sebhal, the genuine desire to protect Rodlakh from seeing any imperfections in him. A mystery, but Dolvid would not accept any explanation including her treachery.

Then, though at Kamin-Tolagh's side, she clearly was not in his confidence; in recounting his and Rheduban's adventures he had twice mentioned the woman thought to be among the outlaws, but given no sign of connecting her to his companion. Besides, as Rodlakh had said, Kamin-Tolagh believed Sebhal was alive, and with Âna as informant he would have been earliest to know otherwise. She knew, too, how Dolvid meant to get Rodlakh into the Residence, surely the first news any spy would bring her employers; an ambush would have been waiting, not one drowsy and inattentive sentinel.

Rodlakh with a grunt grudgingly conceded these facts, without giving up his suspicions. "Not eighteen hours after she left us — she must never have meant to make for Tan Lughsai. And how she was bedecked for that peacock — I never saw her do as much... " and he let that peter out.

Remotely possible Âna had indeed come straight to the New Residence, or in some way set out to catch Kamin-Tolagh's eye, following a plan she guessed the others would never approve. But her way, surely, would have been to tell them about it and defy them to stop her; far likelier, or so Dolvid told Rodlakh, she had been captured, and then taken Kamin-Tolagh's omnivorous fancy.

"She does not behave as a prisoner, or dress like one. She was supposed to love Sebhal, and he is only a week dead. She becomes a whore."

Rodlakh, then, did not know about her coming to his bed. But it was chilling that the sour and greedy assumptions of some unlettered Gabhani chieftain could persist in Rodlakh.   Justice aside, that vilification came too easily.

"Suppose you were travelling alone — unarmed, let us say, and Kamin-Tolagh's celebrated sister, Kamin-Tarú, backed by a dozen swords, wanted to take you to bed?"

"Not so far-fetched, from what I hear about that lady." Rodlakh's attempt at worldliness would have come off, but the tips of his ears became pinker.

"However angry you were at being compelled, you would certainly find some enjoyment in the task."

"Well, a man — "

"A man, yes." Dolvid had experienced how useless it was, trying to set fairness against these surviving tribal beliefs, but had to go on to the end. "And your friends would not think any less of you for submitting to her wants — they would see it as ridiculous if you let yourself be killed resisting her. Should there be so much difference in what we expect of a woman?"

"If Âna had his child — a brat of the Kargul'... "

"She will not," but it was a new concern. "Kamin-Tolagh knows the *Mankh'* way, and they do not want any half-heirs to muddle succession in Kargul."

"Her father would kill her. They never change, those back-country Gabhanil."

"Indeed, indeed," staying grave-faced.

Rodlakh, ready to discuss the exact significance of Shumat's gains in the Northeast, was plainly simply postponing a decision about whether to try to see Ban-Sila. Dolvid said they could turn back from here, return to the Bronze Residence, and be on their way for Tan Lughsai in an hour or so — or, with morning coming, if they would rather travel under shelter of night, they could pass the day in the tunnel before going on.

"I wish we could speak with Âna," Rodlakh astonishingly said.

"So do I, but she is in the Karguli Wing; it would be foolhardy to try." The notion of rescue hovered, but it was not certain Âna would want that, and the outcome of any attempt might be all their deaths.

"It would be stupid," Dolvid made himself say, "when she is sure to be free again before long. He will not harm her, just get tired of her."

"Not everyone is as irritated as you are by Âna's ways. Sebhal seldom was, and she is liked at Kamsilat." Prompt revenge for being lectured by him.

"I was talking about Kamin-Tolagh's ways, not hers. With him, faithfulness means beginning and ending one night with the same woman." All the same, there was a nagging terror this would be different, and Kamin-Tolagh decide to keep Âna.

Sunrise came nearer. Rodlakh said, "We should have brought our packs." They had taken them off getting through the narrowest part of the passageway, and left them there. "Are you hungry?"

Dolvid went into his pocket to bring out and pass over a few sunflower seeds. "As it happens, we should be near food — the night-pantry by the doors into the Court of Nasilú?" It had always been kept filled with cold foods for visitors sleeping in the Rose-Stone Wing who arrived at odd hours, or woke hungry.

"Would that still be?"

"In this Residence? Back in your father's day, the servants had most of the food, but to take it direct from the kitchen and never set it out on the shelves would have been stealing."

Rodlakh was on his feet. "Some of that spiced beef would be good. There was always that, and the flat bran-bread cakes."

Warning it was risky, he went to the door, which opened inwards, and peered out into a deserted corridor. The night-pantry was diagonally across to the left. To the right, three steps led down to a transverse way, and the double-door to the garden-court the Rose-Stone Wing enclosed.

They both darted across. The open shelves in the shallow alcove were not crowded. "Cheese," Dolvid whispered, "Irvati, if you care for it." He shuddered.

"Something here with raisins in it. A barley-loaf, but I cannot find any — "

Echoing voices came to them. Without time to dive across to the door where they had come, they pressed back in the alcove. The sounds were nearing, but along the other corridor at the foot of the three steps.

" — in no mood for small courtesies. Bolan said, `and who has greater experience than I, fighting in the Northeast?'  Tovakh said, `Shumat.'" The little laugh that followed let Dolvid identify the voice; at-Zhâlai.

The double-doors rattled. More curious than wise, Dolvid leaned out a little, as another voice, its stiff, wooden tone familiar from former times, spoke. "These bickerings bore me, but it is no bad thing, to have them goading each other on." At Dolvid's ear, Rodlakh's breathing stopped. The two speakers were about to go through the double-doors, the second broader and taller, but only next to at-Zhâlai. Neckless, stiff, readily recognizable from behind, really of very moderate height, Ban-Sila Rabhsai. The doors closed behind him and his companion.

"No escort?" Rodlakh said.

They went quickly back into the small room, not discarding their booty, and made rapid plans. Rodlakh, now they came to it, was very quickly persuaded into a realism not reconcilable with any of the dreams that had brought him to this place; though ruefully, he was quick to see they would have to use, or at least show, force.

As they left, Dolvid squeezed a short bit of time-wick between jamb and door-edge to prevent its closing completely. Not seen by anyone, they went down the short stair, and through the double-doors into a short vestibule. A second set of doors opened on the Garden Court of Nasilú.

The upper story of the Rose-Stone Wing partly rested on columns enclosing three sides of the court, with its meandering walks, plashing fountain, and stands of small willows, river-birch and other ornamental trees and shrubs. Had the *rabhsai* been planning his own waylaying he could not have done better than to stroll here; the light was dim enough to assist concealment, but less so out in the gardens where the strollers were. Best of all, they were not on the central path, but one near the pillared walk on the left side. By a gap between pillars Dolvid came up from shadows and felled at-Zhâlai with one sharp rap to the back of the neck, catching the limp body before knees touched ground. Attack on the *rabhsai* was best left as a family affair, and the *Valrabh'* did not make any mistakes, getting his left forearm over Ban-Sila's mouth, and letting him see a bared blade. "One cry and you are dead," he hissed ferociously. In boyhood Ban-Sila had been a fair swordsman and good with staves, but possession of an inviolable Person did not encourage training; his muscles were slack, and at his best he could never have matched Rodlakh's lean strength and quickness.

Pulling at-Zhâlai's sacklike form under the colonnade, Dolvid was just a few paces from his own door, the apartments where, as a bachelor, he had his bed. When without real hope he tried the door, it swung open at once, letting out a musty air of desertion.

As at-Zhâlai was hauled inside he was coming to life, or his legs were, and Dolvid drew his knife. Rodlakh was close behind, marching the massier Ban-Sila. In the doorway the forearm slipped for an instant from the *rabhsai*'s mouth, and he blurted "*Who* — ?" before silenced by the point of his brother's knife touched to his cheek.

Dim light let it be seen no furniture remained here. The thing to do was seat the two captives on the floor where light was best, opposite the window. Dolvid took a stance with his back to the door, as Rodlakh bent over the *rabhsai*, reaching under the cloak to remove a dagger hilted in gold and pearls.

As he straightened enough light fell on his features. "Rodlakh — " the *rabhsai* was, perhaps, not altogether surprised.

"I did not want violence. Till today I would not have thought it was needed." That was true; his belief in an innocent, deceived *rabhsai* could have survived everything, except the brief exchange overheard by the food-pantry five minutes ago.

"Oh?" Ban-Sila said.

"No one is going to be harmed, so long as you keep your voice low."

"*Uladh? Kedagh', adani — ul' Rabhsayin owal.*"

"It is not forgotten." Having heard Rodlakh in the Market Square of Burantal, furiously cursing a groom in flawless Owanilú, Dolvid knew tactics, not inability, kept him from following his brother into the Old Tongue. A wise choice, for what had to be discussed.

"I made the journey to find out how much you are truly our *rabhsai*. But it is a silly question. Now, I would rather ask why, but I doubt if you would have an answer."

"Why I am *rabhsai*?" Ban-Sila wanted it seen he was choosing not to be indignant.

"No. Why you are destroying your *rabhsayum*. Why you want to tear the realm in pieces."

Dolvid wished for better light so he could see if the sudden difference in Rodlakh was visible; the quiet sorrow of his questions was far more impressive than rant.

Ban-Sila was slower to see there had been a change, although at Rodlakh's age a year-and-a-half was a long time. As if talking to a child or someone dull-witted the *rabhsai* told his brother, "You have become the dupe of Sebhal and Saidhan. They want a realm where their own criminality is permitted to thrive, where there is no principle, no real virtue. I do not call it preserving the realm if those to whom the Gift and the Descent mean nothing are in positions of power, and true faith forgotten."

"What will you do, pretend four-fifths of our people do not exist?"

"Truth is not decided by numbers."

Yes, but this was strangely frigid. Ban-Sila was not only like, but actually was someone repeating a lesson, yet his teacher at his most calculating had never been without a core of true conviction, and disciples often burn hotter than their masters: the *rabhsai* was reminiscent of a sullen child.

Dolvid did not speak for minutes, and was not recognized till after at-Zhâlai had come back to life, as he did quite soon, with a moan.

Rodlakh was haranguing his brother about the absurdity, considering the admixture in their own descent, of bringing back the outworn Owani obsession with purity of blood, *Lekh'Owan*. As so often with *Mankh'* apologists, Ban-Sila denied his aspirations had anything to do with blood; it was belief, acceptance of the Owani ideal, determination to preserve ancient glories.

The wakened at-Zhâlai said, "*Lekh'Owanit Shei-Owani y'ôl,*" — a slogan descending from the days of the First Empire, when it may conceivably have been true for some: *shei* meant 'free,' and the saying implied that anyone among subject races who could master the lore, learning and faith necessary to count as *Shei-Owani* was just as good as the best blood of Old Owan. A favorite saying of the *Menadhi*, now Patriarch, and often cited by those who claimed Preference, for example, was not essentially a question of race. Yet it was, in the main, untrue as it was condescending; did men who shut themselves away from the world to go half-blind poring over genealogies one morning proclaim bloodlines, after all, meant nothing? They would use the example of someone like Bolan, but Bolan was tolerated because he was useful, and by far the most of the Other Races could never hope to acquire enough lore to qualify as *Shei-Owani* (neither could Bolan).

"*G'Asalladh'* Himself — " the scandalized at-Zhâlai began.

"*G'Asalladh'* Himself lies. I knew the man, as you did, Zhâl', when he was *Menadhi*, and could hardly tell the truth about who would have extra duty. But in those days I was his special pupil, and my blood was right, so about his convictions and aims he had no need to lie with me; he openly exulted in how the Old Blood was creeping back." Dolvid turned to Ban-Sila. "*Deghi*, he habitually called the founder of your house 'the Usurper.' With you I am sure he has had other words."

The light had grown, but he was against the window; at-Zhâlai peered seconds before saying. "Dolvidh. Dolvidh Vidukhat." It took a little longer for Ban-Sila to place the recollection, but once he had done so he could dismiss everything as words of a convicted criminal, a *kaël'rolai*. Inspired, he turned to Rodlakh. "Despite all treasonable acts, I might still pardon a brother who proved new loyalty by obeying the Law of Exiles. Disarm this criminal, and then submit yourself to the *rabhsai*'s mercy."

Rodlakh laughed joylessly, and said, "If I decline?"

"Then your crimes will have to face judgment, with those of the Colony you have adopted."

"What crimes are those?"

"Assailing the Person would do for a start."

"Not my crimes."

"The Colony? You know very well there has been open defiance for years. It all begins with illicit raising of twenty squadrons."

"To defend your borders."

"Only the *rabhsai* can authorize measures for the realm's defense. We cannot have local lords docking their remittances to buy new armies."

"Local lords?" Rodlakh could not resist exclaiming. "Your grandfather, the hero of Banak's accession? Tovakh baKargul must also be a criminal, but you do not outlaw him or his province. Just tonight he admitted to sixteen more squadrons of *péfrapravádal* at Zelkova alone; his province certainly has cavalry in excess of what is lawful."

In better light it might have been possible to see some surprise on Ban-Sila's face (or at-Zhâlai's) over the accuracy of Rodlakh's information, although from the instant he had seen who his captor was the *rabhsai* had been determined not to display any discomfiture.

"Additional provincial forces may be authorized at need; Saidhan would not be outlaw if he accepted that only the *rabhsai* could make such a determination, whereas Tovakh proves he is our loyal servant every day, with our other policies, the new oath — "

Rodlakh resurrected Sebhal's short bark of a laugh. "Kargul being nine-tenths Owani, Preference there has no need of a decree. It is not that simple in the Colony. To give you support against the Colony's crime of having too much cavalry, Tovakh is allowed to maintain excess cavalry, and will soon be permitted to bring it to Kadon Dinul. That is Ulat's hospitality." He referred to a tale everyone knew, *The Foolish Thatcher.*

"Tovakh baKargul is our truest friend — " spoken as if the phrase were a charm.

"Ulat said the same, and they found him in bed with his throat cut."

In a snap of annoyance, Ban-Sila ingeniously reversed the offer made to his brother. "Dolvidhai, you continue to call yourself loyal, and your exile unjust?"

"*Rabhsai*, I am *rabhsayani*."

"You can win our pardon, resume your work, if you will curb your wilder fancies and submit to the judgment of the *Mankh'* when there is a dispute. Your new service can begin at once: my brother, Rodlakh *Asai*, is clearly deranged, and needs restraining, for his own protection. In his madness he has now threatened our Person. You have a weapon; with our help you can disarm him."

He leaned forward, as if expecting obedience. Dolvid was not tempted, but amused by the oddity of what would surely be the last chance in this *rabhsayum* of being back within the law. Rodlakh, meanwhile, gave no sign of even momentary fear Dolvid might change sides, and when his brother began orating about disloyalty said, "Is this what you call rule? *No lord may command the assailing of friend by friend* — " a Patriarchal codicil of enormous antiquity.

"One rules by division, yes."

"Enough division and there is nothing left to rule. The new Loyal Oath is going to destroy your realm — for what? Plakhsila's Oath was good enough for Great Banak." A not-displeasing double meaning lost on Ban-Sila; Banak had both sworn the oath (to its originator's granddaughter) as a new officer, and administered it as *rabhsai*. But this *rabhsai* saw nothing wrong in trying to make men swear by gods not theirs, or rather (as it really was) excluding them for being unable to; for Ban-Sila, the tale of the Gift of Aëlovoi was simply true, and must be true for anyone.

"Give it up," Rodlakh said. "Are we going to let hundreds, thousands die for nothing, an opinion? Would you, not one of your soldiers, you — mount a horse, and hack down a stranger because he had never heard of the Descent of Yoëlladhu? How can we send men to fight and die for such things?"

"No one needs to die."

Plainly, if ever in all history there had been a useless meeting, here it was. Where nothing was heard, nothing was said, and the *rabhsai*'s wooden lack of passion robbed energy from Rodlakh's assault. Neither of them was capable of killing Ban-Sila, the only way this encounter could bring about change, so it was a foot-race on a treadmill, a circle-dance that must end where it began. For the sake of history, it had to be danced out.

Rodlakh spoke about hardships and dispossessions Ban-Sila's policies would bring about if those who stood to lose meekly ended their resistance, as his brother demanded. Quoting Sebhal, perhaps, he was bitter about hypocrisy among the Owanil lords of the Mainland, mouthing pieties about *ga-Yalum*, already picking which lands in the Colony would make a good piece of rough-hunting, after a few little farmhouses had been knocked down. Ban-Sila answered they were grants of land made illegally, gifts never consecrated, all a part of Saidhan's refusal to accept the authority of Kadon Dinul.

When Rodlakh reminded him it was not only in the Colony that men were prepared to resist return of Preference, Ban-Sila, interestingly, minimized Shumat's part in the northern uprising, saying his instructions came from Kamsilat. "Do you suppose I cannot tell who is behind this Free State, and who is to emerge as its would-be ruler, if it is not strangled at birth? Saidhan, for sixty years, has brooded how he should have become *rabhsai* by vanquishing Tobhsila. Now he would love to make his son *rabhsai*, but we have only one Chair of State, so he has to carve out a new realm to do it."

"That is nonsense — " but Dolvid's ear could detect absence of the same conviction Rodlakh had when speaking of farmlands in the Colony, and Ban-Sila's guesses, with a necessary adjustment of outlook, were not that different from Dolvid's own.

Light was growing steadily. "*Valrabh'*, we cannot expect to be uninterrupted indefinitely."

"*Valrabh'*?" Ban-Sila said. "Not so. We were urged to remove Rodlakh from the succession, and kept deferring it, hoping for a return to sanity, but your last letter with its rant about my captivity convinced me. Now we see how wise that was. On his twelfth birthday, Orbanak became *Valrabh'* in your place. He is at the *Mankh'*, out of your reach, under the gracious protection and guidance of *g'Asalladh'* Himself. In the event of my death, there is no chance he can be seized and made a puppet of." Grudgingly, Dolvid had to allow some courage in this; Ban-Sila must see his death as an imminent possibility.

"I would say he is exactly where that is most likely to occur," coolly. "Dolvid, I ask your pardon; I do not know why we are here."

"To learn." Rodlakh had given up his cherished belief in the captive *rabhsai*, although it was, in another sense, quite true; Ban-Sila could not be freed, but he was a prisoner just the same. Better than anyone else could, Dolvid knew the spells cast by the man he had known as *Menadhi*, and while he had escaped Ban-Sila had not; the *rabhsai*'s mind was enthralled and would never be free.

He began to orate, exactly in his teacher's style, decrying what everyone else praised about the reign of his grandfather, calling Pledgings a vulgar fraud that gave ordinary men the illusion of a voice, when in fact the Council made law. Children, he said, would not love or respect their father more if he asked them to decide for themselves who should be rewarded or punished; the wisdom of Ancient Owan would remain the realm's guide.

"You are dead," Rodlakh said, and for the first time Ban-Sila manifested nervousness, tongue wetting lower lip. But the solemn note in his brother's voice was not a direct personal threat, was the echo of history. "You are making the conditions for your death. When you have brought the Old Blood back, Kargul, the Families, do you imagine they will tolerate one of us as overlord? For them, we shall always be tainted with blood of Rodelam the Tanner, and that blood will flow in your veins if you repeat the Responses fifty times a day. One way or another, your reign will be a short one."

"You are not my brother." — with a spasm of rage in his face.

"No," wearily. "And I am not going to stand in the way of anything the Army of the West sees as necessary to its safety, the security of homes and property,"

Ban-Sila stared, but at-Zhâlai smirked. No use asking what made him so sure the Army of the West could be ignored. After all, the

Atarlum could not know Sebhal was dead, or knowing, had not told the *rabhsai*, which was impossible.

"I do not think we shall meet again," Rodlakh said.

Tan Lughsai

Sun was bright on the soaring walls of the Residence. Moving briskly through the garden court Dolvid swung open double doors, and almost walked straight into Bolan in the vestibule.

"I am looking for the *rabhsai*." Bolan was squinting against the light, not sure whether he was addressing lords or minions. A pair of pikemen were just behind him.

"Aye, Captain, he's... " Rodlakh began in a mumble and ended unintelligible, with a vague but vigorous gesture back over his shoulder.

"My thanks." As Bolan continued out into the garden court he glanced back at his informant. One of the pikemen, also in doubt about rank, said, "Your pardon — where are you coming from?"

One foot already inside the Residence proper, holding the door for Rodlakh, Dolvid said, "From talk with the *rabhsai*." The man nodded uncertainly as Rodlakh circled past the other soldier.

From the Court of Nasilú there was a distant cry. Nearer, Bolan said, "A moment — hold them!"

The two leapt up the short stair, pushed open the wedged door, and slammed it shut. Pikemen were close behind, and there was an immediate thud and rattle at the door. With a shake of his head Dolvid reassured Rodlakh; while muddled noises grew outside, they swallowed some mouthfuls of barley bread and something — apple, perhaps — with raisins, standing by the opening to the passage, confident if the room was broken into they would be gone, entrance bolted behind them, too quickly for any capture.

Rodlakh said seriously this killed off any idea of trying to reach Âna. Outside, Bolan's voice came. "We can break in the door."

Unable to resist it, Dolvid crossed to near the door, and called out, "Farewell, Bolan." The door shuddered to an onslaught of bodies, then he was chilled to hear Ban-Sila say, "Wait. There is another way." Heavy footsteps receded, and time for joking was over.

The moving block bolted behind them, they made haste in the passage, Rodlakh leading. "What?" halting, as the *ôdu*-lantern showed a dead end. Remembering, he held the light overhead, and the square hole they had dropped through was above. Dolvid stooped; a block in the floor was hinged to stand on end, putting the rim of the hatch within easy reach. Rodlakh swung up, and after passing him the lights Dolvid followed him, last thrust of his feet toppling the standing block back into place.

He closed the hatch, wishing they had something heavy to put on top, although if Ban-Sila knew the outlet in the Personal Suite, pursuers would not have this hurdle to pass.

"You think he does?"

"I have been uneasy ever since we reached this part of the passage. Not as much dust and cobwebs as when I first explored it."

Very reasonably, Rodlakh said, "Then they will know where the tunnel leads. If Bolan sends fast riders to the Bronze Residence, they will be there before us."

Household men going headlong down the Avenue, the astonished stares of passers-by. "Not much before, if we make haste." Lightly said, but there was an unpleasant feel about being trapped underground between pursuers and others coming from the front. Collecting their packs they sidestepped rapidly along the gallery, General Audience Hall quiet. Everything seemed longer; after the second narrow, when they came to the steps winding down, Rodlakh looked back, questioning whether they had not missed the way. At last there were the many swerves of the descending ramps, and when they reached the long straight stretch that was the Avenue, he caught at Rodlakh's sleeve, so they could stand to listen. Above, not near, but closer than was comfortable, heavy feet made clumping echoes: men in the passage behind them.

Holding inadequate lanterns at arm's length in front of them, they raced over the smooth floor of the unending straight, hardening nerves against tricks their eyes played in unwinding dim, abrupt, horrified conviction of a wall just ahead, or a huge hole yawning in the floor. After far too long the angled stair climbed up, and at first as they paused their own hard breathing was all the noise. Then, above the faint, constant roar of water, a distant boom of voices shaped and colored into strangeness, and again, moving feet.

Then, as they climbed broad, sloped steps, deep-racing water blocked out all other sounds. Every stage was taking too long, and Rodlakh, reproaching his own folly with the ferocity of harsh wakening, was starting to blame himself for their predicament, as they emerged from Plakhsila's tunnel into the more ancient part, where the tunnel went twisting down to their right. "I should never — "

"*Hush*," Dolvid interrupted. Voices reached them again; his heart clenched tight, then leapt. These sounds were from leftward, ahead and above, not behind.

"Are we caught?" holding his light to peer down where they had not been. "Is there another way?"

Pursuers coming from each direction might meet somewhere in the dark, exchange challenges, perhaps blows. "Yes, two others, at least — or there were." He took the downward turn of the tunnel, where quite soon finished stone gave out, and they were between chalk walls that showed little if any sign of working. Soon they came to a remembered part, a widening, a swing to the right, and what appeared to be a dead end, an unworked limestone face. Just in front, a bronze ring was set in the floor, with the six-sided outline of a hatch or cover, largely obscured by dust and debris.

"Leave it," as Rodlakh stooped to the ring. "That is the builder's little joke. The floor is solid rock." Over at the left-hand wall

Dolvid was searching for the only continuation he had found; three interlocking catches held a pivoted block, and it did not work if they were not released in the right order.

The way opened, and there was no dressed stone, only water-smoothed roundness of a limestone cave; they stepped into the close sound of moving water, nearby drippings and tricklings, and the rush and thunder of a large stream not far off.

From inside, this doorway could be closed with big bronze bolts not connected to the outside catches. These were corroded, and it needed some picking and hammering before even one could be sent squawking into its rings. "Unless we or someone else can come back this way, we have probably closed it for good. This was the last escape for a *rabhsai* if the Bronze Residence was ever attacked."

"How could you ever discover all this?" Rodlakh asked. Shouted, rather, and Dolvid realized he too had been raising his voice over roar of the water.

It was as if Rodlakh would not go another step unless he heard an explanation, and while this was no spot he would choose for a lecture, the facts were briefly supplied; Filat, a nephew to Plakhsila *Kímukoi*, had explored, and left a record in a cipher quite easy to decode. He in turn had access to some older writings now lost, or as good as lost; they were probably among many documents the *Atarlum* had secretly removed from the Bronze Residence, and carried off to the *Mankh'* — in some cases, maybe to the Island.

"By Filat's account — " they went forward again, the even-floored cave running downward. "There is or was a way out, into a cellar in the western corner of Kadon Dinul, Old Town, another outside the city, by the Owan Sai road. They used in part natural caverns, which might be blocked or flooded long before now. I did not try the one way I could find. Neither did Filat."

The glow of their lanterns, thrown back by the whitish walls, all at once dispersed; the roof receded beyond reach of the light, side-walls fell back, and they were in a large hollowing where water dripped on all sides, while the larger body of moving water was now very near. In the many years since its partial and rather crude levelling the floor of this cave had accumulated many mounds and small peaks, reaching tentatively for the ragged forest of petrified icicles high overhead. Possibly one of the obscure, twisting recesses might begin a passageway leading off to the south, though they had no guess which way that might be.

"What is that?" — asking about long bronze doors set flush into the floor, stained with blotches of yellow and brown, spatterings of dirty white over the dull lichen-green of timeworn metal.

"Come and see," Dolvid mouthed, beckoning. Where ceiling and wall curved together, not far from the doors, a steep, narrow stair vanished into a low-roofed hole. Half crouched, they edged their way down partly crumbled steps cut from the native chalk, dislodging bits and pieces as they went. Clean-edged steps of some harder stone reached up to meet the others, and the loudness of the stream had suckings and gurglings in it, while a cool breeze fanned their faces.

"Care," Dolvid advised, mouth near Rodlakh's ear, as he came to roughly level ground. This was a lower cave, and past the shelf where they stood the stream rushed, deep and fast, smooth-surfaced and strong out of darkness, into darkness. Dying bubbles crowded in from the right, where, to judge by the roar, the stream must be forced through narrow fissures, while leftward it vanished into what seemed roomier tunnels.

"Shumu Shan'loi," in Rodlakh's ear. "As Filat said, copying from his source."

"The Water Track — Trail," and mouthing the four separate words, "We. Need. A. Boat."

Holding his lantern up as high as he could stretch, Dolvid pointed. The upper parts of the vessel were just under what must be the inside of the bronze doors, the keel a foot or so above the water. In the faint light it was bluish-green, unevenly patched with rust-color, streaks of lime, scattered spots of brighter green. It was, almost certainly, Kanavakh's boat, his final means of escape. He, third ruler in the Gabh'Owani succession, had amply earned his nickname, `Vakh'biSegh,' Red-as-Blood, and the hatred his many cruelties inspired would have been good reason to have a way out kept in reserve.

"Four centuries," Rodlakh shouted. "Will it float?" The idea obviously appealed to him.

There was no sure answer; crafts were finer then, and the boat's hull was completely sheathed in copper; Filat's helpful notes suggested existence of the boat was known within the *rabhsayum* for several generations after Kanavakh, certainly to the reign of Plakhat II, and it had probably been kept in constant repair. That reduced the gap to somewhat more than two centuries, not reassuring.

The question whether it was still streamworthy would not occur unless the mechanism keeping it suspended for so many years could be released. Back in the upper cavern, Dolvid searched for a tool he had found on his former exploration, a long iron bar, the weight of a crow, though one end had the curve of a shepherd's crook, whilst the other was a flattened shape. This fit into a socket in the middle near where the doors met; tugged in a walking circle it was a key and then, after the bolts had gone grinding back, a lever for prying up one door a short way. This done, bar lain aside, they knelt at opposite ends of the door, pushing and hammering against the corroded stubbornness of the hinges. A job with sweat and cursing in it, but in the end one door was fully folded back. The other, held only by the bevel of the first, came up less reluctantly.

Below them, more than filling the oblong space, was the boat, heavily built, a covered deckhouse astern, roof hardly a foot beneath where they were standing.

They looked at each other; Rodlakh said something with *risk it* included, and next moment was crouched on the cabin roof, his boots making a good, solid sound as they arrived. As he scrambled down into the well between the deckhouse and the small area of afterdeck, Dolvid followed him, and felt the boat tremble slightly. Chalky dust was inch-thick everywhere, fragments and water-droppings of soft limestone, but under the deposits the blackened wood of the hull was coated with heavy resin, chased with many fine cracks but evidently sound.

As far as could be told, the boat was held by hangers fore and aft, slotted into the stout gunwales. They had been made to close like compasses, but it was conjectural whether any force could make them do so, with all the corrosion both at gunwales and above where the hangers pivoted. Below that, hung on cross-members, was a ring of heavy metal, and it was clear the arms would close together if the ring could be pulled down.

Now knowing the purpose of the hook at the other end of the tool used to open the doors, Dolvid without much trouble climbed back into the upper cave to fetch it. Standing on a thwart he hooked the ring at the prow end, and pulled down with all his force. He raised his feet clear of the boat, but there was no other effect, and it made no difference when Rodlakh came to help, and they pulled down together.

"Wait — " Rodlakh unhooked the bar and used the key end to hammer at the place under the gunwales where brackets and hangers met. Chips of limestone and some flakes of tired metal broke away, boat giving a small shudder. Rodlakh passed the bar over to the other side and Dolvid hammered away till there seemed clear cracks between arm and what it held. Before resuming the struggle with the ring he went aft and gave the same treatment to both hangers there. The water

roared and gurgled, and the air was thick with the dust they had
dislodged.

At the prow again, he rehooked the ring. "One good tug,"
though he did not see how, held by weight of the boat, the hanger could
come free. He and Rodlakh adjusted their grips, tensed, and on a count
of three threw their combined weight downward. A squeaking jerk,
and one side of the boat was free, wobbling. Another heave, and the
ring came down a long way, nearly closing the hangers, while the boat
leaned to the water very slowly with many threatening creaks and
groans. There was some sort of pivot in the hangers, and once a catch
was released their curve opened like a stiff hand, so the boat could
slide, as it were, from the fingertips.

Once in water the craft began to weave a little, and footing was
difficult as they clambered to the stern. The hangers there had been
loosened by the twist of the prow's descent, and Dolvid was sure he
could move this ring without aid. Rodlakh braced in the small
afterwell; kneeling on the afterdeck Dolvid warned, "Last chance to
change our minds." When the boat was free the current would take
them and they would have no control.

Rodlakh returned his grin, and he gave a sharp downward
pull. The descent was sudden, and there was a heavy splash. Dolvid
went sprawling next to the tiller, losing the iron bar, which was left
hanging in the ring, vanishing at once in the black as the quick current
grabbed them.

No steering could be done. The two small lanterns, starting to
fade, made no impression on profound darkness where they moved, a
pallid island in rushing black. Close walls wheeling through their
patch of light made the pace feel runaway; over and again they nudged
and scraped against rock; after Rodlakh just missed being struck by a
projection from the ceiling they were careful to stay lower than the level
of the deckhouse roof. Apart from a slight side-to-side roll the boat was
steady in the water. Dolvid slid down from the afterdeck into the well

behind the small cabin, an arched extension of the high gunwales. Bent low, Rodlakh came back to join him, and remarked the single long seat was actually a wooden chest inset with heavy bronze bands. He poked a knife-point into the crack between lid and body, wondering what might be inside, and Dolvid noticed Rodlakh's boots were wet.

Going forward carrying one of the lamps he saw between thwarts the sinister gleam of water creeping over dust, creating small limestone islands. The boat bolting on unchecked, he squatted for several minutes watching. Seepage had decreased, increased, stopped altogether; hard to judge how much the lapping advance of wet might be due to the boat's motion. He watched, boat galloped on, and he had to cling hard to his sense of the real, having so often dreamt this rushing journey through the dark leaving baffled enemies behind, lack of either effort or control, the curious comfort of not being able to change anything. When he went back to the deckhouse Rodlakh, on his haunches next to the chest, had fallen asleep. The thump of boots and a sharp nod of the boat woke him.

"Just the same, I am still *Valrabh'*, if I was when I left for Kamsilat. That could not be altered except in Council. Has the Council of Thirteen so much as met in the past year-and-a-half? Not that I have heard."

In any case it took more than a simple majority in Council to alter the succession; surely the nine votes it would need had not been together at Kadon Dinul. Laluvoi's seat had not been filled, and the Household place was also vacant with Bolan's move to the Captain-General's seat; Saidhan surely had not attended a meeting, and Rodlakh himself had a vote, as *Nim'* of the Paowan.

True, but were legal niceties any help? Ban-Sila's normal expectancy would be a further fifty, sixty years of life; if he remained *rabhsai* how much realm would survive?

"Some wisdom went into our lawmaking." Dolvid nodded assent. "The boat is leaking," he said. "Not fast, but it is a leak. We have some hours, if it does not get worse." They had nothing effective for bailing.

Rodlakh had the reasonable hope they would be out of these caverns before then, adding rather shyly he had heard of streams that plunged down to the center of the earth. Dolvid had too, but supposed this one had been navigated before it was chosen as a way of escape for a *rabhsai*. Yet Rodlakh's words were unsettling; dreams could become nightmares, and who could say what changes there might be in the course of an underground stream?

Rodlakh, glad of a distraction, went back to trying to open the chest, while Dolvid sat on the edge of the afterdeck, legs dangling, munching at barley bread from the Residence and a piece of cheese, not the white, briny Irvati, but a tougher yellow cheese from Burantal. Rodlakh at last gave up, and came to sit beside him, accepting some food. Their pace was unchecked, and after a while a narrow glistening serpent of water nosed into the cabin. Forward, water was beginning to creep up the sides between thick ribs.

"We have slowed, haven't we?" Rodlakh said when he returned.

"We may be rolling less, getting lower in the water. The — "

A leap forward, the sensation of hanging on the edge of a precipice, then a fierce plunge that sent their keel grating loudly against solid rock. Swaying, the motion slowed, and they were drifting beam-on, side-walls having faded back into invisibility. Peering, they could not tell what sort of space they were in, but the sounds said a larger, high-domed cave. The current fastened again to the boat's prow; they swooped forward, and ceiling rushed down to bump at the cabin roof once, twice.

With a lurch and a long scrape, they stopped. The boat waggled stem to stern, rocked, shifted, and rested more securely against rock overhead, water bubbling by under their keel.

Dolvid swarmed up to kneel on the afterdeck, cursing boat-builders long dead who, even to pass through caves, could not make a craft for the *rabhsai* without a deckhouse. He put his palms up flat against rough rock, inscrutably changed from limestone to granite, and pushed. His knees, bruised at the launching, were painful against the boards.

Rodlakh knelt up beside him. "Yes, but without the deckhouse, one of us, or both, might have had our heads knocked off."

Pushing hard together they forced the boat down into the water, till it edged forward. Walking hands on the rough ceiling they bounced the boat ahead, and both nearly fell as overhead receded, boat doing all it could to glide out from under them; a rushed, shuddering descent, scrape and whine of rocks against the hull, and they were running free in a noisy channel.

This felt so much like a last lap, they looked ahead, and amazingly there was light. It grew to brightness and arrived swiftly; more relieved than they would have admitted, they were blinking and squinting under sky in a narrow, high-sided ravine.

Not yet possible to tell exactly where they were. The stunted sycamores and beeches peering over the rim of their gorge were like the scrub country southward of the *Mankh'* estates, and that would harmonize with their apparent direction: to judge by sunlight from behind, striking the top of the right-hand wall, assuming it was somewhat past midday, they would be travelling due west, or slightly south of that. All streams in the Heartland flowed either to the Paowan River or direct to Arnan.

The tiller was useless as long as they were drifting with the current. The boat was obviously down by the head, water ankle deep beneath the forward thwarts.

"Not the best thing," Rodlakh, quietly, "to drift out into Arnan, with no sail, no oars, no steering, and a hole in the hull." They had gone forward to watch for any chance of getting ashore without a wetting, and their weight at the bow increased the list. The boat was starting to wallow.

On the verge of beginning the futile exercise of bailing using their small drinking cups, they swept to a turn, where the ravine opened grandly into a rockbound mouth, the sparkling Arnan filling all the background. From the left a low, gravelly spit, edged with smooth blue-grey rocks, jutted into the stream.

They were crouched, ready to spring ashore, but it was not needed; the current nudged them into a slow-winding backwater beside the spit, and the boat came very near running aground broadside on. The hull crunched and grated on gravel and rocks, and as the vessel stuck Dolvid jumped to the spit, while Rodlakh's long legs took him over the gunwale to the top of a higher rock. Not sure it would not be needed again, they hauled up the boat by its blunt, heavy prow. With a weary sigh Rodlakh sat down on his rock.

After a few minutes Dolvid said, "We cannot stay out in the open. We must have cut nearly a third from the journey to Tan Lughsai."

"You said you did not know where we were."

"Till we reached Arnan. I am familiar with all the coastline north of the *Mankh'* to the Estuary, and we are nowhere there. Clearly we cannot be anywhere between there and Owan Sai — we would be facing north, and seeing the uplands of Dramal. So we must be well south of the *Mankh'* — eight, nine miles, at the least."

"Does the *Adanum Plakh'* come here?"

"Not by choice. It is very rough country, south of the Estates, and we must be three miles outside the Outer Precinct. But there will be other troops hunting for us."

If the boat had been undamaged, and there had been a sail, it might have been their best and safest way south. As was, it would have

---

to be given to Arnan; left here it would be too plain a signpost for any searchers.

"A pity," Rodlakh said. "Such a fine piece of old craft. I am still curious to see what is in that chest."

It was unlikely there would be anything of interest, but Rodlakh insisted it could easily be brought ashore and broken into, and climbed back aboard to begin wrestling the chest towards the side. Irritated to have idle curiosity shame his profession, Dolvid went and gave an unwilling hand. He was more concerned with leaving this exposed place, the naked spit overlooked from heights to both sides of the stream, to the southward low cliffs half a mile away.

Lifting the cumbersome chest over the gunwale, they tried to balance it on rocks, but when they let go it toppled out of reach, and rolled down to the pebbles of the spit. Leaving it for the moment, they turned back to relaunch the boat, working it along the spit so the current took it again, turning slowly till the raised stern pointed for open water.

When they came back to the chest, its fall had sprung the rusted lock. Seen plainly the chest was a rather commonplace piece of work, probably from the Island, though the wood was Colony oak. Typical of Owani crafting, the metalwork of the simple bronze banding was superior to the joining of the wood.

"Empty," Rodlakh was despondent. "Wait — no, there is something." He had opened a small, lidded inner compartment. "Documents," in the voice of someone looking for gold.

Now Dolvid was eager. It was a couple of parchment sheets, folded and sealed inside a waxed cover, all spotted with age. Folds would be dangerously brittle, and here in the open, where fragments could easily crumble off and blow away, he risked only a quick, gingerly peep, raising the cover with a cautious forefinger.

"Well?"

"In the Script of Shâl, or a variant. It might be... it seems to deal with family matters. No time now, and this is not the place, for making a translation." Just the same there was a real oddity in what he had glimpsed, and his curiosity was roused and hungry.

"I was hoping for treasure."

"Perhaps you found one." He tucked the documents carefully inside his outshirt. "Now, *Valrabh'*, let us find some underbrush."

When they had climbed away from shore and were in light cover they turned back to watch sadly, as the boat with all its secrets of old craft waddled stern-first into the frilled ripples where the water opened out. A lazy swell ran counter to its slow, turning drift, and the stern was being lifted clear of the water, bow nodding deeper with each wave. It would soon founder.

A rough, tangled terrain was waiting for them, and they had to work their way back eastward some miles, to avoid coastal lands reputed to be impassable. Through warm afternoon they drove on without speech over folded country, thorn and scrub and a tough, dry grass, Dolvid miserably and impotently aware every step took them farther away from Kadon, where Âna was facing unknown dangers all alone. They saw no one except for a boy off in the distance leading a short string of goats on the skyline of a ridge. A boistering breeze off Arnan had the smell of spring, and in moister hollows purple and pale-yellow wildflowers were profuse, as if brought in overnight by the basketload. There were many birds, gulls near the shores, flitting swifts and martins as they turned inland. Though preoccupied and forbidding in his pensive mood, Rodlakh did not miss what there was to see; he strode on seeming to want the ache of driven muscles. They halted only once, drinking all but a mouthful of the remaining *raminat*, and munching some food; four words were enough to start them again. Small sounds could make them break stride for a glance over the shoulder, though fear of pursuit faded as they continued southward, surely least probable direction for a hunt. In deepening evening they came in sight of Dolvid's landmark, the fist-shaped hill, black against a sky smudged with dirty cloud.

They sheltered for the night in a dry cleft out of the wind, just such a spot as he had imagined Âna sleeping. He caught himself looking foolishly for any signs of her camping: it was as if his mind, unable to accept her being with Kamin-Tolagh, was inventing two Ânas, one of them waiting up ahead. Each time, seriously, he thought about her at the Residence, it was more likely she had never meant to make for Tan Lughsai; perhaps after all she had conceived a plan, and decided to do it all alone. What plan he could not guess, but Dolvid was certain he would see her again.

The last mouthful of *raminat*, brackish now, was still a solace to weariness. "Was I wrong not to threaten Ban-Sila openly? Removing him from the Residence would not have done any good. Sebhal told me that, and Âna — you also. Sebhal could be alive, Sett uninjured, Âna in no danger. You have been dragged into it; you are *kaël'rolai*, when you could have been safe in your home."

"But then I would have missed the pleasure of declining a pardon, offered by Ban-Sila *Rabhsai* in person. What could he have done if we had each claimed to capture the other?"

This was good for only a wan smile. "How can he hope to reign? If he puts down revolt, he will be hostage to Kargul."

"The revolt cannot be put down. If Ban-Sila wants Preference, he will have a smaller realm. This Free State they say Shumat has proclaimed is a natural ally for the Colony."

"Saidhan will have to decide that."

"*Saidhan* will?" The discussion had no end, but was not going to teach them anything new about Ban-Sila. Rodlakh would have to see he was, willing or not, his brother's rival, last hope of keeping the realm whole. *"Valrabh'*, Saidhan has spent a long life following and fighting for the House Arbhai-Navu."

In failing light it was impossible to see whether he reddened, but he gave an embarrassed flap of his hand. "Now Sebhal is gone, I am not sure even Galt is going to follow me."

"I have not heard you lie before. You know better than I, soldiers follow rank, and follow proficiency. I have seen you with lance; when rank and proficiency come together there is no question."

"For me the best might be to make my way north, and offer my lance to Shumat. Would he have me, as an under-captain, perhaps? If Bolan and Tovakh can raise all the squadrons they talked about, he is going to need help."

"Your help, but not as a lance. Your rank goes with you, *Valrabh'*, whether at Kamsilat or Yuvakh Din."

Rodlakh could be seen to cause his own shudder. "Commanding in war is harder even than turning against your brother, the lawful *rabhsai*. Telling others to die — those troopers of Kargul, south of Shemugrân; we had to silence them, but they were only men, following their orders."

Though Dolvid had no quarrel, there was an excess about these compound scruples, with men against Preference eager for a leader.

"If the big war Sebhal feared comes to the Frontier, none of these questions exist. Would Ban-Sila call me a traitor if I were at Drin Navuna, fighting off these new *jinzal* that do close-order drill? I suppose he would." But it sounded as if he yearned for the simplicity of such a war, a pure fight for existence.

Continuing to think through the day's events, he chuckled over the picture of pursuers deceived by the ring set in solid rock, made to look like a hatch, in a place with no other apparent way out. "I wonder how long they kept prying at it."

The northern rim of the Preghala Ravine was in line with Kafan Lughsai, the hills with Burantal at their farther end. The southern side of the ravine was sharply lower, so coming to the Lughsai peninsula was stepping down off the shelf of the Paowan, into another land.

The surprise never failed. From somewhere south a chance current swirled into Klam Lughsai, bringing a spring that most years outraced not only the Heartland to its north, but many southerly lands as well. Exposed all sides to breezes that could become fierce storm winds, Tan Lughsai had a milder summer and winters if anything more severe than at Kadon Dinul, but nearly every year, five or six weeks past Fire Days, the snow piled on this southern cape would begin visibly to shrink, heralding onrush of another riotous spring.

"The colors," Rodlakh reminisced. "Late winter when everything has lost its color, and as if someone has beaten the earth with a board, we would come down here. As soon as we crossed Preghala Bridge, it was plum-blossom in the valley all a pink mist, the crocus and daffodil on the slopes, all the budding leaves. We could swim down here only a couple of weeks past Halving Day — chilly coming out, but there would be a big fire, and last year's apples stewed whole in sweet wine, and my mother would have blankets to wrap in."

Considering Rodlakh's history, and that of Saëdhu, his mother, this could not have been very often; it was the way of childhood memories to make everlasting traditions out of anything that happened twice.

They had worked their way before sunrise past the tiny hamlet of Rhutalai. Its chief purpose with Lambarr had been to stable fresh mounts for the fast-messengers that kept the *rabhsai* in touch with his capital, but possibly a cavalry-post was still maintained there. Past the village, going was steadily rougher as they climbed for the north edge of the ravine, winding among immense rocks, clambering up steep inclines, often within sight of the road which, though always empty, they did not dare use. With the fear there was of an invasion from the Colony surely Preghala Bridge would have a garrison, if only in enough strength to warn Kadon Dinul in the event of a landing at Tan Lughsai, an obvious spot, ignoring omens. Away from the bridge, however, the ravine was far from impassable for men on foot prepared to do some hard scrambling. By good luck they hit on a fairly easy way to the bottom, with loose stones the chief danger. The southern side was shorter and steeper, and once it was climbed the ground fell away again, so that the ravine was a crack made in the skin of Paowan, as if the peninsula had tried to snap away.

Descending from the lip of the ravine they were in greener country where birds insistently commanded attention; thrush, starling, lark and swallow, pigeon and wood-dove, fluttering and soaring, debating territory or gathered in trees. Lilac was beginning, and they saw a pair of green-white butterflies in demented whirl; the ants were already erecting their small imitation sand-crumb volcanoes, erupting insects separating into individual bodies of shameless self-importance. Air pressing at the face was soft, space measured and palpable, all vistas predictable, a sheltering and comfortable landscape.

The Estates were to the eastward, inner side of the Cape, on the Lughsai Gulf rather than the wide expanse of Arnan proper. No choice but to veer left and cross the road, in the bottom of a shallow cleft among small trees, field-maple and cherry. The road was not only deserted but looked disused, with broken shoulders and a pitted crown, weeds and grasses threatening to swallow it altogether. On the far side the land tilted upward gloomily; a cloud passing over the sun, a quick interruption in the flow of warm air, a fleeting sorrow, one or all three chilled Dolvid's spine. A little way farther they passed the first abandoned cottage with its overgrown vegetable patch, tiles gone from the neat roof. Tracing the ghost of a trail, they startled rabbits, sending them lopping ahead once, twice, three times before they crashed off into the underbrush. Deft-grappling squirrels sidled trees to avoid being seen, and in a patch of soft ground Rodlakh noted the tracks of deer; all these increased the sense of human desertion; what had been a protective encirclement had become a more threatening clutch. Hard to keep in mind the Disaster was not veiled centuries or decades in the past, but only seven years ago.

Sight of the water might lift this oppression. Long before the Disaster, Tan Lughsai was considered an unlucky place. That reputation had been part of the head-shaking when Lambarr announced his plans to build up the royal estates here, but though there had been criticism, and the time and resources spent became a running joke, all that changed when the Summer Residence was complete at last, largest structure entirely of wood (perhaps ever) in all Arbhal.

"People who knew Lambarr only at Kadon Dinul would not believe the tales of his running races, and helping to pick fruit. Do you know he used to wrestle? Not just with us boys, with some of the tenant-workers on the Estates. Ban-Sila, Banak-loi as he was then, said he demeaned his dignity. He despised the life here. He was always shouting for some quiet, and after he came of age he was never at Tan Lughsai." A small shrug — "Which is why he is alive, and Ban-Sila, and *rabhsai* today. But he never knew our father when he put on old breeches of an evening late in summer, and stood near the need-fire with farm-folk, joined in their drinking and their songs. He had a good singing voice."

Those were the brief flourishing years here, but Tan Lughsai had become ill-omened again. After the Disaster, many of those who had come here to work on the building, or attracted by the prosperity a royal suite could bring, drifted away. The new *rabhsai* did nothing for the workers or tenant farmers who remained; there were accidents, outbreaks of violence, perhaps only what you would find with any people abruptly deprived of their easiest living. But every incident was taken as confirming the ugly myth of Tan Lughsai as a home of death, and new legends with hauntings by some of those who died in the Disaster mingled with older tales. Now, it was said, no one went to Tan Lughsai, not hunters though there was game in plenty, not farmers, though the earth here was deep and fertile. Men scratched at thin soil in Lower Nîv, challenged northern Ân's short summer, wrestled the salt lands near Irbat, but would not come here where there had once been double-cropping; weeds and ferns covered the fields, apples from unpruned trees rotted on the ground.

In mid-afternoon Rodlakh found the driveway to the royal estates, half-swallowed in returning growth. "This is the tenth day. We may find Galt. He might have come and gone; he was told to wait if he could do so in reasonable safety. This he would see as ridiculously easy country for hiding in — his half-squadron can go across a mile of Landegh where you would swear there was not cover for a lizard, and you will not see one of them. I would not want to be the cavalry hunting Galt and his half-dozen best bowmen in these woods."

After winding through dogwood and laurel the driveway climbed a long gradual slope till in sight of the mound where the Wooden Residence had stood. Rodlakh turned aside down a short set of brick steps. Passing through a screen of trees, they came out at the edge of a wide expanse once meadow, now unkempt weedland.

"The Games-Field. Poor Lambakh taught me the beginnings of lance-work here. There were short lengths of fence — well, you have studied arms."

"Swords, knives, staves, two sorts of bow. Mounted, with a lance, I might as well be armed with a hollyhock."

"Oh — " somewhat embarrassed, having made an error of class; Dolvid was neither high enough to have studied lance as a noble art, nor so low as to have trained as a common trooper. But he was familiar with the winding practice course, its piled wooden structures, each with one piece painted red, not necessarily the topmost. The object was to take a *pefrai* through at the canter, using lance to knock loose the red blocks, leaving the rest undisturbed. "Lambakh was very good at it."

"You are no beginner — " remembering the stylish wrists in the fight by Shemugrân.

"In the South, our kinsman Filuvakh was master of all arms."

"Rheduban's father-in-law, as he became."

"I do not think happily. I met Radaghi. The elder sister, Finú — well, she does no harm."

They were making their way quite openly across the field, heading for the conical mound with its one-third size replica of the famous light-tower at Kamsilat. Out of the ground, as it seemed, a man rose, an arrow already at the rawhide string of his short, deeply curved bow. He was wearing a soft cap, a horseman's tunic, somewhat baggy breeches tied above the boots. A short sword, and between shoulder and neck could be seen the haft of a knife, backsheathed like Dolvid's.

"Noldar," Rodlakh called. The man, short, bowlegged as Froghul' were, came down the slope to them, smile stretching as the bow relaxed. At about six paces he slung bow and gave a version of the royal salute, fist hitting his chest. "*Valrabh'*."

The large dark eyes shifted to Dolvid, his face showing he had expected the Captain Sebhal, and was perplexed by the substitution.

"Know the *Bôdhrai* Dolvid." Startled by his new title, Counsellor, he grasped Noldar's tough hand.

"Where is Half-Squadron Galt?"

Noldar indicated the thicket edging the field. "*Asai*, down by the jetty."

"I expected better precautions than this," Rodlakh grumbled, as they left Noldar on guard.

"*Bôdhrai?*"

"Do you object? Better for soldiers to have a rank to recognize." The self-assurance in what was not said here was admirable.

Where a narrow stone-surfaced road curved down through the windbrake of aspen, hazel and poplar, the sheen of water could be discerned past the tenuous screen of pale new leaves. Not less than two more bowmen lurked warily among the trees. "Is everyone on guard? And they left the boat in plain view." The single mast was visible, and in a few paces they emerged opposite the tiny artificial harbor, stonebuilt jetty also a mole. Alongside this the boat was tied up, long, fast-sailing by its looks, low to the water. Camp had been made next to the waist-high wall at waterside.

Instantly obvious far more than half-a-dozen men had come. That many alone were in sleeping-bags, part of a row under a makeshift roof of tarred canvas, the rest of the bedding neatly folded. Another ten or twelve were standing to arms, their dress more various than soldiers of the Household, or General Cavalry. But they were formidable-looking, mostly archers, with a couple of wiry slingers, probably recruited from some of the tribes where that was a common weapon. A good deal of tribal blood could be detected, and in general they were shorter than a comparable collection of men from east of the Arnan. One or two, in whom the Gabhani strain evidently predominated, were taller. A loose-knit, long-necked man with very large hands and feet stood with his Gabhani longbow at the end of the rank, wearing the senior file-leader's insignia. In front, centered on the others, was a man who would have taken the eye in a subordinate position; his feet planted with a firm authority. Not as short as Noldar, his equally black eyes were filled with alert intelligence; his creased face had humor as well as experience in it. This was Galt.

Rodlakh, understandably, was impatient to be done with salutes and greetings and introductions; he did not begin questioning Galt in front of the men, and Galt was too disciplined to blurt out the one overriding question he had, in common with the other soldiers. He had brought Rodlakh's sword from Kamsilat, and handed it over, saying nothing about the other one beside it.

After minimal ceremony he led the way to an open dell in the woods, where there was an old fieldstone hearth, perhaps the same one where apples had simmered in wine for the children of Lambarr. Using well-dried woods the fire was sending up the faintest shimmer of smoke. A very young soldier, tousled and somewhat wild-eyed, was tending both the fire and a large iron pot.

"All right, Truni." Galt's voice was well back in his throat. "We'll feed the fire. See what Sarnak has for you to do." Truni saluted, picked up his grounded sword, and moved for the main camp. Taking a dipper from a flat rock nearby, Galt filled earthenware mugs from the steaming pot. Nettles, mint and dried linden-flowers in goat's milk, a pleasant enough brew.

"Are you hungry, *Asai*? I've got men mud-roasting a pair of does over by the stone building — the Winter Riding School, somebody called it. Mud-roasting does not make much smoke, but I want that cooking-fire away from here."

"This is no time of year for killing a doe."

"No, *Asai*. These were lean, not fattened." He saw Rodlakh's concerns were otherwise. "The herd, *Asai*, has become too large for its winter's feeding, with no hunting here. There's rotted carcasses in the woods, stag, roe, yearling. It is a kindness, *Asai*, to the rest to cull some — we killed healthy animals, but not the best-fed."

Rodlakh, placated, sat on a stone and sipped his drink, and Galt watched steadily. Each had a question, and Dolvid guessed the soldier would be first to ask.

"The Captain Sebhal, *Asai* — ?"

"First tell me what so many men are doing here? It is your own half-squadron, not so?"

"Most of it, and brought up to strength with the few Kamsilat men — Sarnak, who guided the boat, and the men he asked for helpers. We are here by Lord Saidhan's command, *Asai* — I had to send after some of my men who had started for the Frontier."

Rodlakh asked if that meant the Frontier was quiet, the road for Shâl Mines open. Galt replied, ten days ago it was, and the Lord Saidhan said now, too much attention had been given to rumors.

"For myself, *Asai* — " Galt started, and then asked pardon. "The Captain Sebhal always says, speak your mind, it matters less to say something foolish than to leave what may be important unsaid. So, to me, this calm at the Frontier does not feel right — " he rubbed thumb and forefinger together, a man testing soil or a woman the texture of linen. "You get dead quiet after a sand-storm has built up; wind drops, the air clears — but birds don't fly, and there is a weight presses down. The Captain has seen this, often." Galt had urgent messages for Sebhal; they were not written, in case the messenger was captured.

When Rodlakh, after consideration, said Sebhal would not be here, Galt's head went on one side, like a bird.

Rodlakh made up his mind. "He is dead, I sorrow to say. He was killed a week ago, in Burantal."

"Sebhal, *Asai*? Killed, here on the Mainland?"

"It is true, Galt." Briefly, not explaining who Rheduban was, Rodlakh gave an account of Sebhal's last fight. Galt asked one question; what the bow was made of.

"*Valrabh'asai*, he was the only one who would go alone against a *jinzai*. He came back from the Mines on foot, with no water. He took away the knife from the head-man of the Lon-Lovi in the middle of his camp. Is he dead?" He made the Froghuli sign of great grief, right thumbnail lacerating a line down the inside of his left forearm.

"Should we tell the others?"

Galt said, "No. Not before Saidhan *Asai* has the news." He sank his face in his hands, then: "This makes my story so much worse. The Lord Saidhan sent us, hoping Sebhal *Asai* might have word of Lady Aëlu."

This was his news: six days ago, Aëlu, Sebhal's wife, had been abducted from Kamsilat. Her afternoon habit was to walk, in the forest near the Great House, or often along the cliffs on the north side of the Navu Estuary. Though she did it to be alone, two bowmen always followed and kept her in sight. On the day in question she was not missed till near evening. A man found the body of the lad who ran errands for the light-tower, killed with arrows, a pony grazing nearby. Not much farther on the same path they discovered corpses of the two archers, Aëlu's guard.

The man from the light-tower told the fullest story. No fighter, he had stayed in the tower, partly because it was forbidden to leave it unattended, but mainly in fear, perhaps, having witnessed the errand-boy shot down before his own eyes. From above he had seen five or six burly men take Aëlu captive, after killing her bodyguard.

"Aëlu was not hurt?" Rodlakh demanded when the story arrived here.

Her captors, the witness said, been careful not to harm her, even when she tried with a small knife to fight off her captors, slightly wounding one. They carried her off northward along the cliff path, the direction of a cove where small boats could put in. A stranger boat had been working the oyster-beds, with men who, when challenged by patrol-vessels, said they were fishermen of Irbat. Apparently this was doubted even then, because of their accents. Nothing was done because of Saidhan's orders not to provoke open war; later, the boat having disappeared after Aëlu's abduction, it was recalled the men were very well set up for fisher-folk, long-legged and broad in the shoulder, more the build of cavalrymen — but of the *Adanum Plakh'* or of Kargul, since they were all pale-eyed Owanil. It was supposed their boat must have been moored in concealment where cliffs overhung the cove, and there were footprints leading that way.

"There has been, *Asai*," Galt ruefully concluded, "self-cursing on all sides, how such a thing could have been let happen. Lord Saidhan says the men must have been of Kargul."

"No, the *Adanum*," Dolvid said.

Rodlakh said, "No message at Kamsilat, a demand for ransom, terms for Aëlu's release?"

"Not when I left, *Asai*. The Lord Saidhan did not want me to wait any longer, for fear we'd miss the Captain at Tan Lughsai, and he would not have the news."

Rodlakh was grim. "There is always a price — " and then he saw why Dolvid had insisted the *Adanum Plakh'* had taken Aëlu. After all, the Patriarch had not found out about Sebhal's death; He had this other basis for belief the Army of the West would not invade. A hostage.

"He laughed twice, your little schoolmate — at-Zhâlai, when they were talking about threats from the West. I should have throttled him. Aëlu."

Âna had spoken with faint amusement about Rodlakh's virginal adoration of Sebhal's wife; it had been mockingly mentioned in overheard talk between Tovakh and Bolan. To judge by how Rodlakh's hands were opening and closing, arms held straight at his sides, it was about to become either a solemn vow not to sleep or eat till Aëlu was free, or else some rant about taking apart the *Mankh'*, stone from stone, till she was found.

Dolvid observed Aëlu would never be brought to the Mainland, not with the Island so much nearer where she was abducted, so much stronger against any attempt at rescue. Traditional cage for captives of high rank, where Kanavakh the Bloody had died a prisoner of the then-Patriarch, was Drin b'Afon, where the Summer Palace stood, famous City of the Bridge, its impregnable citadel crowning a pillar of sheer rock, guarded by ring after ring of high ramparts.

Rodlakh, who took obscure comfort from displaying what he knew about Aëlu, mentioned she originally came from quite near Drin b'Afon; Dolvid, who had forgotten her Island origin, said it might be used to give the Patriarch's act a spurious air of legality, and saw by Rodlakh's face that was one set of details he should not recite. Fifteen

years ago Aëlu had been a *nôd'yanu* in the *margú* then open in the
Colony, somewhere well west of Kamsilat. Sebhal had met her, and
taken her to be his bride, though some two years of her indenture were
yet to run. Whether Sebhal had ever troubled to buy up that unexpired
obligation was obscure; a law of Plakhsila in any case forbade seizure
(once commonplace) of any apprentice for such a debt. One more
measure Ban-Sila might be in a mood to repeal: Craft families were
always complaining about the difficulty of enforcing indentures; among
the Residence Quarter Families there might be widespread support for
g'Asalladh's action.

"How long would they hold her? Till when?" The Patriarch,
surely, could hardly demand the Colony's capitulation; He must know
Sebhal would never allow such a bargain (Rodlakh nodded vigorously).
What they had overheard at Kadon Dinul suggested the price for Aëlu's
safety would be neutrality by the Army of the West, while Shumat's
rebellion was put down.

"That could be months, a year, years," Rodlakh said. "It may
never come about. Shumat, certainly, could never be expected to
surrender to save Aëlu — this is all impossible."

Galt, having heard the Island's reputation against invasion,
had made a grim face at its mention. "Well, it is a very good half-
squadron. We can try it."

Rodlakh looked wildly at Dolvid, who said, "It has to be faced;
any terms that come or have already come to Kamsilat will have a
threat against Aëlu's life if there is any attempt at rescue."

Hard to say when rescue from the Island began to be
discussed as a real possibility. The roast deer, brought to waterside
cased in its baked mud, was very satisfying, dryer than it should be, a
little stringy, but hot and full of savor. After, both Dolvid and Rodlakh
napped in the deckhouse of the boat, waking to find a light rain

pattering on the wooden roof, as it still was when they sat beneath a lantern for further talk with Galt.

Rodlakh, preoccupied, unnecessarily asked about the mood of the soldiers, and Galt said, "You see us, *Asai*." The joking and boisterousness over their meat-feast had not lessened the impression of deadly effectiveness. Spare minutes were occupied shaving arrows and trimming flights, measuring off extra bowstrings, making repairs to boots and breeches. At this moment, against the wet, blades were being wiped with a film of deer-grease.

Transparently to inform Dolvid, who was being assessed, Galt expanded. "He has said he'll never see us robbed of what we've earned, and we trust old Sai — your pardon, Saidhan *Asai*, I meant to say. However it goes, the quarrel with the *rabhsai*, we've had some respite from double-duty at the Frontier, and they have been able to get their spring planting in, and hoe their winter plantings, too. We don't think *jinzal* are going to trample our crops, but seed was harder to come by than butterfly droppings — thanks to Saidhan, everybody got some."

"Thanks to Sett, also, it was there for the sharing." Rodlakh paused from brooding, "The Colony is going to miss its best smuggler. Let us hope he is on the mend."

"He is in good hands with Mistress Morú."

"Âna," in the high-pitched voice of pure speculation, "if she gets away from Kadon, will be able to go to Sett in Burantal."

"Perhaps," hedging, and Rodlakh took reservation as an attack.

"What, then? I would rescue both Âna and Aëlu, if there were any certainties: Âna may be where she is by choice, and we could not go back to Kadon with a half-squadron — with a dozen squadrons, after what we have stirred up there. Aëlu? I would attempt Drin b'Afon, if I was sure she was there, and men would follow me — freely, not ordered to."

"We would follow," Galt said.

"Otherwise, we might do some raiding. We could march along the coast to Burantal, strike north and east from there to harass supplies going up for Bolan's campaign against Shumat."

"Risky," Dolvid said, as Galt's face brightened, "and not only for us." He was thinking of reprisal against Aëlu.

"Us! You have already done more than was ever asked of you. I want your opinions and advice, but no one demands you go campaigning with us, or expects it."

"Where would I go? My choice was made when I would not try to arrest you for Ban-Sila. It was not hard," (when he showed a wry pretended wonder). "Between two brothers, I would always take the one whose habitual mistake is to think too *well* of others."

He had already admired an Army of the West where very junior officers were encouraged to speak their minds, and Galt was just as impressive knowing when not to ask about what he had no need to know. He was back in the talk when Dolvid had his say in opposition to raiding on this side of Arnan. They had no mounts. Later, as Galt promised, some might be taken from their present owners, but in the meantime they would be going on foot where their adversaries were thickest on the ground; if the General Cavalry was so bad two dozen unmounted armed men could go through the Heartland without being seen and surrounded, then Shumat hardly needed any assistance.

Galt, quickly convinced, was nodding glumly. "Not our country, *Asai*. Here, neither, but let horsemen come by the squadron and play with our bows among the trees, we'll see who's ambushed. Strung out for the march in farm country, that's martyrdom."

He, clearly, would want to try the Island, but Rodlakh was right in saying they could not be certain where Aëlu had been taken, and their most sensible course was to go back to Kamsilat. By now messages might have come with terms for Aëlu's safety: advocating what was prudent made Rodlakh grind his teeth.

Galt, sniffing the air, said he must find Sarnak. "I can't read weather where there is nothing but water. If it clears, we can sail at daybreak, or before." They planned to have the men packed up and ready to embark by the fourth hour after midnight.

Rodlakh had their packs brought on board, where they would sleep, not moving out Galt or Sarnak, who had their sleeping bags here. Sarnak would have the watch most of the night, and when Rodlakh told Galt to be sure to get some sleep himself, he nodded, obviously approving how the *Valrabh'* was taking command.

"You too, before we sail," he told Dolvid.

His part had just come clear for him. "I shall sleep, but I shall not be sailing. Someone ought to stay for Âna. She is bound to make for here, and would not know what has happened. As you tell me, I am not needed as a fighting man."

"I also said, we can use your counsel, your *botadh'*, Bôdhrai."

"Saidhan is at Kamsilat. If Âna comes, we'll go to Burantal, and when Sett's well enough he will find us a boat to bring us there."

"That could be weeks, months. Everything is coming to a head this spring."

"If Âna comes here with news, something important — "

"Then you should leave out Burantal, and make straight for Nambalus. Âna can find the man there to provide you with a boat, Vadirr." All at once Rodlakh had conceded the main point. "I could leave some men here, who would be under your orders."

After some discussion on this question, he accepted two men; any more would only make secret journeying harder. When Rodlakh began to reconsider, saying it would be a waste if Dolvid waited here and Âna never came, Dolvid protested he had been ready to take the whole troop to the Island seeking Aëlu.

"Well, but Âna insists on taking her own risks," a little testy. "Aëlu — Aëlu, besides, is being used to affect policies. Stay, then. If Âna does not come, or if she does, follow us to Kamsilat as soon as you

can. You may need money." Pulling out his washleather purse he
passed over some gold.

"Six days," he fixed. "With Âna or without, I shall start for the
Colony in six days."

He slept poorly. The rain changed to an irregular patter,
coming sometimes in a harder rattle as the wind gusted, freshening out
of the south and west, lengthening the boat's rise and fall, tiny man-
made harbor filling and draining in a long rhythm. Bump of boat
against the jetty kept waking him from shallow sleep and from a dream
of being carried smoothly through tunnels without end, daylight up
ahead never coming closer.

Once when he woke the tall, loose-jointed man, who must be
Sarnak, was talking low-voiced with Galt, beginning with weather.
Flickering in and out of a doze, he heard Sebhal mentioned; Sarnak was
rebuked by the little half-squadron for using the words, *Lekh'Owani*,
and 'Old Saidhan' was put up as a clinching argument: could it be Galt
was defending Dolvid?

In dream or dreams again the boat filled to the gunwales with
water, or perhaps blood, and he was bailing ineffectually with one
small cupped hand, while the other groped for some object he had lost.
The tunnel walls were yielding, dissolving, and above the din a voice
was roaring.

Came a loud crash; the boat might have burst open, and he
was awake (he believed) with all the noises and terrors of his dream
howling on. Pale, eerie upward light came from a fallen *ôdu* globe
rolling back and forth, and Galt was grabbing for quayside as the boat
bobbed like a cork. The view of Galt blurred, quivering like a mirage,
and when the picture cleared he saw streams of water running from
Galt's elbows, his nose, chin. Dolvid knew what had happened, was
happening. A spring squall had come lashing out of the southern

Arnan; huge waves were bursting against and over the jetty, threatening to swamp the tethered boat. Worse danger came from how the small basin was filling and emptying with a rush, back-tow sucking water out with the sound of an immense mop in a giant bucket; chances were the boat would soon be crushed against the stonework where it was moored. The ululation of the wind rose to a tearing scream, while on shore men were shouting over the thundersnap of windwhipped canvas. In the milky wash of the deckhouse floor Rodlakh was groping for his boots.

Outside, Sarnak, the true seaman here, had taken charge. " — more lines on her," he bellowed close to Dolvid's ear, as he, rope wound behind him, managed a new hitch about one of many stanchions on the jetty. Dolvid picked up a line, and as the boat rose could throw a loop around another stanchion. Sarnak, farther forward, was hauling on his hawser, and Dolvid did the same, fighting the retreat of the water. The boat rose again, rasping ominously against stone, and big-handed Sarnak deftly clove-hitched his line to the boat's own bollard. Dolvid, less experienced, was still hauling in when the boat dropped again, and skidding rope burnt his palms. Sarnak came, and together they took in line with the next rise, and made fast. Rodlakh and Galt had begun taking up the original moorings, fore and aft, and now the receding water sucked at the hull, boat high and snug against stone.

Stinging spray bouncing across the jetty had beaten clothes to bodies, flattened hair on faces. For good measure Sarnak made fast another heavy line amidships, roaring his satisfaction the vessel would not be broken against the jetty. Crouching, shuffling gingerly, braced against wind and water, the four made their way to land. Down the shore from their camp they could see the torn white of wind-driven foam folding across the sea-wall, but where they were the harbor was some protection, breaking the worst of the seas, and though the air was thick with spume, wind was the fiercest enemy. The lengths of canvas used to roof over the sleeping-area had gone in sections to wrap around trees; in almost complete darkness men were trying to roll up bedding, cover spare clothing and supplies, stumbling against one another, treading on hands, tripping, skidding and cursing. The coming of just a few ôdu-lanterns, not dazzling, but steady in all the wind and wet, did a great deal to restore calm. Galt was among the men, upbraiding good-humoredly, insisting it was no more than a passing squall. As far as could be told there were no injuries worse than bruises. Galt sent a man, carrying one of the lanterns, to find the guards posted in the woods, calling them back to muster at quayside, away from the danger of falling branches or uprooted trees. One quite near had been wrenched from its shallow grip on sandy soil. But already the wind was failing to sustain continuous savagery; individual gusts might be as powerful, but there were near-pauses now. When the lantern-bearer came back, leading five unhappy sentries, Galt, shivering with everyone else, had a look of vindication: it was a squall, and was passing. Yet to imagine there would ever be anywhere warm and dry was nonsense; sunlight and calm belonged to past ages of the world.

Rodlakh suggested the Winter Riding School, where Galt had almost made camp to start with; only the problem of having to defend two widely separated sites, camp and ship, had prevented him. The roof there, he said, had partly fallen in, but most of the space should be dry. "There are stalls, and a pile of old fences — we could make a great fire."

Dolvid, overhearing, felt his spine creep in an involuntary shudder; Galt had probably only a vague idea of the history of Tan Lughsai, clearly Rodlakh had not heard the eerie echoes that choice of words woke.

Carrying much of their sodden gear, led by lanterns, the whole party filed squelching through windswayed, dripping trees. They skirted the large empty mound of the Wooden Residence on its south side, coming soon to a hollow, mostly filled by a single looming structure, square-built in stone. Skidding down mudbanks they passed through a pillared entranceway, quite dilapidated; this building was already a century old and in poor repair when Lambarr launched his ambitious plans for Tan Lughsai.

Despite holes, relief from wind and noise came at once. The broad expanse of main floor was beaten clay, puddles standing beneath places where the roof had disappeared, but now thought could be unmuddled they concluded that near the waterfront, salt spray driven by the squall had accounted for most if not all of the wet, the patches on the floor here due mainly to the gentle earlier rain.

By pallid *ôdu*-light on the far side, men encouraged by Rodlakh were attacking the rickety boards from a row of loose-boxes, a large stack of planks and fragments growing behind them. Galt produced pieces of tinder-cord and started them with stone and steel from an inside pocket: soon yellow flames were leaping from three separate fires, blazing materials moved deliberately onto wet patches so smoke could find a way out through the gaps above, palely visible as dawn approached. Lengths of fencing were saved from the destruction, and propped up so sodden clothes and bedding could be spread facing the flames. Galt led those not tending fires or breaking up fuel on a warming jogtrot, which Dolvid and Rodlakh joined. The habitual cheerfulness of these men was coming back. As grey morning came Galt sent men back to waterside to gather wind-scattered belongings, while Sarnak took another group to see to bailing the boat and spreading sails.

When enough sleeping-bags were baked dry Galt started the men on two-hour rests, six to a batch, with another six sent to resume guard. Despite the wild and sleepless night there wasn't any grumbling about fresh duties. Rewarmed venison and some kiln-bread were soon being shared out, and as soon as the iron pot was brought up from the wrecked camp lumps of dried goat's milk were crumbled into heating water. Notwithstanding blank window-frames and yawning roof, the

Winter Riding School was warm enough that outer clothing could be discarded.

"Not much loss, *Valrabh'*." Galt, pausing to chide some men for trying to dry rawhide bowstrings too quickly, came over to where Rodlakh was seated on a piece of board, studying his boots.

"Time."

Galt growled in his throat. "But if this storm had hit us at sea, I think there'd be nothing left. We are not rich in sailors — some of my men saw Arnan the first time last week when we came down to Kamsilat."

Dolvid was soon sharing a mug of milky brew with Truni, the young slinger they had seen tending the fire yesterday afternoon. The boy was cripplingly shy, till Dolvid, as not in years, tried some of his Froghulú, and was instantly struggling not to drown in the flood he had released. Froghul remaining in the West could hardly be said to speak the same language he had learnt long ago, but he had since made a study of the changes, finding they followed a fairly regular pattern, and many words for commonest things, man, woman, knife, had scarcely changed at all. Dolvid was able to understand most of what was said, and to fumble together some acceptable replies. To Truni it was an amazing novelty one of the pale-eyed people could speak his tongue; even Lord Sebhal, he explained, never said more than *hello, tell me your name,* and *friend.*

"You are of the Lunu Tezh'?" His dialect was.

"I am, Lord, from the farther-up shores of the Loud Snake, your people call it *River Granu,* Lord. Before me my uncle swore his pledge to Lord Sebhal's big hunt, so I crossed hills and was spoken for to come to the Strong Stone Place and be with the hound-riding arrowfighters." No branch of the Froghuli tongue had ever had an independent word for *horse,* and when they did not borrow from one of the two main languages of Arbhal their compound was something like *big-hound-carry-man.*

Asked whether he planned a farm in the Colony, Truni was proud to say no. "The hunt-company of my grandfather has sleeping-ground in Lunu Tezh'. Someday we'll have smooth roads and built halls as in the Colony, and no more men-without-campfires making forests unsafe. We'll have the *healing*. Learning well how to build, to *heal*, to kill, this can make Lunu Tezh' folk count, also." He meant this, every word.

After trying several directions the breeze settled cool and steady in the northeast, and Sarnak's opinion was it would stay there for some days. A start late that afternoon would give them open water for a night's sailing, and dawn tomorrow for negotiating the southward isles.

Lack of sleep annoyingly caused thoughts to echo like chants in his head, and the clear cool outside might do better for him than the smoky warm of the hall. The world was drying, light patches spreading on the skin of the sandy soil, a disease, he overtiredly thought.

Mind reeling on he soon gave up the attempt at sleep, and went for a tramp, using it, once begun, to fix in his head a clear image of how the Tan Lughsai estate had been laid out. He might, after all, write someday about the reign of Lambarr.

Near the conical hill with its tower Noldar lifted his hand in greeting. Dolvid hoped it was Noldar; he and his brother Guthdar were going to be the two men to stay behind with him, and were very similar.

The toylike square tower made him think of its original, hence of Aëlu's abduction. He could never quite imagine Aëlu; odd that he had been away on the few occasions she had visited Kadon Dinul.

Something in the story of her capture as recounted by Galt needed clearing up; he was not sure what, but recalled this feeling from tackling problems in history, a wrong note in the tune, his ear telling him about a lapse in logic. It would come to him.

Rodlakh was on the lichened stone bench against the wall of the tower, shoulders hunched, hands deep in his pockets. He gave a coldly preoccupied nod, then without warning launched into a savage attack on the *Atarlum*. "It sickens me to have these mutterers using the safety of Kamanta to lord it over law itself. No power not answered for; the *rabhsai* is bound by law, and if the Patriarch cannot keep the Treaty, we should — " He laughed at himself. "I see you have not been given a job, either."

"In a well-run camp a *bôdhrai* is only in the way."

"Galt, however, has decided in your favor, I believe. He — "

"Horseman coming, *Asai* — " Noldar appeared at the corner of the tower.

"How many?"

"Horseman, *Asai*. One alone." Fitting an arrow he ducked away. Dolvid and Rodlakh also removed themselves from the skyline, and edged after Noldar for a look. Across treetops they could soon see the rider on the line of the road, nearing the driveway. Nearly half a mile away, fatigue of the big *pefrai* was palpable. Just before trees cut off their view the upper body of the rider came into plain view, shock of dark hair swinging free, a slender form.

"Horsewoman," Rodlakh said, and then together they exclaimed, "Âna." Both went bounding down, leaving guards gaping. Birds panicked as they got to the trees, and another half-hidden bowman called out a warning. They reached the brick steps as Âna came up the long slope above, bent low to the neck of her near-spent horse, urging it. The flanks were crazed with foam, nostrils laboring.

Rodlakh shouted, Âna flinched, then saw who was there, giving a glad cry of her own. She was swiftly out of the saddle to embrace each man in turn.

"I was afraid you would be gone," she panted. "Or that you — I have been afraid of everything." She was wildly dressed with an ornate robe of golden-yellow brocade over all, undone up to the waist, just possible for a short, polite ride, worn with close, matched breeches in the Residence Quarter fashion, here bizarre over her campaign-breeches, their established stains spattered with fresh mire. The gorgeous robe also had its share of mud, and the once-matching slippers were blackened.

In the joyous excitement of meeting Dolvid saw no noticeable difference between the two embraces Âna bestowed, or there would not have been, for any observer with only casual curiosity. Later when he recalled the reunion it seemed she had spoken mainly to Rodlakh, and that her avoidance of Dolvid's eyes was deliberate.

Her first thing after greetings was, "Aëlu. They have taken Aëlu."

"We know," Rodlakh said. "Galt is here, he brought the news from Kamsilat. What can you tell us about it?"

At the smoke-fogged Winter School, as she gnawed ravenously at baked rabbit, Âna recounted some of what had happened to her since their parting in the Gardens of Kamzhinu.

vi

baKargul

The Gabhani saying, *she can change her mind before she crosses the road* came almost literally true for Âna; as soon as out of sight of the others she wished she had not left them. Seeking a sheltered spot for darting across the Tan Lughsai road she was inconsistently wondering whether, if she turned back, she could find Faëdhal's house in the lane he had described. But she had argued so convincingly for the value of someone going to meet Galt, and meek retreat did not go well with the sense of resentment she had against Dolvid, a feeling she could not exactly account for, and which she was trying to be rid of. Not because he had let her go, not entirely.

The world under cool sunlight was empty. Tan Lughsai was impossibly far away, but once west of the road she resolutely put aside any thought of turning back, counting off three hundred hard paces up the long slope, after which she would be safe from chance observation by some traveller. She let herself be angry with the rough ground she was subduing; she ought to be glad for this chance to be alone, to find out if Sebhal could be properly mourned.

The question might really be whether she, Âna, had any proper capacity for grief. Among her father's folk (they were scarcely less her mother's, but because many polite virtues of Owan were seen as womanly by the Mixed, her father always seemed much the more Gabhani), to be prostrated at loss of one's man was proper in a woman, one with having breasts, or moonsblood. With the old-fashioned, men bereaved were angry, or acted rage; when she was little she had witnessed some of the old funeral rites, now passing away, with their shoutings, mock battles, real bruises, punitive wars against darkness that came as a raider to carry off friends and parents, memory and wisdom. Anciently, women of the Gabhanil had not taken part in hunts or battles, and their part of grief was to shut themselves away, refusing food, not speaking, letting hands and face go unwashed, hair unkempt. For the most part this old ritual had in turn been ritualized, and not many new widows or bereaved mothers would wait out as much as the full three days till their sisters or mothers or mothers-in-law came to ask them in due form to rejoin their kind. Yet even today it could happen the ceremony was lost in true inconsolability, and what was meant to allow release from grief became a prison. She could remember a young wife, not long married, whose husband was killed in an accident, and whose house had to be broken into in the end, food forced on her, her grip on life broken by loss too large to be mimed away. Asana, Âna's mother, had flatly told Konat he need not expect any such extravagances from her, if she survived him. Typically, Konat replied he had few expectations the other side of dying, and none that need concern his wife. The Owanil, part of her bloodlines her mother preferred to follow, had restrained ceremonies, wakes in which men and women joined; older families and those of unmixed blood usually wanted an *atarlai* (of the *Nôdhilum*, whose Order stood for Homecoming as well as Pleasure) for some of the obsequies. For the Owanil, marriage was chiefly concerned with real property, not the ownership of appetites, and when a married man died his widow took from between his thumbs the key the *atarlai* had put there — but Âna had no right to the key to Sebhal's quarters by the Frontier fortress, Drin Navuna, nor, decidedly, to the Great House at Kamsilat.

So far as she had ever heard, women of no race consoled loss in a fresh bed, or if they did it was surreptitiously, and with some feeling of shame. But then, Âna had no firm floor of precedent to stand on, no position in law or recognized custom. Neither wife nor proclaimed concubine, still less was she anything resembling a *nôd'yanu*, making a game and a calling out of perfecting a man's pleasure, whether Sebhal or Dolvid (but Sebhal had not been the very first). Bed-friend, Sebhal often called her, and she had tried to be that. In the Kamsilat days she had been, perhaps, a comrade, surely better than Aëlu at listening to Sebhal's disquisitions on policy, bedding with him in natural extension of agreement about the dangers of *Lekh'Owan*, excited by the pleasure of singleminded accord. And, of course, his eminence.

The expedition to the Mainland, then, might be seen as near-marriage to Sebhal in the realm of action, complementing Aëlu's part in his repose, but outbidding and outflanking her; more of Sebhal belonged to war and danger than ever could to Great House life. If so it had failed before they ever embarked, in the three-cornered talks at her uncle's house. Not that Sebhal and the *Valrabh'* had formed an alliance against her; on the contrary, though always overtly supporting Sebhal, more often than she enjoyed she grudgingly sided with Rodlakh's hopeful innocence against Sebhal's knowing skepticism, and ended by questioning, after all, whether she and Sebhal meant the same thing when they talked about fighting against evil: with Sebhal it became increasingly a simple question of who held the power.

No overnight change in him had brought her fierce and bitter charges against him. Dolvid's easy answer had been, remember what Sebhal did, ignore what Sebhal said, but that could not satisfy Âna; the speaking, scheming Sebhal was the one she knew best, but had become least certain of. Coming to Kamsilat and meeting him had been her rebirth. The real Sebhal was a hero, strong and patient, brave as his fame, but loss of the Sebhal she had imagined was losing herself.

Her shadow bouncing ahead, not bothered by lumpy ground, told her she was bearing too much to the west; over those ridges the *Mankh'* was brooding, hedged by riders of the *Adanum Plakh'*. Half left, a fold in the ground led away, and before long, not wanting to, she struck a foot-trail in the direction she had to take, seemingly not much used. She was not afraid of chance meetings; she could nod to other travellers or farm folk, bluff her way past the idly inquisitive. She felt formidable enough to deal with any individual robber or lecher, and her one real anxiety was military patrols. She hoped the troubles in the north had lessened chance of her being challenged as an unauthorized wayfarer.

She followed her feeble trail up a stony hill, hoping for a glimpse of the road, to tell if her direction was good. Breasting the rise, she saw the road was dismayingly near, not sixty paces ahead, and where her trail, now seen as a mere short-cut, rejoined the road, a horseman was sitting. The mount was a large whitish *pefrai* with a tall cloaked rider looking straight at her; plainly he had been waiting here for her. She backed away, turning to see a whole cordon of other soldiers cutting off her escape. The only cover was over westward, and she did not see how she could outrun the horses to reach where rougher land and denser growth began.

Uncertainly, she left the trail. The single rider, spurring quickly up the slope, was in front of her; the smell of horse was in her nostrils, and a booted foot in its stirrup just touched her arm. She wheeled aside again, and the *pefrai*, well handled, moved with her like a dance-partner, barring the way without touching.

Not going to a weapon, the young rider dismounted lithely. He wore a military tunic, but no helm, slender but by no means slight of build, his face was purebred Owani, not as razorish as some. The hair, longer than the fashion, was a reddish brown. "Hail, Lady," blithely.

"Kamin-Tolagh baKargul." It was out before she could consider it, while one small part of her brain was turning over her chances of sticking a knife into him and stealing the horse. As well as riders behind her, more of his men, all in the long Karguli tunic, were ambling down the road.

His grin widened. "You know me, darling."

"*Asai*, everyone knows Kamin-Tolagh *Asai*." She was falling back on a role half-prepared for any awkward meetings, dimwitted and ignorant in the rural way.

"Everyone? Not everyone, my love, not yet. That will come. Look up, darling. At me."

Reluctantly she did. Frightened, determined to pass as a farmer's nitwit, she still refused to have her eyes beaten down by his gaze, designed to overmaster; a tremor to the long-lashed lids, and his nostrils were quivering — being quivered said it better. The point of his tongue flicked once against upper lip. Absurd, but she did not dare show amusement: this was real, and she suspected he would be maddened by nothing in the world so much as not being taken seriously in his air of conquest. Yet he, in the end, was first to break the eyehold, and let his gaze go wandering down to her boot-tops, then back up to linger at her throat. "Yes," with a sigh of self-satisfaction. "As I said. I said so, did I not, Freighanai." That was to an officer among the horsemen ringed just behind Âna, with a weathered and rather mournful face. He did not answer.

"But why travelling alone? and dressed so drably? Well, why travelling at all, that is the thing; it makes sense to disguise her succulence, with all the goats there are in the world, yes? No use, my darling, nothing but a challenge, for any man with an eye."

He was declaiming, she concluded, for the men of his personal squadron, and they appeared to be enjoying what must be a familiar performance.

"We have watched you for some while, love. Ever since you scuttled across the road below Harbor Gate. I told Freighanai, a wood-pigeon, for a week's pay — he did not take the wager, a prudent man,

Freighanai." Under a large beak of nose the officer creased his mouth into a mirthless smile.

"But I might have said much more." The voice became a caress, and Kamin-Tolagh stooped to let his wrists rest lightly on her shoulders, then ran his hands down the outsides of her arms. With a little humming sigh he hooked thumbs in his sword-belt. "You have a name, darling?"

"Âna, Lord, and I'm — "

"Mixed, your father all Gabhani with his hundred acres and ten words of the Old Tongue, yes? and a wife who thinks she is better, telling you about your cousin who is almost Family." Though well short as to acreage, this was near enough truth to be uncomfortable. She decided Kamin-Tolagh had heard his last fact today; there was a chance when he had done enough preening he would send her on her way.

"And where are your father's acres, my love?"

"Arlemirrstead, Lord." The name came from a mistake by the officer in charge at Tâl Abfekh, when the wagon of Arlimas was halted.

"Âna Arlemirrlayu."

"Lord?"

"Arlemirrs-daughter. And where is Arlemirrstead?"

She waved with flapping vagueness. "Not far beyond Abfekh, Lord, not a large place, but they can speak for us there."

"But you're on the wrong road; you are lucky we found you, Âna. I do not suppose you have such a thing as a passguard token, have you? Didn't have time, I know, I know. Came to Kadon on the back of a feed wagon, because your poor granny is at death's door — is this it, my darling? And poor sick granny turns out to be — who?" He looked all round with a comical expression. "Could granny be a man of the levies, one of those louts Bolan's signing up for the North, pike for pitchfork, go and fight, be a hero. They'll be as useful as straws against Shumat's *péfrapravádal*, but even a lout, if he's a stout lout, can

pleasure a woman — do not blush, sweetheart, we all ride or are
ridden."

He won the laugh he wanted from his men; Âna meanwhile
actually did manage to suggest blushing, with downcast eyes and a
scuffling foot. Her temper held in check might have aided the illusion;
she did not enjoy being used for Kamin-Tolagh to amuse his men.

"That puts you, love, on the axe's edge, does it not? Tell me
truthfully, did you ask your father if you could go on your errand of
mercy? Aha. He is certain to be worried about your absence, and will
give thanks for your return, Gabhani style, with a length of stirrup-
leather. We cannot let you hurry home for that, darling. I too could
have you beaten — oh, all lawfully, for not having tokens to show. Do
you ride? Certainly you do. Kambanal!"

"Sir?" He was an innocent-faced file-leader.

"Âna Arlemirrlayu will ride your *pefrai*."

"*Asai*? How am I to — "

"Walk. This road is in poor repair. I want you to make a note
of places where attention is most urgently needed, so we can give a
proper report to the *rabhsayum*. Come on, man. That saddle is needed."

There were mocking grins among the others as the man
dismounted, not concealing his unhappiness. Kamin-Tolagh caught the
bridle of the animal, a glossy-flanked, dark *pefrai*.

"This steed may be bigger than you usually — " he broke off.
Without thinking Âna had swung up into the saddle. Seeing his
startlement, she let her wrists droop, settling into the farm-girl's typical
slouch, weight back on curved spine. Under her the horse was taut and
unresting, muscles a cocked bow.

She ran eyes over the soldiers. Their mounts were the match
of hers, but she must be less than half the weight of a broad, tall
péfrapravádai fully armed with lance and sword. With a quick start she
might outrun them — but where would she ride for? This country had

little cover, and if she headed south she might lead soldiers to where Galt was.

"A small game of pursuit and capture," quietly, "may be enjoyed. My temper worsens if it goes on too long." He was, she saw, not as much of a fool as conceit made him.

He remounted with the same easy confidence in muscles all his movements displayed. Knee to knee with her he started back for Kadon Dinul, his men falling into ranks and files behind. Behind them, Kambanal trudged, keeping his face down not to show resentment.

"You manage a beast well, Ânaloi."

She kept forgetting to slouch. "Once, Lord, I had a friend in the cavalry, and he let me try his *pefrai*." True, though Kamin-Tolagh would have been surprised to hear what cavalry, and the friend's name.

"Call me Tam."

After waiting: "Well, say it."

Another eight hoofbeats. "Tam." Pleased, he soon began humming, an old hunting song, Gabhani in origin, but adopted by mothers of all races for singing to infants learning their numbers. In the song the day's bag began with `one plump pigeon' and increased, verse by verse, to `rabbits ten, rabbits ten,' the whole roster counted backwards at the end of each stanza, so `one plump pigeon, that was all' came back constantly. Kamin-Tolagh was too well-born quite to leer each time he hummed the line, Âna in her idiot part too abject to show disdain.

"This *péfrapravádai*, then, is your sick granny, not a lout of the levies? What is he, General Cavalry? Not Household? Never mind, darling, you need not say — see if you can remember his name this time tomorrow." He went back to his humming. Hard actively to hate him, but she wished for some course other than passive obedience.

Not challenged, respectfully saluted, they rode in at Harbor Gate, onto the Avenue, Residence noble at the top. The provincial

Pledging she had come for was a third of her life in the past, and she had seen the Avenue only thronged with visitors; it had a listless air about it today. Soldiers of all kinds clattered about in small bands, some new levies in odd single items of military dress. Not many ordinary citizens were on the street, but Kamin-Tolagh gave a jaunty wave to any who recognized him.

More salutes when they reached Pefrai Gate to the side of the Residence, but it appeared the Household men were less than delighted to have the Karguli cavalry here.

Passing through a series of cobbled courts on the south side of the Residence they came to the main stables. "Do not dismount — " putting a hand on the saddle-bow of one of his men. "You will take Kambanal back his horse — you will meet him on the road." He swung lithely from the saddle, and Âna, not wanting to be helped, dismounted quickly as she had seen Frontier bowmen do, lifting right leg over and sliding down, feet together. Galt's men could do this while nocking an arrow.

"Isn't this the *rabhsai*'s house?" The wide-eyed question was to take his attention from that dismount.

"That's right, Âna. You will be with me here. You can have baths, Âna, warm baths, and clothes of shuzi to wear, and a featherbed to sleep on after you have shown me what else you can do there — would you enjoy that, darling?"

Again, she came close to giggling, then imagined what the daughter of Arlemirr might say: "My father — "

"He will be proud to have sired you, when you tell him, and you will have some fine things to keep for your own." They were mounting narrow steps to an arched doorway. "I shall give you some money to take him, and he will praise you for a clever girl, you'll see." The guard at the door, an open-faced Heartlander, startled at the garb of Kamin-Tolagh's companion, saluted late.

"Lord, my father says — "

"If he sees you with new clothes and money to rattle, he will thrash you and put you out. *'Ghai*, they're all the same. It will be different, sweetheart, when he hears his clever girl has stayed in the Residence, the *rabhsai*'s house, and worn shuzi and eaten venison. He will — "

"Venison, Lord?" She was going to be very bored with this ninny she had invented. Only the young man's unlimited conceit made it possible.

"The meat of deer — delicious. You will enjoy venison, Ân'loi. I promise."

The corridor they took was dominated by red, a blood-dark polished stone and a smooth, pinker shade inlaid in complex patterns. It came incongruously to her that without trying she had achieved what Sebhal, then Rodlakh had sought, entry to the Residence. In all the time she had known Sebhal she had never set foot in the Great House at Kamsilat; the wood-carving there was said to be sumptuous, but she did not see how it could surpass the craft here: cunningly masked *ôdul* shed subtle lights on marble pilasters, coffered ceilings measured off the corridors in segments, infinitely various walls, bronze reliefs or softly tinted tapestry in one section, oak panels intricately carved in the next, or the painting of an event from history, a rich mosaic. Windows were wonderfully clear Island glass, and she had view southward over the city walls, all the way to the rim of the Heartland beyond the fertile plain. Or some glass was tinted with rose, pale blue or delicate green, deepening towards the edges, so that tiny panes at the margins were like rubies, sapphires and emeralds.

Kamin-Tolagh made a turn, cutting through the heart of the Residence, Âna in her stout boots and stained breeches silent beside the long-striding young man. At a high hall where ways led off in several directions, after passing another saluting pikeman, they went up broad white steps under a gilded archway, and came to a bronze double-door, snarling Lion of Kargul depicted in relief.

Inside, steps led down to a large, well-lighted room, windows facing north and east. To the right, with three circling steps, there was a corner fire-pit where peat was burning, blue smoke somehow drawn into a chimney-piece, an upside-down funnel. From the steps down from the door she could see a large yellowish cat sprawled by the slow fire. On those curved steps brocaded cushions were scattered, and the room otherwise was furnished with a long table, highbacked matching chairs, a few wide-armed leather chairs nearer the fire-pit with a similar couch and matching footstools, and an immense sideboard opposite the table along much of the left-hand, the westward wall. This was spread with many cold foods, meats and pastries, dried fruits and sweetmeats. A steward was busy there, covering dishes.

"Send Marra to me," Kamin-Tolagh ordered as they passed the man. Beyond the sideboard a doorway opened on a passage, with more doors right and left. She was ushered to the end. His own outer room was very plain, campaign chairs with curved arms, a rush mat that might have been put inside a tent, a serviceable, undecorated desk or table, the room of a soldier, a young Larghai or Banak.

Young Kamin-Tolagh undid his belt, and hung sheathed sword on the wall. He had never seemed to consider Âna armed as a danger, and the notion of attacking him scarcely occurred to her, till he moved behind her and with a swift movement slid the knife from the sheath at thigh-front. "Good blade, a gift from granny?" At the desk, he opened the drawer and dropped in the knife. From a flask there he poured into two cups, and handed one to her. It was good, a pale yellow wine from the Peframi Gorge in Kamin-Tolagh's province.

"Sit. No, wait." Again he circled her, now to slip a packstrap from her shoulder. He helped her from the harness, and weighed the pack in his hands. "You are carrying granny, too?" Not looking inside he stowed the pack in a wall-closet.

"Have you ever been in such a house, Âna?"

"Not like this, Lord, never."

"Call me Tam," waiting once more for her to say it. He moved behind her again, taking away the heavy outshirt, throwing it down on a chair. He nuzzled briefly at her hair and she tensed, but before she could seriously begin to wonder what it was like, being taken by a man not chosen, he was back at the desk, refilling his cup. "Is the wine good, Âna? We have plenty of wine."

"I like this.

"Tam," she added, as his eyebrows demanded.

"My sister's gift. Not the wine, the name. Sit, Ân'loi, sit. When she was small she could not say my name; she called me Tam'tolaf. In revenge I called her Tami-Tú."

"I used — " she silenced herself with a mouthful of wine, sitting down in the nearest chair.

"You what? You may speak, Âna."

"I am hungry, Tam." She was not particularly, but disarmed by his talk of Kamin-Tarú had almost told how as a child she had a habit of half-inverting words, pog-beat, stig-pye, searside fight. Not a reminiscence for Âna the daughter of Arlemirr.

Marra arrived, a young, plain and sullen maidservant. The steward came with her, carrying messages. Bolan, Âna learned, was away from Kadon Dinul, but had sent word he urgently wanted a meeting when he returned. Tovakh was with the *rabhsai*, but had left word about trouble that needed settling, between Rheduban's men and some General Cavalry, regarding quarters or rations, or both. Where Rheduban might be was not known.

"I shall have to look into this." The sigh, to her eye and ear, was the expected thing; she did not think he was altogether unhappy about delay; ever since no longer having his men for audience he had been hunting for a new part to play; when it came to beddings there was no limit to the strangeness of men.

He told Marra this was the Lady Âna (a rank Marra's quick appraisal quickly dismissed) who would have food and a warm bath, and should be brought a robe to wear, the yellow shuzi. "Yes. The yellow." He reached for his sword belt, then faced Âna, jauntiness returning. "Make ready, my love. We shall have good sport when I come back."

Marra did not willingly go beyond proving she was neither deaf nor mute; she answered, "Here," to a question about whether she was a servant to the baKargul, or attached to the Residence. "Three years," was her answer to how long, and she may have thought she was saying too much. Âna's other questions could be answered in one word, and she discovered the unembellished facts that Marra did not mind being here, did not find the work too hard, and had family in the Heartland.

Meanwhile, the bath was wonderful, a single hollowed-out block of green porphyry. There was plenty of hot water, and a shelf had a dozen flasks of scented oils; Âna sniffed at several, ending with a little jasmine. Resplendent as it was, there was an uncomfortable element of capitulation in slipping on the long yellow robe laid out by Marra, but the time for resistance was either not yet or long past, and against her clean and glowing skin the smooth shuzi made a luxurious sensation, after so many days of clothes made for campaigning — as, in its way, this was, she acknowledged with a wry smile.

Without expenditure of a single word, simply throwing open the door with a gesture that was a volume of comment, Marra made clear she was expected to wait in the inner room (was it possible the plain girl was disgruntled she had never had to wait there?). A bemusing contrast with the warrior's room outside, soft and easeful, bed low and wide, curtained in pale yellow, the coverlet a gold brocade, a long bolster matching the bed-curtains. Yellow curtains at the window were nearer in match to Âna; the view was northward across the roofs of the city, descending to the walls, with a distant sight of the grey hills of Dramal across the Estuary. Âna knelt at the window-seat to study the view, then wandered the rest of this carpet-muted space. On a tall dressing-table were hand mirrors, combs, a small brass container of tooth-twigs, a flask of musky lotion, tools for finger and toe nails. Also a few books.

In the corner, next to the bed-hangings, there was a tall pair of doors with long latch-handles of polished metal. She tried them, tugged on the doors, and stepped back with a gasp, her heart giving a sudden leap. For an instant her impression was she had found where Kamin-Tolagh kept a spare woman; a gleaming yellow figure had glided towards her. She realized she was looking into a great glass, clearest she had ever seen, and largest, its polished surface flawless.

Slowly, another astonishment dawned. Not difficult to see why Kamin-Tolagh had desired this Âna — only this Âna was something he had not yet seen. She hardly knew herself. Perched on yellow brocade slippers with slight heels, the slender figure was not uninteresting. She tried for a back view, and could achieve no more than a profile, liking how the hair nodded to a turned shoulder, admiring the fluid drape of shuzi over a hip. The face was pale and serious with sooty shadows under the eyes, but she had never minded how her nose compromised between the overflatness of Gabhanil features, and the Owani beak; hers was cleanly defined and well set, and the mouth beneath had never needed any coloring.

Feeling abruptly near weeping, she laughed. Her allies were probably less than a mile away, and she could not reach them, her instincts telling her to run, even as she appraised herself through the eyes of what she wanted to escape. Other instincts were there. Sebhal had rebuked her for confusing Kamin-Tolagh with Rheduban, and to be truthful she had not heard the much-bedded Heir of Kargul was particularly cruel, not if you ignored the primary brutality of taking unchosen, and of retaining sole right to discard. But then, she had felt passing fear of Dolvid, and certainly Sebhal before that; had never altogether lost that feeling, often dissolving into better sensations, as some well-loved music began with jarring and bitter sounds, or favorite foods with a fleeting pungency — the first aroma of honey, subtly fetid. The contrary concern was it might happen here; her body was pleasant to have so long as she controlled it, and she did not want to surrender the right to decide what she might enjoy.

She shook herself, shimmering. She would not drown in self-pity; in this campaign there was very little chance of her being killed. She used the waist-tie of the robe to catch up her hair, wondering about Kamin-Tolagh's attachment to yellow. A pair of sulfurous men's slippers was stabled under the bed.

Back at the dressing-table one of the small calf volumes was a collection of brief, traditional Owanil tales, cleanly copied in a fine, fluent script, and decorated with witty vignettes. When Kamin-Tolagh came in she was in the window seat, knees under her elbows, reading.

His brocaded robe was blue, not yellow. The long hair was still dark from the bath. He was carrying a flask of wine and two cups.

"Âna, darling, are you tired with waiting?" The tremulous voice told her his earlier urgency had been recaptured. He put wine and cups near the bed, and was back at the window to hand her down. On her bared forearm his fingers were warm.

"Reading?" He took away the book. "You read? in the Owanilú? — " his disbelief mounted a staircase.

"I wanted to see the little drawings." Something was happening to her body; hand-to-arm his heat had infected her. Putting the book back, he turned to examine her full-length, and as before she stared back, not willing to become an artifact or possible mount to be pondered.

"Pigeon — " his voice had thickened. "Pigeon was well short of the mark, my love. A swan, a lynx — do you know what a lynx is? Aha, I knew my eye had not failed."

Conceit, she decided, can hardly go beyond demanding, in effect, she congratulate him on admiring her; she was becoming his achievement. He took her wrists and tugged her to bedside; still only permitting she was embraced, and though her spine shuddered, she held straight when he bent to kiss her throat.

"And my love, my darling, I am going to have you, no doubt about that; your choice is how pleasant it will be for you. Whether or not you see, I do have the means to compel you. Now, Âna — " he was stroking her breasts — "why deny yourself joy? What is the sense?"

Once this would have struck her as sinister; not now. He did not fill her with revulsion, she had known that ever since he had rested his wrists on her shoulders. Perhaps, after all, that kind of fastidiousness was a mannish invention about how they wanted women to be; thousands of women, moreover, though arranged marriages were now nearly extinct, had been obliged to forgo any such feeling. Oddly, the worst of her fears had passed when he began listing the pleasures she could experience at the Residence, and telling her the rewards she would go home with. She supposed others of his current fancies were not far away; there was odd comfort in the idea of being used once and discarded.

And there was no sense in keeping from joy. He was adept, beyond adept, and though he heightened her pleasure only for his own sake, it was not easy not to be flooded with gratitude, and she felt no resentment in following his very exact instructions about what she should do with hands and hips and lips. He must have, somewhere among his books, a copy of the famous *Nôdhuli-Asumanai*, a manual that outraged every decent Gabhani or Mixed, and brought a smirk: Owani filth from the Blossoming Age, but interesting.

He was a talker; "Your breasts," when he slid the robe away, "perfection." Then, "Shuzi from shuzi," as he bared the rest of her body (but she would have wagered he had said that before).

Being a collector he was incurably comparative: "Slender, but with thighs so strong! my last was slack in the thighs, though she had more flesh on her than you."

She kept firmly in mind that when he writhed with his next, Âna would be recalled as too skinny, too short or too serious, and yet she enjoyed his praise and wanted to earn more, absurdly would have liked to obliterate his recollections of all others. After a long bout they rested with wine, and he had her put the robe back on, so he could begin at the beginning again, saying greedily that tomorrow (already her tenure was extended to tomorrow) they would have two different robes for her to wear. She wondered whether, with the hunting-song, it would be progressive, and reading irony in her face, his flickered the same puzzled look as when finding her with the book, or when she had mounted the *pefrai* too confidently. She baby-talked, "Tam good to Âna," and hoped it was forgotten.

"*Yali b'Aëlovoi*, I am glad I was not your first," thick-throated. "They are fools, men who want an unbroken filly, as your men do for a wife. I must send a present to granny in the cavalry who turned you into such a ride — but I cannot believe he taught you what you had not already tried. Âna?"

"We have boys about the farm."

"And ants about spilled honey. But you are not going to forget my ways, hah?"

"No, Tam." She would not. Hating all Owanil, even the Kargul', could only be done successfully at a distance. In detail they all had graces and quirks to charm away recollections of the cruelties that maintained their easy assumption of superiority. An assumption her father never challenged, grumbling as he paid his taxes, asking what the lords were about, not questioning their right to be about it. The real

Konat might even feel some of the pride Kamin-Tolagh had assigned to non-existent Arlemirr, knowing his daughter was at the Residence with the son of a *Nim'*, wearing shuzi, eating their food (though Marra had not brought her any venison). As they did in southern Paowan, Konat hated Kargul on principle; he was also sure his daughter deserved the wrath of very old gods if she let any man touch her outside trothplight. Yet all that might well be transcended by rank, and the graceful way Kamin-Tolagh filled it. He, Konat, would remind her that above all Owanil lords was a Mixed who had begun life with a Gabhani name, his grandfather's.

That was all nonsense, though she loved the old fool (not so old) who spoke it. And she could not hate Kamin-Tolagh. Besides pleasures not anticipated, and the longest of ecstasies, she would remember how all his mastery and skill left him suppliant, wanting what was not there, a prize beyond his own considerable spasms. He began the search again, serious hunting without space for being sure she was pleased. At the very end, when he fell back gasping on the bed and did not renew, she kissed him once with tenderness, consolation in it for the intolerable yearning that owned him. He was scarcely older than she was.

He said to the ceiling, "I am not going to let you go, Âna-Âna."

Flattered, chilled, she guessed but less than hoped he went through this with many of his women, convinced for an hour he had found one he would not tire of. Yet it was only human to hope it had never been quite this for him. Not seriously, she dreamed about being his wife, installed at Inilun Barabhi, mountain-ringed, fringed by water. She would be the one to bring a Mixed strain into the most jealously-guarded of all bloodlines, and surrounded by nothing but Owanil it would be hard to remember what injustice was in parts where the races came together. She would not demand Kamin-Tolagh be tethered only to her bed —

"What are you smiling at?" drowsily.

"I do love it here." She sensed by instinct that would work the other way; he would be put off by any sign she was treading down grass to make a nest for herself.

With a mumble, he fell asleep. Her hunger was painful; it was hours since Marra, measuring out food as if she had to pay for it, had brought cold pork with a cold steamed dish of wheat with raisins. Softly, she slipped past the bed-curtains on the side away from the window. Naked, shivering, she retrieved her robe; the shuzi was cool to her skin, yet she felt a warm stir as the fabric whistled softly over her shoulders; her nipples rose.

In the warlord's room, she went to her pack in the closet, swallowed some mouthfuls of kiln-bread with dried fruits, drank water from her flask, and followed it with two quick cups of pale wine. The quiet was unbroken. The maidservant had left her shirt, breeches and undershirt heaped together on the chair where Kamin-Tolagh had draped her heavy outshirt, and her boots were under the same chair. Gathering it all up, she carried her clothes to the closet, which, with a few odd pieces of military wear inside, obviously was not much used. She piled all her things in a corner, pack on top. Remembering, she went to the desk-drawer to recover the knife, which she added to the pack. Together with the wine spreading slowly through her veins, all this made her feel much better. She went back to the bedroom, where Kamin-Tolagh's breathing had a flutter too faint to be called a snore. Âna climbed into bed, pulled covers over her, and slept sound.

The evening assembly of the baKargul was not called but simply happened. Presumably, together or separately, they all had dinner elsewhere, before assembling gradually in the big room with sideboard and firepit; Kamin-Tolagh brought Âna there.

She had wakened fresh from resolution of a dream-debate, with a new determination not to be distracted from purpose by frivolous conjectures about life with Kamin-Tolagh. A few days would be the term of his use for her, and then he would send her away, with or without a purse and a new gown. She might yet catch the men at Tan Lughsai; it depended how long they tried for Rodlakh's meeting with his brother (and whether they could survive it). She did not expect them to gain entrance to the Residence, or do any good if they did: Ban-Sila was not to be assassinated or deposed, and the best to hope for was that the others would escape unharmed. But that gave her a feasible task; she was here, and her established stupidity might let her overhear plans, intentions it would be helpful for the Colony to learn. If she arrived at Tan Lughsai too late for Galt, her uncle could find ways she could get back to Kamsilat. If neither Dolvid nor Rodlakh was there, she would be a no one, but there were officers in the Army of the West she knew by sight, and they would take Saidhan any information she had.

After that, what she would do at Kamsilat she did not dare anticipate; the only certainty was she would never again wait at her uncle's house for the sound of hoofs in the forecourt, Sebhal's horse. Friendship with Sebhal had been the token that took her into wider issues, and she could never endure again the narrow life at Konatstead. Where she might belong was all doubt, but a war was being fought, and she could do something.

Kamin-Tolagh's mother, the Lady Petakoi, was already occupying one of the leather chairs, in talk with a lean, red-headed woman, whose hardeyed stare when she turned to gaze at the newcomers made Âna uncomfortable, though she felt a sea-wave of the woman's unhappiness: this was Radaghi, wife of Rheduban. Âna did not understand the talk which started again, concerning safety of some relatives in the North.

The smaller, softer, plumper woman on the far side of Petakoi was Radaghi's elder sister, Finú. Dolvid said she might be held to have the best legitimist claim on supreme power, but it was hard to imagine a less inspiring or authoritative figure; Finú's gaze had a vague, muddled anxiety, as she ravelled and unravelled her blunt little fingers. She too, like her sister, deferred to Petakoi, who sat with imperious grace, wearing her fifty-odd years well. In her turn Petakoi gave enormous respect to the little *atarlai* who soon arrived, at-Zhâlai.

All this had to be noted half-surreptitiously, not to interfere with her non-existence. Beside Kamin-Tolagh she was a normal if replaceable part of the furnishings, though evidently because of her — and the servants who came and went — they kept dropping into the Old Tongue, which girls with Âna's eyes did not know; At-Zhâlai, just after his arrival, turned to her and asked in the Owanilú whether she spoke that language. Prepared, she was careful not to overdo ignorance, and used a phrase everyone could mouth, "*Om, loika izhai u, at'ai,*" flat-voiced to make plain those words were the 'little' she spoke. But she was out of practice, and it needed all her concentration both to understand and to seem not to; they would drop back into ordinary speech for ordinary things, and she had to remember which parts not to know about. Kamin-Tolagh, who had captured the large yellow cat, turned from his seat at the top of the firepit and used Owanilú to tell his mother who she was, and Âna sat nodding with a fixed expression of emptyheaded content, giving no sign when he tested her by making a mistake about where Arlemirrstead was supposed to be. After that she achieved invisibility for long periods.

She did not need to hear the next arrival named, bearded and broad, about middle height and Sebhal's age, Tovakh. "Some wine — no, not that, the white Peframi, my mouth is clogged with that syrup the *rabhsai* drinks. '*Ghai,* it's one thing to have a taste for sweet wine yourself, but you have to have something a guest can drink — these touches are important. When I was twelve, Banak-rai asked me if I was homesick for our mountains, and gave me a good apple — I never forgot that."

His wife, speaking the Owanilú, "An apple for the throne, a true Arbhai-Navu bargain."

Tovakh began to describe the meeting, Ban-Sila's concern with events in the north, but he noticed Âna and sauntered over, not having her stand, as she thought he might. "Not bad," he said, himself going into the Old Tongue.

"She knows nothing," prepared for a battle. Âna put her two thumbs together and squinted at them.

"You will know nothing. Your brains will be left in Aëlovoi's purse."

"He will not be young again." Petakoi spoke up for her son.

"He will never have a middle age, unless he learns some prudence. At his age I was in the saddle fifteen hours a day."

"Yes, of a horse. Spare the boy your envy."

These currents were fascinating; Kamin-Tolagh was not so young as to have his mother speaking for him, and most heirs would have their own separate households by his age. In Kargul, everything festered.

Finú, standing was shorter than expected. She said something about a kitten, and went bustling out self-importantly. Tovakh, meantime, spoke about Ban-Sila's private worry whether Bolan was good enough soldier to beat Shumat in the north.

"What did you tell him?" Kamin-Tolagh leaned forward hungrily.

"I did not say he should break a thousand hearts in the Heartland by sending our staunchest couch-campaigner in Bolan's stead. That I did not say. But Ban-Sila has the same worry as Bolan; he holds Shumat's revolt may be only a feint to draw off troops, so Uncle Sebhal can come thundering in from the West."

"There we are — " Finú returned carrying a tiny scrap of a black kitten with no voice and a ruby tongue, and held it out to Âna. The large yellow cat on Kamin-Tolagh's knee made pretence of clawing at the kitten, as she reached up and took it, showing the proper dim gratitude.

"Rheduban," Rheduban's wife said, "maintains Sebhal is the key; disable him and the back of every rebellion would be broken." A bitter irony for Âna in this.

Kamin-Tolagh, unknowing, gave the screw another turn. "I wish Sebhal would meet me in single-combat."

His father was derisive. "You would finish not nearly as lovely as you began. Challenge Saidhan — " he punched his son's shoulder. "Or challenge Aëlu, where your experience and hers both lie. No, but if you want, and the *rabhsai* permits, try single fight with Rodlakh — he's another of your dancers. We shall have music for it."

"Set me against any rider you see as our best fighter," with icy anger, "we shall see who dances last."

"Oh, Hrafi, you'll do, yes, you'll do — some meat on those shoulders and we'll make a lancer of you. But do not talk about challenging a Sebhal, or a Tovakh, not till you see their sinews starting to shrink. Look — " Abruptly, he reached a thick hand under the yellow cat, and held it out unwavering at full arm's stretch. Back legs tucked up, the cat yawned. "You beat swords on body-armor for an hour, and the fighter in middle life is going to have you, every time. Not just strength, Tam — " at last he lowered the cat, neatly leaving it back on his son's knee. "You have to school your body to ignore pain. It takes years."

"Saidhan," Kamin-Tolagh said coolly, making explicit where all this talk of single-combat had its origin, "was twenty-three when he killed the wise, experienced Tobhsila."

"And that was sixty-four years ago," Petakoi said. "Kargul does not yet have its vengeance. Bolan runs from here to there, trying to nip out small revolts: the *rabhsai* must know Sebhal and his father are behind it all. If there is a weed in my garden, I take it out by the root, not leaf by leaf."

"Sebhal," the small *atarlai* said, "has not been seen at Kamsilat for a number of days — or had not; our news is somewhat behind."

Tovakh did not think this particularly important. "He is at the Frontier looking for *jinzal*, then."

"*G'Asalladh'* believes not."

This was beginning of a lengthy exchange she could not entirely follow, though plainly Petakoi, the Islander, was not only more adept than Tovakh in the language of devotion, but more concerned with acting in accord with the desires of the *Mankh'*. Apparently there had been some past discussion of an expedition against Kamsilat to subdue the Colony, but the Patriarch had advised patience. With uprising in the North, it was clear He and Tovakh had been in accord, though at-Zhâlai was not pleased when Kamin-Tolagh, departing from his mother's careful hints and understandings, referred openly to Kargul's former idea of letting Shumat and Bolan batter each other to death. Now, however, *g'Asalladh'* was inclined to take a graver view of Shumat, and to see his defeat as a strong priority, to the extent, at-Zhâlai said, that if an alliance was required to keep Bolan from the chance of failure —

Tovakh saw where this led. "The Patriarch expects men of Kargul to go north, and keep Bolan from making a mess of it? To save Bolan?"

At-Zhâlai answered with his complicated and allusive murmuring, leaving Petakoi to translate for her husband. In order to ride north, the Cavalry of Kargul would have to be permitted to cross the Nanakh and Kôbh Rivers, to ride through the Paowan, bypassing fortifications at Kanzan Tâl and elsewhere. Tovakh, rubbing great palms together, exulted at the prospect of achieving what in war would be costly and perhaps impossible.

At-Zhâlai then went off to see if fresh word had come from the *Mankh'*. They were expecting news, he said smugly, that should make it feasible to ignore the threat of Sebhal's Army of the West. Kamin-

Tolagh took this to mean trouble at the Frontier, and at-Zhâlai did not quarrel with that guess. His last piece of advice to Tovakh was to be not over-anxious to offer his squadrons to Bolan, who would think better of himself if convinced he had laboriously persuaded Tovakh to help him.

"No pretense in that," Tovakh growled. "The *péfrapravádal* of Kargul have their price."

When the *atarlai* had gone he improved this for his wife and son. "There is a good chance I can bring squadrons here, then persuade Bolan to hunt alone, leaving us the center of the board." His chuckle was sinister. "Ban-Sila *Deghi* should be protected by reliable men."

Âna's tale was not told in order of happening (most of what happened and almost all of what she felt with Kamin-Tolagh was never told at all), and for Rodlakh everything was secondary to the more urgent news about Aëlu. But here Dolvid took a second to be puzzled about the exact role of at-Zhâlai. As a boy at the *Mankh'* he had prospered through ingratiation rather than intellect, and now he was the Patriarch's representative, both with Kargul, and at state meetings. "He is an Islander," to Rodlakh. "The man who is now Patriarch used to joke about Zhâlai's supposed relationship with Petakoi's family, but here he is deep in the confidences of Kargul. Where is his first loyalty? We also saw him as a personal companion to your brother the *rabhsai*."

"I heard about that," she said. "He told everyone how brave he was."

A muddled night of sleeping and waking; she did not know why Kamin-Tolagh roused her so she could be at his side for the meeting with Bolan in the big, draughty hall with one wall made of wonderful wood-carving, but resented being banished by Bolan just when she was about to learn something. When Kamin-Tolagh came from that meeting dawn was near, and she, sleepy, made another mistake, asking whether Bolan's news had been so important, after all. Seeing the frown in his eyes, she said, "I wish I could see Tam's sister," reestablishing a reputation for butterfly-minded inattention.

"Tú is not at Kadon Dinul."

"She must be a fine lady, with lots of gowns."

"Are you your mother's friend, Âna? Never mind; it is different with your people, you both live in the same fear of your father. We have gone a thousand years beyond those ways."

He did not sound convinced Owani progress was an unmixed benefit. The picture of her real mother going in fear of her actual father was so fascinating she was distracted from curiosity about Kamin-Tarú (and, it seemed, her less-than-friendship with Petakoi). Kamin-Tolagh said in an unconvincing and unconvinced tone, "At Inilun Barabhi, the *Nim'* my grandfather is ill, nearly blind. Someone has to stay there for him."

He did not return to bed, and Âna had only closed her eyes when there was an eruption of excited voices.

"The *rabhsai's* brother?"   Kamin-Tolagh's voice, utterly disbelieving, came from his outer room, and for dread-filled moments she was sure the news must be about Rodlakh's capture. Tovakh's voice was a menacing rumble, but by getting out of bed and creeping near the partly-open door she soon heard enough to enjoy the truth, Dolvid and Rodlakh had for the present escaped. But they were being hunted.

For Kamin-Tolagh, much more for his father, the crowning wonder was that Rodlakh, having found a way past Ban-Sila's defenses, had not killed him, and declared himself *rabhsai*. "Oh, aye, a strong law," Tovakh growled in irony, reminded in at-Zhâlai's gelding voice about the so-called Law of Parricides, intended to withhold allegiance from those attempting to benefit by assassination. "But no measure is better than the swords to enforce it, and Rodlakh is going to have this war to fight, whether Ban-Sila is alive or dead."

"And where is he," Tovakh said. "Where are they all, the two or the three of them?"

"The *rabhsai*, also," at-Zhâlai said, "wants the answer to that question."

"If Kargul had all its squadrons here, we would show them a search." After some discussion on the chance the intruders were still concealed somewhere in the passages and tunnels, Kamin-Tolagh asked if Dolvid did not have some friends at Kadon who might give him refuge. His father growled that there were severe penalties for giving aid to a *kaël'rolai*. "If there is any doubt, we'll bring them here, let Rheduban have his pleasure questioning them."

"If Rheduban honors us with his attendance again," Kamin-Tolagh said.

She felt sweatily sick; Faëdhal was an obvious suspect. Surely the *rabhsai* would not permit torturing of his Master of Tongues; Faëdhal was, however, so quaintly aloof from the conflicts in the realm he might simply admit the chance-meeting in the Gardens of Kamzhinu. Supposing her safe, he might also mention a slender, dark-haired girl named Âna. Kamin-Tolagh first saw her a short distance from the Gardens, dressed as Faëdhal could report her dressed.

He would kill her, she was quite sure; his pride would be assailed by her having fooled him. Death could be the best of it, since they might think her worth torturing for what she could tell. She settled with herself that she would volunteer everything she knew about Sebhal, Saidhan, the Colony, Rodlakh, the readiness of the Army of the West, make something up if they expected her to know about Shumat: there were no secret plans she had heard of, and to withhold information would be no help to her friends, only agony for her.

The voices outside the door receded, with talk of breakfast and meeting with Bolan. Knowing only that her friends had survived so far, wondering in what way Ban-Sila had been, as at-Zhâlai said, "splendid," She rinsed hands and face, brushed back her hair, and went to the large outer room. No one was there; she had assumed the talk of breakfast meant this place, and there were fresh dishes on the sideboard, but the men must be elsewhere in the Residence.

She took food, and was eating barley-bread with honey when Radaghi came in, the one Âna most distrusted. Petakoi was clearly more formidable in terms of power, at times openly controlling Tovakh, but Radaghi had another sort of menace. A sense of aggrievement hung like a mountain-mist about both sisters, but what with Finú came out as a damp-nosed self-pity with this one was rancid and dangerous. She was large and angular with the big-knuckled hands of a dyer.

She leered. "The men are gone?"

"There was an alarm, *Asayu*, Lady, madam."

"Some men have tried to attack our *rabhsai*, Âna. What do you say to that?"

"They must be wicked men, madam."

"And still at large. One of them is his own brother. What do you say to that?"

What Âna Arlemirrs-daughter might say was anyone's guess. "Who in his right mind would try to harm the *rabhsai*, *Asayu*, let alone his own brother? Though my two brothers have no use for each other, it's true."

Without any change of expression Radaghi went into the Owanilú to say, "*The mongrel* rabhsai *has the love of the mongrels, why not?* These wicked men are not coming here, Âna," back in ordinary language. "You are safe."

"Thank you, madam." To be safe with Radaghi from Dolvid and Rodlakh was a strange enough idea. The pallid, carmine-lipped woman reached out one of her wheelwright's hands to stroke her upper arm lightly. No comfort in the smile she gave.

It was surprisingly easy to yawn. "I hope Tam may soon be back, madam."

"Tam wants you to be nice to me, Âna." Odd that close up, where the harshness tended to fall into its parts, the woman started to seem younger; she could hardly be past midway in her thirties, for unmixed Owani blood not much past a girl, the same age as Aëlu (another strange notion). She was doing her best to make that face agreeable, flickers of uncertainty in the shallow-set, pale eyes.

"Tam would want me to be nice to everyone, madam." Yet there was little doubt what Radaghi meant; dwarfing Âna's wrist the strong hand was closing.

"Why don't we go to my rooms? We would be comfortable there."

As from a bangle, her hand snaked from Radaghi's grasp. With monumental oblivion she sauntered away to put furniture between them. "Madam, I am to wait here, so Tam said. I'm hungry."

"That's all right." Radaghi advanced with her swaying walk. "Tam said you should be nice, and do everything I asked, *pevruloyun vi-mômai.*" No change from the cajoling tone for this last, `brainless filly,' but much more insulting in the Owanilú. Across the back of a chair she reached to grasp Âna's arms. If Radaghi was as strong as she seemed Âna could see being lifted clean over the chair. Then the woman sidestepped, and there was no choice but sidestep with her; there was a traditional, ridiculously solemn Owani dance that went something like this. Hands walked towards each other behind her back, and

Radaghi gave a gentle tug, parting her lips to display the wet tongue. In the dim character Âna was obliged to maintain she was not fully a person in this woman's eyes, and could not think of a way to elude her. All that was delaying things was Radaghi's evident preference for consent; she was burbling, "Come Âna, pretty Âna be nice to 'Dahi."

Possibly she was cautious, too, about an all-out assault, here where interruption could come; Âna begged for it to come, although the baKargul', for all she knew of them, might stand by and contemplate rape. Radaghi was horribly strong.

Âna was not shocked or revolted in principle (these neat thoughts went on side by side with desperation); there was no reason why two women, friends, surely, should not fondle and give each other pleasure. When her filling body had begun to hold men's eyes she'd had a girl-cousin for friend, and they had whispered together their ideas about what men might be pleased or maddened by, gently exploring meanwhile; that had been very sweet. It was this particular woman, quite powerful enough to do murder without a weapon, who repelled her. Hands were sliding down her back, the stretched mouth bore down, and the revolt in Âna's body was an incipient seizure.

Radaghi, offended, undecided whether to beseech or threaten, placed her back at half-arm distance. Breath went chuffing in her nostrils. "Do you want Tam to beat you? He said you must be nice to me. I shall be nice to you, because you're so pretty, pretty Âna." Her right thumb was bruising Âna's left forearm.

"I want my Tam — " going as near a wail as she dared to.

"He is not coming yet. Am I not nice?" Radaghi was speaking with an hysterical sweetness a bubbleskin away from uncontrollable rage. Âna, very afraid, would have yielded, if her body had let her.

A quiet voice spoke the Old Tongue, and no one could remotely have guessed at the words from the calm tone. It was Petakoi. *"Leave the child alone. You have been told before. You will be sent back to Thenimala, and we shall tell Rheduban why."*

Thenimala, not Inilun Barabhi: interesting that for this woman whose lineage was far more illustrious than Petakoi's, being with Kargul counted as a privilege.

The face, very close, acquired a maniacally thwarted expression that terrified, and then faded. Trying to control her breathing she took her tone from Petakoi, pleasantly inconsequential. *"This is no child. If I have the little mongrel, why should it matter to you?"*

"It matters to my son; you upset his women, make them no use to him." She was a stablemaster chiding someone for mistreating a horse, though Âna knew she was in fact of less consequence than a good horse, which cost money to breed and feed, and could not just be plucked out of the fields. Keeping face blank, not giving away she understood this exchange, was enormously difficult.

A grating note she could not quite control came into Radaghi's voice. *"He will be done with her soon enough."*

"You can have her then, if you still want. But you should not forget Rheduban is angered by your beddings with women."

"Rheduban! What would he be, if it were not for my birth? And what about his whores?" Nevertheless, there was fear in Radaghi's voice. *"You would not say anything to him?"*

"Leave my son's pleasures alone."

Radaghi's hold had slackened and deadened, and at last she let go, turning to face the older woman, and with a lightning change of mood in defeat, sneered derisively. *"Two years ago I might have told you the same. Poor Tam, so young to have lost so much."* Straight-spined, without another glance for Âna, Radaghi left the room, going inside.

Obviously Petakoi had to master anger. She did so, dropping into ordinary language to suggest Âna enjoy some of the food while waiting for Tam.

"Asayu, I wish I could have a bath."

"Yes. Yes." She blinked once. "Marra will have fresh clothes for you to put on for Tam." Most girls of her supposed standing would have to be persuaded to wash properly; some might have to be washed, like a dog. A bad mistake; even among her own real people she was considered remarkably fussy about cleanliness.

"The water is so nice and warm, *Asayu*," she babbled, "and there's all these oils that smell lovely... "

"Yes, yes; enjoy a bath." A step closer. "My cousin's games can be misunderstood. You must not tell Kamin-Tolagh, Tam, about this with the Lady Radaghi. I'll see to it you are not frightened again."

"Yes, Madam."

"Oh — " Petakoi called her back. "And if Captain Rheduban comes while you are here, he must not be told any of this."

"Is Captain Rheb — "

"Rheduban."

"*Asayu*, is he Lady Radaghi's husband?" Even Âna Arlemirrs-daughter would understand that much.

Petakoi nodded. "You do not have anything to be afraid of."

"I wish for Tam to come back, *Asayu*," she mumbled, rather dismayed to find how true that was.

"Rheduban," Kamin-Tolagh sprawled wearily after a day in the saddle, "would make a better officer of cavalry if we knew where he was once in a month or so." He had in fact returned, and was with Radaghi.

"Oh, aye," his father made faces over a cup of spiced *raminat*. "Well, we can't all be Kamin-Tolaghs, martyrs to duty. What self-denial — this lad, madam, went unpleasured for all of eight hours — unless you found something better than ducks down by the Paowan."

Âna sat by the firepit giving no sign she understood, leafing though a sheaf of pictures, block-prints on traditional subjects, given her by Finú. Earlier, ridiculously resplendent in ankle-length brocade of a close-fitting surcoat she had tried to go for a wander in the Residence, but Petakoi stopped her at the door, saying she would only get lost and cause trouble. Since then she had been very bored, but with

Kamin-Tolagh's return was cheered to hear the fugitives remained uncaptured.

Tovakh repeated his view they had gone to ground with confederates at Kadon Dinul, while Kamin-Tolagh insisted their only sensible course was to make for the North.

"What about Sebhal?" he asked suddenly.

"What about him?" and the son confirmed her impression of a potential for intelligence by putting together disparate incidents into a coherent if incomplete story, quite accurate. Sebhal had been lost sight of in the Colony, and at about that time some outlaws from the West came to consult Dolvid Vidukhat, who was certainly travelling with Rodlakh now. In the fight south of Shemugrân the man who had survived said he was unhorsed by a master, a tall, slender young man with a light hand for a *pefrai*. Clearly, Rodlakh. Then, among others of the party he described, there was a man of middle height but very broad in the shoulder, not unlike (the man said) their own Tovakh *Asai*. Sebhal, Kamin-Tolagh insisted, but if Sebhal came to the Mainland, why was he no part of this raid on the Residence?

"Why, indeed — " Rheduban was by the inner door, and Âna first heard his droning voice. "He might not have been so merciful with his nephew as the younger one was."

"Hush," Petakoi reproved, glancing at the other door, as if at-Zhâlai might appear there.

Kamin-Tolagh, growing steadily more excited, started answering his own question. "In Burantal," to Rheduban. "The curfew-breakers you fought."

"Worse than curfew-breakers."

"Five days ago — well, it will be six. You did for one before you fled."

Rheduban's tight lips drew back from long front teeth. "I *fled*, as you call it, because my only ally, who had my sword, promptly gave up the fight. When you take on four knives in half-light with nothing but a little bow, you may talk about *fleeing, Asai*."

"You must pardon me, Captain," Kamin-Tolagh soothed conflict. "I meant nothing by the word. The one you wounded — you would call him a fighter?"

"I would call him dead, with an arrow clean through his breastbone. Oh, they were all fighters — why else would I have *fled*? He was no youth, big in chest and shoulders, like our Tovakh *Asai*," Rheduban made a half-deference, "but light on his feet, quick."

"The others," ignoring his father, who was ready to proclaim his own agility. "One a tall man, very slender?"

"He came at my back, and was very near wounding me."

"Another, a man of moderate height, but lesser build than the one you wounded — "

"I killed. If I'd had men of my own at hand there, I would have taken hostages and lopped a limb an hour by the fountain till someone told me where the body went."

"You killed Sebhal."

"Oh, come — " his father protested. Kamin-Tolagh, three fingers on his left hand standing for Rodlakh, Sebhal and Dolvid, went through all the history again, but Tovakh stayed skeptical. "What in the name of Zhunoi was Sebhal doing cat-and-mousing about Burantal?"

"What was the *Valrabh'* doing, sneaking into the Residence dressed in dirty campaign-clothes?"

Tovakh asked Rheduban, who was surprisingly neutral: Âna would have expected him to want credit for such a feat, but he would only say he could not swear it was not Sebhal he shot.

"Plain as the Mountain," Kamin-Tolagh insisted. "And with Sebhal dead, the Army of the West — "

"I'll need better proof before I start counting out the Army of the West," Tovakh snarled. "Banak-rai was also said to have died at Burantal — a hundred saw that. Thirty years after his tragic demise he was leading troops against Kargul. Let us not give the West the start of a legend, where Sebhal can come back from the dead."

"In any event," Petakoi comforted him. "You already have the assurance of *g'Asalladh'* the Army of the West can safely be disregarded."

"*Atarlum* hints and winks, by way of at-Zhâlai. Not eight hours after telling us not to mind about the West, he was cowering under Rodlakh's knife. A flaw in *aën'modha*, was it?" Petakoi showed affront.

"Could the *Mankh'* have heard about Sebhal being dead?" Kamin-Tolagh unknowingly came to the same explanation Dolvid had.

His mother shook her head. Clearly she was the one closest to the *Atarlum*, but when Tovakh said he would not be put off by hints and winks from her, she leaned forward to say in a confidential tone, "The *Adanum Plakh'* has captured Aëlu. They have taken her to Drin b'Afon."

She spoke in the Owanilú, and Âna, who, during all conjecture about Burantal and Sebhal, had been displaying a keen interest in her stack of pictures, could not prevent a jerk of her head, or be quite certain she had heard right. But Kamin-Tolagh, with the others, was held by the news. "A hostage?" not exulting.

"The *nôd'yanu*," his mother said, "comes home at last." Finú giggled, then covered her mouth with a plump hand.

It was Radaghi who offered that Aëlu's value as hostage was diminished if her Rheduban had really killed Sebhal. Petakoi did not agree, saying Saidhan would be no less solicitous than his son for Aëlu's safety.

"Nor Rodlakh," Tovakh barked out. "If his feelings for auntie are all they say."

"Is this how to make war?" Kamin-Tolagh, irritably, and of all people Rheduban was with him.

"War against wives. We want to see the Army of the West out of action, good, then bring them here, and let us cut them to pieces in the open field; hostages are for eunuchs and half-men. The crops of the Heartland will be all the better dewed with some good blood."

"Oh, there will be fighting, fighting enough for everyone. Even you, Tam — we can be heroes without taking on ten at once."

Tovakh rubbed his hands together. "At last, the *Mankh'* is giving us something better than a pat on the head. We'll give Shumat safe-conduct to his own slow hanging."

Petakoi warned everyone not to let at-Zhâlai know she had told them about the abduction. The little *atarlai* had been expected before this, but when he did come, filled with officiousness, he explained he had been talking with a Household officer, Dorrmas, who said the fugitives were dead. Drowned. He had taken a patrol westward, and with his men had watched the end of a strange boat on Arnan, not far from the outlet of a stream which came from underground, always said to begin beneath Kadon Dinul.

"That is all?" Tovakh added these to the list of deaths for which he would want proof. Dorrmas, after all, was of those mongrel Household officers whose loyalties might be suspect in a choice between Ban-Sila and Saidhan (or Rodlakh, Saidhan's parrot); what better than this rumor to blunt the edge of a continuing search?

Kamin-Tolagh thought even less of the report. For Âna in her isolation any bad news seemed true; while she knew the purpose of his scorn was not to console her, she was grateful to Kamin-Tolagh, who simmered on when they were alone.

"And none of them tried to save themselves by swimming? What, were they asleep, or did they die of boredom underground?" He was offended, she realized, that his father gave equal disbelief to this thin tale and his own elaborate analysis of Sebhal's death.

In the afternoon, returning from patrol and the abstinence sardonically praised by Tovakh, his ardor had been fierce enough for a month's separation. Now, happily, he was overtaken by fatigue — or perhaps his interest in her, already by his standards abnormally sustained, was starting to wilt; by now he should be looking for her successor.

The news about Aëlu was something Rodlakh should have before sailing for Kamsilat; she surmised if undrowned he must be in

Tan Lughsai by tomorrow. She had wondered about trying to make contact with some of Rodlakh's potential allies in the Household; this Dorrmas, or Kizhunai, the captain, whom Dolvid had called a decent man. It had been in her mind this afternoon when she had attempted to leave the Karguli Wing. But there were dangers; Rodlakh (she resignedly knew) would not expect those officers to forget their oaths to the lawful *rabhsai*.

The better way was to carry the news herself, and for that an escape, or being released by Kamin-Tolagh, was not enough; she needed a horse as well. But travel was restricted, and given a horse, she would need means of getting past the various guard-posts and patrols.

"Another day's hunting tomorrow, darling," sleepily; he might be explaining-away his failure to rouse tonight.

"Tam, I would love to go and see horses. I've been all shut up here. It would be nice to go down and see the big horses."

"We shall see. If you please me." He put a flaccid hand on her hip, and just so, open mouth reaching for her, fell asleep.

After hasty mouthfuls from dishes on the sideboard, he went down to the Court of the Ram where his men would be waiting, bringing Âna to the attention of yawning Household guards, so she would be able to return. He had wakened her at dawn, and their passions were hurried by his need to be with his patrol. This too was a hunt; the word was *ransack*, as he panted after what was always out of reach. *So young to have lost so much*, Radaghi had said, annoying Petakoi. Radaghi was mad, but old rural women held the utterances of the demented could at times go right to the heart of truth: it all had to do with his sister, Kamin-Tarú.

Outside at the head of the narrow steps they were hit with a slap of rain, a cool and blustery morning. Down below by the stables Freighanai was waiting, and other junior officers were assembled, already mounted, by the huge buttress at the eastern end of the cobbled yard. Kamin-Tolagh would evidently lead men of the Household today as well as Kargul, and even without their distinguishing tunics it would have been easy to tell which were which, from how the men watched Kamin-Tolagh descend the steps with her, the Household men with lidded looks that accused him of conceit, Kargul with faint grins and near-nudges the opposite of envy, as if by being his men they shared in his conquests, his prowess. Evidently there were qualities other than courage for men to admire, hence more ways than Sebhal's of making them want to be led. That might put Kamin-Tolagh too high as a potential leader in war.

Making her own strategies, she played up to the atmosphere of mannish boast, keeping pressed close to Kamin-Tolagh as he strode to the stables, though she would not have forecast how much she would despise herself for the deceit.

His near-white *pefrai* was led out by the stablemaster, a Mixed, not as elderly as he initially appeared, who glanced at Âna with amusement somewhere softened with sentiment. He handed the horse over as if passing on a treasure, and approved when she reached up to fondle the beast's nose. Kamin-Tolagh, reins in hand, stooped to kiss her, less vulnerably than he kissed when they were alone, a display kiss, which brought sounds from his audience, between a murmur and the ghost of a cheer, quickly suppressed.

So the stablemaster could overhear, Âna said, "Soon, Tam."

"Yes, soon, Ân'loi." Foot in stirrup, mind already on soldiering.

It was still very early. Tovakh, belted, noted her passage through the common-room with the faint dip of his bearded chin; he showed no interest in her as a woman. No one else seemed to be stirring, but Marra was already cleaning in Kamin-Tolagh's rooms. Going for a bath, Âna did not linger, coming back to find everything quiet.

Nothing had been disturbed in the closet in Tam's outer room. She took her soft undershirt and heavy breeches, hesitating over the long knife, reluctantly concluding the lesser danger was to leave it. While stowing it in her pack, she took a fistful of dried fruit for her pockets. Over shirt and breeches she put on the long brocade robe once again.

On the first day, retrieving her knife from the drawer, she had glimpsed what she hoped was going to be the talisman to frank her past gates and guard-posts, turn away inquisitive patrols. It was still there when she looked, a hinged clasp to fit on the upper arm, enamelled in sky-blue, Kargul's provincial color, the bronze metal of the actual clasp embossed with the Mountain Lion, their emblem. Such a token would be worn by a courier carrying messages to or from the *Nim'* or his immediate circle. In ordinary circumstances a rider wearing the provincial emblem would never be challenged, except perhaps attempting to enter the gates of the Residence; elsewhere, no guard or officer would risk the insult to a *nim'*, whose dispatches, too, might be for the *rabhsai's* own eyes. Today, there was war and suspicion, but that might actually help, with Kargul in the ascendant at Kadon Dinul; her appearance might not matter, unless she was stopped by men of Kargul. She put the clasp in the wide pocket of the brocade robe.

" — but reduced to provincial exile for Bolan's sake." The voice coming from the common-room, not one she knew, sounded aggrieved. "He did not want it said that he had a man sent to the Island so he could take his wife." The subject being discussed appalled her. The door was already open, and she could not retreat. Rheduban was nearby at the sideboard, while the speaker was seated at the table.

"Are there many of these exiles?" Rheduban asked. "I would think at the onset of fresh trouble, it would be a simple thing to execute ones who have known associations with rebels and outlaws. Trusted officers could be given standing orders — " Here Rheduban caught sight of the hesitating Âna, and stretched his lips back from the predator teeth in what passed for his smile. "Oh, I frightened you," he droned. The other man was bending over, using food for bait, trying to attract the large yellow cat.

"No, not so, Rheduban *Asai* — " knowing very well the honorific was incorrect. She was trying to wish, after all, that she had her knife, but knew in truth she would never be able to strike Sebhal's killer, numbed as she was by his cold stare.

"This would be Kamin-Tolagh's newest?"

"My wife says she is ditch-filth. Are you ditch-filth, Âna?"

"I cannot say, Lord."

Rheduban glanced over his shoulder to be sure the other was paying attention. "Do you bite? Does Tam enjoy claws that wound? I could show you some ways to draw blood that would devote him to you, but he would not love himself for it. Hm?" He let out a breath between sigh and shudder. Aroused, what he was doing had something in common with Kamin-Tolagh, strutting for his troops.

Rheduban reached to take her wrist, leading her farther into the room, his long, strong fingers unpleasantly dry on her flesh. "She is only a small thing, and he a lamb who thinks he is a great he-goat."

"Sir, he will be waiting for me," she managed to say.

"Oh, we don't want that. Ask leave, then."

Her heart leapt with new hope. "Your leave, *Asai*?"

"Not mine, uncouth — " he gestured at the other. She had never seen the face before, though it was familiar to her. That seemed nonsense, till, beseeching the cat, the man turned in full profile. Familiar from coinage; Ban-Sila *Rabhsai*.

Flustered, genuinely so, she made full deference. "*Deghi*."

"You have leave." Ban-Sila was not interested, scarcely glancing her way. She repeated her deep deference, and made weak knees negotiate the steps, feeling Rheduban watching, hoping she had hitched her breeches high enough not to show under the hem of the gorgeous robe.

"But present law on exiles — " Ban-Sila was saying, as she shut the door behind her.

She did not dare do what she most wanted, sit down and tremble for a while. Need kept her going past friendly acknowledgement of guards she was passing for the third time this morning, letting her eyes flirt. Once again she came down into the Court of the Ram, where the stablemaster was instructing a couple of grooms. Seeing how patiently he made his point about rubbing down

the flanks made her sure she could count on his kindness. Her mother
had told her always to watch how men were with those who worked
for them, and that seemed sound.

He came to her, wiping hands on the front of his breeches.
Not sure of her standing he compromised, bowing his head a little,
which might be only to listen, though he was hardly a handspan taller
than Âna. Worn rather than elderly, not so much older than her father.

When she told him she needed a horse he rubbed his chin with
the back of his hand, and she could hear the roughness of stubble that
could not be seen, here in the shadowed stable entrance. "Well." He
scratched beside his eye. "You see, madam, I have to have a warrant.

"No horse without a warrant, that's the *rabhsai*'s own orders,
you see. These from the south, well, their cavalry brought enough
mounts, but the lords, and there's spare horses needed, Zhôl knows
where I'll find them."

The arguments were starting to multiply, and she saw with
persistence she could win. The stablemaster cited his responsibility to
the Captain Bolan, to all the ladies here at the Residence, to mounts he
must not let be overridden. He would say exactly the same to the lord
and captain of Kargul he had seen madam with earlier.

"If there's questions," he resumed, just when she was sure he
had finished, "giving out horses, right and left, no warrant to show, it's
old Norlum who is to blame, as usual. I've got my place to keep, you
see, madam. See, I can't let the saddle-horses go, when the ladies call
for them almost every afternoon, and a lady such as yourself, madam,
you wouldn't want to be straddling a big *pefrai*, now."

"I am not a lady, I'm a farmer's daughter, and anything that
eats hay I can ride. You saw me on a *pefrai* when I came here,
horsemaster."

He was wavering.   Anxious every moment, her
shoulderblades shrinking from imagined recapture, she withdrew
farther into the stables, and began unfastening her long robe. Perhaps
the stablemaster supposed she was about to offer her body as bribe; his
face lit up like a lantern with relief when he saw she was in breeches
beneath. Now she could reach her pocket, and as the man began again

at the *rabhsai*'s orders, she cut him short with a quick movement of her hand to his, passing him one of Rodlakh's gold coins.

A bashful grin. "Didn't recognize you right off for the one who rode in with Captain Tolagh, dressed so different, and him having so many — comings and goings, I mean to say." With no change of expression he watched Âna put the enamelled clasp on her arm, and shortly was leading out a black *pefrai*, less large than some, though still a big, powerful animal. With fixed face and a certainty she would soon scream she had to listen to a recital of the *pefrai*'s 'little ways,' aware every second Tovakh might come here, or any of the women, Rheduban.

At length the stablemaster finished talking, shortened the stirrups, took in the girth a fraction, and with resignation handed over the reins. She kissed his grey-stippled cheek, and hoped he would see her trembling as anticipation of the supposed reunion with Kamin-Tolagh. She was up, kicking a glossy flank with the heel of a brocade slipper the horsemaster had not omitted to observe was never made for riding, begging her pardon. She clattered onto the cobbles, and no one challenged; the pikeman at the head of the narrow stair to the doorway, a fresh-faced youth who had thoroughly memorized Âna as she passed and repassed him, gave a gesture near a wave.

Not breathing she came to the gate, and was passed through without a check, out onto the Avenue of Treaties, rose-colored stone solid under hoofs. She maintained a walk, her back stiff with dignity — a terror she hoped would pass for dignity.

Getting dizzy with the idea of freedom she swung left by the Disc, riding down to Market Gate. From the market-place to its gateway was packed with five or six farm-wagons, great-hoofed draft animals impatient for the road; seeking such a prize as Rodlakh, the searches were more diligent than formerly. With disdain proper to a clasped courier she swung out past the line and came down to where the outward half-gate was shut.

"Where are you bound?" an officer barked, and in prudence, "Madam."

"Zelkova." That was southward, a long way.

"A good road, madam." Soldiers pulled away the barrier. Down a short slope and up the opposed incline, and she was passing the hostelry. There, when they chattered their way out of the compound, she had learned boldness was the key — that, and a sense of mad laughter. Terrified, she had enjoyed every moment of this escape.

Taking a lane that led right she must have passed near Faëdhal's house, and hoped Tovakh's idea of questioning Dolvid's friends at Kadon Dinul would remain forgotten.

As Kamin-Tolagh had observed, the southward road, which she soon came to, was not in best repair. There were puddles and mudholes from the rain, blown away from a sky where cloud was high and smooth, though tattered squalls could be seen ahead where the way wound up into low hills. The horse took to the road, and she had to hold him from dancing into a gallop; it was a long ride, even for a *pefrai* with half its normal burden.

She settled into the saddle, the mount into a steady gait. Wind made her cheeks glow, and the weight of the Residence rose from her shoulders to go spiralling away into the colorless sky. Day was dull, country scrubby, she was the carrier of bad news, but she exulted in being free, and felt like singing. Standing in her stirrups she did sing, hair blowing across her face. Whatever reason or rumor had to say against it, she was certain her friends were somewhere ahead, and she would catch them. She sang for joy.

"The Summer Palace, beyond any doubt," Dolvid said. "Where they have kept prisoners of the Patriarch, from earliest times, within the citadel where they say no enemy has ever entered. No captive has ever escaped, either."

"She will be lonely," Âna, out of experience.

"*Never* only means, *till now*. The Patriarch is here on the Mainland, not so?"

"As far as we know," seeing his drift; by far the best soldiery the *Atarlum* could command was the *Adanum Plakh'* and most would always be with the Patriarch as his bodyguard.

He ladled out some warm goat's milk for Âna, who was wiping grease from her hands. Animated, Rodlakh argued the news Galt had brought of present quiet at the Frontier, added to the difficulties for Bolan and Tovakh trying to work in harness, gave him the chance for a quick visit to Kamanta.

Âna said, "Will that not put Aëlu in danger?"

Rodlakh had already worried that through and through; his answer was ready: she was in absolute danger, now, every second; it might be months; he was uncertain the *Atarlum* could be trusted ever to give her up. Terms, whatever they were, for her release would be carried to Kamsilat, and if any attempt at rescue was expected, surely the Island's defenders would be watching their western shore. "If we are swift and secret, we may land without being seen."

Deciding he must discuss their tactics with Galt, navigation with Sarnak, he jumped up and went striding off in search of those men.

Âna had an enigmatic face. "It seems I came just in time. If there had not been the storm he would have sailed before now."

"For Kamsilat. Without your news we could not be certain Aëlu was on the Island. Thanks to you we may catch them unprepared."

This was stiff; the ease of Burantal had gone. He admired how she had seized the opportunity Kamin-Tolagh had given; himself not a coward when it came to a fight he recognized here a calm and abiding courage that was out of his reach; he was suddenly shy.

She mistook that. Not having told everything, enough was understood for the lingering ghost of her Mixed inheritance to whisper that he would not want her now, after Kamin-Tolagh. Her father would have expected her to die defending what it was women defended when they were no longer virgin — property-rights of some man, she supposed.

"You are tired," touching under her eye. "We shall not be sailing till dark, or just before. You can sleep."

I shall sleep through till dawn, after you sail. I am not going with you. You will be a raiding-party, and I would just be an *encumbrance* — " the remembered word was deliberately chosen. "Sebhal was right. I do not want to be like Sett, cause of a disaster."

"You are not safe here on the Mainland. Kamin-Tolagh may hunt for you."

"So you offer me instead a holiday on the Island and a stroll through Drin b'Afon." A flash of the Âna who had challenged his manhood with words, but unanswerable, even if he knew it was not fear that was keeping her from the voyage. If asked what he thought their chances were on the Island he would have to say, nearly none, almost certain death; how could he invite her to suicide?

"Then I shall stay too, we'll go to Burantal together." That had been his plan, but everything was changed.

"You know you cannot." She was right. "You have to go, to stop Rodlakh from challenging the entire *Adanum*, so he can clamber to Aëlu on their piled corpses. Look at him — have you ever seen anyone so happy his lady is in peril?" He was by the fire, his face in the dim of the hall lighted by yellow flames. Elated, he punched at Sarnak's bony shoulder.

"It is not that. He is muddled about making war on his brother, the lawful *rabhsai*. This is a job he can attempt, with no conflicts of honor."

She nodded. "We all have our jobs. I'm not going to Burantal, I am going back to Kadon Dinul — to the Residence."

He searched her face, and she meant it. It made him sick to think of her being back among Rheduban and Radaghi, Petakoi and Tovakh. "Rodlakh will forbid it."

"Don't tell him. As far as he knows, I am making for Burantal, to be with Sett."

"That is where you should be." Âna herself had said, at Kadon Dinul there was the chance Faëdhal would be questioned and in all innocence give her away. When Dolvid tried to talk about danger, she said she was too unimportant, then reminded him of what she had said before, that if interrogated she would tell anything she knew rather than suffer pain.

"You would have told them about Galt and Tan Lughsai?"

"Yes," with the momentum of her anti-boasting, then, truthfully, "No. Everything but that."

"Well, that would have been all right, then," with irony that weighed a ton. "Rodlakh's intentions after he left the Residence — why would anyone ask you about that?"

There was going to be some anger between them, and she tried to steer past it. "Besides," she said wryly. "The food is better at the Residence."

"For you, perhaps. All we found was something wet with raisins."

"Apple and pear with raisins and wheat. The cooks must have made a mountain of it."

After a thick silence he said, "This abduction is improvised, a hasty plan."

"Even Kamin-Tolagh was shocked."

Through more cleaveless air Dolvid said, "Âna, do not become attached to him."

"To a Karguli, a baKarguli, to that coxcomb?" then because of the steady gaze, "Yes, that would be stupid, you are right. As always. Besides — " it seemed a possible joke, went sour in the telling, and was rancid between them once uttered: "He will never love anyone but Kamin-Tarú."

Here, Rodlakh returned, with news they would have to start rather sooner than they had said. With the wind where it was, Sarnak estimated eight to ten hours to make the eastern coast of the Island, allowing some time for hunting out a landing-place. They needed light for actual landing, first light would be best; Sarnak hoped they might get ashore unseen if they could tuck in under the cliffs by sunrise.

"About sunset, then, we shall sail," making the calculation.

"Âna — " Rodlakh was tremendously earnest. "You have already done your part, and much more. I wish I could persuade you to make for Burantal."

"Very well, *Valrabh'*."

Marshalled arguments died in Rodlakh's mouth. "After Sett is well again, he will want to come back to Kamsilat, and we shall look for you there. There will always be a place for you in the Colony."

He meant, though Sebhal was gone, and this attempt at graciousness obscurely irritated her; when such things need saying they can never be altogether true. "As what? Can I have a squadron from the Army of the West to play with?"

"I would wish to have your advice, as well as Dolvid's." The simple answer shamed her, but was also a sign he had begun to see himself in the space Sebhal's death had left empty.

"*Valrabh'*, I heard somewhere he believed a hen in a rainstorm had more judgment than I have."

"I am beginning to see you better."

"Or my judgment to be better?"

"Both, it might be." Their smiles met, and were the most warmth Dolvid had seen between the two.

A little later he walked down to the jetty with her. Rodlakh was already there, vigorously overseeing the loading.

"It will be lonely here tonight." She brushed that away.

"What more can you hope to learn there?"

"*Bôdhrai*, what is going to be your advice to Rodlakh? With his brother's ally making war on Aëlu, everything may change."

"One decision he cannot be advised in; he has to make up his own mind, though I think he is there, all but the last step. You realize, the moment Rodlakh declares against Ban-Sila, he becomes a rival claimant to the Bronze Sword, whether he wants that or not."

"It nearly drove Sebhal mad — Rodlakh's nail-biting, I mean."

The sun had gone for good, into a low bank of cloud on the western horizon, but fading memories of scarlet and gold bobbed in the depths of Arnan. Within the miniature harbor a white radiance of ôthu-light was shed on the water.

Dolvid said, trying not to make it sound a task assigned, "I wish we knew what gave g'Asalladh' His confidence — it shows even in the little fish — at-Zhâlai. The abduction is something apart, but He believes He can control either Ban-Sila or Kargul — I cannot see what tile He is holding, but I know the man's mind, g'Asalladh's."

"So you have said." Rapidly she kissed his cheek and he took her hand, wishing they could make love. Rodlakh came from the jetty to take her other hand, and together they walked to the boat, where Rodlakh jumped down, and climbed up again with one of the ôdu-lanterns. "We shall not have much use for these. You take this."

She thanked him, and he kissed her. One foot hovering above the gunwale, he said, "Give our best wishes to Sett."

"When I see him."

"Tomorrow, the day after at the latest."

"Valrabh', I am not going to Burantal." She told him her actual plan, and Rodlakh, grim-faced, got out of the boat once again, to tell her she could not.

"My task. You have yours."

He made a harried movement with his hands. "We have to catch this wind. Sarnak says it might not last, here on the leeward side. Âna, I cannot stand seeing you minister to the needs of that — " no adequately contemptuous word came.

"He will get rid of me soon, and then I'll make for Kamsilat. In three days, four at most, he will throw me out of his bed."

"How can you be so sure of that?" A short, communicating moment, and the Valrabh' was almost certainly blushing. Only the dimmering, perhaps, had let him be so outspoken. "The breeze," apologetically. "We have room for you."

"I may be in Kamsilat before you." That, surely, was true. "Good hunting."

"And you. Keep safe." This was abrupt and almost harsh, as Rodlakh stepped with finality into the boat.

Again with the feeling something large was being left out, Dolvid faced her as Sarnak began casting off. Her eyes were on the spot where Rodlakh had descended. "Bad Âna."

"No, no; he does not think that. He is divided, again."

"Friend, Dolvid."

"Friend, Âna." He pressed her hand. She did not know, of course, he had decided to stay here, that if there had been no storm last night and the boat had sailed, she would not have found Tan Lughsai deserted. Too complicated to tell her, and too near demanding her gratitude for what he had wanted to do. This might be their last sight of each other alive. When, having jumped into the boat, he turned, she was already walking back slowly along the jetty.

In the waist eight men were manning oars. Big-handed, Sarnak tossed down a coiled rope, and took the helm. Nearby, two men pushed off with poles, and the half-hoisted mainsail stirred and rippled.

Under roof aft of amidships Rodlakh was regaining his epic spirit. "Have you ever imagined setting sail for the Island — *Kamanta*, Dolvid!"

"Oh, yes, I have. I am just twenty years late."

The water was lapping against the side. On shore the small white light was still, as Âna watched them out. That lantern, not reflected in the water, was the soul of loneliness in the gloom of the land, a faint cry with no one to hear.

"All the same," Rodlakh said, "we owe her our gratitude."

The Island

Steadily they sailed through a night too bright, wind at their right cheeks. Presumably, with Estuary and Royal Port at Owan Sai to guard, few patrol ships would sail so far south, and any that did would be watching mainly for an invasion-fleet from the West, not for little vessels going there. Yet the moon that rose stark behind them, a nail-paring away from full, made them feel unduly visible on the black and silver-ribbed sea. In his high-pitched, cracking voice Sarnak said any pursuer would be "bridegroom lucky" to catch this craft with its shallow draft and narrow beam, built for speed, its large spread of canvas, as well as space amidships for up to eight pairs of oars.

"'Sides which, if we did get outsailed, Galt's jolly crew'll see to it we're not outshot." But the larger worry was that in this white radiance, which did not lessen as the moon overtook then glided ahead of them, their best chuckling pace would not run them out of sight of a pursuer, so any landing they attempted on Kamanta could be observed without their knowing.

But, after all, that might be overestimating their abilities. Not only live defenders had kept Kamanta safe through so much of the long Night of Owan; its cliffs were as hostile a coast as any. The safe anchorages, especially Pavani at the eastern, Doniftu the western end of the Forbidden Road, would be closely watched and heavily garrisoned; other lonelier harbors of the south were too far away from central Kamanta, dangerous days of marching till they could be where the Mountain, Karg' Kamanta, rose, and Drin b'Afon watched over the Valley of the Patriarchs.

In the deckhouse, Galt, not aware he was returning Sarnak's admiration for his fighting qualities, said, "He's best of sailors; if there is a landfall to be made, he'll find it." He had with him his own men, Uttar and Muranak, and they were all deep-water fishermen when they

could be. Passingly Galt mentioned it was Sarnak, no blame to him,
who had taken a patrol-boat out to challenge the feigned oystermen, the
men who kidnapped Aëlu. Sarnak had been cursing himself ever since,
though it was hard to see what he could have done differently; it was
not yet Colony policy to sink boats or try to capture them because there
was something about the faces of the men in them.

Rodlakh went aft to stand beside Sarnak, asking him a number
of questions, a friendly pat on the shoulder taking away any hint of
interrogation. On the foredeck men lumped in sleeping-bags slept or
talked in low voices; some of the Lunu Tezh' men in the waist were
playing the Froghuli game with lengths of knotted cord. Either as this
gambling game, or when (usually with a woman making the tosses)
used for foretellings, Dolvid had never grasped the principles, and all
explanations made muddle worse, though the youngest Froghuli had
no trouble reading the lie of the cords and agreeing who had won.

After long hours divided between anxiety and tedium they
sailed into a measured swell on a sea scarcely ruffled, and there was a
large thing not a cloud coming up to blot out the radiance below the
impassive moon. Truni, now the watch in the prow, leaned forward
impatiently, but as the ship climbed a fresh wave the shadow slid from
sight. Minutes passed, and then the Island's heights were cut cleanly
out of sky's luminescence, a black hole in night.

The boat's rhythm altered, becoming irregular, in patterns of
waves impossible to predict; the mainsail kept spilling its wind to flap
slackly in the swirling breeze.

Sarnak called out to Galt, "Wouldn't do harm for some rowers
to be standing by." The little half-squadron officer went hurrying
forward, as the sail rattled startlingly back and forth, and the craft lost
way. Casting about, Sarnak found wind, and they resumed their
course, though now the backtow could be felt. With the moon
westering they were coming into the shadow of cliff-walled Island, and
no one was sleeping. Moon vanished for good behind the central
heights, while to aft, on an eastern horizon lower than would have
seemed possible, there was a faint chink of pale yellow, a parting under
frosted indigo, new day pacing behind retreating night.

Ahead was the ghostly white line where cliffs stood in surf. A southerly gust and a strong northward surge of current struck at once, and the ship heeled, almost dipping a gunwale. Men grabbed what they could clutch, and Sarnak, throwing the tiller, cried out, "Reef, then — reef!" Two men stationed at the mainsail were clinging on for life, but as the ship righted and Sarnak's order came with added urgency, ropes were hauled, sails furled, and the boat settled, head coming into the current. Sarnak, with slight assistance from slow-dipped oars, was content to follow the flow northward, very gradually approaching the line of cliffs.

"Need more light for finding a landfall," he observed.

"I am worried about watchtowers," Rodlakh said. "Can we come in closer under the cliffs?"

"Not that much, *Asai*, if you're fussy about hitting rocks."

"Near as you dare, then."

Giving the helm to Muranak, Sarnak went forward with the other of his men, Uttar, to keep watch for rocks, stopping on the way to instruct the eight rowers as to signals: they were seated reversed, using a short pushing action. Due west appeared what, if not a dream, could only be the cap of Karg' Kamanta floating up, a wedge of ivory on an ocean of black.

The shoreline they were converging with was unbroken cliff, and oars dipped unevenly in the short chop of the waters. Streaming black tips of rocks were bared, and Sarnak's right hand went up with a cry of "*Ho!*" Helm went over hard, and they were bobbing past a headland jagged with rock-spires. Less urgently Sarnak indicated a portward correction. His left hand shot up again; spread like a dark-blooming water-lily, rocks were dead ahead. "*Ho!*" Sarnak sounded, and the helm answered at once, while the portside oars, slower to respond, lifted.

So they pivoted about the headland, and Sarnak signalled with his right hand; the starboard oars went in once, twice, coming up dripping. They were inside the main barrier of rocks, nosing westward into a deep fissure in the shoreline, though the cliffs gave no sign of relenting.

"Push, then," Sarnak called, and all oars went in nearly together, as the boat lifted forward on the swell. Giving quick little signals Sarnak guided them deeper into the cove, grazing rocks, oars often bumping and clattering. Light was palely gathering, and Dolvid noted now Rodlakh had been up in the prow, shielding an *ôdu*-lantern with his cloak so light was shed on Sarnak's hand-signals.

Now they could see that above where the black wall opposite came back to meet the one they were following there was a notch, a break in the line of cliffs, perhaps only a rockfall, or the outlet for a small stream.

Sarnak questioned Rodlakh with a look.

He did not debate. "Yes, try it here." They were bumping on rounded rocks, swinging in on the breakers, then dropping fast, shuddering, to lean forward once again. Wind in cool and gusty fragments had no settled direction, and rowing was a scramble, though the oarsmen were struggling bravely. A larger wave came to fill up the end of the fissure like a giant bath, and carry them, heeling dangerously, towards the right-hand wall, then straight down, oars jammed back into the boat. They were certain to be smashed to pieces, and the hull did strike, making boards creak. With Uttar showing how, oars were used to fend, pushing at the wall shiny with slime and weed, while waves carried them forward a few feet, and so receding back half that distance.

They were only yards from where the break mounted, a steep, littered stair, and Sarnak in the bow had a coil of rope at his feet, a three-pronged grapple in his hands. The starboard oarsmen crouched to shove away the cliff, and Uttar yelled for them to pole the boat forward too. With the next large wave the nose of the boat hovered in the gap before falling back on the undertow; it was likeliest by far they would be caught up and smashed against the cliff. A lesser wave swung them up again, and Sarnak made a toss, catching nothing, very rapidly bringing back the hook. With the next wave the boat screech-scraped bottom; Sarnak, clawing wet hair from his eyes threw the grapple neatly up over a notch between rocks. He paid out line as they receded, then hauled in, at first steadily, then with a grabbing rush.

Wrapped around the left-hand rock, the rope came free with a whipping motion; grapple slipped, then caught again. Uttar had rejoined Sarnak, and they braced themselves, hauling hard as a new rise began.

This was a big wave, biggest yet, throwing the stern sideways against solid rock. Their helmsman went sprawling and thudded against the gunwale; Dolvid who had gone back to help him fight the tiller now grabbed at it to save himself. The boat leapt forward, water splashing and foaming over the stern. He hung on to the tiller, spitting out salt water, fairly certain he was going to drown. The jarring crash as the boat came down squarely in the gap had no connection with his own problems.

Retreating sea tried to suck them back, but Sarnak had evidently made fast, and the line held while the hull ground against rocks. The thought, if Âna had come with them it would only have been to share their deaths, came very plainly to Dolvid, who then found he was neither drowned nor drowning. Even Muranak, scrambling up, was aboard and alive, though probably bruised.

Dolvid went forward up the steep slope, and in the waist joined Rodlakh in hauling a former oarsman back aboard from the milky waters. Disarranged, twenty-seven men had far too many arms and legs — and this was not twenty-seven; some were already out of the boat at the prow. Dolvid clambered down to help, and was knee-deep in water next to Galt, who was thigh-deep. Water began rising, waist, chest, and all hands thrust upward on the hull. Galt, immersed to the chin, stumbled and went under, but was there on hands and knees as the water ran off, and the boat's stern crashed down again, prow jammed in the cleft where the grapple-line had gone. The half-dozen men found new footings higher up, and as water came roaring they hauled, slipping and cursing, those on the starboard side having to scramble clear, as the boat rolled over on a level shelf above the two rocks, stern jutting well clear of water. Rudder was in tatters, boards were punched through, and the bow was crushed, but the vessel was firmly aground, and their baggage safe.

In the past moments everything had been water, and it was amazing there were things unsoaked, some unwetted — packs and bedrolls stacked in the deckhouse were practically dry, though shipped water was streaming from the tilted deck. Galt, standing on a flat rock next to the trickle of fresh water that came down through this cleft, was starting a roll-call.

Rodlakh called out as Dolvid came back on board. The back of the *Valrabh*'s hand was bleeding, but he looked carefree. In his own pleasure at being alive among the living Dolvid was slow to register fully where he was standing. Rodlakh, gazing up at the cliffs, said, "Kamanta."

"To stay, *Valrabh*'," Sarnak put it. He was getting a coiled rope to take ashore, and enumerated the boat's mortal injuries. "She won't float again, not by any repairs we could do."

Dolvid said, "We shall steal another boat on the far side of the Island, when we get there." Sarnak took that as settled fact, and shouldered his rope with a brisk nod.

As the men gathered in improving light it became apparent Rodlakh's hand was one of the worst injuries; there were bruises and scrapes, other minor cuts, some torn clothing, and miraculously that appeared to be all. They were completely within the cleft, the left-hand cliff curving over to give concealment from above.

"That watchtower by the headland," Rodlakh said. "Would it be garrisoned?"

He had not seen a tower, but offered if there was one it would be manned by not less than a watcher or two; the *Atarlum* did not depend on *ga-dazhai* alone to defend their Island. The term caused Rodlakh to fidget uncomfortably, and Dolvid was glad to define *ga-dazhai* as a fraudulent weapon in the *Mankh'* armory, "sacred dread." Yet for him there had been all those hundreds of days and nights at the *Mankh'* when *ga-dazhai* had been real, the proper feeling for what should be reverenced; contemplation of the Mountain, awe for the Island, the Forbidden Road, Shuf'Oëladh, icy waters fed by the undying snows of Karg' Kamanta, the Stream of Being, where he would have bathed his feet on his pilgrimage. The quality in things that caused *ga-*

dazhai was simply called *mai*, a particular and awe-giving state of existence; for someone trained in belief it was unmeaning to ask whether *mai* was really there: it could be perceived in a sunset, a single note of music, touch of a hand. What fighting men they would have to deal with on the Island was an unknown, but his stay here would be a battle against the *mai* he had been taught to find.

Rodlakh asked who, legally, could garrison watchtowers, or for that matter guard the walls of Drin b'Afon; there were not enough of the *Adanum Plakh'*.

"Your grandfather — " relieved to be dealing with tangible facts — "had questions about this. Under the Treaty, according to the Patriarch, the Island has the right to raise any numbers for its own defense. Banak-rai said, the Treaty intended to limit the size of the *Adanum Plakh'*, but the levies here freed the *Adanum*, potentially for aggressive actions. He was angry, I think, because of rumors — quite true, as it happens — some squadrons of the Patriarchal Guard were borrowed by Kargul in the War of the Widowed, and fought under Kargul's colors."

"But the Island goes on levying its troops."

"It would take a hundred thousand cavalry to force them to stop. But Banak-rai also conceded with the poverty there was, and still is in remote parts of the Island, militia-duty was a way of putting bread in some mouths."

"They are in arms over a Free State outside the *rabhsai's* authority, up in the Northeast," Rodlakh, grimly. "The Patriarch has maintained one here on Kamanta for generations. Well, it does not matter who we have to fight." He brushed hair back from his forehead, leaving a streak of blood from the back of his hand.

But it very much did matter. They were sure to be vastly outnumbered, and their chances in a fight were not good, but if it came to that, better to fight someone who would surrender when beaten, rather than those whose Death Oath made them fight on, with hope or without.

"Surrender. That is good to hear."

Following the example of some of the men Dolvid sat on a rock and unlaced his boots so he could wring water from his socks. Rodlakh soon sat beside him. "They say Drin b'Afon has never been taken. But it is also said no invader's foot has ever stained the sacred soil of the Island. If that is true, why make a fuss about how strong the city is?"

A man in his middle thirties, Dolvid, after two dozen years, almost touched his own backside in pained reminiscence. "Clever boys at the *Mankh'* who ask that same question do not sit in any comfort for several days."

Not too complicated for those who could master the art of *knowing, not-knowing*. The inviolability of the Island was a political and religious assertion, and a racial one as well; it was dogma that on the Island all through the Night of Owan the bloodlines of the Owanil had remained unsullied, so at the Return they could resume their rule by right. In history, on the contrary, the Island had experienced several invasions, some mere raids, a few serious attempts at conquest.

The earliest, coming just a short while after collapse of the Mainland empire and realm, very nearly succeeded, and was finally defeated only after a number of years. That, and a subsequent plundering raid in strength by men the *Atarlum* chronicles called corsairs, caused the Islanders to begin fortifying their towns, and especially Drin b'Afon, a site of great natural strength, made apparently impregnable through craft. It easily withstood an assault about the year 2000, and endured a siege of more than a year when invaders fleeing from the growing strength of the Mainland Gabhanil were in alliance with rebellious elements on the Island (this was during the Years of Rival Patriarchs, a secret history contained in books no one who had not taken all the Oaths was allowed to see). The Island had other fortified cities, both its main ports, the southern city of Kred Taknai, the True *Mankh'* itself; only Drin b'Afon could truly boast it had never fallen to an enemy.

"We are not going in the front gate."

A stare. "We have to cross the Coastal Hills without being seen. Then there is a full day's march at the least, in open country, before we can see the Summer Palace planted on its rock. There may be a way, but we have to get there."

Galt cleared his throat and broke in to insist apologetically there must be a way. "You can make a cave safe, but not a whole city. Too large. Our handful can't take this 'Fon, but a few of us may get in, and out again."

From below there was a snarl. "Goat of the Tezh', watch where you're going." Sarnak, bringing up coils of rope from the boat, had accidentally been sent sprawling by another man, unsighted by the pile of bedrolls he was carrying. It was young Truni.

So did Sarnak, and he became sourer. "Can't understand a plain order, all you can think of is saving your own stinking skin. No good as a lookout, but you knew what to grab when we thought we were foundering, didn't you?"

"I did not understand what was wanted when I was lookout." Truni's tone was far less apologetic than the words. "When the boat started leaping — "

"Argue with me? I should have thrown you in the Arnan, it might have washed away that goat-stink. You give signals, it has to be in time — "

"I made the signals as soon as I could see — "

"Argue!" This was pure snarl. Sarnak's hand went to his side, and steel flashed. Dolvid, barefoot, Rodlakh, boots gaping, both started in that direction. Galt was quicker. The small officer ducked between the two adversaries, straightened, and made Sarnak's knife roll into his opened palm. That was how it looked, a magic trick. A fast catch at the tall man's wrist, a dipping turn with the knife plopping into Galt's left hand, while Sarnak, released, took a backward step, letting out a percussive yelp of pain. He and Galt locked eyes, till Sarnak's gaze faltered. Reversing the knife in his hand, Galt gave it back to its owner, putting his hands lightly on his hips, and coolly turning his back on knife and knifeman, as Sarnak's fingers fondled the haft.

"When an officer makes a charge," Galt told Truni, "you do not argue."

"Half-squadron, I was — "

"You do not argue. If you think it unjust, you can ask to speak to the highest officer, to me, and I can call you both together and talk. Isn't that how it always is?"

A sulky pause, then Truni allowed, "Yes, Half-squadron."

Now Rodlakh took part, saying danger often made for short tempers, just when comradeship was most needed. Certainly, Truni had not meant to knock down Sarnak, but Galt might have him ask pardon.

Galt nodded, but Truni did not move, lips sullen. Sarnak was making a new career out of sheathing his knife.

To him Rodlakh spoke direct. "You had most of the responsibility in bringing us to shore, and that was well done." The man stirred. "But in the Army of the West there is no talk of lesser and greater races. You will ask Truni's pardon for your name-calling."

"*Valrabh'*, I never meant — " It stuck in Sarnak's stringy throat, but he stepped up to the young slinger. "I've been frayed with worries. I ask your pardon — Truni, is it?"

The large eyes lighted. "I ask yours for my clumsiness, sir."

"Granted, granted. This quayside would be none the worse for some smoothing."

"Hands," Galt said, grabbing the right of each man, and clapping them together. Truni gave his shy smile, Sarnak the grin that threatened to split off his lower face. All the others, watching tensely, began nodding and smiling. Rodlakh's breath escaped slowly with relief.

"All my fault," as everyone returned to a task. "I should not have taxed Sarnak with questions about Aëlu's kidnappers, and I should have been quicker to praise his navigation — Sebhal would have been punching him in the ribs, calling him a fucking wonder, the moment we struck shore. This name-calling lays up troubles for a fight, when we all need each other."

"Just the same, *Valrabh'*," finding pomposity unavoidable here, "may a *bôdhrai* say you did well?" Rodlakh's authority had been confirmed, and the cost might have been far higher.

At the *Mankh'* all mapmaking began with the Island, and Dolvid knew the shape of the land better than many places he had actually been. He told Rodlakh they must be well south of Pavani, and probably north of a village called Daëni Tâl, where the road from Drin b'Afon reached the coast. The village was on a wide bay, Klam Nampai.

"*Nampai?*"   Rodlakh was pleased.   The word meant `contentment,' and he was taking it for an omen.

With Galt who could read ground Dolvid went forward for a look, while the others made a meal and did what they could, short of lighting a fire, to hurry drying of clothes and equipment. Going up the cliff and the stony end of the long spur beyond, Dolvid found Galt his match for rock-scrambling; the man had a quick eye and made his choices assuredly. No one would call Galt graceful, but economy is a kind of grace, and so is competence that knows itself; Galt was effective.

Needing an overview they went to the top of the ridge, and crouching on the skyline saw their landing-spot was indeed within the broad sweep of a bay that could only be Klam Nampai. Not far south, beyond the headland with Rodlakh's watchtower, there was a huddle of stone houses perched along the cliff; Daëni Tâl. They could clearly make out the saddle in the coastal hills, through which the road must pass. This side of the village the road, some way back from cliff-edge, came winding down towards them. Nothing was moving there.

Galt asked what the land would be beyond the smooth hills, and Dolvid told him; the central plain of Kamanta, higher ground than here, but mainly flat.

"A high plain. Another Landegh, then."

"Not as dry, or as rocky. South of the road farming soon begins. Here, there should be tall grass." Kamanta-grass! old dreams coming back to life; Kamanta-grass, imagined since childhood, found nowhere else except this central plateau. The poet Bronal, when he loved a woman of Kamanta, called the plain in summer `shadow-green sea where my hopes are sailing.' More to the present point was that head-high grass would hide them.

Pointing out a pass through the hills higher than the saddle of the road, and perhaps two or three miles northward of that, Galt sketched out a route there that might keep them largely under cover. The man, though he did not boast, was quite aware of his talent, here unlikely to be challenged.

His troops, too, were wonderfully trained, as was seen when they moved silently from close-order double rows to the wide-spaced single file used for crossing the coastal road in its shallow cutting. Each man exactly imitated the man ahead, and this must be taught everywhere in the Army of the West, since Sarnak and his two helpers, not a normal part of Galt's company, did the same, and Dolvid, after Rodlakh, followed as well as he could. Though often in sight of the village as they climbed a hillside mainly bare, they reached the chosen pass apparently unseen, certainly unchallenged. Quite possibly Galt's bowmen could defeat any forces in the immediate region, but they needed secrecy, not a victory that, alerting defenders, would doom them to defeat before Drin b'Afon.

This part might be the worst risk, as they moved up from the poor shelter of sparse scrub. The watchtower, now below their level, had dark window-slots on this landward side, but they trusted its job was to watch seaward. Fifty sideslipping steps around a bulge in the hillside, and Galt, leading, broke into a trot, heading diagonally down into the windgap, better chosen than they had realized. With these dull hills it was hard to judge distances, but they discovered what from below was a mere dent in the crest was really where opposing hillsides overlapped, making a wider and lower pass. They all jogged down, sweeping rightward on the skirts of the answering slope. They were entering the plain with its subtly varied ripplings of the great grass, dun grey now, stretching to the huge massif where Karg' Kamanta rose, 'brave island in the sea no keel divides.' The lower juts and bastions of the Mountain were shadowed in blue, and the symmetrical summit, dazzlingly clad in snow and ice, rose high beyond eye's belief. The base was lost in tumbled brown foothills, browner and tamer as they came down to meet the plain. There somewhere would be Drin b'Afon.

Leftward, the line of road could be discerned, but beyond that the patterning of farmlands was surmise rather than a sight. All this was one quick, marvelling glimpse, before they dived into the sea of grass.

From above the grass appeared a continuous carpet of growth, but in fact it grew in close-spaced, many-stemmed bundles. New silvery-green shoots were pushing up, some knee-high, among the drier old stalks, thick as a man's wrist at the base. A whispering rasp and rattle sounded constantly, as grasses stirred in the breeze; feathery tops where seed had been swayed softly, higher than the heads of Rodlakh or Sarnak, their tallest. Cover was complete.

They closed back into double file as soon as they were deep enough into the grassland. The ground was ridged, and where grasstops parted there was usually a view to Karg' Kamanta. Galt was told they must aim somewhat south of the mountain's base, but not so far southward they ran into the road.

"Will there be farms? Fences?"

"North of the road is all Patriarch's land, and kept open for the hunting."

Rodlakh said, "Tovakh has hunted here often, and Vinilat of Dramal. They ride down boar here — jackal, for those who are not proud, perhaps a leopard."

Galt was satisfied none of those animals would trouble a good-sized party on the march. He asked about snakes, but Dolvid did not know. With bow-hunters it was the best country for the Kamanta pheasant, a pale-feathered, pale-fleshed variety, occasional visitor to the Mainland, and very good eating, saved for feasts.

Galt wanted to say something, checked himself, and had to be persuaded into what he was obviously afraid might be indiscreet. "It's this, masters. What do lords who can put aside lands for their hunting want with our little plots in the West? Land here to share among a hundred families for a thousand years. *Valrabh'*, no one of the Frontier begrudges the lords their herds and pastures, their rough-hunting — not till they start to covet our barley-patches as well. I am speaking too plain."

"Not so. When I am back in the Colony, when we are at Drin Navuna, I mean to repeat Sebhal's pledge to the men of the West. He said as long as he could hold a weapon, no one was going to take away your title to lands you have fought for." Rodlakh's eyes were tear-bright again.

"This," Dolvid said, "seems to be the only road back to Drin Navuna." Taking the hint, formation tight, Galt moved out.

Cautiously Dolvid and Galt edged their way to the tree-capped crown of a small knoll, last islet in the rustling sea. The sun was sliding down near heights ahead.

Through this white day they had made good going, not checked by small streams in sudden fissures, finding ways past other barriers of rock, and crevices concealed by the bland sway of the grasstops. Once, under the perpetual chafe, they heard distantly the roll of horses' hoofs, and the company halted, crouched, while the drumming loudened. But it stayed some way off, and soon began to fade; the march resumed, men uncocking bows never breaking stride.

With all their care they put up a few birds, and there had been brief sight of the bristly hindquarters of a wild pig that vanished in a flicker, a fat fish retreating in seaweeds. They crossed faint, uncertain paths; a dilapidated shack of brush and woven grass turned out to have been a blind for bowmen put up in a hunting-season long past, now occupied by birds, and one sleepy-eyed shape that yawned in the dim and resolved into a vixen before slipping away through a gap in the side wall.

A cloudless day, with wind eddying tamely out of the southeast, though once or twice the coming of a stronger gust was an old excitement (a small boy, crouched for concealment in the Gardens, on an early spring day) with the gradually growing rush and roar of the grasses. The air was dry; rough, whitened patches came out on breeches and outshirts, their packs. When they stopped for food Galt moved from man to man, examining boots and weapons, discussing the condition of bowstrings. Pieces of fatty skin from the deer killed at Tan

Lughsai were used for rubbing leather and rawhide, and trimming of arrow-flights was another constant activity.

Past midday the ground had begun gradually to rise again, with another line of bare brown hills rising to block the view to Karg' Kamanta. Pebbled open spaces began appearing, bare ribs, small knots of wind-tormented trees. From where they were perched could be seen how the Kamanta-grass thinned to pale streaks, advancing along the gullies, failing completely where the brown ridge climbed; the slopes were held only by scattered bushes and scrub, and the crest far above appeared naked, with squat watchtowers breaking the skyline at intervals, surely the outer defenses of Drin b'Afon.

Leftward the ridge soon petered out, merging into rolling downslopes. There was a plain windgap, improved by working, with the road ascending on a smoothed slope like a ramp. Dolvid remembered being taught the road here passed through a small, tough outer fortress built from hillside to hillside.

He explained to Galt what he expected on the farther side of the ridge; Lunu ba g'Asalladhi, Valley of the Patriarch. A long, cold lake curving about the eastern flank of the city, road crossing at its foot where a stream issued, Kematakhi, known for its seven rapids. At the head of the lake the inflow was Shuf'Oëladh, the Stream of Being, a torrent in the narrow slash of a stony gorge.

Galt shook his head. "But you've never been here?"

"If I had, I might have some ideas about getting into the city."

Plainly they needed a longer and more daring reconnaissance. Meanwhile Galt had spotted, over to the eastward, a gully Dolvid's eyes, assuming tops of small trees to be a clump of bushes, would have missed. Improbable they would find a safe haven any farther forward, and they decided to make at least a provisional camp.

The steep-edged dell was larger than it looked from above, sown with slender trees, clustered thicker near the middle, where a dark pool was apparently fed from beneath. Despite care, the descending column caused an irruption of startled birds, and Galt let out a quiet imprecation, mindful of watchtowers above. He cheered up when he saw a well-trodden trail leading to water's edge, and how branches arched low over its course; "Pig-run." Watchers would be used to the birds being disturbed by animals coming to drink.

This made a good place, Rodlakh concurred, to wait for darkness.

"You and Galt have a plan?"

"So far, only not to cross that ridge by daylight with two dozen men."

"The *Bôdhrai* and I will go forward and see how things are, *Asai*." Flattering, though it was only sense to put his map-knowledge together with Galt's craft. But he foresaw there was going to be trouble with Rodlakh, who was itching for action.

"I shall go with you this time," elaborately offhand.

"No," too quickly, then patiently explaining it would be poor policy to risk Galt and Rodlakh, the two men who could lead the company, on a single patrol; if this one failed Rodlakh could make his own attempt. Useless to leave Dolvid, who could not command troops, and Galt must go, because he had to learn the ground.

"I am not going to let others take all the risks."

"That has already been seen, *Valrabh'*."

"How long will you be?"

Galt eyed Dolvid, who said, "Give us till an hour after dark."

At the westward end of the gully the sentinel was Rongar, the same mixture of races as Galt. "Try not to shoot me or the *Bôdhrai* when we come back," Galt said cheerfully, and gave a low, warbling bird-call by which they could be recognized, no bird Dolvid could name.

The country approaching the ridge was more broken than it had appeared, at least with Galt leading the way. The sun had dipped behind the heights, and in the shadow Galt used unfamiliar ground as a good and trusted friend, going from hide to hide in swift, smooth darts. When they reached the end of what most would call plausible cover, the upslope beginning in earnest, Galt made a point of reinstructing Dolvid to imitate him exactly, adding apologetically,

"Only that I've hunted in this way before." They had to diagonally cross and recross the slope in front of one of the stubby watchtowers, and once having fixed its position Galt never let himself be tempted into looking up at it; a face in this failing light would show much more readily than their drab and grimy clothing. Wriggling on their bellies up a long, gravelly scoring across the slope took an age, but covered a great part of the distance. From there Galt went to a tuft of growth like dead iris, to the waterscooped hollow behind a rock too small to hide a rabbit. After that, elbows and belly again; Dolvid followed, not seeing much more than the soles of boots. He almost missed the moment when Galt turned with a wink and a wave up towards the tower. On his feet, but crouched over, he ran directly to the bulged bolster of rock where the tower sat. That bulge created the blindspot, well out from the tower wall, which Galt had aimed for from the start; at the point where he had made his gesture only part of the cupola roof could be seen. Dolvid scrambled quickly up that last stony slope, and leaned against rock to pant. Below, the shimmer of Kamanta-grass was gold-grey in evening light, the far line of the coastal hills an oranged brown, soft and woolly. Southward they could see the close-set squares of farmland, and a long way east there was a blur on the road that might be horsemen. A brilliant spark showed for an instant as sunlight touched a breastplate or polished helm.

On the level, the ridge's summit, there were untidy tufts of a thick broom never seen elsewhere. Growing in a fanlike form they made with the rock where the tower stood a kind of tunnel by which the reconnaisance could continue. At the far end the gold light of westering sun was startling, the ember-caverns in a long-burning wood fire, where landscapes and magic cities, cliffs and fissures, pulsed and quivered in a rich glory.

Near tunnel's end, eager for a first glimpse into the Valley of the Patriarch, which must be here, they had to pull back at the sound of tramping feet. A crunching sound, a dozen or so feet on loose pebbles, direction hard to determine. Galt jabbed downward with a thumb. Evidently a pathway for the watchtower; prone, they saw helmets pass by, tips of a dozen pikes, lastly the yellow crest of an officer from the

Adanum Plakh'. On the shifting flints of the path this small contingent made enough noise for a company or more.

"Change of watches," Galt, softly, staying drawn back from near the brink. "There'll be some going off-duty, too." Dolvid had not had a real view of the valley, and from where he was could see only sky.

Backs to rock they deduced steps up to the tower entrance, a wooden door rapped with the butt of a pike, a challenge from inside. At an upper window, perhaps, a trumpet gave a short, bright call. The door thumped open, feet again clattered on steps, passwords were exchanged. Soon the march resumed, but the path must continue on to further posts; those marching feet receded. Meanwhile, loosely paired, four men coming off duty came down the path in a slithering saunter. That way must lead back to the city; in the men's chatter Dolvid plainly caught the word *wineshop*. Dusky gold dappling his cheek, Galt licked his upper lip, and reached for his skin bottle. Mildly surprising these soldiers were permitted to make their own way back, not joining the main formation, and yet it was encouraging to assume men not of the *Adanum* enjoyed some laxity of discipline, or simply were not very well trained.

After some quiet minutes, nothing further happening, Galt and Dolvid edged forward again, squinting. Cliffs opposite loomed dark and near, a long, stark promontory thrusting clear from the lesser peaks that jostled at the knee of Karg' Kamanta, filling the northward sky, though still miles away.

Straight across was Drin b'Afon, not to be mistaken by anyone knowing any of the history and legend of the Island; the high rock of the citadel to the right, behind that the slender line of the bridge that gave the city its name, *Afonu Asalladhilu*, Bridge of Patriarchs. It curved gracefully across the chasm dividing the rock of the citadel from the main spur, sole fragile access from the north to that uppermost level where the Summer Palace was. Some surrounding hills were higher — this place must be level with the roof of the palace — but did not seem so, due to of the isolation of that rock. On the lakeward side the cliffs of the citadel fell three hundred feet straight down from wall to water, with an overhang directly beneath the walls.

Letting the gaze return leftward, the city descended in broad steps, of which the first was highest, a straight drop of some eighty feet from the court of the Summer Palace to another walled enclosure, rock face scaled only by a narrow stair mounting crosswise, overlooked by embrasures above. From there southward building spread on slopes and terraces to the valley floor, taking in wider territory than expected, but not a large city in terms of dwellings: enclosed by lower rings of wall were swathes of pasture, and perhaps some growing-land as well. These bottom courses had a disordered look, the vast web of a slovenly spider, walls, often incorporating natural rock outcroppings, following contours of the land. An army, a large one, investing Drin b'Afon, taking its defenses line by line, would be contained in spaces that kept narrowing, struck at from every side by missiles of every sort. It would require breaching four major and durable walls to deprive the city of its incorporated pastures, and no doubt there were stores of food and water in the citadel.

"Strong enough," Galt remarked.

"And beautiful." He had expected to be overawed, not simply moved. Their view from commanding heights might somewhat tame sight of the city; for a traveller crossing the stone bridge at the foot of the lake the predominant impression would be soaring strength, the towering remoteness of the citadel. From here, though the walls capping them were evidently a little mouldered and shabby, the savage chop of cliffs from bastion to lake was magnificent, stone crowning stone. The Patriarchal Palace with its many windows had nothing to rival the splendor of the New Residence at Kadon Dinul, nor the dour impressiveness of the Paowanu *Mankh'*. Neither was it mellowed and benign in the way of the Old Bronze Residence. Made of a light, hard stone, its lines were bold and simple, as if an architect long ago had made up his mind that where windows opened on the stunning sight of Karg' Kamanta, on the sweep of that valley, there was no need for an elaborate setting of worked stone.

Galt's observations were more practical; he noted yellow crests of the *Adanum Plakh'* could be discerned where pikemen walked the walls of the citadel, but in the lower levels such defenders as could be seen were in plain round helms or soft caps, their weapons various. On the uppermost level the *Adanum* had nothing to guard except the Palace. There was also a small, squat building set in isolation in the broad court, perhaps a guardhouse.

Dolvid let his eyes wander down to the lake which wrapped about the city's eastern side. In shape, an elongated kidney-bean with a distinct narrowing to a waist, somewhere about the middle. This narrowest part was spanned by a trestle-bridge, and leaning forward Dolvid could just see the near end, at the bottom of the steep slope beneath where he and Galt squatted. As he watched, four men, obviously the ones from this watchtower, emerged from the farther end of the covered bridge, marching in step and with less languor as they approached the city. The track went curving left past a great dome of rock, to reach a small postern-gate in the lower levels.

"The bridge is part of it," Galt, following his eyes. "The small wooden one there."

It must be, but the path beyond went to a strong gate, and on the other side of that, most likely a barracks. If, using the trestle, they could somehow enter the lower levels of the city, there would yet be wall after wall to pass, till they came to the court beneath the sheer front to the bastion rock. From there the only way was that narrow, easily defended stair.

Something in that progress was not quite sense, but before Dolvid could hunt through it for what caused that vague nag of unreason, his attention was held by the squat building in the Palace forecourt. He noticed there were guards posted at its doorway, two pikes.

Galt was again frowning over the strength of the fortress. "Ten thousand, with six months to spend... "

"Why not a hundred thousand, and ten years?"

"That many could not be fed. Still, *Bôdhrai*, if a big army kept knocking at the front gate, and picked men, meantime, went up into the heights behind, they might take the thin bridge up there."

"Defended with massed bows."

"And in the end, it could be broken. Oh, it's a strong nut. What's that other bridge?" He indicated where, farther up the cliffs behind the city, another arched line leapt across the chasm, connecting to the roof of the Summer Palace.

"Aqueduct," Dolvid guessed, "but closely watched also, if it would take the weight of men."

Though he was squinting against the sun, a shadow advancing from the hills behind fell across the topmost court, and he asked what Galt made of the small, lonely square building. Galt agreed it must be a guardhouse, but before they could discuss the two meanings of that word, a trumpet sounded, a falling sequence of three notes. A guard-post down in the city echoed it, and then others in the valley and up on surrounding heights, candles passing flame, one to another. Brave and sad it swirled in purpling ravines, spiralling at last to silence in shadows suddenly chilly. Up on the citadel rock guards were being changed, and there was a flurry of activity by the small guardhouse. Dolvid stared till his eyes watered, trying to read what he saw.

"Men," Galt said, "brought something and took something away. Food? and taking away plates and leavings of a noon-meal?" It might well be for prisoners, or a prisoner and the guards there.

"Why would the *Mankh'*-father be so unkind, if it is Lady Aëlu? Any captive could be kept safe in the Palace."

"If the Patriarch," working it out, "Remains on the Mainland, the men of the *Adanum* might be fearful of bringing a prisoner into the Summer Palace. It is *ga-dazhu*, of course, more so while He is away."

"I don't know a thing about that."

He explained; not so different from stone-gods of the Landegh, who said some ground must not be walked on. "Here, rites have to be performed before one can enter."

"Like getting married."

"If you will." Dolvid was slow to see the witticism as intended, and that only made Galt's grin broader.

"But are these *Adanum* men not purified? I saw one go in the Palace just now. And they would shut the Lady Aëlu up like an animal?" Galt might well be anticipating Rodlakh.

Feeling safe where they were they had a drink of water and a few bites of food. Continuing to learn what he could of the terrain, Dolvid began to form a plan of desperation, but devoutly hoped Galt might magically invent a saner way.

"Well," the soldier said. "No use going north to find a way across the stream — Owad, you called it? If we could climb up behind the citadel, we would never take the bridge by storm. If we could, they would break it."

"We don't want that. It might be our only way home."

Galt gave a slow nod, as if Dolvid had been playing a cat-and-mouse game. "The *Bôdhrai* has a plan."

"The ghost of one."

Both more and less, worked out in some detail, but all the more impossible for that. He asked Galt whether, by night, the guarded trestle-bridge could be taken, without raising a general alarm. Galt was sure so, if lakeside could be reached, avoiding detection. "In such places, with watchtowers to one side and city walls to the other, never an enemy seen, guards must get bored and careless. Half a dozen good men could take the bridge quietly."

Assuming the plan from there was to break into the lower city, he mentioned diffidently that while Dolvid, perhaps the *Valrabh'*, might pass for Islanders, none of the soldiers could.

"We could not risk so many challenges. We have to go up the cliffs."

Not straight up, and not entirely by darkness, he answered Galt's worried question. A conceivable route climbed beside the city, after many suppositions, reaching the face beneath the citadel where the cliffs receded in a deep bay, before swinging back at midpoint of the courtyard. Some of this inlet was out of sight, but where the face came in view again there was a diagonal fault, which might be continuous in the section they could not see. Over two hundred feet, best estimate, above the base of the cliff, but lower than the bulged overhang.

"If we could be beneath the citadel by the end of night, we could wait for some light, and then our best climbers carrying coils of rope might be able to get to the base of the city walls, where it looks as if there is a small level bit to stand on."

"I see. A man could set himself there and let down his rope for others. But they would be seen climbing."

"If timed with first light, they could only be seen from over here, and the citadel could not be warned in time — we would be across the walls before the guard suspected anything." He hoped he was not being influenced excessively by memories of the Pass of Perus, fourteen years ago, when a daring rush over walls had overwhelmed surprised defenders.

He was a disappointment to Galt. The man had expected more cunning and less pure physical risk.

"Then that's what we do," at last.

"The *Valrabh'* will have to rule." There was a profound half-hope the *Valrabh'* would call it what it was, lunacy.

"So few men in the citadel," Rodlakh pondered. "You would expect them to fill it with troops. What if she is not there?"

"We shall have made a long climb for nothing." But the defenders must be certain the place was impregnable, and either of the obvious ways in, bridge and narrow stair, could be held by a couple of dozen against hundreds. Conceivably, the Patriarch wanted only those He trusted close to Aëlu — but when Dolvid said that, Rodlakh misunderstood, saying with pompous dignity Aëlu was not one who would give herself to an enemy to save herself from harm.

"No," ignoring the implied slight to Âna. (Keeping to her plan, by now she was back in Kadon Dinul. She had never said how she would explain her absence.) "I would be less anxious if she were."

"Her past is never forgotten. She was *nôd'yanu* for one year, and since then she has been married and faithful to one man for fifteen. I had heard you *Lekh'Owanil* saw no dishonor in serving at a *margú*? But when it comes to Aëlu — " Sensing he had offended Dolvid, Rodlakh broke off.

"As a spokesman those called *Lekh'Owanil* would hardly acknowledge," ice-keen with anger. "Let me say there is no dishonor in *nôd'yanum*. Men are often stronger than women, men make threats with weapons, dishonor is a word men use, but the injuries of rape resisted are real."

In the quiet, Galt cleared his throat. Dolvid was still trembling, but there was room for wonder over a man this late in the world's life who yearned for a married woman and boasted how faithful she had always been to her husband.

"This morning I reprimanded Sarnak for bringing up race; now I am guilty. Leaders should — oh, that is no use — " the voice lost its distant, conventional tone. "I said stupid things to Âna, too, about wanting her as an advisor. What I want is your friendship, and to deserve it. In time I hope to be wiser."

"Everyone hopes that — " not meaning the ambiguity, but letting it stand. "I hope my heat will be forgiven, *Valrabh*'"

A mock-shiver. "Your heat I do not know, but your cold could give chills to a *jinzai*. Have you done this sort of climb before?"

"Years ago, not so hard, in good light and at my leisure."

"For sport," Galt said. "In the West, we climb sometimes, but never when we could go around."

"You are a soldier. If a bookman does not do more than he has to, he becomes a fat bookman with short breath and piles."

"No mockery was meant, sir. Truni comes down to Kamsilat with some time of his own, and he might take a boat on the Navu, for pleasure. Sarnak would ride a horse for sport, and call Truni's boat work. Not what makes us sweat much or less, but whether or not we have to do it, that's how work is different from play."

"But can this be done?" Rodlakh meant, the whole plan. Dolvid, trying to hold off the old feeling, half fear, half joyous excitement, soberly went through all ifs; if the full force could be taken past the watchtower undetected, if the trestle could be taken, if the climb could be made, a long and tiring business, with a fight at the end —

"For the fight," Galt, solemnly, "blood rises. The men will be ready for some killing, and no one will feel any weariness."

"You will see to it," Rodlakh said, "everyone has some sleep before then?" Trying to work out how long it all would take, they had decided on an hour past midnight for their start. His plan, as plans do, was getting a life of its own. If only someone would shout *no*; it was a madman's idea. He did not want responsibility for two dozen lives.

"Everyone, if you sleep, *Valrabh'*, and the *Bôdhrai*."

So, quietly, it was all settled; Galt went off to instruct the watch. Dolvid said, "Galt and I with twenty men could try this. Then, if we fail, you could make your way to the western shore, steal a boat, and return from Kamsilat with a stronger force." The last part was not among his better inspirations, and Rodlakh gave a weary laugh.

"My friend, once the Island is alerted all the Army of the West might not be enough to rescue Aëlu; one covert attempt is all we can have. Great Odi, we have to be honest gamblers — you are risking it all on one draw, and now you want to take out enough of your stake to make a fool of you if you lose."

"I was thinking about the realm. Preference — "

"I am not needed — " sounding sincere. The Army of the West, he said, had its officers, soldiers who led their men against *jinzal*; Saidhan was there for their emblem of resistance.

"Besides, it is unfair," lightening the mood. "You say not a word about stepping aside yourself. You have every right; a *bôdhrai* is not required to go up mountainsides and into battles. But I am not enough of an idiot to tell you you cannot go. Galt, we know — " the man was back from his rounds — "Galt would go over to *g'Asalladh'* if we told him to stay behind. But you want to romp off and make a new epic, while I sit here and wait, like Kukkuk's Devil-Bride." That reference delighted Galt; in the West they loved the Odi Kukkuk tales, especially the bawdy ones.

Dolvid had not expected any other answer. All the same he could feel a half-wish someone would be enough of an idiot to try telling him not to go.

The Assault

Above the hills a dense bank of black cloud, silver-edged, had been building, and there the moon vanished early. When Galt led the silent file of men out of the gully night was at its blackest, dawn hours away. Yet still overbright; in the doings of the past week Dolvid might have begun growing night eyes, huge, round and yellow. The moon's abdication left the sky crowded with points of light and a tenuous frosting, while to the south shooting-stars arched down. The earth itself might be breathing out a faint radiance, gone when confronted direct.

Two dozen fully-armed men moving with their packs and gear across uneven, pebble-strewn ground made less noise than a night breeze. Blades were muffled, archers also winding strips of cloth among their loose arrows. The sound of careful feet was practically drowned out by soft breathing, creak of a knee-joint, rustle of clothing.

Dull yellow light from the watchtower kept bobbing into view; once Dolvid imagined he could pick out the shape of a head and shoulders at an upper window-hole. Galt had recommended they begin with a swift attack to negate this outpost, but Rodlakh stood firm; the risks were too great. Though it might be possible, as Galt urged, to silence everyone there before an alarm was given, there was no knowing whether at intervals all the watchtowers made signals to the city to say "all is well;" silence from this post might itself be an alarm. It went against Galt's grain to leave live enemies behind, but he agreed they could never find and assail all the posts along the ridge. This would not in any event be their line of retreat.

Galt went as if he had known the terrain all his life, and watchtower notwithstanding, ground already covered, not merely surveyed, was bound to be the easiest part; night cloaked them enough so they could go at the crouch, instead of on knees-and-elbows or bellies. When Galt, Rodlakh next to him, straightened, the tower lights were gone, and they hastened up the steep slope to assemble men at the base of the big rock. Teeth, whites of eyes came out of the gloom, and when everyone was there Dolvid shouldered his way to Galt, and with him found the start of their leafy tunnel. By night the light at the end was a blue-white radiance enough to define the curving stems of the tough broom.

Now, Drin b'Afon was a surpassing sight, lower levels in a well of ink, a skein of scattered lights, watchfires at gates, lanterns in the towers. Above, the use of *ga-ôthu*, here on the Island of its origin, was prodigious; hundreds of globes to trace cornices and windows of the Summer Palace, curve of its arched entrance, many more to turn the Bridge of Patriarchs into spiders' strands on a dewy morning, draped with gems of light. The entire length of the citadel battlements gleamed cool with *ôdul*; reflections burned deep in the polished lake, but the city floated on night, raised on a cloud of darkness.

"Pretty," Galt admired. "Too pretty for a war-camp. They blind themselves, and see nothing. Wait a quarter-hour after we go down the path."

His five picked men behind, Galt lowered himself over the edge, down to the sloped surface of the path. He carried a blanket outside his pack, and its use was now seen; after his feet came down with a slight crunch he spread the blanket to muffle the sharp flints. A flicker of shadow against lights of the city, he moved across to the outer rim of the path, where loose stones gave way to earth and solid rock. Going carefully, not dawdling, Galt vanished down the path, and five crouching shadows followed. If they failed in this attempt to take the trestle undetected, Rodlakh's notion was the full force should go forward and storm it, go on as far as luck and prowess would take them; once an alarm was given nothing could be gained by retreat, since they would soon be hunted down among the long grasses.

Hard to be patient; preserving night-vision, Dolvid tried to ignore the city, a heart-stabbing sight, the Palace floating gauze. Lower, where black shadows were soft, lesser lights picked out a segment of carved stone arch, a fretted casement, swelling round of a tower, rising.

Rodlakh touched a wrist. "How can men who can prize this beauty —
" The soft speech was full of pain, and there was no need for a
conclusion, or expectation of an answer.   Silence lapped back
soothingly.

Judging at last the agreed time had elapsed, Dolvid alerted
Rodlakh, and with a thumping heart slipped over the edge onto the
spread blanket. Cushioned, the crunch sounded loud to him. From
here he could see the watchtower, its entranceway at the top of a short
curve of stone steps, door recessed out of his view. Looking up where
he had just dropped from, the dark was absolute, no embankment, no
face above, nothing but dense black, till he made out what could be a
spark of reflection in Rodlakh's eye. Waving at nothing, he gestured,
and in a moment the *Valrabh'* was next to him.

"You'll lead them?" He wanted to count the men down onto
the path, and obscurely thought he should be here in case there was
trouble with the watchtower. Rodlakh nodded, and imitating Galt
stepped to the quieter outside edge of the track.

Every arrival out of blackness a fresh surprise the men
descended steadily, without question imitating the man ahead. Good
troops; some grinned — he could see the gleam of teeth — and he
found himself patting shoulders, breathing words of encouragement.

The twentieth had an accident, something causing him to half-
stumble, so he landed awkwardly, knee and elbow. A pouch of pebbles
— he must be one of the slingers, then — jerked loose from his belt, and
went rolling a short way down the path. The noise was immense.

The man, or boy — probably Truni — straightened slowly,
while all others froze. A taut wait, then from above, muffled sound of
a voice, words unclear, tone of frowning enquiry unmistakable. The
reply was even more indistinct. Brief quiet brought hope, till there was
a sound foreheard in his mind's ear and feared, scrape of bolts drawn
back, squeak and rattle of a latch.

The door came open with a bang. No longer masked, voices
sounded, and boots moved out doubtfully. Not fifteen paces from
where Dolvid and the young slinger were, yellow lantern-light struck
the path. Two men appeared on the bend of the steps, the first with the

lantern in his left hand, bared sword in the right. The other had a longbow, slack, though with an arrow fitted. Hesitantly, the two came most of the way down the steps. They looked up the hill, then straight down at the men on the path.

"Who's there?" the man with the lantern called, caught between fear and fear of seeming ridiculous.

"A rabbit, I tell you." The bowman's Island accent was thick, his eyes full on Dolvid.

"No rabbits up here."

"Whatever you've got up here, then. Jackal, that dog thing." A voice from inside the tower called something, and the man with the lantern turned to say, "Aye, there has. Loathe the mangy things, we all do."

"Cursed death-eaters," the bowman shuddered.

It was numbing; they were starkly, lavishly visible; the gleam of hands, twitching for weapons, while the scuffed and salty toes of boots were beacons. It was easy to see the eyes of Truni, glisten of hilts on his hunting-knife. If he turned Dolvid knew he would plainly discern the shapes of several of the men farther down the pathway.

"Getting chilly," the bowman said. Talking about a late spring, the two went back up the steps.

Dolvid almost bounded after them. It was a trick so they could slam the door and give the alarm. These two could surely be killed; they would turn to meet him, giving the Frontier bows clear shots. Equally, unless those inside the tower were slow, they could bar their door and sound the signal trumpet before an entry could be forced, and then the city would be wakeful and waiting.

The door thumped shut, bolts scraped home, and no alarm came. Dolvid made himself accept that the two men had not seen him or the others. With his back to the city he had been staring into perfect dark for minutes, but coming from the lantern-lighted interior, struck full by the gleaming city, lamp throwing as much light in their own eyes as anywhere, the men had no background against which to see the raiders; *they blind themselves and see nothing*, Galt had said. Yet it was hard to give up the conviction visible is visible.

He had clenched his fists tight enough to drive fingernails into his thumb-pads. Trembling under control, he gave a quick tap to Truni's elbow, waving him on. Deft now, the slinger stooped for his pouch, and glided to the edge. Next man, and the last, was Sarnak, readily told by his lank height. "Too near," he muttered, and moved on.

Over-early for relief, and there were too many dangers ahead. They went soberly down the steep path, which with several turns twice crossed the full face of the slope, ending in a dozen uneven stone steps. Beside the lake, the way wider here, Rodlakh had held the men, well back from where they might be seen in light reflected off the water. The city loomed high across the lake, yellow slits showing in black towers.

Rodlakh was squatting at the head of the men, perhaps sixty paces from where the trestle-bridge spilled a patch of lantern-light from its entrance. Against the far wall inside was the shadow of a helmed head, and nothing was moving.

"Can Galt have missed his way?" Rodlakh began, having found Dolvid. Just then the guard leaned out, shorter-legged than any Islander, Galt. He beckoned urgently, then vanished again.

Skirting the puddle of light the raiders filed onto the planking of the bridge. In reply to Rodlakh's question about the original guards, Galt jabbed his thumb at the waters flowing black, smooth and powerful in the space between walk and sidewall. Sharp eyes might have noticed two standing as guards at the far end were in growing puddles of water; they must be chilled to the bone from their swim. Later Dolvid learned these men, Noldar and another, had lowered themselves into the current above the bridge, and drifted silently down till they could grasp pilings of the trestle.

Here in mid-bridge he tasted a first feeble sip of hope; lake and trestle had haunted his brief sleep, but Galt's efficiency had made this initial hurdle absurdly unworthy of dread.

Past the bridge the path swung left, and Dolvid, leading, went right, up the rounded rock, part of the bulge nipping the waist of the long lake. A quick, straining spurt brought him to the mound under city walls, ascending as they fell back from lakeside. Going hard he climbed crosswise to bring the raiders as soon as possible close under the walls. Away to his right he imagined there might be a feeble sign of lightening sky. Surely not yet, but dawn would not wait for their climb.

From the opposing heights there had not looked to be so much room between lake and city, and down to the right the lake had shadowed their path, wrapping close at the base of the mound. In gloom leftward pricks of light were here and there, not as many as expected; walls cutting off most that could be seen from above. No sentinels were in sight; unless the raiders were careless the earliest likely alert for the city would be the unguarded bridge. By now Galt and his picked men had joined the end of the line.

Sweating, he paused. He must not drive the pace; fatigue could be quite literally fatal when real climbing began. He had been following a slight levelling of the side-to-side slope, which had almost merged into contours of the incline; he stood with one bent knee, right hip thrust out, left hand resting on left thigh. He was seized by a dreadful conviction that since his survey of the route everything had changed; nothing confirmed what was observed and surmised. Just ahead, the hillside was interrupted by a deep, black gash.

No ground, he reminded himself, controlling panic, is ever what it seems from a distance. Rodlakh, just behind him, was breathing with measured control. High above, a radiance against the sky might or might not show where the Summer Palace was.

Urgency came back. He went forward to the edge of blackness, and threw a leg over. Deep down there was the gleam of water, and he guessed this must be outflow for one of many streams rising within the city's perimeter, one more reason it could withstand endless siege. Left, at the end of the cleft were the walls, rising hugely high, resting on rock that must be the roof to a natural tunnel. Briefly tempting as a way in, but there was sure to be a grille blocking the way, and if that could be passed the old objection held; entering the lower levels was useless. The climb was a nightmare to come, but its logic was that while the approach from the city gave the citadel line after line of walls, on the lakeward side there was only one. One wall, a sheer three hundred feet high.

After a few nervous, shuffling steps, Dolvid grudgingly surrendered some hard-won altitude, leaping down onto the tunnel roof he knew must be there, a bad moment, trusting what his mind, not his eyes, told him. Across the cleft he hurried on, stumbling a little, certain there was a lightening away to the east. Overhead star-pricked black was melting to profound blue. Glancing back he could see shapes of the men, and also something to make him hug himself. They had already passed beyond a line of defense, a short, crenellated wall, culverted for the stream, that closed the mouth of the cleft.

He headed up again, making for where the main wall followed the backbend of the cliff, start of the wide uneven curve of bay. This was a tough hillside, bare and broken, but still only hard walking; real climbing would begin when the corner was rounded. From there should be a view to the citadel high above.

The corner he was coming to was set with a turret. Thirty feet up he could see a figure in lantern-light, probably looking out and wishing for dawn and his relief. Under the overhang of the turret he was only a handsbreadth from where the city walls were welded to natural rock. A stir came from the city, a muffled rustling now and again broken by harder sounds, as if Drin b'Afon was a drunken ogre, sleeping restlessly. Sharp and near a shrill whinny was answered by snorts and flutters, hoofs testing paved ground.

Luck held, men flattening one by one up against the rock beneath the walls. In this position there was small chance of being seen before the final climb was under way.

At the turn the hillside ceased to exist; there was nothing. Dolvid had his glimpse of the Summer Palace or its top course, hovering dizzily over greyed absence, a pit with no bottom. Cautiously edging farther, he straddled the corner, one foot resting on space, while he did what he could to examine the face. Where wall and cliff came together was a secure handhold, and by inching up a little he could grasp the ledge. Below, the face was not quite vertical, and sidling feet could find projections. The other side of this stretch was next to where the front of the citadel bastion was, and there would be a second sharp turn into the corner invisible from across the lake, the place he hoped to strike the start of the main diagonal fault.

Breath hard to come by, heart surging right under his chin, he edged back to give Rodlakh the news. "Room in this section for all of us, with at least secure handholds."

He seemed to understand, and grunted assent. The face, dimly seen, surprised Dolvid; there was anxiety, but also excitement, eyes lively. He might be smiling slightly.

"This turn needs care. Reach for a firm handhold, and feel out with your right foot. Have that passed back."

"Very good."

But after that one blind commitment it was not as bad; the rock's natural formation had horizontal ribs so toes were never without a purchase; his body pressed to the rock-face he could have stayed with no handhold, and wind was negligible. His coil of rope interfered, but though his sidling step was deliberate, he could force a belief there was no real danger.

Next was a difficult patch, where wall met upsoaring rock of the citadel bastion, which bulged out to make a cramped little corner. Becoming tenser, Rodlakh sighed, "Can this be done?" Looking back it could be seen the turn must be giving trouble, lumpy shapes wavering as they came into view. On the face some moved more surely than others; that all were still following was a triumph in itself.

Yet night was being eaten away faster than he had hoped, and light was coming steadily. He must not be greedy beyond what absolute need demanded: if the fault was as well-defined as it had looked, good visibility would be needed only for the very last, and that might be unclimbable in any light.

About ten feet over his head the corner he was hemmed in dipped back, making a sloped step to bevel the turn. Every instinct and all his experience told him that would be the spot for surveying the main cliff, and perhaps for launching the assault on it. To his left the last stones of the city wall were pitted and pocked; not waiting any longer Dolvid went up, very deliberately placing hand, foot, hand, and making sure Rodlakh saw each move.

No longer any need to lean back and crane to see the recessed part of the cliff; with joy he recognized exactly the fault they had been aiming for, like finding a miraculous short-cut. Not far from here, the fault slotted back into the cliff to become a low notch where a man might go on hands and knees, perhaps a crouched walk. Higher, it might narrow to a foothold.

Hands and knees, he worked up quickly. Three sidles and he was where rock was substantial under his feet. His knees were trembling only a little as he went on, turning to bend low, going up a steady slope. Where half-roof above tapered into an uneven overhang that threatened to nudge him into space, he stopped again, waiting both for a little more light and for those who followed to close up. Room, he hoped, for all to be safe in the notch of the fault; it would not do to leave anyone on that awkward bevel, nor the awkward climb to it.

To Rodlakh he said, "I should be told when last man is up and past the turn." Rodlakh started the message on its journey back. No one yet had fallen or stuck, and if this next bad part could be managed the final stage would be up to the best half-dozen climbers. If they failed the raiders would be so much lichen there on the cliff, waiting for sunlight to display them fully. Their enemies above would hardly need to waste arrows or dropped missiles; some combination of hunger and fatigue would take them all in the end. Probably you would fall asleep, fall, truly! and wake up already doomed. He was not going to glance downward to his right, knowing what was there: space, and the gleam of the lake, two hundred feet straight down.

"What are we waiting for?"

"The last man. Look — " He sketched out how, as the cliff returned from the deepest part of its bay, their ledge continued, broadened perhaps, under where bulged overhang hid everything above except sky. But the ledge was a good stretch higher than their present level. "This is going to be a nasty part."

"What has it been?"

"Practice — " using a rounded edge to help keep his leg-muscles loose, rocking heel-and-toe, stretching away the start of cramps. Anxieties about that final climb were beginning to trouble his belly; morning was no warmer but he was soaked with sweat. Greyness kept seeping in with its odd, swarming effect, like tiny insects or particles of dust, swirling madly. Textures of rock were becoming plainer, and there were tufts of plants, a smaller version of the tough broom up on the ridge. Here it seemed rooted in living rock. Dolvid reached to give one of the plants nearby a cautious then a firmer tug, but it clung to the rock even when, getting a secure hold with his left hand, he wrenched as hard as he could with his right.

A murmur came up the line, and Rodlakh touched his arm to report Galt said all were aboard. Galt himself, it seemed, was at the end.

The sky was losing color. The light would have to do. "Here we go." Flattening against the cliff he leaned very gradually, right hand sweeping to find the hold, good rock. Knowing Rodlakh was watching him with absolute concentration, he could slide his left knee up over the jut of layered rock the roof above them had dwindled to. Thrusting off with that leg as his right stepped up, he made a fluent half turn, pulling himself up. His belly brushed, then came down on the ledge. A right knee, painful, a double handhold, and he was up on a space surprisingly ample, room enough to turn and proffer a hand to Rodlakh, who came up with his face showing exaggerated distaste for this. As he in turn aided the next, Dolvid went on; the ledge, climbing, canted inward slightly, and was the best so far, but over it beetled the mass of overhang that had to be crossed.

At its widest three men could stand abreast on the ledge, but past there it narrowed sharply, levelling off. Another corner was ahead, and at last to confirm their position Dolvid risked a downward look, south and east, directly to the trestle-bridge, watchtower high above, rightward the arched stone bridge where the road went at the foot of the lake. Bringing his gaze back the length of shining water he could perceive the inflow, so he thought, of Shuf'Oëladh, foaming white in the mysterious shadow of its deep cleft. Little doubt that where the cliff turned its next corner it swung back to form the rear of the citadel bastion, head of the famous bridge. Where he stood must be beneath the courtyard of the Summer Palace. This was the final stage.

Among those assembling on the ledge was Haun, one of the Lunu Tezh' men, carrying a coil of rope, as was Guthdar, Noldar's brother. Galt had originally named himself as a climber, but seeing the fatigue in the man's face Dolvid was glad they had agreed no one who took part in capture of the trestle would also lead the climb. Nearby, back to the cliff, Sarnak was taking off boots, stringing them together for handing to Muranak, stuffing socks in his pocket. "Twice as much to grip with," flexing his long-toed feet.

The climbers were to pick routes they thought best, or least awful. They shuffled to and fro on the ledge, frowning back at the rock. "Not hard, not hard," Haun kept chanting.

There was a place nearer the northern end where a faint shallow channel crossed the overhang. Dolvid wiped hands on his shirt.

"What is it? Are you hurt?"

He had not realized his face was so indiscreet. "No, terrified," and Rodlakh's half-smile was disbelieving. "I'm off," to Sarnak, and Dolvid launched himself at the face.

A bad climb, and surely among the worst times of his life. The rock punished fingertips and fingernails, but without its roughness the climb would not have been feasible. After half a dozen tense moves he almost decided it could not be done; every hold so far had been near failure. His body was complaining, and ahead was the sickening back-bend, where tender fingers would have to cling like leeches.

From where he was it would be possible to drop tamely back to the ledge. What he told Rodlakh was true; he had never climbed except in terror, and had no head for heights. That, not enjoyment, had always been in his climbing, the need to drive back fear that otherwise might be his master. To his stretched nerves and hurting muscles the idea of returning was very good. Cunningly he tried to say he would begin again, with a better choice of route.

Just to his left came Sarnak, hauling up spider-armed to take the lead. In his spasm of murderous anger at the fool's wish for early death, Dolvid's breath went out in a sobbing near-whimper, and the sound of it shocked and shamed him. Perhaps it had been heard on the ledge below. He was not going to be beaten. New blood pumping, he stretched for a hold, and of its own accord the other hand went past, feeling for grips.

As settled, each climbed for himself. They had nothing to spare for sentiment and if all but one fell, that one could still unwind his rope for others to begin climbing. All of life narrowed to the few inches of rock-face to be kept close.

Anxious to be past the overhang with its sensation of hanging upside down, body sucked at by nothing, Dolvid hurried a foot-movement, bypassing a projection, left side, hoping for a higher one to give some relief to his bloodstained fingers. The foot skidded off plain rock, swinging out sideways into space, while his right-hand grip, throbbing with strain, fractionally shifted. Sweat running into his eyes and dripping from his elbows, he achieved a mighty convulsion of the spine, bringing left knee, then foot, back to the rock-face. Even now, the weakly scrabbling toe could not hit the missed hold. His right knee began wobbling, and the right hand, all at once greasy, shifted again.

Clouds came into his head, where one of his selves was nodding satisfaction; yes, this was what it was to fall, very easy; actual comfort to lean back on the void, give his weight to space, get relief from this agonizing and foolish struggle.

He said *No* out loud, forcing thought, ferociously denying hysteria's insistence he was slipping steadily left. As if instructing someone else, he said where the missed hold must be.

His left leg would not go there. Teeth set, right hand in cramping pain, he made the left hand grasp upper leg, and push it into place. Just as the hold on his right was no longer tenable his left toes slotted home. With a blind and unruly snatch, eyes filled with sweat, he grabbed back his left handhold, and clung. Under sobbing breath, body and mind swung back together. He instructed himself to count calmly to twenty, and needed three starts to remember what came after fourteen.

As always happened in mockery, the next hold he found was a lavish one, a slot in rock for both his hands to grasp at. Next, one of the firm-rooted tufts of green, where the cliff tilted back to merely vertical. His knees bumped over the hump, and he was sprawled spreadeagle on the sharp slope to the base of the walls, a slope anyone who had not negotiated the overhang would call a sheer drop.

Guthdar was winning the race; he must feel either personal grudge or passionate lust for the rock-face, and whichever it was worked for him. He was in his last flailing stretch as Dolvid began the final steep, and when he sighed his knee onto the rim by the walls, Guthdar was unwinding a rope. The situation was better than had appeared from a distance; it was as if the rock had once been soft like a pillow or fresh mortar, and the walls had been plopped down before it hardened; between walls and brink there was a swell of rock where feet could comfortably be planted. Shoulders braced against the walls, they could give much help to the rope-climbers who followed. Sarnak came panting, accepted a hand up, and unhooked his rope. "Haun, hung out — wet washing."

Dolvid was paying out his line. Sarnak did the same grimly. "Did he say something about an easy climb?" making his rope swing gently to and fro across the rock-face, lowering it where he hoped Haun still was. "Moss," he said, "a barnacle."

Dolvid felt a tug on his rope. A coil taken about his body, he braced, and the rope went taut. Then Sarnak's line also tightened, but went slack again when the lanky man tried a tug. He worked the line slowly back and forth again, sending lazy waves swishing down. It twanged straight. "A bite."

Haun's face with all blood gone out of it rose past the overhang. Part-climbing, he was part-hauled up the last feet. Just then Rodlakh appeared, leaning back well, walking, making good use of the line. As Noldar came up on his brother's length of rope, trumpets sounded in the city.

The raiders were sure they had been seen. Then, as at sunset the call was taken up and passed from post to post, valley filling with the re-echoed three notes, rising as the evening signal had fallen. Morning was being declared.

Though sky was bright above the hills, no sun yet found the men gathering at the base of the wall. Rodlakh, stepping up beside Dolvid gave a brief hug, and took over his line. Others arriving had ropes of their own, and soon the cliffside was swarming with climbers. Galt, quickly up, began spacing men out, facing the wall. He laughed out loud when he saw the surface of the masonry; "A stair." Undeniably, making repairs here would be difficult; binding between stones had rotted away, and some of the stone, too, was deeply pitted. The walls were built with a backward lean, or more likely a taper. A child could climb them, if he could ever get to this place.

Men were unwinding and discarding strips of cloth that had muffled their quivers, cocking their bows, lifting swords and knives to be sure they were free in the sheaths. Faces, tense as they climbed, were taking fire from the morning, and knowledge battle was at hand. As Galt forecast, the blood rose, fear surging into an expectancy. Rodlakh, near the middle of the line, was eager, even glad.

Rimming the hills the sun came, light slicing across the valley, displaying smoky layers of mist. At last from the far side there came the expected alarm, a single trumpet note, high and hammering.

"Too late," Rodlakh, not losing his blithe face. All the men were up, most of the ropes coiled; the others could be dropped over the cliff. Galt confirmed the count, "Twenty-seven, Valrabh'."

Rodlakh drew the sword Galt had brought for him from Kamsilat, and waved at the ramparts, resheathing for the climb. Everyone went forward and up; climbing lefthanded Dolvid reached for the knife at his back.

Some sort of second sight was needed, for a trumpet call from across the valley to cause sentinels on these ramparts to look straight down. Shading their eyes, squinting against the sun, trying to make out what was wrong up at the watchtower, they were completely surprised and instantly overwhelmed. Not one attacker was thrust back, and most crossed the wall unchallenged. Noldar, just to the left, knifed down a pikeman, Galt another. Rodlakh, quickly over, redrawing his sword, unhesitatingly charged down the platform at a knot of three pikemen, but more attackers appeared to reinforce him. In less than a minute the guard on the eastern side was annihilated, and bowmen were kneeling on the platform to shoot down reinforcements running across from the far side. Dolvid found Galt, and with a few others quickly enlisted they jumped down to the flagstones, running to assail the small, boxy structure in the middle of the front parapet, where the stair came up from below to an iron gate; a handful of defenders were there. Two fell to arrows shot on the run, but one, ducking inside the little gatehouse, wounded an attacker with a jab of his pike before falling to the knife-thrust hooked around the door-pillar. Another man threw down his pike and called for quarter. Since his helm had the yellow crest this might be called breaking his oaths, but the oath the *Adanum* swore was to die defending the Person, and *g'Asalladh'* was safe, many miles away.

The officer on duty slipped past the heavy gate of iron grillework, and went bounding down the steps crying the alarm. An arrow caught him at mid-stair and he crashed to the foot of the long flight to lie broken, an unnecessary killing.

"Now the city knows," Rodlakh came up. His sword was meat-stained, but he was unwounded and calm.

"Doesn't matter." With Galt and Truni, Dolvid dragged aside the body of the pikeman who had fought, and pushed the grumbling gate shut; three stout iron bars held with pins secured it. The stair was barely wide enough for two men abreast, and above bowmen could sit in embrasures, aiming their arrows down through guarded slits. Unless the lower city maintained siege-engines for assailing its own citadel, this side was close to impregnable.

That was also Galt's assessment. He posted four of his bowmen at embrasures, telling them not to shoot needlessly — "Only if they carry tools to break the gate, or ladders to scale it." Guthdar among the archers nodded sullenly; men who had taken these risks were not glad to be told, hold their hands; the rise of blood demanded a release.

All the courtyard in front of the Summer Palace had been cleared of enemies able or ready to fight. Uttar had taken a pike-point in the left forearm, and his eyes were blazing for battle; two other attackers had wounds, not counting a superficial scratch on Galt's cheek.

"What now?" gathering up his men. Dolvid suggested there was probably a guard on the near end of the bridge. A rear court could be reached passing through the central archway of the Palace, and Sarnak was sent doubling there with eight men, some already armed with pikes taken from fallen defenders. They had strict orders to come back for help if outnumbered.

Meanwhile wounded prisoners and two unscratched were shepherded against the eastward wall, watched by a single bowman, too far back to be rushed. The rest of Galt's men ranged in a semicircle facing the front of the Palace, bows ready. Last night when the guards were changed they came from and returned to the archway entrance.

"So this is the deadly *Adanum*," Galt growled.

"They are not finished with."

"Oh, we're wary."

Dolvid joined Rodlakh at the little guardhouse. The fear was of guards locked in with the prisoner, perhaps with orders to kill if there was any attempt at rescue. The presumed prisoner, that was, though they were absolutely convinced Aëlu was here in this squat structure of hard stone. Windows were heavily barred, made of a thick, unshattering glass, opaque from outside as the surrounding stone, though they must let in some light. The door was a slab of solid iron, with a thigh-thick bronze bar across, double locked. The two men put their shoulders to it, but it did not budge. Skidding in blood they turned over the two guards who had died by the door; as expected neither had any keys.

"Keys must be nearby," Dolvid said. "They brought food here last night. Probably the guardroom of the Palace. We shall not break in that door without a ram, or smith's hammers for the locks."

Rodlakh gnawed his lower lip and grumbled about time draining away, though on the other hand he did not see why, if the bridge could be secured, his little force could not hold the citadel indefinitely. Not eternally, however, and any retreat would be doomed if the enemy was given the chance to gather forces. Rodlakh was half-abstracted, trying to get an arm far enough through the bars of a window to rub at greenish glass with his sleeve. Again, Dolvid was trying to form an image of Aëlu, to imagine how she would endure captivity. Loved by all, Âna said, not caring about policies or statecraft, and Rodlakh agreed, in different words. A famous beauty, who went for lonely walks in the absence of her hero-husband. She had never borne a child; not her failing, perhaps; neither had Âna, probably not Sebhal's first mistress, and there were no rumors of natural children. Loved by her father-in-law, adored by her nephew, and Dolvid might die not knowing more than that. At least Galt and his men had seen the woman they came to rescue.

Rodlakh angrily shook at the thick bronze bar. "Where is the guardroom?"

Before any answer, battle reopened. Over the frontal parapet nearby there came a dense flight of arrows, obviously shot at random from the lower court, clattering on flagstones, hitting nothing but the body of one of the fallen enemy. The man watching prisoners found it good to move farther up, and was kind enough to shepherd the prisoners away from harm. Safe in their embrasures the Frontier bowmen replied, choosing their targets, and a second volley of arrows was much fewer.

At the same time there was the clatter of iron-tipped boots in the Palace archway; above a dozen fully-armed men of the *Adanum* charged the ring of archers. With their breastplates, crested helms and long, steel-tipped pikes they should be an overmatch, man to man, for the lightly armed men of the West, whose numbers were about equal. Had the *Adanum* been trained to think they might have fanned out to make this a collection of single fights, but instead they trotted in close formation, as if breaking through the ring would be a victory. Archers on the flanks let loose shafts unimpeded, hands going from string to quiver with magical speed. The leading pikemen met, muddled with and overran the center, but they had lost half their number. Rodlakh came up with blade whirling, and Galt was there with Noldar as the charge spent its force. It was a wrestling, skidding, cursing melee. A bearded pikeman sidestepped Dolvid and he was obliged to take the next, expecting to be spitted from behind as he prevented the wounding of one of the archers, going for gap between breastplate and leather collar. Not able to bring his pike across the man went down with a knife-wound in the side of his throat. Dolvid whirled back, and the man who watched the prisoners was coming to observe with interest how his dart had punched right through the body-armor of the bearded man, a file-leader.

Rodlakh had broken loose, sword to sword with a senior officer. An overhead parry, and Rodlakh came with a lightning underhand thrust that went in under the man's breastplate. That, practically, was the end of the fight, but the raiding force had two dead and three more gravely wounded. First to die had been their youngest, Truni. He had discarded his sling and gone for his knife, dropping to one knee and never flinching from the path of the charge. Too much atonement for his stumble on the ridge, and he would never teach the Lunu Tezh' what he had been taught as a soldier.

Now shouting and clash of weapons came from the far side of the Palace. With the feeling their plan was coming apart in many places, faster than it could be mended, Dolvid ran for the archway, and Rodlakh was with him, and a few men who again carried pikes of fallen enemies. As he leapt down broad flagged steps beyond the arch Dolvid was thinking he might acquire a sword in the same way.

A narrow band of green gardens, startling after so much bare stone, separated bridgehead from Palace. Here another detachment of pikes had driven most of Sarnak's band into a small fort-like structure where the bridge ended or began. Sarnak's men were defending with spirit, and their adversaries, caught in rear by the fresh attack, were soon routed, two dropping their weapons and giving up at once. Yet here again their forces had dead and wounded.

Sarnak was unscathed. He had not yet found a minute to put his boots back on, and had defended himself with a captured pike, singing scurrilous sea-songs.

The bridge, he said, had been quiet; two men had started over earlier, and the Frontier bows had caused a change of heart. Dolvid allowed himself briefest glimpse of the famous structure, *Afonu Asalladhilu*, woven metal and wood swooping gracefully across the gorge, narrow and no less delicate at this close range. The farther end was apparently enclosed by containing walls, but no garrison could be seen there. Higher up, the other span across the gorge did indeed seem to be an aqueduct, skillfully made of bricks and stone.

"We could break the bridge in five minutes," Sarnak said, "if they tried to come that way."

"Don't do that. It is our road home."

Leaving extra archers with Sarnak they hurried back to the archway. Galt was grim-faced, seeing their small force whittled away; they had beaten off perhaps the only counter-attack the citadel's garrison could muster, but four were dead, seven wounded, not less than three of those lost to the fight.

As they spoke a quick bowshot from a Palace window struck a man in the throat. Before a second shot, before the man was on the ground, the Frontier bows let loose a volley; glass shattered, points smashed into stone. No more arrows came; in the courtyard the man died.

Galt's remaining men, together with prisoners, were brought back under the archway, a tunnel through the heart of the building, a number of doors on either side. Effective force here was at most half-a-dozen, subtracting men watching the bridge and bowmen over the stairway at the front parapet. Asked whether four were enough there Galt said they had to be, and his remark about the narrowness of the stair made something come clear in Dolvid's mind; it had troubled him ever since last evening when they had surveyed the city.

He asked Rodlakh, "Can you imagine the Patriarch making His way up that steep little stair? No room to carry a litter, and three of the last four have lived to a hundred. It is said to be a rough road down from the north past Lunu Midhi."

A frown. "You mean, there must be another way into the Palace."

At the Mainland *Mankh'* a tunnel ran from quayside to the personal suite of the Patriarch, and there must be something of the sort here, probably from the lower city. It would be *ga-dazhu*, that was certain, but there might be an *atarlai* in the Summer Palace to lift the ban with appropriate words, or a city annoyed enough by this raid might steel itself to sacrilege. Though it would take time to bring them together and arm them, every able man in the city could be levied.

Rodlakh said, "Then we should not waste any time finding the keys."

On the right-hand side of the archway tunnel, the door where the pikemen of the *Adanum* had emerged for their ill-conceived charge remained open. Inside, steps ran down, worn into a marked hollow by the boots of an agelong guard, never tested till today. Rodlakh posted a man at the door and hurried down, Dolvid just behind, now armed with a sword, counting casualties as they went. Killed, disabled and disarmed, they had accounted for some forty men of the *Adanum*, and the question was whether that was all or nearly all of the standing garrison for the citadel. The shortage of bowmen here was not surprising considering a company of archers was always part of the Patriarch's guard, and there were plenty of ordinary soldiers or citizens of Drin b'Afon who could bend a bow, judging by the deluge of arrows that had fallen in the forecourt. Very properly Galt feared archery above anything, particularly if another force could enter the citadel, because duelling at close quarters made the range and power of the Frontier bows go for nothing. In simply practical terms the raiders could not afford further casualties if they were to have any chance of reaching the western coast and seizing a boat. Less hardheadedly it was to be hoped those who had died or who were badly wounded understood the connection between this desperate venture and their homes and livelihood in the West; men should not die or believe they were dying for the whim of a lovesick lord. Muscles had gone cold, and that he had killed one man and wounded two others was troubling Dolvid.

At the foot of the stairs Rodlakh threw open another door and strode in boldly, more concerned with haste than safety. A long low-ceilinged space lighted by lanterns assisted by a row of half-windows on one side, up near the ceiling. A long table of scrubbed stone was flanked by many short benches, some lying where they had been knocked over, presumably when the alarm came. Cups, bowls and some hunks of bread were left on the table, while on pegs along the wall shirts, belts, a cap or two were hanging. Rodlakh stooped to pick up a broken length of fine chain with a luck charm, a bronze bee, hung on it. Face rigid, he put it down on the table.

"The *raminat* is still warm," feeling the big kettle with the back of a hand, deliberately affecting insensibility. Finding two unused cups he ladled out drinks and passed one to Rodlakh. The tartness of *raminat* was wonderfully refreshing, and it arrived none too soon after all their exertions. Rodlakh went back to the doorway, and told their sentinel, Nam', to bring another man down here.

Rough doors halfway down this common room opened on a dim space where mattresses on the floor and tumbled blankets had the look and smell of recent use.

"Keys," Rodlakh muttered fiercely. Off the sleeping-quarters was a latrine with a long trough they both made use of; it was sluiced continuously, quite possibly from the aqueduct. Beyond, a wash-house had pewter tubs to be filled from an immense slimy stone cistern with large dippers hung at the rim. A few laundered clothes were hanging dispiritedly.

Back in the common room Nam' and Rongar were waiting for orders, and Rodlakh told them to carry up the big pot of *raminat*, and let the men share it out. They could drink from ladles if there were not enough cups.

Nam' took a handle. "Should prisoners be let drink, too, *Valrabh*?" shyly.

"If there is enough. As Galt wishes." The two men with the heavy kettle between them went awkwardly for the stairs.

The one door remaining led to a workshop, not equipped as a full-scale armory, but adequate for making repairs; a much-used grindstone, and a bench strewn with dented body-armor, a sword with the cording of the hilt coming loose, a breastplate with a broken strap, scraps of leather and pieces of golden-yellow piping. Rodlakh took up a short-handled but weighty square hammer, and a short, thick crow. "Without keys, the door must be forced." Picturing that stout bronze bar and iron door, Dolvid said nothing.

Passing the open doors to the sleeping-space on their way back to the stairs there was the flicker of something moving, a soft sound of scuffling feet. Rodlakh put down tools to redraw his sword.

Nothing could be seen in the dim as they moved cautiously between rows of mattresses, but Rodlakh tensed and sprang, reaching into heaped blankets, which began a violent threshing. Assisted at the last by Dolvid he pulled to his feet a ragged, frightened boy of perhaps twelve, whining he was no soldier, did not want to be killed, and knew nothing. The Island accent was very strong. A much-mended smock of stained linen was belted with greasy rope. The boy's hair was matted, face smudged with dirt as they pulled him into better light, his fingernails black and ragged. An orderly for the guards, perhaps, or a kitchen-boy — though surely the most slovenly cook might demand cleaner hands than these.

"Who keeps the keys?" keeping his hard grip on the boy.

Who tried to go limp. "I don't know, I am not with the *Adanum*." Pale eyes rolled up in terror, and Rodlakh shook the boy as he might a piece of wet clothing, demanding, "The keys!"

This would not do it; Dolvid had the boy placed. He loosened Rodlakh's hand where it clamped the collarbone, and addressed the lad in the stiffest, most formal Owanilú at his command. The language, fit for raising a new Patriarch, rolled in rich incongruity in these mean surroundings.

"This lord who speaks to you is Rodlakh Lambarrati bi-Arbhai-Navu, brother to the Lord Ban-Sila *Deghi, Rabhsai*. Know him!"

"*Asai*," the boy moaned. Tottering since out of Rodlakh's vise, he sank to his knees, bent head showing signs of ringworm. Hand to threadbare breast he said, "Your pardon, I knew him not." The Island accent was still there, but overlaid with the *Atarlum* tones. Rodlakh, not having Dolvid's knowledge of these Island families bred to Patriarchal service, had been impatient with the choice of language, and startled by the boy's instant response. Now he took up the game himself.

"Come," taking the boy's arm and half-lifting him to his feet. "For journeys we must sometimes clothe ourselves meanly; you could not recognize us." Mud-stains, patches of salt, spatters of fresh blood, and ragged rock-clambering tear in one knee of his breeches made *mean* a succinct description of Rodlakh's attire. His Owanilú was less ornate than Dolvid's, who noted the *Valrabh'*, while fluent, made some minor mistakes Faëdhal would never have let pass.

"Say quickly, for we are in haste, who is it keeps the keys, those of the guardhouse, where we hear there is a notable captive being kept."

"It is so, *Asai*." Sly-faced, the boy tried to be ingratiating. "A choice captive."

He was very near being clouted; about to swing a clenched fist Rodlakh saw the boy was merely parroting what he had overheard. The word *ifnaku*, choice, might be used of a ripe pear or succulent fowl, only crudely of a woman. But Aëlu, offence aside, was found.

The boy's name was Larghai, his father Vedrughi, Steward of the Palace, therefore keeper of keys they were looking for; his son said he would be somewhere about the Palace proper. Steward sounded grand enough, but these families were kept eternally poor by their *Atarlum* masters, whom they continued to regard with an awe never lessened by familiarity. On the contrary, there was a proprietary affection only increasing their worship; Vedrughi would be able to reel off names and chief deeds of the Patriarchs for the past fifteen centuries.

When they came to the Mainland they despised servants at the Paowanu *Mankh'* who did not have their fluency in the Owanilú, though they themselves spoke only ceremonial forms. Every few generations these service families would proudly produce a boy alert enough for training as an *atarlai*, a girl with the grace as well as the beauty to be considered for schooling as a *nôd'yanu*. Zhâlai, now the officious at-Zhâlai, came from just such breeding.

Thoughts of the *Mankh'* brought back fear of a secret way into the Summer Palace. The boy was going to lead them where his father might be. "But before that, show us the Secret and Hidden Way of the Patriarch." The boy of course would have only one meaning for this, a kind of pun that might also refer to beliefs and policies.

Larghai (the name came from the greatest military captain of the First Empire) showed fear. "The Way, your pardon, the Way is *ga-dazhu*."

"Do you instruct us? Lead us there."

Rodlakh became the kindly one, taking the boy's hand. Outside, Larghai's eyes rounded at sight of sullen prisoners with their wounds; most of them must be men he knew. The bloodstained court with the tangled bodies of those felled in the charge of the *Adanum*, the short, serious-eyed Frontier soldiers cleaning weapons, binding wounds — Larghai was taking it all in, and trying to make it fit with Rodlakh's claims of rank.

Galt, eyes red-rimmed, a patch of blood dried black on his cheek, came to report all was quiet; the arrows coming over the parapet had ceased, and that lower court was empty. That did not reassure Dolvid, who wanted to know where those men had gone. Next to the lake, Galt said, and on the main road, there had been some riding to and fro of horses to no apparent purpose, the milling of ants when their nest is disturbed. Learning what Rodlakh intended, he gave them a couple of men, Noldar with his short bow and one of the Lunu Tezh' men, a pike as weapon added to his sling.

With Dolvid, Galt obviously had a terrible sense of doom gathering for them. "Must we stay much longer, *Valrabh'*?"

"I can't tell, can I — " Rodlakh's testiness was part of shared anxiety. "Till we do what we came for, I suppose."

"Well, a rest is welcome," Galt placated. "And the *ram'nat* went down well. The men also want our purpose to be achieved, *Asai*."

Rodlakh gripped his forearm. "However the day ends, your men have achieved a great feat. Drin b'Afon, Galt!"

"Oh, aye, there'll be some fame here," trying not to seem too proud. "Names that won't be forgotten."

They left him. On the far side of the archway, down by the bridge, Sarnak, leaning against the wall of the little fort gave a jaunty wave to say all was well, then used interlinked fingers to make a roof over his head. He was right; clouds were spreading to meet the sun's climb, and rain looked certain.

Hush of the Palace was ominous. The five went up a broader stair, coming to a hallway where nothing was moving. Under *ga-ôthu* stonework was austere greys and blacks. Larghai, going with the assurance of familiarity, took them past doors, across the corner of a high-ceilinged dining-hall where *ôthu*-light shone in the polished brown of a vast horseshoe table of smoothed stone. Glimpse of a window entirely filled with the soaring sight of Karg' Kamanta brought a new attack of wonder and awe at being here; *mai* was everywhere.

A big heavy door and eight steps down brought them to an extraordinary place, the central stairway. Here the skilled builders had been able to omit inner walls across the entire depth of the Palace, using stair-column as a pillar, poised rather than massive, wrought in rare stones and burnished metal. Soaring, it climbed to the very topmost levels, linked to each stage by slender arched bridges. High above eight slim arches joined stair to circular rim of a broad skylight, slightly domed, divided like rinded southern fruit into segments to match the arches, Patriarchal Seal depicted at the center. Both front and rear the mounting windows made this space very light, as if emerging into an outside court. The illusion was added to by a curious structure jutting out (or rather, in) from the front wall at ground level, roofed and windowless, a blind house within a palace, its stone cleanly cut, with recessed panels of lighter stone to suggest windows. At its inner end, right opposite the foot of the central stair, it had a tall double-door of smooth bronze, all the way from floor to peaked roof of this inner house. From doors to stair a stripe of floor was made of polished black stone bordered with golden tiles.

"*Moragh', Asayal!*" Larghai declaimed. "*Ga-Zhanu b'Asalladhit ô.*"

Rodlakh could be more decisive than Dolvid. Easy to speak lightly of *ga-dazhai*, out in the open, to men whose gods were comfortable familiars to be chided if they brought storm when there should be harvest weather, anger instead of desire. For Dolvid, trained among chafing echoes of the *Mankh'*, the *mai* of this place was paralyzing. Except at Rodlakh's heels he could not have stepped out onto the black stone, where the *Valrabh'* was already trying the doors. Larghai's shocked gasp spoke for him, too.

Somehow balanced on bearings of shuzi, a door swung out with dream ease. They were looking down shallow steps in two flights; eight, a landing, and most likely eight again. Feeling his step contaminated what he trod, Dolvid went with Rodlakh down the first flight.

Right under the outer wall of the Palace, as they judged, there was an actual portico, beyond, a long passage, sloping down gently, feebly lighted with *ôdul*, of which many needed restoration or replacement. Dressed stonework was very similar to the older sections of the passage at the Old Bronze Residence, as if one had been imitated from the other, though Dolvid, with dates of construction and renovation revolving in his head, could not work out which way it would be: the Bronze Residence was much older than the Summer Palace as it now was, but there had been an earlier edifice here.

He estimated the straight stretch of tunnel must run to, or very nearly to, the face of the citadel cliff, and where the passage appeared to make a sharp turn rightward there were shafts of light that might be coming through vents in that rock-face.

Came another reminiscence of that other tunnel. "Can you hear something?" Rodlakh's voice was piercingly sibillant in this rockbound space.

"Feet." Distant, but a rolling, rhythmic sound that could not be mistaken, many feet. As they strained to hear, perhaps they heard voices, too, and the clink of weaponry.

"If the bronze doors can be locked — " he started back, but Dolvid stopped him. There must be a stronger way to close the passage; such a pathway into the inmost halls of the Patriarch would never be left with only bronze doors and *ga-dazhai* to guard it against, for example, an uprising in the city.

Down at the portico to the actual tunnel he found what he wanted, a row of deep slots across the floor. Above could be seen sharp spikes of a big portcullis, hung within the wall of the Palace.

"Very good. How is it brought down?"

"It must be held up by counterweights." At the inside corners of the portico plaques of bowed metal ran from floor to ceiling, and might well conceal chains. The mechanism could be pictured, pulleys up above the portcullis in the Palace wall, chains coming down on each side, great weights of stone or solid metal, at present resting at the bottom of wells beneath where they were standing. But portcullis had to be made to come free of its counterweights, and somewhere must be a device for winding it up and locking it in place.

Dead center just before the lowest step there was an inset stone, light brown in the surrounding black, about one pace square. Dolvid knelt for a closer look; on the side nearer the stair there was a clear slot. Using the tip of his salvaged sword, watched by Rodlakh, he pried at the slot. The waves of sound coming up the tunnel were growing, and there was no longer doubt about voices, or the clank of arms. Dolvid poked, and the inset started up quite easily, proving to be a bronze plate cleverly faced with a thin-sawn wafer of the brown stone. Helped by Rodlakh he lifted it aside, and had the mechanism he was looking for; a heavy iron pulley-wheel wound with chains with a keyslot for a crank, an inner cogged shoulder held by an iron double-escapement. With the hilt of the sword he rapped at the escapement, trying to make it release the teeth of the cog. As he did the noise of feet and weapons surged, and vanguard of the enemy appeared at the far end of the straight section. That corner was now seen to be the head of steps or of a ramp, climbing across the inside of the rock-face, matching the steps outside, but probably not as steeply. Pikemen were in the lead, but surely there would be bowmen, too.

"Noldar," Rodlakh called. He came down and nodded coolly when he saw the advancing enemy. On one knee just inside the portico he bent his bow.

"Is he clear of the portcullis?" Rodlakh looked and nodded, sword drawn again. Under furious hammering the escapement jerked free; the big pulley squeaked a quarter-turn, stopped, then went a little way farther, stiffly. Shouts boomed in the tunnel; they had been seen. Noldar's bowstring slapped against horn, and another arrow was in flight before the foremost of the enemy had dropped with a shaft buried in his abdomen. Encouraged with a hard kick at the pulley, the portcullis creaked down a foot or so, and stopped.

Noldar, having shot twice more, glanced over his shoulder for instructions. Another bad-tempered kick gained another few inches of drop, then all Dolvid's hammering and kicking achieved no further result.

With several of them down, the enemy hung back in momentary indecision. "Is the cursed thing free?" Rodlakh said. "Pull it down." He jumped to catch at the bottom crossbar of the portcullis, a foot above the grim iron spikes. An arrow passed by his shin, missing the unwavering head of Noldar by a fingerspan or so. As the bulky gate came down a little farther Dolvid could leap beside Rodlakh. The portcullis jerked, trembled, and came with a rush, clanging and booming down. Several arrows came rattling against the close-set grille.

"Can it be lifted?"

"Not from that side." Dolvid, in fact, had no idea how it could be raised from any side. Behind the tapered points of the spikes he had noticed slots, and the notches in the floor seemed to work as spring-locks, a catch fitting into those slots. Besides, as designed to, the escapement's other claw had swung into the cog-wheel, and once released the entire weight of portcullis and chains would remain to be lifted; he had heard the counterweights come thudding up under their feet.

After a yell of bafflement, feet were running for the barrier. Not wanting to be shot between the bars, the three men, Noldar clearly enjoying this, hurried up the steps, and two arrows smacked into stone behind their heels. A ferocious hammering came at the portcullis as they retreated through the bronze doors.

Larghai, wide-eyed, was being watched warily by their pikeman. Rodlakh said the bronze doors also might as well be shut, and did so with a decided click, lifting long gilded handles. No drop-bar, but there had been such doors at the *Mankh'*; at about eye-level parts of the relief, if centerd, would form a replica of the Seal. He tugged at the upper panel, and it slid smoothly to center. As if grooved in shuzi the lower came across beneath the other. Larghai choked out a scared warning it could not be opened again. It came together, and there was a smooth, solid and satisfying *chunk*, as a well-made lock took hold. Now the only gap was a six-sided socket, part of the Seal.

"Once shut, Lords." Larghai was persistent in his ornate Owanilú, "these doors can neither be opened nor broken; a priest must come and speak a *kolukezh'*, touching his pendant to the Seal. I knew this not, Lords, when little, and thus was whipped for their closing. But that was many years since."

Dolvid nodded, and said quietly, "The key-pendant does more to open them than the chanting, but unless there is an *atarlai* with a key about the palace, we are not going to be interrupted very soon. Larghai!"

"Lord?"

"Is there any other outlet for the Sacred Way in the Palace?"

The boy was puzzled there could be anyone so learned who did not know that. "None, Lord, which is why this closing is such a dire matter. From within, not the Blessed Father Himself can open it. There must be a *kolukezh'*, and then the priest — "

"We barred the way to rebels," Rodlakh invented.

"Drunken rebels," Dolvid improved. Still needing the boy's cooperation, it was best to keep him on the near side of panic.

"My father would keep all wine from soldiers," sententiously, "all soldiers from wine. By this are they made beasts, Lords." He went on to speak cheerfully of the many floggings there would be.

"Father!" the boy shouted suddenly, going into ordinary speech with a clogged Island sound. Before anyone could grab him he darted away, hurling himself at a door leading off the central hall, which had been closing quietly. Pulled on both sides, the door wavered, while Larghai stammered a garbled account of his adventures — "and the *Adanum* men left their breakfast, father — "

As the men came up the door was abruptly released and Larghai nearly went sprawling backwards. In the passageway beyond, a bent and cringing figure padded away.

"Steward! Vedrughi — " Rodlakh said loudly. Either that or the creak as Noldar's bow was bent made the man halt and turn. Larghai ran to him. "Father, here is the *Valrabh'* come on a long journey to see to the punishing of drunken rebels." Dolvid admired the ingenuity in weaving together elements into a coherent-seeming tale. The Island accent was stronger than ever.

The Steward was unexpectedly ancient for such a young son, so Dolvid wondered trivially whether Vedrughi's strictures against soldiers who drank might have a personal origin. Less conjecturally, he had a sharp nose, stringy neck, cheeks beginning to fold in on themselves. The eyes were bleary and frightened, but not stupid. In excitement Dolvid saw the bristling ring of keys at the man's belt, and wanted to warn Rodlakh to be tactful; it would save trouble to have this man's unforced help.

"You are the Steward Vedrughi?" No need to have worried; the voice rang out so cold and regal Dolvid felt abashed; habits of subservience would surely hold Vedrughi.

He made full deference, and Rodlakh demanded the keys to where the prisoner was being kept. His contempt sounded genuine, as it might well be for a father who would run away leaving his son in the hands of men he must assume to be killers.

The steward shuffled his feet, fingering his keys, licking his lips, and despite abject deference, said he lacked the authority. Rodlakh, freezing the man with his eyes, strode forward and grasped his shirt. "We are your authority. You have the keys here?"

"*Asai*, yes, as they were entrusted to me." Without more resistance he started with them for the guardhouse. It was interesting to wonder how often and in what other circumstances this Rodlakh might appear, impressive, more than a little frightening.

The boy skipped sideways with them as they went, taking a different way. Dolvid asked the steward where the people of the household were. Even with the Patriarch not in residence, there would have to be a considerable staff. With the unerring instinct of the servile Vedrughi concluded this one was no one in particular, and called him *sir* with a near-sneer. His tale was, servants, when the fighting began, as was not permitted, took refuge in the *ga-Zhanu b'Asalladhi*, which, as also should not be, was now closed and not to be opened again without vexatious trouble. Others, he believed, fled to kitchens below.

Provisions for the retreat, when it came, had been a concern; asked whether the kitchens had food for a journey, the steward first said no food fit for the *Valrabh'*, but under questioning admitted a supply was kept for patrols, often made ready in cloth bags for a horseman to carry.

Dolvid turned to the two soldiers. They had been unhappy when the talk was in high-flown Owanilú, and possibly did not follow much more of the steward in ordinary language, with his thick accent. Using his halt Froghulú, Dolvid said the boy Larghai would take them to the kitchens, there to seize all food ready for travel. They could use any servants they encountered to help carry food up to the courtyard.

"Go with care," again. "Some among the — the *flesh-cookers* may dream as warmakers." Noldar, happy to hear his father's language, promised they would be cautious. Dolvid's term for cooks had tickled both soldiers: once it would have meant civilized men, those with camp-fires.

Larghai self-importantly led the Frontier men away, and his father self-importantly dared to take up the question of the Sacred Way again. The Patriarch alone, he said, could order its closing —

"And to the Patriarch alone shall I answer for it, wretch — " in this flinty vein, going again into the Old Tongue, Rodlakh was not to be fooled with, but in his face the strain of all the delays was showing. The steward did no better with his stammering attempts at explanation or apology, which was cut short with a curt, "*Rughoi!* Enough!"

Outside, nothing had changed but the day; between bloodstains the stones of the courtyard were being darkened by a fine drizzle. Vedrughi stood, trying to disdain the Frontier soldiery; Galt did not hide joyous relief at seeing Rodlakh again, and came over to report all was quiet, quieter than he enjoyed. From the Bridge Sarnak had sent word something was happening on the far side, he did not know what, but there were enemy troops moving about. Galt had spared him one more archer, taken away from the front embrasures, where they had nothing to shoot at.

Rodlakh took a moment to explain how the enemy's best plan had been spoilt. Dolvid, unbearably anxious to get back to the little guardhouse, could only imagine the effort Rodlakh's patience cost.

Two bodies were still lying in front of the guardhouse; before, Vedrughi might have been considering a last officious protest against unlocking the door without proper authority, but the glazed eyes of corpses had their effect and the steward only sniffed disapproval as he began holding keys up in front of his nose till he found one he liked.

The first lock on the bronze bar was opened. The choosing was repeated, and the second lock fumbled open. Together Dolvid and Rodlakh lifted out the bar and laid it down. A last prolonged sorting-through, and the rather larger key for the door itself was found, not needing confirmation of close scrutiny. The steward inserted and turned it. Rodlakh slipped out his sword. The door opened inward.

It was murky in there. The main thing to be seen was a man, an officer of the *Adanum,* seated on a chest in the narrow vestibule, facing the door, a bared sword in his hand. Rodlakh sprang forward, the man's feet hit the floor with a double thud, steel sliced against steel.

"No, no, no — " as swords engaged a woman's voice came. Rodlakh and the young officer were nose to nose and knuckle to knuckle.

"Sunabhal — *Rodlakh?*" — a glad and baffled exclamation. Dolvid paused to call himself stupid for letting Rodlakh go blind through the doorway, for not having had bowmen standing by; the guard could as easily have been an archer with an arrow ready.

The woman appeared from a door opening off the small vestibule. She spoke a couple of calm words, and the two young men disengaged warily. "He has been kind," Aëlu told Rodlakh.

Tension between the swordsmen broke as Rodlakh turned to the woman. His face was kept guarded, but the posture of his body was eloquent; relief, triumph, joy, residual concern. "You are unhurt? Well?" His voice was oddly flat and weary.

"Yes, yes — I am not hurt. I have been afraid. How can you be here?"

"We came to find you." Rodlakh at last put an arm behind the slender back and kissed her forehead, not having to stoop. Her low-voiced calm was impressive, and Dolvid hoped, as seen with some bereft women during the Narn Campaign, she was not binding down feelings only to have them burst out the more violently. Aëlu was bereft, and did not yet know.

"I do not see how you can be here," again.

Rodlakh brought her out into grey light and the tingle of rain. She shivered, dressed as she must have been for her walk on the clifftops, grey cloak over a long whitish gown, now rumpled and dingy. In consideration of the retreat to come, it was good her shoes were not fashionable to the level of immobility, but made for walking.

She was looking left and right; as with Galt at Tan Lughsai it was not hard to guess for whom. Large eyes coming to question were very eloquent, and he was not sure he welcomed the return of what had not happened in years and never very often, conscious exchange of confidences with a woman he had not yet spoken to. Not short, the poise of her head made her taller.

"Dolvid Vidukhat, whose plan got us here, who led us up the cliff."

"As a change," after brief consideration, "from sifting through ancient manuscripts?" Dolvid inclined his head. Cool, and anything but cold, this Aëlu.

Rodlakh persisted in asking if she was harmed, and she decided, hungry; the disturbance that came with sunrise had robbed her of breakfast, though she would have minded less about that had she known just what the noise was about. Sunabhal could not open the doors from inside and knew exactly as much as she did, the faint sounds of a fight between who-knew-what adversaries.

Rodlakh began explaining why it had been so long between that and her release. Sunabhal meanwhile came to Dolvid. "I am your prisoner, I suppose."

He suggested the half-squadron leader surrender the sword Rodlakh had failed to collect. "We have bowmen who shoot when they see armed men in that tunic."

Sunabhal reversed hilts, and passed over the sword, an excellent one of an old pattern, such as Dolvid had often practised with in youth.

Galt was coming across the courtyard to greet Aëlu, and she called out his name. The men gathered at the archway raised a cheer, and Galt was holding down a whoop as he saluted Sebhal's wife.

More serious with Rodlakh, he said Sarnak was reporting numbers of men moving up the hillside on the far side of the ravine. "What this means I can't tell, *Asai*, but if our business here is done... " He looked happily at Aëlu.

Just for an instant Rodlakh could be seen to catch some of that joy. "Are you fit for a journey?"

"After I have had some food," gravely.

Seeing she would go with Rodlakh and Galt, Dolvid wanted a word with Sunabhal. "Your father is Silnath?"

"You know him?"

"I did, long ago." Amazingly, the sword actually was one used in practice, belonging then to this young officer's father. Very fresh in memory was Silnath's pride when his son, this son, was born. "He was kind to me. Before him, I had been taught to believe the *Adanum* drank blood and cracked human bones for the marrow."

"That's us." Sunabhal Silnadhi mocked, then was earnest. "I have not broken any oath as I understood it. If anyone can tell me how killing a defenseless prisoner, a woman, is part of protecting the life of *g'Asalladh'* — Let us ask the *kímukan*."

"The one who was in command here? He is dead. He fought the *Valrabh'* sword to sword."

"Oh, Rhonalai should never have done that." Sunabhal looked about. "Your fellows are going to have some boasting songs. I can't see how you broke into the citadel."

"We climbed in."

"Where was it you knew my father?"

"At the Paowanu *Mankh'*. I was to have been of the *Manadilum*."

"You broke free? How have you made your way? They say the *Atarlum* never forgives its deserters."

This was near to Sunabhal's own worries. Dolvid said, "Who would want to be part of those who ordered murder of an unarmed prisoner, a woman they have abducted."

"Yes, but — " Sunabhal made the pious sign. "Those orders never came from *g'Asalladh'*." In a way curiously like Rodlakh's with Ban-Sila, he had invented evil advisors to surround the Patriarch, carrying out policies He would not have approved. His, Sunabhal's, failure to do away with Aëlu would be held against him, he had no hope of putting his case to *g'Asalladh'* direct, or to the "true friends" he was sure somewhere existed. He wanted to join the retreat, nominally as a prisoner, but with the understanding he would have an opportunity to sign on with the Army of the West, keeping (or improving) his present rank.

Dolvid did not answer immediately, and Sunabhal said petulantly, "You were glad enough of my *unreliability*, so far as it kept your lady alive. If this raid had been outlaws or mutineers, I would have defended her."

Clearly they could not leave him to face possible death by torture, and it was unfair to despise this man, with so little of his father's blunt virtues. Dolvid wished he could have seen Silnath again. He could remember him saying, when asked about another relative, "We've always been *Adanum*, us."

That, too, was part of Sunabhal's pragmatic attitude. Silnath was about half a mile from where they stood; he and Sunabhal's mother kept a small drink-shop in the lower city. With the *Adanum*, as his son sourly recounted, he had never reached higher rank than acting-*kimukan* with a squadron-leader's pay. He had ended by selling the small lands earned in a half-lifetime of service, ending too stiff in the joints to make anything of farming. Yet by the standards of his Owani race, he was not so old, a few years beyond seventy.

Perhaps to be expected that a boy growing up as Sunabhal had, watching the *Adanum* use up his father, would be something of an opportunist. What was hard to stomach was unfeeling acceptance of the death of comrades.

"Guarding the lady," Sunabhal leaned forward confidingly, "was not the reason I was here — I arrived the day she was brought from the coast, but I was in charge of the chest in there — " He indicated the guardhouse. The chest, he said, was filled with money, no fortune, silver and bronze, not gold, but altogether a good sum already done up in small bags, this quarter's pay for a hundred of the *Adanum* here, and a company of bows on its way from the Mainland.

In the few years when it had been his job to assure food supplies for the Heartland Dolvid had learnt the sound a dishonest proposal makes; he could not count how often hints had floated that if he overlooked an irregularity both he and the speaker would profit and no one would lose. When Sunabhal went on to mention again his desire for rank in the West, Dolvid's apparent influence with the *Valrabh'*, it was familiar ground. Not giving any answer he went into the guardhouse. A key was in the lock of the ironbound chest. Inside, as Sunabhal said, there were many small cloth bags lumpy with coins, somewhat fatter ones tagged to show the rank they were intended for.

"You will speak for me?" Sunabhal, from the doorway. He had found and was munching a piece of bread.

"The *Valrabh'* will probably agree to your coming with us — but you will be weaponless, and I assume there will be a man assigned to kill you at any sign of treachery."

"Understood," almost winking complicity. He was probably going to survive several future changes of side.

Under the archway Aëlu was using an upturned barrel for a seat, being urged to eat cold rabbit and venison. Obviously the Frontier soldiers adored her, and she was completely at ease among them, as they with her, far beyond Rodlakh, who was stiff and self-conscious. Dolvid took him aside to tell him about the chest of money in the guardhouse, and was pleased when Rodlakh, after first wanting to dump it over the cliff, decided with only slight prompting it could properly be divided among their own men as booty; Galt was brought in, and details of the sharing left to him; among their lesser numbers it would come out to better than a year's pay, a windfall not to be despised.

Aëlu at last, with Dolvid and Rodlakh together, asked flatly, "Where then is Sebhal?"

Rodlakh went blank. "He could not be here."

"Could not?" Full-face to Dolvid, and he acknowledged for the first time the extraordinary refinement of her features, cut and planed.

Rodlakh had flushed; Dolvid, certain the telling could not be put off, said, "He is dead. He was killed in Burantal, by Rheduban."

His bluntness got him a tight-lipped frown from Rodlakh. A catch came in her breathing, and she leaned a little on the arm her nephew had given her. Her eyes stayed with him till certain, though he could not help feeling he had only put words to something she had already guessed. Or being married to a Sebhal, year after year going out into danger, she had over and again prepared herself for this moment when he was not going to return.

"I knew. I knew, that is, he would have been here, if he was still walking."

Rodlakh said, "Of the men only Galt knows, so far. We have to remake our policies, and Saidhan has to be given the news."

Aëlu touched the corners of her eyes with a little-finger. "Then we cannot start our mourning." She pressed Rodlakh's hand. "But the *Bôdhrai* was right to tell me. It would have become worse for every moment of expecting Sebhal at the end of our journey."

"The officer of the *Adanum*, Sunabhal — " Dolvid began.

"He will come with us, I suppose. He was courteous to me."

"As our prisoner, then. And if he wants to."

"He does."

The city was baffled, a fierce bull with cattle-ticks between its horns. Just before the bowmen at the front parapet were to withdraw a fresh, desultory shower of arrows came arching up from below; it might well be some of those who had tried to gain entry through the tunnel, impotently expressing their frustration. Horsemen had been seen hurrying eastward on the road; others were riding north along the near side of the lake. There could be ways up into the hills behind the city; the retreat might have to face ambushes.

"We may get clear before they can organize a large force," Dolvid said, watching with Rodlakh from the eastward parapet. "According to Sunabhal you killed the highest-ranking soldier now on the Island."

"Was it wise to tell her, so soon, after she has been through so much?"

A hopeless gesture, not able to match his feelings to those terms. "It was necessary."

Hailed, Galt who was bustling by said, "Ten minutes, *Bôdhrai*. We want to lay out our dead decently, if they cannot be buried. We're not going to leave their talismans for the *Mankh'* mumblers to make spells over. Nor their bows. The food is packed; we're better-supplied than we were this morning."

"And more encumbered." He meant wounded, the prisoner, even Aëlu who, though she might not flag on the march, was one more without a weapon, one to be protected.

"Aye — " Galt indicated Noldar, who went by with pike as well as bow, wearing a helm from which the hated yellow crest had apparently been burnt away. "We are not corsairs who fight for booty, but a soldier who refuses a fair prize is a fool. Well, they'll throw away anything that begins to weight them down. What's the plan?"

"None, except get across the Bridge as quick as we can."

The reverie was only apparent. "We shall need some of the best bows bringing up the rear, behind the wounded. We cannot have any stragglers. How are we for arrows?"

"Richer than we began there, too, *Asai*." The men from the front parapet had proudly carried back fat bundles of gleaned arrows, hundreds, it must be. They had neither weight nor length preferred by the Frontier bowmen, but were all usable.

Rodlakh, who intended to lead the crossing, asked Dolvid if he would take charge of the rear for the Bridge part; after it would be Noldar's job.

The steward, Vedrughi, bullied into bringing hangings from inside the Palace, helped with covering the dead, six of the attacking force, one of the wounded having bled away. Dolvid took personal charge of Truni's wristband of painted leather; kin somewhere would be glad of a small memento. He would never make the rejoinder to Truni's ideas about greatness: soldiers may keep order, he wanted to tell the youth, not always by killing, but by being hard to kill.

The dead of the *Atarlum* were also covered and left where they lay, undespoiled except of swords and pikes; those not taken by the invaders were sent clanging down the cliff. The prisoners were herded into their quarters beneath the Palace, and left to chew over the difficulties of vigilance in a place called invulnerable, where nothing much had happened for several centuries. Some men of the West, Sarnak in particular, talked wistfully of setting fires to teach the

Patriarch not to come marauding at Kamsilat, but Dolvid's regrets were just the opposite; with so much here never seen by anyone outside the Patriarch's immediate circle, he had no time for rummaging.

The Retreat

So, quietly, they left their triumph. Rodlakh led a handful of pikes to support the leading bows for crossing of the Bridge.

A marvel deserving its fame; three hundred paces from end to end, the bridge was supported on slender piers of stone, while from towers near the ends an intricate mesh of twisted ropes helped hold the long central span. The walkway was of wooden slats laid crosswise, and there were sides of rope and wood, with a polished handrail at waist height. Travellers usually went single-file, though there was room for those meeting on the bridge to pass — or for Rodlakh's pikes to pass the bowmen for the assault, if there was to be one, on the stronghold at the farther end. No defenders could be seen there, and Sarnak said they had all been moving higher up the hillside.

At a brisk pace Galt's picked bows moved out on the span. Rodlakh, sword in hand, followed. As he did an arrow came from the left and looped lazily to drift down the gorge towards tumbled rock hundreds of feet below. Dolvid, not yet having passed through the small fort at the Palace end of the bridge, looked left to see a line of figures against the sky, men moving on the narrow roof of the aqueduct. Diving past two of his rearguard, he took Aëlu's wrist and hurried her inside the bridge-house. Men too badly wounded to manage weapons, five, were also installed there.

The Frontier archers had recovered from surprise, and as he emerged again a man fell from the aqueduct with a yell, either struck by an arrow from the bridge, or losing his footing in ducking one. The aqueduct, despite its higher elevation, was an idiotic position to take up. With no good level surface, no sidewall or rail, most effort would have to go to keeping one's balance. Some there, with arrows flying near, were lying flat, or crouched on their hands and knees.

He could count some twenty or two dozen on the aqueduct, a few of the *Adanum* among them, and saw it must be not an ambush, but start, too late, of a counter-attack, meant to attain the Palace roof, where bowmen could have shot straight down into the courtyard. No doubt there were ways down into the building from the roof. For all the Patriarchal forces could tell, the invaders had meant to occupy the citadel indefinitely, and this attempt at dislodging them might well have succeeded, if the retreat had not already begun.

Now, while the foremost on the aqueduct roof either froze or attempted to turn back, the yellow-crested men of the *Adanum*, near the middle, were still trying to urge others on. A flight of arrows from Galt's bows settled debate, toppling three of the *Adanum*.

Dolvid frantically saw an opportunity being squandered; there was no need for this duelling; now, while so many enemy were up in the hills by the aqueduct, was the chance for crossing the ravine. If you could walk on air the distance between aqueduct and Bridge was probably ninety paces at the closest, and at the farthest, double that, but on the rocky bluff where both began it might take an hour to get from one to the other. He went through onto the bridge to bellow out, "Galt! Never mind them — go on!"

The same decision had already been made; Galt waved. A message was called back, and knowing what it would be Dolvid was already instructing his little band of excellent archers, when one of the wounded leaned out from the bridge-house to say, "Galt asks if the *Bôdhrai*'s men can keep some heads down for him."

Crouched behind rear wall of the citadel the Frontier men with only a few arrows were able to prevent any on or near the aqueduct from getting set to shoot. Galt's archers, meanwhile, moved forward, followed by pikes, and the wounded were started across.

Last of all were Aëlu and the brothers Noldar and Guthdar, whose bowmanship was admirable. As he called for them to leave their positions and bring up the rear, Noldar pointed almost straight up. Two men were on the Palace roof, one with a bow already bent. Noldar, quick as thought, sent a shaft which missed the man by a hair, skimming by his ear. He jumped hastily back from the roof's edge, as Noldar shot again, and hurled curses after his miss.

The downward shot, involuntarily released, whirred down between Dolvid's legs as he stood straddled. He felt a sharp burning sensation near the right knee, and looked down to note with interest he could be counted with the wounded. Above the knee, but at the inside, not the front, there was a tear in his breeches, and a trickle of blood that spread quickly, creeping through the cloth.

"That's nothing," he said, not to anyone. He wanted to proclaim he had gone through the entire Narn Campaign in '28, including the bloody Pass of Perus, without a scratch (remembering sand fleas, he could not say, without scratching). He felt unreasonably mortified in being hit, though the arrow could have gone anywhere. Now he knew why men wounded in battle were often so crestfallen.

Though the wounded moved very slowly the enemy on the aqueduct were for the most part simply holding on, and Dolvid, with a surge of compassion for their ineffectual position, told his four not to shoot except to frighten any who showed signs of using a bow. No arrows came while Aëlu was on the bridge, and at the far end there was no battle; defenders had gone, leaving behind two dead.

This stronghold was made for keeping people off the Bridge, not on it. Steps from the end of the bridge descended into a compound on natural rock, somewhat levelled. Against rough walls to the left were some small structures, and one, with its row of half-doors, was apparently a stable for ponies, or, as it turned out to be, small horses, half a dozen of the tough little animals, hill-horses the men of the West called them, saying they used very similar mounts on Landegh.

They must be kept here for the Patriarch's journeys up to Lunu Midhi and the True *Mankh'*; that road began here. Sunabhal said, "Let's not go that way," and seemed to give a shudder. But the objections he voiced seemed reasonable; there was never less than a half-squadron of the *Adanum* guarding the True *Mankh'*, and besides, the trail ended there. Dolvid, though he did not want to pass through that more than hallowed vale, was sure Sunabhal was wrong; an apprentice *atarlai* making his pilgrimage to Yoëlladhu's Watch-Rock and the Home of All

Beginnings did not have to go through Drin b'Afon, but after landing at Pavani went westward on the Forbidden Road, coming down to Lunu Midhi from the north, passing through an ancient arch that marked the head of the valley. Aëlu, born not ten miles from here, was equally sure; the path that joined the Forbidden Road went around the western rim of the valley.

Sunabhal had been born at Drin b'Afon, but conceded he had never spent much time in this country. "Besides, Lunu Midhi gives me the cold sweats, to tell truth. No one want to serve up at the True *Mankh'*. They see things there."

Galt growled, "Let us hope they're too busy with *things* to notice when we go past. *Valrabh'*, couldn't we mount the worst-wounded?"

"If they can manage a beast on this path — " Rodlakh gazed at the wild landscape northward. "The Lady Aëlu, too — "

"I shall walk," firmly. "Uttar is carrying his weapon, but that wound on his head is a bad one."

Horses roped together so they could be led, the march resumed, wary of ambush, for which this was ideal country, path seldom visible ahead for more than a few dozen paces, broken stone everywhere to conceal bows. The path itself was scarcely less a marvel than the Bridge, a broad, smooth surface with never less room than for two or three abreast, in parts chopped out of solid rock by more-than-human effort, a hewn shelf across a pillared cliff-face. Elsewhere blocks of stone had been shaped to mortise snugly to broken escarpments, and crevices bridged with chiselled slabs, not a trace of mortar anywhere. Heroic rather than graceful building, but there was beauty in defying what was not possible, and the victors of Drin b'Afon left their triumph on a road made of the same spirit that had subdued the citadel.

Climbing continuously, they passed where a stair cut into rock curved up to their left, soon passing from sight, conjecturing this might be the way to the head of the aqueduct. If there had been a guard, they were gone.

The clouds were breaking up, rain done. Whenever the column rounded nearer obstructions the entire view north was filled with Karg' Kamanta, or rather with its huge central peak; in fact this whole rocky upland was part of the Mountain, a dwarfing excess of tormented and broken stone, not so much a natural landscape as the sculpting of insane giants. Here it would be easy to believe tales of the world's beginning, the war of Draha the Rock-Lord, chief ally to Hranakh, Lord of Darkness, against Raëdh' in His aspect as Adhi the Grower — these were true only as words and in their spawning of words, yet not lightly to be mentioned, here within a few miles of time's beginning.

Not challenged, after an hour's tough plodding they emerged high on the eastward flank of the main spur. Steeply down to the right the scar where Shuf'Oëladh had carved and was still carving its gorge; distantly to the northeast other heights, stark and rounded, with tufted murk of clinging rainclouds hiding the plain in the direction of that coast. The way divided. The narrower option went straight ahead, but then curving right, looped down to where a short stone bridge took it high across the river-gorge. Farther, some of its wide-swinging descent into kinder country could be seen. The main path, wheeling left, made for the opposite flank, across a face clean-cut as a vast step.

"Last chance for Pavani," Sunabhal said.

"No use to us," Rodlakh said. "We want Doniftu, on the west coast."

"The *Adanum*," Sunabhal, shading his eyes, "keeps a small cavalry stable where the trail reaches flat country. We say, a day's march and a half-day's ride to Pavani this way. If you take the main road from Drin b'Afon, to Daëni Tâl then north up the coast, the distance is longer but you can ride it all. What saves feet ruins the love-life. We might be able to capture some *pefral*."

Mysterious why Sunabhal was so much against going to Lunu Midhi, unless he was having second thoughts, so soon, about which side he should be on. "If you want to go that way," Dolvid said, "the

Valrabh' might permit it." Any news Sunabhal carried about them would be out-of-date by the time he could deliver it.

"Why you want to go taking on more of the *Adanum* — "

"We do not." Besides himself and Rodlakh there were fourteen effective fighters. "The full complement will not be at the True *Mankh'*." The men of the *Adanum* who had been in charge at the aqueduct must have come from somewhere.

Rodlakh, frowning, asked both Dolvid and Galt to imagine they commanded the Patriarch's forces here on the Island, and work out how to deal with the invaders. As a question it belonged more to a campaign involving armies, but Dolvid gave what seemed the obvious answer, in which Galt quickly concurred; do all they could to watch the ports and coasts, hope to keep the raiders on the Island till enough cavalry could be assembled to hunt them down and encircle them. Meanwhile, if some horse was available, shadow the retreat.

Sunabhal added, "And try to put new heart in soldiers swapping scared tales about men who walk up mountains and archers who can put out wrens' eyes at a quarter-mile."

Galt, who had drifted away for a look back the way they had come, returned. "Are we going to move on? I think we are being followed."

Increasingly ready to stop, legs increasingly were sullen about starting again. The weather was brightening, and the sun breaking through was overhead; astonishingly, this crowded day with all its feats and fights, its debates and standstills, had only just passed noon. There had been some discussion of continuing to occupy the citadel long enough for rest, but while they were sure they could do so safely, perhaps till dawn (this was before they knew about men crossing on the roof of the aqueduct), it would have given the enemy too good an opportunity to collect and deploy forces. Swift retreat was the right choice, but how long they could expect to keep marching after all their exertions was a question; they knew nothing of the country ahead, but they would need darkness to be safe from the hunt, and that was many weary and dangerous hours away.

After hesitation about which of the spur to take, the way made a steep climb about a rounded mass of rock, and with the magic of dreaming they were at the rim of the scooped valley, lying like a lap between knees of Karg' Kamanta. The sun found its opening, and topmost slopes and ramparts of the mountain were dazzling white, impossibly high; a whole continent of raised rock, with blue-shadowed vales, stipplings of woods, glittering glacial plains above. No guide was needed to show Dolvid *Murutrakha Yoëlladhani*, the Watch-Rock of Yoëlladhu, a pinnacle standing apart from the main mass, exactly where he knew it would be, its top flat as if cut away. There, two thousand, nine hundred and forty-two years ago, the Founder had stood to survey all the boundaries of an empire not yet dreamed. Not far away was ga-Midhúrai, the Table, a vast squarish thrust of rock made squarer by enormous labor. Its smooth top, with room for a fair-sized city, was directly across the valley, and nearly level with where they were standing. As if a fantastic outgrowth of the mountain, the True *Mankh'* was set back on the Table, squat towers at the corners, but the eye went most readily to the graceful dome near the outer edge of the Table, a curve of bright marble, its arched entrance facing true south. A gleaming circle of gold marked the opening at its crown.

"*Ga-Tembúrai —* " he could not keep his voice from trembling.

"I expected it would be larger," Rodlakh said.

"When they talk about its measurements, it is not for the size." The numbers flooded back with no searching. "The base consists of eight hundred and four equal blocks of one *rodukh'*, and there is a gap of one *bedai*. From north to south, door to door, the distance across the Dome is two hundred and fifty-six *rodukh'*, the Number of Wholeness increased by itself its own number of times — "

"Four to the fourth power," Aëlu said.

"What makes you remember all this?" Sunabhal, impatiently.

"These numbers are the beginning of measuring, of building. In any true circle the proportion between its outer measurement and the shortest line crossing its centre must always be the same, eight hundred and four and a quarter to two hundred fifty-six. But dozens more measurements and proportions are kept in the stones of the floor, where black and golden and blue tiles trace out the lines a builder, a surveyor, a geometrist needs to know. This Dome is also our true calendar." He went on to explain how the golden ring at the crown measured 365 *rodukh'* and a *bedai* — or really a *betuloi*, little-finger, less than a fingerspan. To be seen by night, there were many piercings for the sighting, at various seasons of the year, of particular stars, while by day the sun's image was projected on the floor, and special plaques and stones told the date where the sun's image would rest at noon — or, if the date was known, could be used to tell the exact hour by means of a simple calculation. At the centre of the floor where black path and gold came together there was a disk of pure gold, where the sun's image came to rest at noon on midsummer's day, and illumination of that disk was sign for the start of *Shuda'sai g'Asalladhi,* for the *kolukezh'* to the Goodness of Raëdh'. Though he did not give the proper name for the chant he did make the pious sign with his thumb, then noticed Aëlu doing the same.

"To me it was always like a big beehive," Sunabhal said, and Dolvid was incredulous an Island-born officer of the *Adanum* could be so ignorant, either of his religion, or simply the Owani language; the name, *tembu-rai* meant exactly that, a great hive.

Aëlu explained that as with the device on the Patriarchal Seal, where double loops represented bees-wings (as also the proper way for an *atarlai* to tie his waist-cord), the shape of this edifice, lined inside with six-sided tiles of tawny gold, commemorated Yoëlladhu's encounter with the wild bees who led him and his starving followers to abundant honey, not stinging anyone who feasted on it.

"The beginning," Dolvid observed, "for the Owani claim of lordship over others, a sign, Yoëlladhu is supposed to have said, many not of their own kind would labor for the welfare of His children, and not expect any return." Abruptly embarrassed to be repeating so much lore that was hardly secret, he apologized for his wordiness, but Rodlakh admitted that though of course he knew the tale of the wild bees, he had never seen what it was made to stand for.

Galt was clearing his throat. "We are being watched, *Valrabh'*." Along the outer edge of the Table, behind a low wall, about a dozen of the *Adanum* could be discerned, mounted, sitting still. They were armed with lances and evidently observing the march; though there was no easy way to traverse the bowl of the valley, from eminence to eminence across was barely half a mile.

Sunabhal's opinion was these troops would stay where they were, hoping the raiders would try to plunder the True *Mankh'*, where many treasures were said to be kept. As the march continued along the valley's rim, seldom out of sight of the lancers, it seemed he might be right, but as pure defenders they had no need to be in the saddle, and would doubtless become part of whatever force shadowed the retreat. For now, the terrain was poorly adapted to ambush, and Galt was a little less grim. As he confessed, he was used to attacking in the open, defending behind walls, while helping to hunt down many parties of tribal raiders out beyond the Frontier had made him miserably aware how vulnerable a small column was on the march.

Ahead at the top of a long slope was the wide, corbelled arch that counted as entrance to the valley. Past there, free for a while from baleful observation, they might be able to find an opportunity for leaving the trail; though fatigued, everyone's pace quickened. Aëlu went with the long light step of a walker, her face showing neither worry nor grief. Serenity was often overrated as a virtue, or else overpriced; the serene were often just too simple to know why they should not be, as sheep grazing next to the slaughterhouse were. But Aëlu was neither stupid nor oblivious, like someone who existed outside ordinary time, so tidal waves were far-off ripples, a holocaust the tiny flare of a remote star. Fanciful, but that distance was certainly in how she regarded Rodlakh's adoration; she saw him as a boy, as faintly amusing even in the midst of her gratitude for his coming to rescue her. Her Rodlakh was as he must have been when he first came to Kamsilat, more inexperienced and unsure than two weeks ago when he returned to the Mainland. Since then, very swiftly, he had changed, forced to shed both illusions and dependencies; he was quite different from the half-shy youth met a dozen days ago; there were no limits to what he might accomplish, if he could survive this Island adventure.

But none of that maturing was yet in his dealings with Aëlu — if he could be said to have any; the Aëlu he stammered over was only his own dream.

The archway sprang from rock to rock, its position cunningly chosen so that in its opening as they approached nothing could be seen but pale sky; it could be world's end. Bowmen led the way cautiously; this might be the last chance before Doniftu where the retreat could be struck at in confined space.

There was no sound but faint hissing of wind. Carvings on the face of the arch were weathered down to a muddle, and Dolvid could not stay to read inscriptions inside, selections from the Tale of Yoëlladhu, carved in both glyphs and the syllabary, with some later additions in the Script of Shâl. Those reminded him to wonder whether, as he had asked her, Âna had found a way to send Faëdhal the small sheaf of documents they had rescued from Kanavakh's boat, and he tried to tell himself it was praiseworthy to keep his scholarly concerns in the midst of killing. But Âna might have other preoccupations, and about those he could not permit conjecture: to do so would paralyze him with apprehension that became a ravenous guilt no amount of insistence on her resourcefulness could satisfy; they should never, he should never have let her go back into that Karguli den.

For the traveller coming, as most did, in the opposite direction, the change in landscape, first sight of the Valley's stark beauty, would be awing, after passing through these gentler lands. Downhill on the farther side of the arch the road curved left. North and east the ground climbed on in pillars and towers of stone mounting to the mass of Karg' Kamanta, but north and west vistas opened to the plain and the sea. From the right a long arm of the central massif thrust across to bar the northward view to where the port of Doniftu must be. Westerly, the soft sweep seaward was interrupted by hard bars of hill, blue mists coaxed by hazed sun. Strays from the main herd, rocky piers here and there jutted up; warm air pressed in, and not far down there were trees in full leaf. Up here new grass was edging the path, and tough-stemmed shrubs putting out new shoots.

"Kamsilat — " Galt breathed it in.

"We are going to do it," Rodlakh, not in specious encouragement, but as a man struck by irresistible conviction. Dolvid was cheered, although it did not conform to logic. If they must have a boat, and the enemy knew so, the broad country in front of them was a funnel, small end aimed north, for Doniftu. Stopping up that narrow end should be an easy job for their adversaries.

Following the path down the crest of a fading ridge, they soon turned aside to find a small hollow, not well-hidden, but adequate for the brief rest that was a necessity. Under warm sun the wounded were suffering, and except for Galt's wish they had better cover no objections were heard to the stop. On hillside sparsely grassed they flopped gratefully, planting weapons near to hand, unlacing collars, loosening boots. Noldar used his short bow in imitation of a stringed instrument, strumming to accompany a snatch of song mocking their feats.

As Dolvid sat Aëlu said, "*Oh!*" eyes widening. Blood had spread from his little wound to stain most of the lower leg of his breeches. Both Rodlakh and Galt came to look at the nick, which, except for an occasional sharp pricking, did not hurt. Inside and just above the knee the fleshy bulge had been torn, probably by the tang of the arrow. Aëlu moistened a kerchief from Rodlakh's flask, silenced Dolvid's protest with a formidable glance, and washed the wound, which started bleeding again. By folding she found a clean spot on the kerchief to press against the tear, but when she started to tie it he stopped her.

"It is muscle, it will bleed more when you start walking again."

"I cannot march with a bound knee."

"Very well, *Bôdhrai*," her face mocked heroics. "Wear your manhood in scarlet, then. Hold this — " She took his fingers and placed them on the pad of cloth, her cool hands momentarily taking him back to boyhood, when Esodra would make sure he had washed before a meal. Aëlu told him to keep the kerchief pressed to the wound till they moved again.

Rodlakh had watched, squatting on his heels. "When we do, the ways divide — "

"We should take neither." The branch that stayed on higher ground over to the right must come to the Forbidden Road, and that was sure to be patrolled. Bearing left, the lesser path would soon strike the main road as it came curving up from Drin b'Afon; that would be at present the busiest thoroughfare on the Island, and if they crossed it they would be squeezed in a narrowing strip between road and clifftops. Only in rougher country dead ahead, even if it was mouth of the funnel, was any chance of eluding the hunt. They did not need roads for finding Doniftu, which should be easily recognizable by its headland, a wedge-shaped rock, visible well out to sea, used by all ships as a landmark. Sarnak, certainly, could never mistake it.

When Dolvid estimated they were perhaps twelve to fifteen miles from the port, Rodlakh was on his feet ready to resume the march at once. Galt reminded him the men were very weary, and may yet have to fight again; it would be good going to make another five miles.

"I was not thinking of trying for Doniftu today. I wish it could be missed altogether, but we must have a boat. It can't be helped."

"Great Hrafi!" Sunabhal was nearby, using a small knife he was not supposed to have to slice yellow facings from his tunic. "Here you have achieved one of the feats of all history, and you say it can't be helped."

"And with an historian in their ranks," Aëlu teased. "What foresight."

"He is more than that," Rodlakh, very earnestly. "He was first to set foot on the rock of the citadel."

"No, second, *Valrabh'*. Guthdar was first." It was old experience, how early a sober historical account began to merge into something else: those who actually participated could start to make legends within hours. If he got to Kamsilat he would demand a quiet room and two days of peace to write it all down.

They decided to have food, then go on only long enough to reach better country for hiding in; lower down cover could be seen to deepen. Halting for the night quite soon, they could make another start at dawn or before. A pity, as Rodlakh said, to allow the port so much opportunity to prepare a welcome.

Sunabhal said, "Your chance of surprise is long gone; is it so bad to give them some time for stewing? They don't have any senior officers, and it's always a muddle anyway while the Patriarch's away on the Mainland."

This was chilling; Galt hawked and spat. The two men were the same rank, and Dolvid tried to imagine the callow officer of the *Adanum* on the reconnaissance he had made with Galt, or stepping into the quarrel between Sarnak and Truni, calmly counting heads before assault on the citadel, or, best of all, quietly taking the trestle-bridge away from its owners.

"Why we had to go picking fights with the Colony, when everyone knows you've got the best fighters in all Owan — I would be proud, *Valrabh'*, if you could find a place for me."

Rodlakh shook his head. "This is a lean spring for enlistment. If we reach Kamsilat it might be possible. If you do join us, you will remember the name of this realm is Arbhal."

"I'll try, *Valrabh'*."

"You will have to do better than try."

While they ate Rodlakh asked more about Lunu Midhi, about the apparent ruins he had noticed, between the flat rock of the Table and the course of Shuf'Oëladh. Dolvid had also seen the broken masonry, and assumed that was what was left of the *Manai*.

Aëlu said, "There were numbers of *manal*, surely, in various parts?"

"One original, *Ifaka Manai, ga-Lakha Manai, Manayit-balakim-manal*, the School of schools, however you name it. An age ago, before the *manal* became just another tool of Owani power, its teaching was a fine aspiration. Most evils are a perversion of noble beginnings — even *Lekh'Owan*." He could imagine what Âna might say to that, but all the same it was true; men put hard shells about their tender dreams and the shells came to be prized for themselves instead of the good they protected. In the days of the First Empire the *Atarlum* was devoted to teaching Owani belief about the arts of living, and nobles of conquered Vrobhan studied at the *Manal* in Dônshei. When the *manal* spread to all the provinces, that the One Realm could come only from a single language, a single law, an agreed tale of the world's beginning was (he liked to believe) a sincere conviction, not, as it became, a formula merely mouthed, a covert way of advocating Owani supremacy.

"But every folk," Rodlakh objected, "has its tale of the Beginning. What Froghul have is good for Froghul. They do not try to make Owanil believe as they do, or force them to renounce Yoëlladhu."

Dolvid gave a faint but audible moan, wondering if there would ever again in any age be space to discuss all difficulties of what Rodlakh had said. "Patriarch after Patriarch struggled with that question. Some wanted to expunge all rival faiths, others to keep streams of belief that flowed side by side, unmingling. Several tried to be workers in metal, making of two or more separate beliefs an alloy stronger than any. Take Zhôl," he said, and instantly wished he had not. "He began, as far as I can tell, as a Vrobani god, named Jalef."

"That cannot be right. Zhôl is firstborn son to Raëdh and Aëlovoi. You are not going to tell me it was the Vrobanil who — "

"As I say, it is a difficult question," hastily. How tolerant people were, so long as they were talking about the beliefs of others. "In any event, the *manal* deteriorated to what Plakhsila *Kímukoi*, and later your grandfather, wanted to reform — hatcheries of Preference and of hatred between races."

"What about *Shei'Owani*?" Sunabhal said. "They taught us anyone, of any birth, once given true teaching, was as good as — well, was not any different — "

"Was entitled," rescuing him, "to all rights and privileges of Owani birth." This had also come up with Ban-Sila, and it was amazing how such a condescending notion could strike sane people as just. Merely, in any case, another deceit. "Before you could ever enter a *manai* you had to be able to answer questions of custom and lore only an Owani child of good family would ever be taught. Ban-Sila *Deghi* might count as *Shei'Owanai*, but if so he must be the only one in all history."

"But a strong *rabhsai*," Aëlu said, "could surely end Preference for ever."

"So long as he did not have to go to the Families for money. So long as he really wanted change." This was very interesting. Everyone had agreed Aëlu did not concern herself with policies, but here, well beyond simply entering the discussion, she was lecturing Rodlakh, or goading him.

He knew it, and was burning with self-consciousness. "It might be the battles he fought after hanging up his sword were what made my grandfather great."

"And he had the dauntlessness of Laluvoi beside him —" quoting the end of a passage in his unfinished book.

"You knew her well, did you not?" Aëlu said.

"Late in her life, yes. She was shrewd as well as wise." He admired the unsentimental way Laluvoi had used the feelings she evoked: the Families had never been able to reconcile their distaste for most of her policies with their pride in her as one of their own.

"Then a Ban-Sila comes along," Rodlakh, despondently, "and all the battles have to be fought all over again. But if not Ban-Sila, why not Finú, or Tovakh?" He fell into a reverie. His conclusion was valid: the lawfulness of Ban-Sila's accession could be challenged only at the cost of querying Great Banak's right to rule.

Noldar, on watch, came down the slope to speak in Galt's ear. A small detachment of horse had appeared well above them, between them and the path, moving at a walk, about a quarter-mile away. Their long lances had gold pennons of the *Adanum*. Eight in all, and they were keeping watch on the party resting in the hollow.

"Will they charge?" Rodlakh said.

"Not unless there are more than we see, *Asai*," Galt, grimly. "None of these will reach us if they do." His men already had arrows nocked.

After the two forces had stared at each other for a while Galt suggested the men of the *Adanum* might not know the range of Frontier bows. If these eight men were part of a trap, he wryly conceded, it made no difference whether or not Rodlakh's forces took the bait; they were trapped, stand, fly or fight. They could not outrun *pefral*.

Watched steadily, they packed up again, and prepared to advance in the direction of the *Adanum* men. Every wounded man took a weapon of some sort, and Dolvid went to Guthdar, who was carrying a spare bow, taken from one of their own dead.

"You shoot, *Bôdhrai*?"

"Longbow — Gabhani bow." He tested the stiff horn weapon. "I can't speak about these *zhin'pefral* you carry." Guthdar grinned: *zhin'pefrai* was a siege weapon, a beamed catapult for throwing giant boulders a third of a mile.

From each of half a dozen authentic bowmen Dolvid asked an arrow, and put the sheaf at his back, under his pack-strap. Rodlakh also equipped himself with a bow; Sunabhal asked for one, and was given a pike. If anything, being armed would make it harder for him to change sides in a hot fight.

So, with their best bowmen leading, they marched straight for the waiting *péfrapravádal*. Next to Dolvid, Sarnak, at last in boots, brandished a pike and kept up a loud commentary on the character, fighting qualities and parentage of the *Adanum*; Sunabhal, next to him, was in no position to differ.

If attacked from all sides, their object was to let fly with as many arrows as they could before the cavalry could close. Otherwise, if the eight watchers let them get as near as two hundred paces, Galt was confident they could all be killed. He was insistent on keeping formation on the hillside, as if that could hold off a charge by well-trained cavalry; these were toy tactics appearance of just two squadrons of enemy would instantly expose as laughable.

The range closed steadily. At three hundred paces Galt called, "Ready," swinging his bow into position. The officer of the cavalry half-stood in the stirrups, and leaning back to tug on his reins, issued a sharp order. He left the crest, and one by one his men wheeled to follow, quickly disappearing.

"I did not want to show them our range," Galt told Rodlakh, "till I was sure we could bring them all down."

After the retreat went back to the track for the short distance they would need it, the tactics of the enemy became clear; to follow, not to challenge, staying out of bow range, perhaps to hope stragglers could be snapped up. Near a fork in the trail, and again a short way farther on, Rodlakh halted to see whether their shadows would close. Each time the cavalry also stood, slouched in their saddles, not as they believed entirely out of range, but on its margin.

This was a wild place. The main trail clung halfway up a long, stony escarpment, shored up with stacked rubble where original stonework had aged away. All at once the Arnan was in plain sight, pewter under the hot, hazed sun.

"Doniftu Headland," Sarnak pointed, half-right, more northerly than Dolvid would have anticipated, a bluish arrowhead of rock, sharply defined. One of the wounded, a man of Galt's build who had taken a pike-point in the neck, slumped forward in the saddle; Sarnak put up a hand to hold him as he swayed sideways.

"Down there — " Rodlakh indicated a steep and broken but negotiable route. "Let us make for the thickets." Some stray tufts of Kamanta grass, then a gully was filled with brush and thorn, a few scattered alders to be seen.

With the horses, progress was slow, but small-footed and short in the leg, each individually led, they showed no sign of refusing the hard slope, picking their ways with care that was instinctive or instilled by long practice. Galt said, "They'll never risk a *pefrai*'s ankles on this." He seemed to be right; after a wait by the fork the cavalry ambled along the upper trail, above the course of the retreat, which only gradually diverged from theirs.

Digging in his heels, leaning back against the pull of a horse, Sarnak said, "Odi's armband! You ever do it on a three-legged bed?"

"Do what?" one of the wounded men baited, and Sarnak silently mouthed the word he had left out in deference to Aëlu's presence.

"Tomorrow," cheerfully, when they reached the fringes of the brush, "someone will have to lend me some breeches." Rodlakh opened his mouth, and closed it without a word.

They were still in plain view of the watchers above, yet this inadequate protection was a comfort. Galt led them on a swing to the left, and had picked up what had been a watercourse, a pebbled hollowing where going was easier for horses, the cover deepening with clumps of alder and hazel. Pleasing to imagine anxiety up above as they passed from view, though they could not be far lost; they were moving deeper into the narrowing funnel, here no more than five or six miles wide. Off left where the road must be the ground was much balder.

In a short while they unexpectedly came out into a short strip of meadow between thicket and the dry watercourse, enclosed by tangled undergrowth and trees with their leaves well-developed, though in the fresh colors of early spring. Not far ahead their gully dipped, and there was a live stream chattering down to the northwest.

"Well," Rodlakh said, "we are not going to pry off our shadows. We may as well rest."

Galt quickly approved of the place, and the men, filing onto the grass, were grey in the face, more than ready to close books on the day's adventures. Dolvid, with Rodlakh and Galt, pushed through some dense growth and climbed a gravelled embankment for a view upward to the track, half a mile away. Almost exactly above, four of the *Adanum* were sitting still, and they started to dismount as the other four went slowly back to where the ways divided. After some discussion they took the coastward way, moving into a lope and soon out of sight.

Though the watchers above had taken care to surround themselves with nothing, Galt was sure he and a few of his best men could use what cover there was and get close enough for their bows. Rodlakh considered whether it was worth doing; their chief object here was not to kill men of the *Adanum*, though he would not flinch from doing anything necessary to the escape. The other four plainly had gone to fetch reinforcements, perhaps enough to encircle this hollow; to kill the watchers and slip away was a tempting idea, except there was nowhere to slip to; they could not vanish, and must continue making for Doniftu. Where they were would be very poor country for a cavalry attack, and on the whole Rodlakh would rather risk being surrounded here by night than chance being caught in open country in their present state of exhaustion. If, then, they were staying here, it meant nothing to kill the men up above.

To Galt, obviously, any enemy was fair game if he did not take proper precautions, and Rodlakh's wish to spare lives was too complicated. But he acceded, seeing a full-scale attack would be unlikely here. The horse, he predicted, would be used as shepherds, to keep the retreat headed into a well-laid trap in front of the port, with every bow the Island could muster.

"I won't have the love, *Asai*, of those who have to stand the early watch," as they started back.

"Begin with half-watches. Dolvid and I will be part of the watch."

Aëlu had not much to tell about her captivity. She was kept blindfolded on the boat, fed, allowed to rest, bundled ashore, guessing it must be the Island, because the journey from Kamsilat was so short. "Short in actual hours, not for me with my eyes bound." When they let her see again, she saw and recognized the stair to the citadel at Drin b'Afon, confirming her conviction about who had abducted her. She had so far been told nothing except she would not be hurt if she obeyed orders, and now she became subject of a hot debate, with Rhonalai, the senior officer, nervously unsure whether she could be kept in the Summer Palace while the Patriarch was absent, and the Steward

Vedrughi quite sure she could not; it ended with her installation in the guardhouse, a little later with Sunabhal for a companion.

"How did you know I had been taken to Drin b'Afon?"

"We guessed," Rodlakh said.

"And had some confirmation — " not wishing to be the one to explain to Sebhal's widow who Âna was.

Rodlakh over-explained how they had come to Tan Lughsai from Kadon Dinul, after words with the *rabhsai*. She, however, was after something else. "Burantal was where Sebhal died?"

Rodlakh tried, but an excess of tact made him tongue-tied. He had, in any case, not seen much of Sebhal's last fight. Dolvid took up the tale, finding Aëlu already knew who the trader Sett was. Impossible, he discovered, to lose a feeling of failure, and when Aëlu searched him with a frown he knew she had caught the note of self-blame. Lips pressed tight, she shook her head, and Rodlakh told about the Marionette Guild and Sebhal's death, still leaving out Âna.

"Did he speak?"

Dolvid repeated words that had embittered Âna, and reflected it might be equally sour for Aëlu to know her dying husband had spoken them holding another woman's hand. But she cupped her face in her hands and wept gently: Rodlakh rather clumsily put an arm about her as they both knelt on the ground. She did not lean to her nephew; Dolvid stood awkwardly and went the few steps to where his sleeping-bag was spread.

Limply exhausted, he expected profound sleep. Muscles stiff, hurt knee throbbing, he dozed fitfully, hearing the watch exchange muttered comments, watching the sky darken. Not dreams but waking pictures of the day's events nagged in his head, pushing him back from the borders of sleep. Staring up at a treetop blacker than the indigo sky he perceived he could never separate glory from horror. What they had accomplished today ought to soften revulsion for all the butchery, but instead his pride only made him guiltier.

Hardest to admit was the joy brought by killing itself; did that make him a monster? Blood squeezing between fingers as he rammed a knife into a pikeman's throat, the majestic joke of half-a-dozen men swept from the aqueduct by a flight of arrows — men as full as he was of blood and brain, gut and feeling, spinning down into that abyss. When blood was hot, there was no doubt killing was fun; that was real. Yet he was horrified by someone — by Rheduban, who openly acknowledged that pleasure, indulged himself in it. Was it hypocrisy? the same as what he had told Neldron about Kamin-Tolagh's licentiousness, that Rheduban was different only in that he had power to do what others desired?

No: the horror was real, too, and that, for the Rhedubans, was left out — or perhaps also to be enjoyed. No moment lives only in itself; it becomes a memory while it is happening. Pleasures with no bad aftertaste (vanquishing a stubborn bit of translation, a mating without bitterness, dear Âna) extended happily in time, but blood-lust, like the passing joy of anger, well-phrased abuse, drunkenness, turned to shame.

But, oh, it was unwise to use rasping thought to erode away the satisfactions in a period of necessary killing. They had met a great test, and triumphed, and any man in Arbhal would envy them. Their cause was a just one, if ever it was possible to be sure that was not merely an excuse for indulging in the heady joys of murder.

Something white was gleaming at the edge of sleep. The two men who had lain so long in their blood at the guardhouse door: with one the upper lip had drawn back in death, letting out a small dribble of blood and vomit, leaving the eye-tooth exposed. That was not the worst, but entrails spilled through slit bellies were nastier in words or in memory than when real; to recall such things on the march could make his step a mincing one, as first the soles of his feet and then his manhood shrank in revulsion, a wave of weakness he would do anything to conceal.

A warm yet clammy dawn struggled with an overcast that had made the night moonless. Dolvid shivered; he had been up since midnight, plenty of dank hours for despondency to capture him. He hated this narrowing strip of country they were caught in, and their attempt to reach the coast was bound to mean more fighting, more deaths.

Galt said, "Aye, *Bôdhrai*, this is a mad craft, when men have no quarrel with one another. Myself, I'd as soon wrestle with a man, and whoever took the fall would be beaten."

"If it was for your land? If you were the one thrown, that would be the end of it, and he could take all you owned?"

"If that was the bargain we made. I have seen hill-goats battle for their matings — there's a winner and a loser, and the loser doesn't go on fighting till he is killed, though losing he may go without a mate — can my land mean more to me than ram-ram does to a billy-goat? Mostly they don't really fight, just snort and butt a little — they've made some sort of bargain there. Anyway — " he grinned. "I would not be the one thrown. And so long as men try to kill me, this — " patting his bow — "is a craft I'll do well at. But, *Bôdhrai*, I don't care for soldiering on foot, and I don't care for islands. You do not know Landegh, *Bôdhrai*?"

"I have wanted to see the West."

"It's — no one denies it's a dry land, hard — " shy of showing too much partiality. "Days there will already be hot at noon, but nights can be cold in high summer. No one's ever sorry to see the walls of the old Drin again." He meant Drin Navuna, the Frontier fortress. "Landegh's a horse too wild to break — it takes skill to stay on its back, and if you let down your guard for one instant, you'll be thrown."

"Those who can stay on such horses come to love them."

"Not losing their respect." Out of stubborn night Rodlakh joined their talk. "It is true, you can fall in love with that harshness in the West. Someday it would be good to ride to the borders of the First Empire with a few men, men like Galt, who know how to live on Landegh. They say you can come to green country in the end, beyond Minshei, and then the Western Ocean."

"Somewhere there is the grave of Lost Plakhan."

"We could go and find it. What can they not do, the men who subdued Drin b'Afon?"

No response; Rodlakh's rather forced exuberance was not lighting any fresh fires. "Is night over?"

"By the time-wick, *Asai*." Galt showed the glowing stub.

"The men should be wakened."

"Aye."

Cold food and drink, icy waters of the stream for washing in, did not much to cheer the general waking. Aëlu wondered if she could beg spare breeches from one of the less short-legged Froghul. "Their shirts are too broad in the shoulders for me."

Rodlakh said, "There is a shirt and outshirt in my pack." When she observed he was scarcely narrower in the shoulders than most of the men, he became confused, and Dolvid knew why. At Kadon Dinul when they redivided the food to give Âna more, she had made space by giving some spare clothes for Rodlakh to keep.

"A woman's clothes," shaking out the fine wool shirt.

"They belong to another one that was with us — Âna. She stayed on the Mainland."

"Âna, Sett's little niece?"

"She came back from the Colony with Sett."

"No need for blushes, *Valrabh'*. Wars would go out of favor if they were nothing but warring."

"She has not been — " he struggled, "my particular friend." In Aëlu's level look he was caught between conflicting motives, to explain away Âna without bringing in Sebhal, but also to maintain his own pure fidelity to Aëlu.

Dolvid offered faint support. "Âna's home is in Lower Paowan, not far from where I was living in exile."

Aëlu turned from one man to the other, perplexed. "When I saw her at Kamsilat, I thought her pretty enough for any man to be proud to call his — particular friend. Well." She went off to change clothes.

Into tension Rodlakh threw, "How is your wound?"

"Shiny." Except where the flesh was open, it was bright pink. When Aëlu came back she insisted on careful washing, and persuaded all the hurt to bathe their wounds, even at the expense of some fresh bleeding, which some of the fighting men muttered was all wrong. But Aëlu, her coercion given force by whose wife she had been, urged also that they bury yesterday's filthy bandages and if necessary sacrifice a shirt or two to fresh dressings. In her own right, she was admirable. "With Frontier patrols, not one man who kept his wound clean and changed dressings has ever been lost to fever, or the maggots." The last word convinced any who had been hanging back. Every officer of the *Adanum Plakh'* had to carry a flat box of the ointment made with *garaminat* in oil of sheepskin, and Dolvid asked Sunabhal for his, so all wounds could be smeared with the thick brown unguent. On his knee it stung far worse than the arrow ever had.

"It will deaden in a minute — " carefully expressionless as she held down the new dressing.

"Have you been to the Frontier often?"

"No, seldom. He wanted them kept apart, husband and warrior. Put two fingers there."

Galt had been out scouting with a couple of men. He came back perplexed. Their watchers had gone, and there was no enemy to be seen. It might mean only they were satisfied the retreat would not continue by darkness, in which case they could be counted on to return. But when Rodlakh hoped they might be able to shake off pursuit, Galt jutted a lip, and said there were bare ridges to be crossed, which could not be skirted, so he perceived it, without meeting the road.

Every start was different. This one was reluctant; no one was trying to create delay, but one man or another fussed a little longer with boots or packstraps, had forgotten to pack a cup or a sock, needed a brief visit into the bushes before falling in. "Out of spirits," Dolvid confided to Aëlu, and when she looked a question; "This is a dreary business, after Drin b'Afon, where they were giants."

As Rodlakh, showing irritation, went past, she caught at his sleeve. "Tell them something. It is needed."

His puzzlement lasted only a second or two. He nodded understanding. Calling the men in close as he stood in the middle of the clearing he gave a quiet-voiced, light-toned address, saying he expected his next sleep to be in Kamsilat. He told them they were within ten or twelve miles of the port, Doniftu, which they all knew was a short way from their home, across the western Arnan. "At Doniftu, we shall have to take away one of the Patriarch's ships. They will all be guarded, naturally, but not so well guarded as the Lady Aëlu was." This caused general laughter, and he finished by asking for one last day of wide-open eyes and taut bowstrings, to bring them all home.

The change was astonishing; Dolvid was invigorated by the new confidence the men conveyed as they shouldered their bows, boosted the hurt into their saddles. Apparently Rodlakh had succeeded in heartening himself.

They went as before with badly-wounded in the middle, horses fed and watered, moving their heads alertly. Dolvid's knee was stiffer, and abruptly he realized he had been distracted into letting Aëlu bind it. She was loping beside him, bare-wristed in Âna's shirt, her dignity not lessened by the bagginess of borrowed breeches.

Going was easier as cover thinned, but also more nervous, and soon they came to the bare ridges Galt had mentioned, a series running down from the high ground eastward. Above, they began blade-sheer, gentling as they descended, becoming mere swells of land down leftward where the road must lie. Only there could any growth be seen at the crown.

"Cavalry country," Rodlakh, grimly.

"Cavalry-hunting country, *Asai*, for good bowmen who can hide." Galt had been up far enough into the highland to say the hollows between rows of ridges were spattered with clumps of brush and patches of tall weed on a flat, pebbled base.

Above and behind, following windings of the track on that precarious hillside, riders of the *Adanum* appeared, and there was no use making for cover; the retreat had been seen. Not moving at any great pace the cavalry, intermittently vanishing against a background deep in shadow, was rapidly overhauling their quarry. Galt, peering, said, "More than before. A file, I think." Twelve.

Vigilant for enemy ahead, the retreat crossed the first of the ridges. The next was lower, intervening dale a little less than a half-mile across. From the summit they could see the third ridge was succeeded by the soft roll of farmlands, and after that the barrier swinging across from the central highlands, cutting off their view of Doniftu Headland. Down to the left it was all a kinder country, though the line of the road could not certainly be identified.

Before the last of the retreating column was across the ridge and filing down into the hollow, the enemy horse had begun slowly descending along the spine of that same ridge, big *pefral* very cautious, held back hard. The twelve enemy were all lancers, and not eager to challenge Frontier bows, holding again where the slope was less extreme, watching the retreat go in among islands of bushes and shocks of a tall, unfamiliar weed, with a spreading top, resembling a ragged elm seen from a distance. Not till Galt and Rodlakh, the leaders, were mounting the second and least of the three ridges did the *péfrapravádal* move again, coming along the former crest to align themselves behind the marchers. Once the retreating column had filed down into the second, more thickly grown dale, the cavalry, forming a well-spaced double column of their own, came ambling after.

Galt, Dolvid and Rodlakh had ducked down and doubled back to lie on the backslope and observe the enemy as they threaded the bushes, lances upright.

"*Asai*," Galt exulted in low-voiced contempt. "I did not see anyone report a count of our number." Elementary to him, trained in Frontier wars, that enemy were counted whenever they came back in view, to be sure some had not slipped away, or concealed themselves.

Rodlakh understood at once Galt wanted to try an ambush, and their plans were made swiftly. The column, turning farther westward, made for where the crest of the third ridge was broken and irregular, flank scored with bold lines made by water. Before the leading enemy had climbed to the top of the ridge behind, the retreat was diminished by five, Galt and his four favorite bows, the most they dared use for their trap; any more and their followers would notice the shortage at a glance. Ascending the last ridge the column went single-file to make the change in numbers harder to detect.

On the backslope the able men turned and quickly spread out to lie just under the crest. Below, the wounded dismounted to hold horses, and Aëlu was there, watching anxiously.

The men of the *Adanum* were not coming on without any precaution. Two riders had watched from the second ridge till the column was out of sight, and the double column advanced with as much as eight to ten paces between horse and horse; head to tail in a normal tight formation they would be far more vulnerable to concealed bows.

On the ridge waiting bowmen laid out their arrows, and beside them the captured pikes, in case it came to close quarters. Rodlakh had again borrowed a spare bow, Dolvid had never relinquished his, and that made eleven in all, waiting.

"Not too soon," Rodlakh entreated, as, a quarter-mile away, the leading horsemen bobbed into a sandy dip before starting the upslope. Timing was crucial; revealed too early for the bows on the ridge to join in, the ambushers could be hunted down; too late and the cavalry might close with the men on the ridge, making Galt's bows useless.

The insignia of the officer could be seen, half-squadron, young and very nervous, constantly half-standing in his stirrups to look around, or back to be sure his men were with him. He must be cursing his superiors for sending him out with numbers too small to be sure of winning a pitched battle; there might not be many of the *Adanum* left on the Island, but his force could surely have been stiffened with some auxiliaries who knew how to ride. Finding himself sympathetically in his enemy's mind, Dolvid wished there was no need for renewed dying.

The last cavalryman came up out of the little hollow. Rodlakh's breathing was noisy; the nearest riders were within a hundred and twenty paces. One of the rearward riders suddenly jerked and fell sideways from the saddle.

For an endless three seconds it seemed to make no other difference, then two more men were struck, both towards the rear of the double column, one letting out a sharp cry. The officer and his other file-leader turned; *pefral* were beginning to shy and sidle, and one of the lancers gave a shout. Five seconds of stunned indecision cost the officer the chance of salvaging anything from the fight.

"Now," Rodlakh barked, standing, bending his bow. Dolvid's spine twitched as he stood, imagining an ambush for the ambushers, a much larger force of enemy emerging from the farmlands behind. He glanced over his shoulder to prove that was absurd, and when he turned back the officer had been first to fall to the bows on the ridge. A nearby horse was hit. The second-in-command roared an order and tried to wave his men forward, but only three could follow him. Two had already been brought down by Galt's skirmishers, while others with lances levelled were wheeling in a frantic search for their adversaries. A thrown man stood, sword in hand, while his wounded *pefrai* ran wild, and one of the rearmost was circling, trying to decide which fight if any to join.

Dolvid's attention momentarily left the action down below. The men on the ridge were yelling ferociously; he had not realized how much these proud western warriors hated being chased by an enemy they could not turn and fight, and there was a vindictive joy in their bowmanship against the shrunken parody of a charge. Two men fell quickly, a third at the foot of the steep slope. The file-leader, crouched in his saddle, weaving, was for moments unhittable; his *pefrai* broke pace as it challenged the slope, and another arrow passed inches in front of him. Just as Rodlakh dropped his bow, reaching for his sword, Dolvid, with a half-pulled bow, shot the man in the upper arm, and another arrow, coming from the left where Sarnak was, hit him in the leg. The *pefrai*, burdenless, snorted by, and one of the Frontier men darted forward to knife the officer before he could roll over.

The other fights were as good as done. Empty-saddled *pefral* were loping aimlessly, and the unhorsed man had vanished. Rodlakh shouted; racing away westward was the one man never engaged. His horse took clumps of vegetation in reckless jumps, rider bent to the animal's neck. Galt appeared, ran to a slight eminence, drew his bow sighting carefully, waited, then let go his shot. It was prodigious, and everyone watched the race between arrow and *pefrai*. The bolting man swerved past some tangled branches, and the watchers on the ridge groaned as the arrow passed his right ear, not a foot from the target. A second from Galt's bow was in the air, but would obviously fall short. Rodlakh had tried to capture the file-leader's *pefrai*, but had to admit the fugitive had too good a start. The battle was over, but it would not be long before word of it reached Doniftu.

A victory with no loss, it seemed, but then two men below were assisting a third, Noldar. Rodlakh, after getting his men off the skyline, went down to meet Galt.

"Shall we capture the *pefral, Asai*?"

Tempting, but Rodlakh soon shook his head. "We have to get under cover; *pefral* would only hinder us. You have wounded?"

"Noldar's thigh. He dodged a lance and caught a hoof."

"A trade I'd do every day in the week." Noldar came up in pain but walking, helped by his brother Guthdar. "Kuno made sure the lance didn't get another go."

If the rider who escaped did not break his neck, there would be aid for the *Adanum* wounded soon enough. Galt regretted that one survivor, and Dolvid the start of killing that had no finish; the only object in ambushing the cavalry had been to lose pursuit. Sunabhal, however, held the chief effect of the one man who reached safety would be to add to tales of the fearsome Frontier bows, and with the unendearing callousness he had for his own comrades-in-arms, asked how many of the *Adanum* there could be left on the Island. "The garrisons were all stripped down, nobody knew why, to send a few men each to Drin b'Afon — they have to maintain a seaward watch in the ports. The high officers are on the Mainland, and hardly anyone on the Island knows how to deal with this raid — I honestly doubt there's much left between us and the Arnan but a rabble, with a few *Adanum* giving orders they hope will be obeyed. Who would want to fight battles with half-trained farm-boys for the job? Troops with ten thumbs can be more trouble than the enemy."

"No doubt you have fought many such battles — " Rodlakh's level-eyed gaze put Sunabhal in his place.

Yet what he said about strength mustered against them might have some truth; for two hours, skirting pastureland or stealing across its margins, they saw no one except a couple of cowherds who stopped talk to stare at what they might think was a dream, the column of war-worn soldiery passing from trees to trees a quarter mile away. The day stayed dull, the view west uncertain, though the road could not be above two or three miles distant, following the same line as low, dark hills. Their own way began climbing again, along the skirts of a long spur, leading to higher hills beyond which the Forbidden Road must be. Trees here were too evenly spaced and too much of an age to be natural woods.

"These must be the tree-plantations of Pedhival," Aëlu said — "Pedhival the brother of Petakoi, Tovakh's wife. These were her father's lands; she was brought up near here."

"Are you somehow akin?" Dolvid had the temerity to ask.

"All Island families are, one way or another, but also Petakoi's first husband was my father's cousin. We were the landless branch." That was the husband whose opportune death in a suspicious accident left Petakoi free to marry Tovakh. Aëlu must have been a very small girl at the time.

"She was not much loved in her youth. In her hunting days she killed more than one horse, and that was remembered later."

After conferring, Galt led them almost due west, staying well upslope among the trees. In a mile or so Rodlakh called a halt and they sat on soft ground for a meal, horses munching quietly at spring grasses. Past the slender, spaced tree-stems, the plain below, pasture cleanly divided from plowed lands, was seen with somewhat the effect of a leaded window, a series of panes; a knot of buildings belonging to a prosperous farm, stone-built villa at the centre.

"We shall have to climb the ridge, and attempt to cross the Forbidden Road before cover this side gives out," Rodlakh said.

"*Bôdhrai* — " Galt squatted down. "What do you make of that — right of the barn there?" He meant, where the land folded, presumably to the course of a stream, and where, sticking up above the fold was a row of spikes that might be taken for a fence, unless closely studied.

"Lances?"

"So I would say." Mounted, or perhaps standing next to their horses, a dozen cavalry, at least, were concealed there.

That there were enemies here began to create them; the innocent landscape darkened with soldiery waiting in ambush. This side of the flat and colorless Arnan, the line of the coastal road was unmistakable, and where a shoulder of the hills jutted out, what till now had been only a patch of shadow had the glint of weapons in it. At the end of another farm building were hindquarters of horses never bred for plowing or pulling wagons, and where a small hedge behind the villa divided neat gardens from barnyard, an archer stood to kick cramp from his foot, and was at once pulled down by two others.

"Hrafi!" Rodlakh said in a low voice. Along the road, barely a mile away, more cavalry was moving very slowly south.

"All this for our handful?" Galt spat. "Why haven't they ridden out to make a search?"

"They wanted to choose the ground," Dolvid said. "In front of those dozen *péfrapravádal*, we were to walk into the middle of this welcome."

"If they didn't run away, seeing us coming."

"That's just it," Sunabhal said. "I tell you, you should hear what tales they're telling about your prowess. They are defending Doniftu, and wishing you would try somewhere else."

"If there were no *Adanum* there, we might try parleying for a truce and a safe-conduct."

Sunabhal agreed. "*Asai*, if it weren't for the *Adanum*, they would give you a boat and wave goodbye," but this was an alarming return of the Rodlakh who thought he could negotiate with Ban-Sila.

A good bet there would be enemy lookouts on this actual hillside, and probably archers lurking somewhere in the fringes of the trees. Best chance of avoiding them was to go straight and silent up and over the ridge, but before they could move again, Galt hissed, "What's this?"

From westward three riders of the *Adanum* were coming in a hurry, cutting across tilled land as well as pasture, taking a hedge at a leap. They vanished by the fold where the stream was, and reappeared near the villa. Two waited while one dismounted and bustled inside; meanwhile others of the *Adanum* came out of concealment to gather by the new arrivals, perhaps questioning them. At a guess, this was first news of the fight that morning and its outcome.

Soon a group emerged from the villa, an officer of the *Adanum* putting on riding-gloves, and several subordinates, including a trumpeter. A horse was brought for the officer, and he was handed a helm.

"Under-Captain Kaëfanai," Sunabhal breathed. "When did he come back to the Island?"

Reason to be gladder they had not acted either on Sunabhal's cheerful pronouncements about a dispirited remnant of the *Adanum* here on Kamanta, nor Rodlakh's desire to parley; Kaëfanai, nominally second to an aging Captain, effectively commander of the entire *Adanum*, would not have been likely to bargain with g'*Asalladh*'s enemies.

The trumpet was sounded, and a force of archers and pikemen began appearing from many hides to form up in the yard. The lancers spotted by Galt rode up out of their gully, while farther to the west some other horse, not regular cavalry, trotted from concealment in a patch of orchard. Very quickly, two-and-a-half to three hundred armed men were assembled. Many obviously were not real soldiers, but there was about a squadron of regulars to stiffen them, besides those over by the road.

Another sounding of the trumpet began what was meant as a general advance. The bowmen gradually disentangled and formed groups of about twenty, each with a few pikemen. Cavalry was behind foot at the centre, with contingents sent trotting out to the flanks; a file, looking everywhere but up into the trees, passed not sixty paces from the watching men.

A nervous army; men of the *Adanum* kept approaching Kaëfanai for further instructions, and he repeated an embracing gesture. No group of foot wanted to be in advance of the others; it was relatively open farmland where they were, but with hollows and patches of denser growth that might conceal the deadly bows they had heard so much about.

Soon, except for a slow-moving line of horse on the distant road, and an uninspired rearguard, makeshift cavalry on farm horses, there were no enemy left in sight. Rodlakh straightened from his tense crouch. "There could not be a dozen men with weapons left between here and waterfront."

Tying horses back together to lead them, giving badly wounded all help they could, they went straight up the slope, a new urgency the wind filling their sails. The planted trees ended abruptly; through an evergreen hedge and across a band of grass, they came to where they looked down on the Forbidden Road, hard-stoned and empty. Behind, Karg' Kamanta had again risen splendid from its foothills, clean-edged today against cloud. Front and left, the blue-black wedge of Doniftu Headland was very near. Dolvid shivered a little, but the Road did not overcome him with its *mai*, and that might be because he knew it was not immemorially *forbidden*. Well after the Return it had been part of the normal route between Kamsilat and Kadon Dinul, shortening that journey by not less than half a day, even for cargoes, allowing for unloading a ship at Doniftu and loading another at the Island's eastward port, Pavani. Closing of the road had nothing to do with rites of the *Atarlum*, but had been a weapon in disputes between *rabhsai* and Patriarch, only later surrounded with the *ga-dazhai* of holier forbiddings, so the Island home of the *Atarlum* could lie like a dead tree across natural paths of the realm.

They slipped over in small groups, crossing bare embankment into better cover on the north side. Here, they could come down into Doniftu, as Sarnak advised, from north of east, to the larger and older of its two harbors, used by traders and fishermen. South Harbor, with better quays, was Patriarch's property, and used mainly if not solely by the *Atarlum*. It also had a garrison, but Sunabhal said that was on the spit dividing the two harbors.

The houses surrounding Old Harbor were drab and huddled, small-windowed, all built of the same dull stone. Sunabhal said there were some grander buildings up on the ridge by South Harbor, but Dolvid was inattentive, pondering the marvel an officer of Kaëfanai's standing would permit this retreat to walk clear around his left flank. He had often toyed with the idea that in war, when superior forces lose, the primary failure, whatever other elements may be, is of will. Was it possible Kaëfanai, hearing tales of his enemy's exploits, had wanted, in depths of his heart, to avoid the fight?

Marshfire, he told himself sternly. Here and now they were crossing long-crumbled fortifications, passing between small, close houses. The few in the street, women, children, an old man or two, quickly vanished, and it was easy to see why, the unkempt, bloodstained, weapon-ready band they were. Their close-packed march to the harbor went unopposed, though Sunabhal was still letting his eyes dart, as if again undecided whether he should stay with these men of the West.

They would soon have to abandon the horses, and some of the wounded were near collapse. Haun, the little Froghuli Sarnak had hauled off the cliff at Drin b'Afon, twice wounded in fights by the Bridge, suddenly shouted a fierce string of curses, mixed with words about death and dying. Rodlakh angrily told the man to be quiet, but as the words tailed off moistened a square of cloth from his water-flask, and reached up to wipe Haun's face.

The harbor was a backbend with a low wall, and guarding the small gateway was an uncertain group of pikemen, not soldiers, rough-clad working men armed for the occasion, keeping their ground tentatively, too scared to run, as the men of the West approached.

"Wait — " Rodlakh ran ahead. Dolvid, guessing his mind, went after him, and as they came to the end of the dwellings it occurred to him the hapless pikes could be bait in a trap, with bows massed in the shelter of the houses. He drew the sword that had belonged to the *kímukan* Rodlakh fought, a fine blade, notched a little in its owner's last fight.

Well in front of his own men, some dozen or fifteen paces short of the pikes, Rodlakh reversed his sword and laid it at his feet: Island fishermen, no matter how ignorant, could understand that. "Clear off," he called, not angrily as when he cursed the frightened groom at Burantal, but still commanding. "We do not mean you any harm. Go!"

Shifting, glances were exchanged, some hopeful that after all they would not have to stand here and be killed for reasons beyond their comprehension.

"Go," Rodlakh, with a quick glance back to be sure no one would shoot needlessly. "We'll let you go; go now!"

It worked. With some muttering the men edged then half-turned to shamble away, jostling, need to save dignity resulting in a kind of ragged dance-step, with many backward glances. One called out, "Who are you?" and was told by several others to shut up. Dolvid came up beside Rodlakh. "That was not wise, *Valrabh'*," but he was glad what would have been slaughter had been avoided.

Distant shouting came. As Sunabhal had tried to describe, the high ground dividing the town in halves continued out as a rock-spit between the two harbors. Battlements and a low, craggy tower fused into the spine of the rock, and there yellow-crested soldiers were gesticulating, yelling both general alarm, and particular abuse at the retreat of their auxiliaries. They were too distant to be any immediate threat.

From the gateway in the wall a steep stair went down a low cliff-face to where on a new-moon strip of silvery sand a dozen or so vessels were drawn up, mainly tiny fishing-boats. At the far side, against a breakwater rough-built of stone, a larger ship was moored, a two-masted coastal vessel, broad in the beam and with a shallow draft. Half a mile farther north the stark headland cliff stood.

Sarnak said of the stout cargo-ship, "She's ready to sail. You see the canvas is hung. She won't give us good legs if we're chased."

"You can sail her?" Rodlakh was keeping anxious watch on the garrison.

"Sail herself, *Asai*. Galt could sail that one." Sarnak got the face he wanted out of the half-squadron.

They took the steep stair as rapidly as they could, Aëlu helping to calm the wounded, telling them with more optimism than logic could share that this would be the last of their trials. Rodlakh was first on the beach, and as Dolvid joined him he saw women, a thin man, ducking out of sight behind fishing-boats. Nets hung for mending stirred slightly in a breeze Sarnak would have to assess.

"They have at least one *zhin'pefrai* — " Rodlakh nodded at the fortified spit between harbors. Against white sky the beam of the stone-throwing device was being wound back by urgent men. Other helmed figures, carrying longbows, were moving landward. High trumpets sounded on one repeated note, like the alarm at Drin b'Afon, as the retreat moved down the beach. A small boy stood tranced between two boats to watch the fighters pass, and was yanked back by a mother, the terror in her face beyond reach of the reassurance Rodlakh tried to convey.

"Come," he said to Sarnak, and with another seaman, Muranak, ran ahead. Furled sails were already being hauled to masthead when Dolvid arrived with Aëlu.

The waist had space for several pairs of rowers, and the weighty oars were aboard: in their shortage of men two pairs with two men to an oar would have to suffice, if there were to be some bows for defense. On either side of the aftermast the decking of the poop was extended to make a sheltered place, with provision for a canvas to be stretched above oarsmen amidships. On the wide deck forward where the mainmast was, cargo was piled in sacks and cases, a hold beneath.

As the slowest of the wounded were handed aboard, Sunabhal was still standing on the beach, keeping an eye on the men of the *Adanum* out on the spit. The moorings were cut, men on the starboard side were pushing off, using the breakwater to give them some way.

Rodlakh called Sunabhal's name, and at the same time a shout came from the top of the cliff, highest here. Sunabhal looked each way, made up his mind, and stepped towards the scarcely moving ship. A scatter of ill-aimed arrows came from clifftop, one thudding into the foredeck, others splashing into the water or hitting the beach. But Sunabhal went down, hit high on his back.

Cursing as he heard Galt also was, Dolvid was about to step back onto the breakwater when Sunabhal, having managed to kneel up, was hit again. Wretched luck when any good archer had a better angle for targets in the ship, where nothing but deck and mainmast had been hit. Sunabhal was flat on his face by water's edge, and Rodlakh grabbed Dolvid's arm. More arrows were falling: on the poop Galt took his bow and sent back a couple of quick shots, to disconcert marksmanship rather than with any real killing purpose. The boat rocked into better water; *Push!*, Sarnak was urging. Another loose volley of arrows showered down. A man near Dolvid, Kuno, held up his forearm where an arrow had passed through, but not for display; he wanted Dolvid to snap off the head. That done, he sat down using his free hand to press at the larger wound where the arrow had emerged. Aëlu, kneeling, gave the hurt man a wad of cloth so he could staunch his bleeding.

The other wounded were urged to take shelter under the projecting poop-deck. The vessel was clearing the breakwater, and sails were up, rippling to a breeze that must be all wrong, pressing from the left as they faced what ought to be westward. Sarnak was at the tiller, and oars were coming into use. On the beach the body of Sunabhal was quite still, and Dolvid turned his mind away from Silnath's grief. The ship cleared the end of the breakwater, nosing for open sea. Half a dozen arrows splashed short.

"Give us a wind, *Zhavukindhrai* — " the Gabhani Sarnak invoked Zhôl by an Owani title, Gale-Master. At their slow pace archers could come down to the beach, run out on the breakwater, and

have ample time for several shots. They were discouraged by Galt and
Guthdar, who stood next to Sarnak, facing the other way, behind the
high taffrail, and as men started down the harbor steps, let go with
aimed arrows that found targets. They could outshoot the longbows by
fifty paces.

Snap and heavy thud both at once, the *zhin'pefrai* was tripped,
and from the direction of the spit a big smoothed rock was soaring long,
toppling to send up a waterspout well beyond the ship. Rodlakh
remarked calmly he would have been happier to see them short.

Sails at last drew wind, steadying out of the south, and Sarnak,
leaning on the tiller, came close to the breeze, keeping them aimed for
open water, and for Kamsilat. Eight rowers, beginning to catch the
rhythm, heaved mightily. Some archers had reached the foreshore, but
they shot well short, and there was no need for duelling.

"To the chest," Guthdar, with unspeakable scorn. "The ones
with short-bows pull to their chests, like children." Unknowing, he
must surely be echoing over fifteen centuries the contempt of his distant
forebears: in the armies of the First Empire the Owani bow had for
centuries not been strong enough for drawing to the ear, a Froghuli
practice which amazed all early chroniclers.

Perhaps in fear of those same deadly bows, no enemy ran out
on the breakwater. Too soon to be the first one rewound, what must be
a second *zhin'pefrai* thudded, and again there was the agonized wait
while the missile soared. The shot was long again, and wide, but some
of its spray reached the ship.

The first *zhin'pefrai* shot again, and at the top of the missile's
flight, stone hanging, it was certain the ship would be struck. Everyone
flinched, but the stone hit water a few feet astern, sending up a
drenching spray. After its violent lurch the broad-beamed vessel settled
back, a smug duck. Sarnak said, "Do you mind if I run her out of range,
Asai?" He threw over the tiller to run before the wind; the keel steadied
and sails bellied bravely. Unless the artillerymen had a way of
increasing their distance, one more shot from the second engine and the
ship would be out of range.

It never came. "Fighting-ship," Galt said. Out of the New Harbor, nosing past the spit, a low, quick-moving shape emerged, a long and narrow ship, dark and sailless, a menacing water-insect with eight pairs of oars for legs; these, worked by prisoners, were chained so as to move together.

"Rammer," Dolvid specified, "to a design of Dromladh's." There was another kind of fighting ship, a slow floating fortress, used to protect entrance to ports. With these quick rammers, amidships on a platform there would be archers, and they became pikeman ready to board any vessel not sunk by their main weapon, the hard bronze beak jutting from the prow, low so as to hole a ship's timbers near the waterline. Behind that beak the hull was complete, so the rammer could leave its sting in a victim and survive. It was rapidly gaining on a curving course that would take it to seaward of their ship.

"Dromladh?" Rodlakh was hoping for an omen. "Did he not drown?" Something everyone remembered, but though an irresistible piece of folklore, the vessel in which the "Ship-*Rabhsai*" went down was not one of his own design; it was an ordinary cargo-ship caught in an unforeseen storm.

"If nothing else, this silences the *zhin'pefral*." They watched the glide of the low pursuer with interest. Well, but that was puzzling: the big catapults did not have to be accurate to a span or so to keep shooting for some time without endangering the fighting-ship: perhaps they had been stilled for another reason altogether, such as someone all at once remembering Aëlu was not supposed to be harmed. Galt was with the archers, sharing out arrows equally, and telling them how they would shoot at the sky so their arrows would rain down on the enemy.

"When they are nearer, could we shoot the helmsman?" Rodlakh asked.

From his exposed elevation Sarnak said, "The lucky worm sits under a shield, or hood, and has orders called to him. The rowers have a roof of sorts over them, too."

In half a gale with rough seas to hinder rowing they might outrun the rammer, but here they had no chance, as he quickly admitted. "The only thing, with that beam and drawing so little, they can't come about as smart as they'd want, otherwise they'd capsize. It's a craft well made for the one thing."

The fighting-boat, now seaward, began to take the long gradual curve that would bring their courses together. A few arrows came, none well-aimed; the narrow craft was in open sea, and rolled too much for good shooting. Rodlakh freed bowmen by leaving the oars to one man apiece; they could just be managed so, and speed was not the best ally.

Eleven bowmen waited, eyes on Galt. Glancing back to see what more might emerge from the harbor Dolvid was surprised how far it was left behind. Already they were up beyond the headland, where the coast of the Island lunged back sharply, making for ample searoom. Gulls scolded raucously as they swooped down and banked away. Despite the terrifying pace of the fighting ship the gap was closing slowly. Sarnak told the port oars to be ready to check and push forward when he gave the word.

The gap closed to one hundred, to eighty paces. More arrows came, and better-aimed, one sticking in the mainmast, another bouncing off a gunwale to rattle down by the rowers, whose heads were kept low; Sarnak leant over as far as possible, making some shelter out of the high taffrail. Dolvid and Rodlakh were on the poop with him, while the main body of archers crouched in the waist by the deck-cargo.

"Push!" Sarnak hissed venomously at the port-side oars, throwing the tiller over as the rammer leapt at them. The slower ship lost all way, and surely their evasion was left too late. Painfully, pivoted on oars, their head came around, Sarnak keeping grim watch on wind in the sails. The two ships rushed together; "Pull!" Sarnak bellowed, and at last the rammer also veered, passing near enough to clash oars, while Galt's archers stood for a shot into the lower, heeling vessel.

At once Sarnak threw his helm over again, widening the gap, as the fighting vessel struggled to come about. Too tight. Sarnak howled orders at the oars, cursing in despair as he lost wind, sails flapping slackly. The fighting-ship, heeling hard, nearly grazed the bows as the two craft crossed; Sarnak had eased off to find the wind, and Rodlakh, with that air of benign abstraction which for him did for battle-fury, stepped up high on the taffrail, ignored arrows which came humming, and leaned as far as he could to take dead aim under the cowling where the enemy's helmsman sat. Chained oars dipped again, and then the long ship slewed violently, almost broaching to.

In a confusion of cries and orders, the rammer, rudder jammed, continued its crazy, tight circle. The oars were lifted, but its forward way carried the ship, dangerously heeled, right alongside, where Galt's bows had an open target in sprawled and tangled enemy. They poured in arrows mercilessly, and then the fighting-ship was astern. Sarnak again eased into wind freshening out of the south, lifting small curls of white from wavetops. Far to the south was a band of pale blue sky. An arrow had stuck in the woodwork inches from where Rodlakh's waist had rested; another had left a long scar in the wood.

"Had enough," Sarnak, more plea than statement. Someone down by the deck-cargo had taken an arrow in the upper arm, and Aëlu was there, tending the man. Climbing up to the poop Galt reported they had about a couple of dozen arrows left among them.

Astern, the enemy boat drifted as if derelict. At last, oars stirred again, and there was doubt and apprehension about its course. The rammer came about and was laboring for its anchorage. Sarnak was right; they'd had enough.

The gangling helmsman gave a loud crow, and called the news to those below who did not have a view. They raised a cheer, but Aëlu was frowning up at the afterdeck.

Sarnak asked permission to lay a course for Kamsilat.

"How is your breeze?"

"We'll make it do, *Asai*, but it'll be a longish sail."

"You can be proud of your seamanship."

"Aha, *Valrabh'*, this is not such a bad old wallower." Sarnak, in his element, began shouting orders and teaching lifelong landsmen what they meant.

Aëlu, mounting steps to the poop, told Rodlakh quietly, "What you did was very brave, too brave. Especially now Sebhal is gone, your future is not just yours, to throw away."

He answered only with a shrugger's mouth, but his animation was beginning to fade into former perplexities. This raid, with all its dangers and glories, the triumph of the citadel and miseries of the retreat, had been separate from the larger reality; Aëlu had been rescued, but that only returned Rodlakh to his dilemma. In the Northeast men were or soon would be dying in a fight against his brother for what he believed was justice, and the outlawed Colony needed only a word to join that fight, which was also theirs. Respite for considering was not unlimited; delay could lose the war, not only for Shumat's so-called rebels, but for the West as well.

"Home," Rodlakh, dubiously, looking west. Factually, of the five on the afterdeck, only Sarnak, about to break into a song, was truly going home. Galt had farther to go, to the Frontier, and perhaps beyond it, a man of Landegh. For Dolvid the refuge most like a home, with his manuscript left to molder under the floor, was no longer possible. Rodlakh had taken to the Colony, and would probably wish it could be his whole realm, but Kadon Dinul would remain his city too, his and not-his, so long as his brother ruled. Aëlu had lost what made the West her home, and the place of her beginnings was falling away astern; mostly they were wanderers.

"Things I overheard — " she was thoughtful, "make me think the Patriarch has a spy at Kamsilat — more than a spy, someone who helped them abduct me." She explained: "People talk freely when you are blindfolded, as if you were deaf-folded, too. But I could not tell who it was."

"We shall find him," Rodlakh, with a grim nod. Not only what he had learned at the Residence, but Âna's report as well, certainly confirmed Aëlu's perception.

"Or her," she said.

This chimed, too, with Dolvid's reflections. Briefly he had conjectured Sarnak might be the one in g'Asalladh's pay, but his service at Drin b'Afon and his handling of the ship made that absurd. What still had to be considered was a flaw, something wrong in the tale of Aëlu's abduction as Galt told it. They would have to go through it again, point by point, with Aëlu present. He yawned.

Down in the waist Guthdar had been examining deck-cargo, trying to discover what they had incidentally stolen from the Island. Loosening ties to a sack, he plunged a hand in, and brought it out heaped with a golden-brown mass, fragments of dried leaves.

He sniffed and crowed. "*Raminat*," he called. "Whole sacks of it."

"A treasure," Galt said.

"Then the boxes will be *ôdul* packed in straw," Dolvid predicted. "This is one of the coasters up from the south of the Island." Its cargo would have been shipped across to Pavani on the Forbidden Road, then by boat to the Mainland. Probably they had been ready to unload when the alarm came. "Any guards there were might have been made to join Kaëfanai's forces. Though these cargoes are protected mainly by *ga-dazhai*."

Aëlu was also of the *Mankh'*. "*Ôthu* and *raminat*, light and renewal, all for the Colony."

The value of this cargo had saved them, not only as the likeliest reason why the *zhin'pefral* had stopped their shooting. Sarnak's seamanship had been superb, but even he could never have evaded the fighting-ship if it had seriously tried to ram them amidships, instead of the much more difficult maneuver of coming alongside to grapple and board them.

Injured thigh forgotten, Noldar was with his brother, enjoying the wealth of so much golden *raminat*. He called out, "Enough for a whole realm, *Asai*," and Rodlakh turned away impatiently from Aëlu's keen eyes.

The great fires Galt's men had made inside the Winter Riding School had died out long ago, leaving the sour smell of cold ashes. Dawn came clammy, mist eddying in through every gap; tethered to a rusty ring Âna's *pefrai* stamped and nickered unhappily. There might be nothing to Tan Lughsai's reputation for bad luck, but she was sure it must be the dreariest place in all Arbhal. Her misery came mainly from stiffness, cold and hunger, but confused with it also, an anger she knew was unfair.

They had left her tinder-cord, firestones and steel. She blackened her hands salvaging part-burnt wood likely to be dry, and argued with herself as she huffed up a small, bright flame.

She had been the one to insist on staying on the Mainland. The men, moreover, had not gone sailing off to a comfort and safety she was denied, but to certain danger and probable death. At this moment their boat might be battering to bits on the cliffs of Kamanta. She did not believe that, and wondered if her irrational certainty Dolvid and Rodlakh would come through safe was because otherwise she would be unbearably ashamed of her feeling of injustice, the sense of being abandoned.

Outside there came a heavy slithering crackle, a good-sized creature, possibly man, moving through woods. She took out the knife she had been given and crouched by her small fire, watching the doorway, half-afraid someone or something would use a window-hole to get in. Only a pallid light came in through those spaces; peering out she could not see anything but mist, not the ghost-shape of a tree.

Alerted, she could detect many small noises, twitches of morning itself. She knew there were deer and rabbit in the woods, probably foxes and a badger or two, besides squirrels and other smaller beings. When nothing with any purpose seemed to come closer, she heated milk in a metal cup, and squatting by flames swallowed pieces of bread and cold deer-meat, amused it was here, not the sumptuous Residence, that she had found her promised venison.

Though she had put the pail near the fire the water was still excruciatingly cold when she came to wash. Chafed dry, face tingling, she took wasted care in folding up her bedding, which, with everything else not brought with her (except the documents Dolvid wanted to go to Faëdhal), was going to be left here.

Sitting to think through her best course, she was shocked to find she had dozed off. For no more than a minute or two, probably — the light had not changed much — but she could not risk it happening again, and guilt took her hurrying outside.

In a grey, damp world with nothing solid, her unbordered loneliness came pressing in, and she was holding the breath in her nostrils so as to listen to the throb of her heart. At the dell's edge tufts of grass were dull with moisture, while a far bird piped on one bleak note.

Light and vision improved as she climbed, and at the top of the rise she caressed the soft nose of the horse, and mounted. He bent back his head, not displeased to have a rider again. Apprehensive, all landmarks changed or invisible, she took what must be the right direction, and soon was moving down the main driveway, in brown dank between softly dripping trees.

The mist as she neared the road began glowing like *ga-ôthu*, and soon she was climbing up into watered sunlight. Her hands were cold, but courage started coming back as she emerged into open land where the road mounted in a notch beneath lilac and horse-chestnut blossom. To the near side of the Ravine the small ill-kept coastal road joined with this, and at the junction she halted to reflect. Coming south she had used the clasp on her arm to frank her past the guard on the far end of the bridge, as earlier past the guard-post at Rhutalai. Since there should be no reason for her to make for Tan Lughsai, she had taken care to ask about this coastal way, saying she had missed the earlier road eastward. It was fairly sure she would be remembered, and how much magic was left in the clasp was doubtful; whether it let her share in the surly reputation of Kargul and escape close questioning. Had she been a man muddy clothes and general disrepair would have been natural to a courier in haste, but it only weakened her pose as an important lady about her own business. No one slept at Tan Lughsai these nights.

She could take the right-hand road, and ride the long curve of Klam Lughsai, coming to Burantal by the little-used back way; it tempted her with the idea there might be chance for a word with Sett. She was seized with a desire to let loose the *pefrai* short of there, and slip into the town on foot. There, she could vanish; Dolvid's friend Untimarr could shelter her, too, and later when Sett was well his boat-owning acquaintance at the fishing-village with the name she forgot could take them both back to the Colony. The men had urged her to do just this, and no one could accuse her of not having done her share. Chances were strong that Kamin-Tolagh, tiring of her, had netted a new bed-friend on his patrols, and all the risks of returning to Kadon Dinul would be wasted.

She did not yet know whether she had been missed; her pounding journey made absence feel longer than it really was. But if she meant to face a return to Kadon Dinul and to Kamin-Tolagh, delay increased her danger, and Burantal took her almost a full day out of her way. Besides, when she turned north there would still be challenges to face, and on the whole she preferred the sleepy posts on this road to the well-manned and alert one at Tâl Abfekh, and all the soldiery moving at present on the Burantal road.

The *pefrai* rattled his bit. Once the Ravine was crossed, there were no more branchings before Kadon, but there was no sense of unalterable decision as she touched the animal's flanks with the ruined slippers, and rode northward, carried, if nothing else, by simple curiosity.

HOSTAGES

The End

www.ingramcontent.com/pod-product-compliance
Lightning Source LLC
Chambersburg PA
CBHW031419240626
47154CB00001B/115